# THE
# CHANEL
## SISTERS

## JUDITHE LITTLE

**REVIEW**

First published in 2020 by
GRAYDON HOUSE
By arrangement with Harlequin Books S.A.

First published in Great Britain in 2020 by
HEADLINE REVIEW
An imprint of HEADLINE PUBLISHING GROUP

First published in paperback in Great Britain in 2021 by
HEADLINE REVIEW

1

Cataloguing in Publication Data is available from the British Library

ISBN 978 1 4722 7959 0

Offset in 12/15pt Bembo by CC Book Production

Printed and bound in Great Britain by Clays Ltd, Elcograf S.p.A.

Headline's policy is to use papers that are natural, renewable and recyclable products
and made from wood grown in well-managed forests and other controlled sources.
The logging and manufacturing processes are expected to conform to
the environmental regulations of the country of origin.

HEADLINE PUBLISHING GROUP
An Hachette UK Company
Carmelite House
50 Victoria Embankment
London
EC4Y 0DZ

www.headline.co.uk
www.hachette.co.uk

For Les

And for Antoinette, so she won't be forgotten

# THE
# CHANEL
## SISTERS

PARTS OF AUBAZINE WOULD STAY WITH US FOREVER. A NEED for order. A fondness for simplicity and clean scents. An enduring sense of modesty. An insistence on craftsmanship, of stitches perfectly made. The calming contrast of black and white. Fabrics, rough and nubby, of peasants and orphans. The rosaries the nuns wore around their waists like chain-link belts. The mystical mosaic designs in the corridor of stars and crescent moons that would reappear as *bijoux de diamants*, as necklaces, bracelets, and brooches. The repeating patterns in the stained glass of interlocking Cs that would become a symbol of luxury and status. Even the old monastery itself, so vast and empty, that gave us room to imagine, to let possibility soar.

All those years on the rue Cambon, in Deauville, in Biarritz, people thought they were buying Chanel, glamour, Parisian sophistication. But what they were really buying were the ornaments of our childhood, memories of the nuns who civilized us, the abbey that sheltered us.

An illusion of riches sprung from the rags of our past.

# CHARITY CASES

AUBAZINE

1897–1900

# ONE

IN LATER YEARS, I WOULD THINK BACK TO THAT COLD MARCH day in 1897 at the convent orphanage in Aubazine.

We *orphelines* sat in a circle practicing our stitches, the hush of the workroom interrupted only by my occasional mindless chatter to the girls nearby. When I felt Sister Xavier's gaze, I quieted, looking down at my work as if in deep concentration. I expected her to scold me as she usually did: *Custody of the tongue, Mademoiselle Chanel.* Instead, she drew closer to my place near the stove, moving, as all the nuns did, as if she were floating. The smell of incense and the ages fluttered out from the folds of her black wool skirt. Her starched headdress planed unnaturally toward heaven as if she might be lifted up at any moment. I prayed that she would be, a ray of light breaking through the pitched roof and raising her to the clouds in a shining beam of holy salvation.

But such miracles only happened in paintings of angels and saints. She stopped at my shoulder, dark and looming like a storm cloud over the sloping forests of the Massif Central outside the window. She cleared her throat and, as if she were the Holy Roman Emperor himself, made her grim pronouncement.

"You, Antoinette Chanel, talk too much. Your sewing is slovenly. You are always daydreaming. If you don't take heed, I fear you will turn out to be just like your mother."

My stomach twisted like a knot. I had to bite the inside of my mouth to keep from arguing back. I looked over at my sister Gabrielle sitting on the other side of the room with the older girls and rolled my eyes.

"Don't listen to the nuns, Ninette," Gabrielle said once we'd been dismissed to the courtyard for recreation.

We sat on a bench, surrounded by bare-limbed trees that appeared as frozen as we felt. Why did they lose their leaves in the season they needed them most? Beside us, our oldest sister, Julia-Berthe, tossed bread crumbs from her pockets to a flock of crows that squawked and fought for position.

I pulled my hands into my sleeves, trying to warm them. "I'm not going to be like our mother. I'm not going to be anything the nuns say I'm going to be. I'm not even going to be what they say I *can't* be."

We laughed at this, a bitter laugh. As the temporary keepers of our souls, the nuns thought constantly about the day we would be ready to go out and live in the world. What would become of us? What was to be our place?

We'd been at the convent for two years and by now were used to the nuns' declarations in the middle of choir practice or as we worked on our handwriting or recited the kings of France.

*You, Ondine, with your penmanship, will never be the wife of a tradesman.*

*You, Pierrette, with your clumsy hands, will never find work with a farm woman.*

*You, Hélène, with your weak stomach, will never be the wife of a butcher.*

*You, Gabrielle, must hope to make an adequate living as a seamstress.*

*You, Julia-Berthe, must pray for a calling. Girls with figures like yours should keep to a nunnery.*

I was told that if I was lucky, I could convince a plowman to marry me.

I pushed my hands back out of my sleeves and blew on them. "I'm not going to marry a plowman," I said.

"I'm not going to be a seamstress," Gabrielle said. "I hate sewing."

"Then what will you be?" Julia-Berthe gazed at us with wide, questioning eyes. She was considered slow, "touched," people said. To her everything was simple, black and white like the tunics and veils of the nuns' habits. If the nuns said it, we would be it.

"Something better," I said.

"What's something better?" Julia-Berthe said.

"It's..." Gabrielle started but didn't finish.

She didn't know what Something Better was any more than I did, but I knew she felt it just the same, a tingling in her bones. Restlessness was in our blood.

The nuns said we should be content with our station in life, that it was God-pleasing. But we could never be content where we were, with what we had. We came from a long line of peddlers, of dreamers traveling down winding roads, sure that Something Better was just ahead.

# TWO

BEFORE THE NUNS TOOK US IN, WE'D BEEN HUNGRY MOST OF the time, our clothes torn and dirty. We spoke only in patois, not French. We could barely read or write because we'd never gone to school for long. We were savages, the nuns attested.

Our mother, Jeanne, worked long hours to feed us, to keep a roof over our heads. She was there but not really, her eyes turning flat over the years so that they seemed to look through us. They searched instead for Albert, always Albert. Our father was usually on the road, peddling old corsets or belts or socks. He was incapable of staying in one place for long, and our mother, a fool for love, was always chasing after him when he didn't return when he'd promised, pulling us down country road after country road with her whatever the season.

They were together just enough that our mother was always pregnant, Albert leaving us for months at a time to fend for ourselves with no money. She was a laundress, a maid, whatever she could find until she died at thirty-one from consumption, overworked and brokenhearted.

When she died, no family members wanted us, especially not our father. That shouldn't have been a surprise. How could he travel from market to market—and bed to bed—with all of us? Still, weren't fathers supposed to take care of their children?

We were three girls and two boys. Julia-Berthe, the oldest, then came Gabrielle, then Alphonse, then me, then Lucien. Alphonse had been just ten and Lucien six, no bigger than spools of thread, when our father had them declared "children of the poorhouse." He'd wasted no time turning them over to a peasant family as free child labor and delivering us girls to the nuns. We hadn't heard anything of our brothers in the three years we'd been at the convent.

Meanwhile, our father was off living the free life, as he always had, caring only about himself.

"I'll be back," he'd said to my sisters and me with the gilded smile of a salesman as he left us at the convent doorstep, patting Gabrielle's proud head, then disappearing into the horizon in his dog cart.

Julia-Berthe, who didn't like change, was inconsolable, not understanding where our mother had gone.

Gabrielle was too angry to cry.

"How could he leave *me*?" she'd say over and over. "I'm his favorite." And, "We can take care of ourselves. We have been for years already. We don't need these old ladies telling us what to do." And, "We don't belong here. We're not *orphans*." And, "He said he's coming back. That means he is."

And me, then age eight, I cried, confused, not used to the strange ways of the nuns, skirts swishing, rosaries clacking at their sides, clouds of incense drifting by like ghosts, the pungent smell of lye.

The convent was the exact opposite of all we'd known. We were told when to wake, when to eat, when to pray. The day was allocated into tasks: study, catechisms, sewing, housekeeping. The passing of time marked by the ringing of l'angélus, the prescribed prayers of the Divine Office. "Idle hands," the nuns repeated endlessly, "are the devil's workshop."

Even the days of the week, the weeks of the month, the months of the year were partitioned into what the nuns said were the seasons of the liturgy. Instead of January 15 or March 21 or December 19, it was the twelfth Sunday in Ordinary Time or the Monday of the first week of Lent or the Wednesday of the third week of Advent. The afterlife was divided into Hell, Purgatory, and Heaven. There were the Twelve Fruits of the Holy Ghost, the Ten Commandments, the Seven Deadly Sins, the Six Holy Days of Obligation, the Four Cardinal Virtues.

We learned about Saint Etienne, a hunchbacked monk whose tomb was in the sanctuary, his stone figure lying in repose on top, more figures of monks carved into the stone canopy. During Mass, I would trace with my eyes the knots and loops in the stained glass windows, the overlapping circles that looked like Cs for Chanel, for my sisters and me forever intertwined. I didn't want to think of what was in that tomb, the old bones, an empty burlap robe.

"There are ghosts here," Julia-Berthe would whisper to me, her eyes wide. There were holy ghosts, unholy ghosts, ghosts of every kind making the flames in the votives sway, hiding in corners and narrow passageways, throwing shadows on the walls. Ghosts of our mother, our father, our past.

Sometimes in the mornings while we bathed or in the evenings when we were to say our prayers silently, Julia-Berthe would grab my arm and squeeze. "I have dreams at night, frightening dreams." But she wouldn't tell me any more. I wondered if she had the same dream I had, of our mother in a bed with no coverlet, a bloody handkerchief in her hand, bitter cold seeping in through the thin walls. Her eyes closed, her thin body unmoving.

I taught myself to wake in the middle of these dreams, to shake off the image and climb into bed with Gabrielle. She'd let me curl into her as I did when we were young—before Aubazine we'd never had beds of our own—and be comforted by the heat of her body, the rolling rhythm of her breathing, until I fell asleep again.

Then too early in the morning, the sun still not up, the bells would sound. Sister Xavier would burst into the dormitory, clapping her hands and announcing in her too loud voice, "Awake up, my glory! Awake, psaltery and harp!"

After that, the chiding would begin.

"Faster, Ondine, faster. Judgment Day will come and go before you have your shoes on!"

"Hélène, you have much to pray for. Make haste!"

"Antoinette, stop talking to Pierrette and remake your bed. It's slovenly!"

The nuns of Aubazine gave us shelter. They fed our stomachs. They tried to save our souls, to civilize us by filling our days with order and routine. But they couldn't fill the empty places in our hearts.

# THREE

DAYS, WEEKS, MONTHS, ORDINARY TIMES, UNORDINARY TIMES.
Routine, soothing at first, grew tiresome. Then one airless
morning in July, the year 1898, our third at the convent of the
Congrégation de Saint Coeur de Marie, everything changed.

"Mesdemoiselles," the Mother Superior said as Gabrielle, Julia-
Berthe, and I cleaned dishes in the kitchen. "You are wanted
in the visiting room."

Us? We were never wanted in the visiting room. Unless—
My heart shot up to my throat.

Could our father have come to get us at last?

We followed the Mother Superior down the hall. I smoothed
my skirt, felt the plaits in my hair, hoping they were neat. I saw
Gabrielle reach up to pat hers too. She was the one who'd said
all these years he would come back, convincing herself that he'd
gone to America to make a fortune and would return once he
had.

When at last we reached the visiting room and the nun opened the door, I held my breath, anticipating a man with the grin of a charmer, the hands of a peasant, our father. Instead all I saw was an elderly lady with a kindly expression on her face. She wore carved wooden shoes called sabots, a coarse gray skirt, hempen stockings, and a faded print shirtwaist.

Grandmother Chanel?

"Mémère," Julia-Berthe said, rushing to embrace the old woman as if she might disappear as unexpectedly as she'd appeared.

I stared at her, more surprised than if it had been Albert.

"You don't know the peace we've had all these years," Mémère told the Mother Superior, "traveling from market to market knowing our dear granddaughters were in your care. It's not an easy life out on the road, and now we're too old for it." She clucked her tongue as adults did and offered us lemon pastilles.

She and Pépère had taken a small house in Clermont-Ferrand, a village just a short train ride away, and we were invited there for a few days to celebrate le quatorze juillet, the holiday commemorating the storming of the Bastille prison. At last we were getting out of the convent, for a little while, at least.

I didn't say out loud what I was thinking, what I was sure Gabrielle was thinking too. *Maybe our father will be in Clermont-Ferrand. Maybe he's waiting for us there.*

Somewhere deep in the empty places inside of me, where love was supposed to reside, I couldn't quash that dash of hope, foolish as it was, that Albert would return. Not the old Albert but a new one, who wanted us.

We left, and Mémère ushered us aboard a train. At Clermont-Ferrand, she led us to a crooked house with just one room cluttered with an array of objects to be sold at the local market—flat bicycle tires, moldy boxes, crusty pans. Rows of chipped, mismatched crockery lined the walls near the cookstove. A collection of old, broken dentures, yellowed and gruesome-looking, turned my stomach. It was as if nothing was ever thrown away.

There was so much clutter that at first we didn't see the girl near the bed. She was about fifteen, the same age as Gabrielle, or maybe sixteen like Julia-Berthe, and she moved toward us with an excitement and warmth we weren't used to. "Gabrielle?" she said. "Julia-Berthe? Do you remember me? And little Ninette! It's been so long. One of the fairs, I think, that's where we met. Look how pretty all three of you are."

She had the same long neck as Gabrielle, the same fine features and thin, angular frame, but with kinder, gentler edges. She wore convent clothes, like us, but with an ease and poise so that they didn't seem like convent clothes at all. I noticed Gabrielle tucking loose hair behind her ears. We must have been staring at her dumbly because finally Mémère spoke up.

"You daft girls, this is Adrienne. My youngest daughter. Your father's sister. Your aunt."

"Aunt?" Julia-Berthe said. "She's too young to be our aunt."

"Indeed she is your aunt, and I should know," Mémère said. "I've brought nineteen souls into this world. Your father was the first when I was sixteen. Adrienne, the last."

"The *grande finale*," Adrienne said, performing a charming little curtsey.

An aunt in convent girl clothes? An aunt who was our age? Gabrielle and I seemed to have swallowed our tongues.

"Ah, girls, don't look so confused," Mémère said. "Adrienne is just like you. She goes to a convent school in Moulins. Before le quatorze juillet is over, you'll all be more like sisters."

Maybe it was the confusion of being in a new place, but for a strange moment Adrienne appeared to me to have an aura, a cloud of golden light emanating around her like a saint on a prayer card. I glanced at Gabrielle. She didn't usually take to new people right away, but she was smiling. Adrienne looked like a girl we could learn from, and I found myself smiling too.

# FOUR

BLESSED ADRIENNE. HER FIRST SAINTLY ACT WAS GETTING US
out of that dark, cramped house. "Because, Maman, I'm their
aunt," she said with authority, convincing Mémère that it was
appropriate for her to take us to see the town. "Which means I
can be their chaperone."

Before Mémère could disagree, we followed Adrienne out the
door. Julia-Berthe stayed behind, helping sort buttons.

In town, as we walked the cobblestone streets, everything
came alive. Tricolor flags and bunting swung cheerfully from
the buildings and the lampposts. Horses clopped along, pulling
carriages. Delivery men with rolled-up shirtsleeves shouted and
unloaded sacks of flour or jars of mustard from wagons. Sidewalk cafés were crowded with old men stopping for a cup of
coffee, and markets bustled with women inspecting apples and
melons. Closer to the center square, workers assembled stages
and booths for the next day's celebration, hammers pounding.

Adrienne led the way with confidence, and I tried to emulate her, half smile on my face, shoulders back. In the reflection of her light, the darkness inside me faded. I could feel it floating off in the breeze.

At the sight of a train car propelling itself along the street, I stopped suddenly. There were no horses at the front. There was no steam engine. Passengers sat calmly inside as if it were nothing. Cords poked out of the roof like antennae on a bug, running straight up to more cords that ran parallel to the street. On top a giant sign said *La Bergère Liqueur* in fancy lettering.

Adrienne noticed me staring. "*Le tram électrique*," she said. "Don't you have a tram in Aubazine? We do in Moulins."

Gabrielle scoffed. "In Aubazine all we have are goats. And cows. Many, many cows. And pig breeders and plowmen the nuns think Ninette should marry. Nothing *électrique*."

"Aubazine is so dull. What else do you have in Moulins?" I asked Adrienne.

Her eyes lit up. "The cavalry. There's a barracks with soldiers. Handsome ones. They wear tall leather boots and jackets with brass buttons. And bright scarlet breeches. You should see them. They strut about like roosters in the henhouse. We admire them, but only from afar."

I sighed. "I wish we had something to admire."

"But you do," Adrienne said with a mischievous smile. "I'll show you."

We followed her until we reached the end of the road. There Adrienne turned and waved us through a tall brick archway that opened up into a park.

"*Voilà*," she said.

We paused inside the entrance to take in the sight. Curved gravel paths cut through lawns of emerald green. A pond glimmered, and two white swans glided idly near the shore. Trees rustled in the gentle wind. The busyness of the town dissolved, and men and women in fancy dress strolled along the paths. People who, unlike those outside the park, appeared to have nothing to do at all, as if they, like the swans, strove for nothing more than to be picturesque.

"They're all so...so..." I wasn't sure of the right word. Grand? Decorative? Exotic?

"Rich," Adrienne said in a reverent tone. "They are all so rich." She took a step forward, but Gabrielle and I hesitated. "Come on," she said with a laugh, "they don't bite. In fact, they won't notice us at all."

She took us to a shaded bench near the pond, where we watched these people who were even more fascinating than *le tram électrique*. The gentlemen wore elaborate suits despite the heat, with fine coats and striped trousers and straw boaters to top them off. They carried canes in one hand though they had no limp, and they strode with noble assurance alongside delicate-looking women swathed in layers of intricate white lace. Lace ruffles. Lace collars. Lace-trimmed skirts. Lace parasols. They wore wide-brimmed hats as large as the nuns' headpieces, adorned with oversized flowers, enormous plumes and, in some cases, colorful stuffed birds. Despite the weight, they somehow managed to walk with a graceful sway, a careful sashaying from side to side.

"Who are they?" I asked.

"The *élégantes*," Adrienne said with a flourish. "And their dashing *gentilhommes*."

I couldn't stop gawking, but it didn't matter. They didn't ever glance our way. Adrienne was right. In our convent clothes, we were as noticeable to them as blades of grass.

Only Gabrielle wasn't watching them with wonder and admiration as Adrienne and I were. She had a look on her face that made my stomach drop.

"Giant cream puffs," Gabrielle said, shaking her head. "Life-sized dust balls."

"What?" Adrienne twisted around. "Where?"

Gabrielle nodded toward the ladies on the path. "Volcanic

eruptions of lace. The Puy de Dôme has nothing on them," she said, referring to the largest of the old volcanoes that encircled Aubazine.

"Gabrielle!" Adrienne said. She put a hand to her mouth, her eyes wide. I froze, worried Gabrielle had offended her, and she wouldn't want any more to do with us. But beneath her hand, Adrienne was trying to contain laughter. She said in a put-on serious voice, "Archaeologists will find them someday preserved for posterity like the bodies in Pompeii. Buried not under ash but lace."

Now we all laughed together. It felt good, poking fun at those who wouldn't acknowledge our existence.

"They must get headaches, balancing all that on the tops of their heads," Gabrielle said.

"How nice it must be to have nothing to do but dress up like bonbons and stroll through the park with no cares at all," I said.

"But, Ninette," Adrienne said, her expression turning solemn. "These are more than just strolls through the park. Don't you see? Look at them, how they move and how they eye each other. See how the men push out their chests and the ladies bat their lashes at the men but glare at each other? This is business, the business of love and courtship." She sighed and put a hand to her heart. "Isn't it marvelous?"

I peered closer, trying to make out the batting eyelashes and glares, but before I could, Adrienne stood up from the bench and smoothed her skirt. "And now, *chéries*, we should get back before Maman sends the gendarmes for us."

She linked her arms with ours, but instead of taking us directly to the brick archway and back to town, she headed toward one of the gravel paths, pulling us into the promenade, where we stifled laughs and swayed and sashayed as if someday we too would be in the business of love and courtship.

# FIVE

THE NEXT DAY, THE FOURTEENTH OF JULY, WE WANDERED about the fair, past booths with wheels of fortune and other games of chance, stages with bands playing, people young and old moving about as far as the eye could observe. Everyone was there, except the élégantes.

"Where are they?" I asked Adrienne. After yesterday's walk in the park, the élégantes were what I most wanted to see. Not puppet shows and men trying to climb greased poles to get the ham at the top.

"At their châteaux," she said. "They don't come to village fairs. Fairs are for the common people."

Of course. That was why *we* were there.

But not for much longer. Adrienne, as usual, had a better idea. "There are other places to see élégantes…"

We stopped in a tabac, and with the one-franc coins Pépère had given each of us to spend at the fair, we bought magazines with beautiful ladies on their covers for fifty centimes each: *Fe-*

*mina, La Vie Heureuse. L'Illustration.* At the house, we went up to the garret and nestled among sacks of grain and herbs hanging from the ceiling. The far-off sounds of the bands drifted in through the open window.

"You see," Adrienne said, holding out the magazines. "Here are our élégantes. Everything we need."

"Need?" Gabrielle said. "For what?"

Adrienne smiled. "To become an élégante, of course."

Gabrielle and I exchanged a glance. *We* could become élégantes?

Adrienne turned the pages, and there they were, men and women of high society, of what Adrienne called "*la haute.*" Page six—élégantes strolling arm in arm through the Bois de Boulogne, handsome gentilhommes eyeing them behind jaunty mustaches. Page eight—élégantes gathering in the most exclusive salons in Paris for charity events, buying flowers from little girls in frothy dresses. Pages eleven and fourteen and fifteen— élégantes posing in the great couturières' latest fashions.

"Look at this hairstyle," Adrienne said, pointing at the glossy pages. "Isn't it sophisticated? Later we'll get out my pins, and see if we can copy it. Oh, and this hat—enchanting! My sister Julia buys plain straw boaters then trims them herself. I think she could make this."

We shared a pair of scissors. Adrienne and I cut out the wedding photos, the brides clutching trailing bouquets. Their grooms stood next to them, tall and proud in military uniforms covered over with ribbons, sashes, medals of stars or suns. What was it like to be so ordained, a golden burst upon your chest?

Julia-Berthe chose a photograph of the Queen of Romania and her children, well-kept little girls with soft hair and the blasé gaze of the pampered. Clean, fluffy little dogs sat at their feet and on their laps, not the wild scruffs we were used to.

There were articles about plays, images of actresses holding dramatic poses, their eyes large and full of emotion. Gabrielle collected these.

It felt as if a shroud had lifted. Thanks to the magazines, the élégantes weren't just a fleeting glimpse in a park, a vague blur of white lace and parasols never to be seen again. These élégantes we could keep, cut out, study, tuck inside the empty Vichy pastille tins Adrienne saved for us from one of Mémère's piles because "it's easier to sneak them into the convent that way." Rather than mimicking the lives of the saints, as the nuns wanted, now we could mimic the lives of the élégantes, their style, their attitude, their expressions, everything about them.

As evening crept in, I tried to put out of my mind that we were leaving the next day. Still, the heaviness slowly descended, as if it had been waiting, hovering behind me like a cloud of gnats. Only Julia-Berthe, who worried no one had fed the birds in the convent courtyard, was ready to go back.

Adrienne promised we'd see her again. For every feast day, she said, we'd come to Clermont-Ferrand. She also gave us a souvenir to take with us: Monsieur Decourcelle.

"But who is that?" I whispered, Julia-Berthe now fast asleep.

"He's a writer," Adrienne said. "Surely you've heard of him."

"We only hear about saints and apostles," Gabrielle said. "The nuns make sure of that."

"But you have to know of Monsieur Decourcelle," Adrienne said. "Life is too sad without him. He wrote *The Chamber of Love* and *The Woman Who Swallows Her Tears* and *Brunette and Blonde* and so many others. He writes about convent girls who marry counts and peasant girls who become queens of Parisian society. The poor become rich, the rich become poor. *Voilà.* You can't put it down."

We were startled by the crackling of fireworks in the distance. The feu d'artifice had started. From the garret's tiny window, we watched the fluttering pieces sparkle, a snowfall électrique.

"Convent girls who marry counts?" I said, not moving my eyes from the bursts of light.

"They're just stories, Ninette," Gabrielle said.

I ignored her, turning to Adrienne, my hand on her arm. "Where can we find these stories?"

She reached into her bag and pulled out a small book. "They come in parts in the journals. They're called mélos. Melodramas. My sister Julia waits every week for the next installment, then sews them all together and gives them to me. This one is *The Dancing Girl of the Convent*. A rich, beautiful ballerina at the Paris Opera gives up everything to become a nun and join a convent and—"

Gabrielle snorted. "No one would ever do that—"

"Shhhh," I said, annoyed at the interruption.

"—she bequeaths all of her worldly goods to a beautiful peasant girl. This peasant girl moves to Paris and steps into the ballerina's life of wealth and handsome suitors, jewels, and silk dresses. She becomes the toast of the city and she saves her family from poverty. There's passion and romance and they wear the most exquisite ensembles and live in the most luxurious villas."

I couldn't help but sigh. Outside the window, silver and gold flashed again.

"Do the nuns in Moulins allow you to read this?" I asked.

Adrienne shook her head. "I have hiding places. There's always a loose floorboard somewhere. And now you'll have to find one too. Here. Take it back to Aubazine with you, Ninette. I'm done with it. And maybe between the three of us—you, me, and Monsieur Decourcelle—we can convince Gabrielle that a convent girl really can marry a count."

That night, my dreams weren't haunted by ghosts, by my mother, cold and gray on a cot. Instead, I was back at the park, wrapped in layers of the finest lace as if I were something to be cared for, something to be treasured. A miniature garden sat regally on my head as I swayed and sashayed, handsome gentilhommes carrying useless canes by my side. I was an élégante. I was a heroine in a Decourcelle mélo. I was Something Better.

It was so much easier to dream when you knew what to dream of.

# SIX

"WHAT ARE YOU DOING?" I GLARED AT GABRIELLE IN THE DIM light and swirling dust motes of the convent attic, my voice a screech. We'd hidden *The Dancing Girl of the Convent* under a floorboard like Adrienne suggested, and here Gabrielle was, pulling out the stitching, taking the book apart.

"Shhhh," she said, glancing back at the door. "All of the Massif Central can hear you. Relax. I'm doing this for us. This way we can read whenever we want." She took a few pages and folded them into her pocket. "We'll bring them with us to class, to the courtyard, wherever we go. We'll hide them in our composition books and history books. The nuns will never know. Don't you see, Ninette?" she said, a mischievous smile spreading across her face. "We can read Decourcelle all day long."

*We.* It hadn't taken long for Gabrielle to fall under Decourcelle's spell.

Now we covered the tales of devotion and persecution in *Lives of the Saints* with Decourcelle's more earthly passions, switching out the pages when we were finished. He was our teacher, not the saints or the nuns. We read during recreation. We read during rest time. We read whenever we could, so much so we were held out by the nuns as examples to the other girls.

"Margueritte, stop staring into space," the Mother Superior would say. "Look at Gabrielle, how intently she's reading."

Or, "Pierrette, wake up! Your book has fallen over in your lap! Why can't you be more like Antoinette?"

We didn't tell Julia-Berthe our secret. Julia-Berthe, the rule follower, wouldn't have been able to keep it, confessing all in a burst of overwhelming guilt. But at night, before I fell asleep, I'd crawl into her bed and recount stories from *The Dancing Girl of the Convent* and pray that rather than those dreams of our mother, she was dreaming, like me, of ballerinas and handsome counts and love at first sight.

Just as Adrienne had promised, after le quatorze juillet, we were invited back to Clermont-Ferrand for Assumption Day in August, then All Saints' Day in November, Noel in December and Candlemas in February. Each time, we bought more magazines, keeping up with the latest styles. We cut out more pictures and brought new mélos back to Aubazine. *The Chamber of Love. The Woman Who Swallows Her Tears. Brunette and Blonde.* As our secret library grew, possibilities broadened, our world expanded.

When we were there for Easter the following April, it rained like *les vaches qui pissent*, as Pépère liked to say, keeping us indoors. He gave us each a coin, then headed to the café. Mémère was away, and we girls had the house to ourselves.

"We'll have a tea party," Adrienne said. "All the élégantes take tea in the afternoons. We need to practice."

We ran out in the downpour to buy the tea. Adrienne and

Gabrielle spent the rest of their money on ribbons and lemons, the juice of which was said to even the complexion. Julia-Berthe spent her remaining amount on tins of sardines for the feral cats that prowled around our grandparents' house. I decided to save mine.

"But there's nothing to buy in Aubazine," Gabrielle said.

"It's not for Aubazine," I said. "It's for after."

Gabrielle laughed. "After? That's too far off. I want something sweet now, before we go back to the convent where the nuns say anything less bland than the Communion wafer is gluttony. Besides, what will a few centimes get you anyway?"

I ignored her, enjoying the solid weightiness of the coins as if I were holding a piece of the future in my pocket.

# SEVEN

ON SUNDAY AFTERNOONS, WE WERE MADE TO FOLLOW SISTER Xavier up and down the hills of the Massif Central to "fortify our constitutions," which, according to the nuns, were weak from the poverty of our early days. During one of these winter treks, as I tried to imagine it was spring, that I was in the Bois de Boulogne like the élégantes in the magazines, strolling at a leisurely pace in the shade of a ruffled silk parasol, I heard Gabrielle say to Hélène, "Our father is in America. He made his fortune and is coming back soon to get us."

I nearly tripped over a jutted wedge of volcanic rock, catching myself just in time to avoid tumbling to the ground. Hélène snorted. "If he's made his fortune, then why are you and your sisters here?"

Gabrielle's chin was high. "To be educated. I wrote him and asked him to bring me a white dress made of chiffon. He promised he would."

"You're lying," Hélène said.

"You're jealous," Gabrielle said.

Hélène crossed her arms in front of her. "You're just like the rest of us. An orphan nobody wants. Stop claiming to be better."

"I am better. Anyone's better than you."

"Actually, you're worse. My parents died. But your father is still alive. And he doesn't want you. He probably never did."

It was all I could do not to kick Hélène as hard as I could. I wanted to shove her off a cliff and listen to her scream the whole way down.

I pushed myself between Gabrielle and Hélène and reached into my pocket. Sometimes I carried the coins I'd saved from Pépère with me. "He is coming back for us," I said to Hélène. "And he sends us money too. Look."

I held out my hand, the coins reflecting in the sun for a split second before I put them back quickly. Hélène's face was bright red.

"You see," Gabrielle said to her. "I told you so."

"Hmph," Hélène said. She moved closer to Pierrette, the two of them veering sharply away.

Gabrielle and I walked on in an uneasy silence, her words echoing in my head. Our father was coming back? She'd written to him?

That couldn't be true. It wasn't. I knew it wasn't, and a sick feeling came over me. After all our trips to Clermont-Ferrand, all the time we spent with Adrienne, all the stories in the mélos, I'd thought Gabrielle didn't think as much of Albert, that she'd stopped hoping for him to return. I was glad Julia-Berthe was up ahead, closer to Sister Xavier, so she couldn't hear. She would believe every word.

I adjusted the scarf around my neck as dark thoughts swirled. I was dreaming of princes. Gabrielle was dreaming of Albert. To her, he was a prince.

"Maybe he did go to America," she said finally. "Maybe he did make his fortune. Maybe he's on his way to get us right now."

I shook my head. My mouth and throat were dry. "You've heard the conversations at Mémère's." Sometimes when we were there, neighbors or other family members called Albert *le grand séducteur*. One said he'd heard Albert was in Quimper selling women's shoes. Another said he was in Nantes selling women's underthings. "He's not so far away," I said to Gabrielle, "and still he chooses to have nothing to do with us."

The look Gabrielle gave me then was that of someone far older than her years. It was hard, like a scab, protecting something raw beneath. "All the more reason to make him something he's not," she said.

Trees bowed, and leaves whirled up in clusters as if trying to take their rightful place back on the branches. Back at the convent, a strong gust had knocked the latch loose on an old iron gate, sending it swinging back and forth with loud, ringing clangs. I hated the wind, always pushing its way in, making everything creak and shudder.

Later that day, I ended up in the infirmary, the Sunday walk in the cold worsening my constitution. One minute I was hot, as if my insides were on fire, then just as suddenly my teeth were chattering with cold. "Sickly, just like her mother," I imagined the nuns whispering, crossing themselves as they did when they spoke of the dead.

Sister Bernadette, the nun in charge of nursing, wrapped me in a wet sheet to lower the fever. She put a balm on my chest, gave me a draft of strong wine, and dabbed holy water on my forehead as an extra precaution. I would live, she declared, but better safe than sorry.

Gabrielle offered to sit at my bedside. This way she could avoid catechisms and needlework and read instead. She held

*Lives of the Saints* close, her voice low so that Sister Bernadette wouldn't hear that it wasn't the trials and tribulations of
the sainted she was reading but the trials and tribulations of
Decourcelle's *The Dancing Girl of the Convent*.

As the medicine of the wine sank in along with Gabrielle's
words, a drowsy feeling took over. I almost didn't hear the
Mother Superior and Sister Xavier come into the sick room
just as Gabrielle was getting to the part where Yvette, the peasant girl who switches places with the ballerina, arrives in Paris.

Gabrielle stopped reading, closing the book quickly. The nuns'
expressions were grave. Was I going to die after all? Was that
why they were here? The Mother Superior stared at me, one
eyebrow raised so that it almost touched the white band that ran
just below her hairline.

Gabrielle jumped to her feet. Her face was so colorless I could
make out traces of blue veins on her forehead like the whorls of
mold on the rind of a cheese. "What are you doing with that?"
she said to the nuns. "It's not yours."

I pushed myself up on an elbow to see that the Mother Superior was holding my blue-and-white tin, where I'd replaced
the coins after our walk. The nerves in my stomach seized. I'd
hidden the tin in a dark corner under my bed in the dormitory.

The Mother Superior cited *Matthew*. "Lay not up for yourselves treasures upon earth, where moth and rust doth corrupt,
where—"

"—thieves break through and steal!" Gabrielle said, cutting
her off. She flew toward the nuns, her elbows jutted out, her
jaw thrust forward. She was no longer The Dancing Girl of the
Convent, whose posture we both tried to imitate. She was the
peasant girl who grew up on the streets of Auvergne. "That's
Antoinette's money," she said. "You have no right to take it."

I shuddered, as much as for my coins as for Gabrielle's daring.

"What is to become of you, Gabrielle?" Sister Xavier said.
"You know your verses well. Which means you and Antoinette

should know that treasure, if there is any, will be in heaven, not here with earthly things."

I wanted to cry out, but I was too woozy, fever swelling my head. My coins. My precious coins. They were for the future. For Something Better.

The Mother Superior opened the tin. "And what about these?" she said, pulling out my paper élégantes, my brides and grooms, my princes and princesses. "It's prayer cards you should collect with images of the saints, not false idols."

Outside, the wind howled, rattling the windows. The broken gate clanged like an old, worn-out church bell. In my feverish state, the wind, the sounds, the scorn on the Mother Superior's face echoed through me. I felt too ill to fight back.

But Gabrielle wasn't giving up. She turned to the Mother Superior, her voice more controlled this time. "Please, Ma Mère. Our grandfather gives us each a coin to spend when we visit. I've spent all of mine on selfish things. But Antoinette always saves hers. She could waste it on candy and ribbons and trinkets like me, but she doesn't. She saves so that when she leaves here, she'll have something to help give her a start."

I watched the Mother Superior's firm expression, hoping it would change, but it didn't. She took out the little bit of money, held it in her palm, and then closed her old crooked fingers around it.

"We are to give alms to the poor and needy," she said, "following the example of our Savior. The priests are taking a collection for la Mission Catholique in China, to feed the starving children of Shanghai. This shall go to them as an exercise in piety."

The two nuns turned and walked out, the underskirts beneath their holy habits swishing against the floor, the rosaries attached to their belts swinging at their sides. They motioned for Gabrielle to go with them.

I started to cry, the kind of tears that fall silent at first. Somewhere in the back of my fevered head, I thought that at least the nuns hadn't mentioned the lie about our father. But sobs quickly followed until my pillow was wet, my nose running. I wasn't The Woman Who Swallows Her Tears.

I cried for Gabrielle who still longed for Albert but covered it up with pride and lies, for Julia-Berthe, who saw ghosts in every corner, for the brothers I didn't know. And I cried for the loss of my blue-and-white tin, that tin like an extra chamber of my heart, the most sacred one of all.

I stayed in the infirmary for a week, chills coming and going. Julia-Berthe brought me broth, warming me from the inside like a soft blanket. Eventually I got better, but if the nuns entered the room, I still coughed and groaned. I didn't want to get out of bed. I just wanted to sleep.

When Sister Xavier walked in at the end of the week, I winced, trying to sink back into the bedding and disappear. I waited for her to clap her hands, to shout and force me out of bed. *Awake up, my glory! Awake, psaltery and harp!*

But for once, she wasn't too loud. She didn't call me weak or slovenly, didn't chide me that I would end up like my mother. Instead, she told me she'd talked to the Mother Superior and convinced her not to give away my savings to the starving children in China.

"It was wise of you to save your money," she said. "To not be wasteful like Gabrielle. I'll hold your savings for you, Antoinette, until it's time for you to leave here, when you'll really need it. Starving children in China? The poor and the needy, we have enough of that here in France. When you and your sisters first came to us four years ago, you were so thin and dirty.

You only spoke in patois. You didn't even know the Apostle's Creed. And now, you recite it by memory."

She rested a hand on my head, and I swallowed hard. All the bad thoughts I'd had of Sister Xavier, and now she'd done this kindness for me.

I'd always believed the nuns meant only to torment us. But the picture of what we'd been when we came to Aubazine and what we were now materialized before me. The nuns had shaped us like the streams carving the Massif Central. They'd given us the only home we'd known and prepared us for the world outside the convent walls, and we were better for it. Even in Decourcelle, a prince didn't marry a girl who spoke only in patois.

# EIGHT

WE FELT SURE OUR TIME WAS COMING TO LEAVE AUBAZINE and start lives of our own. Julia-Berthe was almost eighteen, Gabrielle almost seventeen, and I thirteen. Our forays in the outside world with Adrienne made us all the more eager.

For the third year in a row, we celebrated le quatorze juillet in Clermont-Ferrand. But I no longer saved the money Pépère gave us. Despite Sister Xavier's assurances, I worried that the Mother Superior would change her mind and send my savings to China. But also, I didn't save it because I found another use for it. While Julia-Berthe helped Mémère at her market stall, Gabrielle, Adrienne, and I visited the gypsy who lurked around the fringes. Julia-Berthe, the rule follower, thought it was all blasphemy and sin. But I was guided by the verse from Jeremiah: "For I know the plans I have for you." Maybe God etched these plans on our palms. It seemed like a good way for Him to keep track. Or maybe in the placement of a gypsy's cards the divine let itself be shown.

Superstition came from our father, who always carried wheat in his pocket. "For prosperity," he'd say. When he'd come home after being away, he'd make a dramatic scene, putting a hand on each of our heads in turn, Julia-Berthe, Gabrielle, Alphonse, me, and Lucien, and then counting us. "One, two, three, four, five. *Five.* My lucky number." I knew now it was all talk. He never believed anything about us was lucky. But Gabrielle had adopted the number five as her number too, drawing it in the dirt with a stick when we were little. At Aubazine, she etched five-pointed stars and crescent moons like the ones in the mysterious mosaics that we always thought were lucky, stepping on each one whenever we passed through the corridor as if it would give us some celestial power.

The gypsy wore a purple-and-gold headscarf, her thick hair long and wild as she shuffled Lenormand cards with mysterious pictures, then spread them out. There was a ship card, cloud card, tree card, cross card, coffin card, and they meant different things in different combinations that only the gypsies could interpret. Clouds meant trouble. But clouds already sat on the hills of the Massif Central like sacks of flour. We were used to them. Money, love, that was what we wanted to know about.

"You will have great riches one day," the gypsy said, reading Gabrielle's fortune.

"She says that so I'll spend my money now, on her," Gabrielle whispered under her breath.

"You will have a great love affair," she said to Adrienne when it was her turn.

Adrienne leaned forward. "But who will I marry?"

To get more answers, she and Gabrielle went off to the palm reader while the gypsy read my fortune.

The rings on her fingers clacked together as she shuffled the cards. She spread them out, revealing a coffin stacked on top of a cross. I waited for her to tell me what that meant, but she stared at me without speaking as if she could read my face, her eyes, dark and limitless, peering out from beneath the headscarf pulled low on her forehead.

"I know the coffin can be good," I said hopefully. "The end of something bad, for instance. Or the death of something un-wanted..."

She took the cards away without giving me a full reading.

"What was it? What did it mean?"

"Sometimes it's better not to know," she said with a warning look.

It felt like everything inside me stopped. My heart, my lungs, even the blood in my veins. Was something terrible going to happen? "Please, tell me."

She studied me. "Are you sure?"

"Yes."

Her voice was hushed. "An early death."

She wouldn't say any more. Instead, she slipped a small ring off her pinky finger and held it out. "Take this."

It had a thick gold band with a round yellow stone, beautiful and opulent looking, something I imagined an élégante might wear. I'd never held anything so magnificent.

"The stone holds the power of the sun," the gypsy said. "It brings warmth and light to the darkest places." She said something else in a language I didn't recognize, then her eyes went flat like curtains drawn over a window, and she turned away.

*An early death.* Someone would die young. Someone would die before their time. Then, with relief, it dawned on me. Our mother. The cards were about Jeanne.

When I showed the ring to Gabrielle and Adrienne, Gabrielle examined it as if she were an expert on gems. "It's not real," she said.

"How do you know?" I asked.

"Because it came from a gypsy."

Adrienne jumped in. "But that means it really could be

real. Gypsies have a way of getting their hands on things. Oh, Ninette, just think, it might have once belonged to a queen!"

Gabrielle shook her head. "Queens have fat fingers. The band is too small. It would never fit a queen."

"Well then," I said, refusing to let her ruin this. "It's just the right size for a princess."

# NINE

GABRIELLE AND I HAD OUR SHARED SECRET: THE MÉLOS BENEATH the floorboards, Decourcelle's pages hidden in books. And I had my gypsy ring, tied to a piece of string around my neck, resting beneath my shirtwaist.

But as summer turned to fall, Julia-Berthe surprised us with the biggest secret of all. Gabrielle and I, so caught up in the world of Decourcelle, had missed it. Everyone had. Until the day Sister Geneviève finally went in the garden shed for a rope to tie up the gate and keep it from clanging.

Hélène, Pierrette, Gabrielle, and I were huddled around the warming stove in the sewing room, practicing our stitching for the ten thousandth time as Hélène went on and on about a boy who worked at a produce stand in the town she visited on holidays with her great aunt. His fingers had touched hers when handing her a plum, which Hélène claimed meant he was in love with her. As Hélène droned on, a loud wail from somewhere inside the convent rang out, startling all of us.

My needle and thread slipped from my hand and dropped to the floor. It sounded like Julia-Berthe. In the past she'd been inconsolable when a hawk sailed down from the mountains, snatched up a baby rabbit, and soared off with the poor creature between its claws. And there was the time she found a bird's nest on the ground, cracked eggs, pieces of shells, two unhatched babies, pink and wrinkled, never to grow feathers or fly.

But this felt different.

I jumped up in a panic, headed toward the source of what were now loud sobs, Gabrielle close behind. We hurried along the corridors and down the worn stone steps of the broad staircase to the hallway that led into the Mother Superior's office, stopping outside the closed door. We could hear the low murmurings of the nuns. Julia-Berthe crying, repeating over and over again, "But he says he loves me."

*He?*

Gabrielle and I exchanged glances, catching only bits and pieces of what Sister Bernadette was saying.

"…it was the old blacksmith's son…the one who was supposed to fix the gate…no wonder it hasn't been fixed…if I hadn't walked in the garden shed right then…on the verge of carnal knowledge."

Then, "Jesus, Mary and Joseph" and the sound of rosary beads clacking.

For a moment I didn't breathe. Julia-Berthe, the rule follower. Julia-Berthe, who saw the world in right and wrong, good and bad. Julia-Berthe had been sneaking off with a man?

"But he told me he loves me," she sobbed again to the nuns. "He loves me, and he wants to marry me."

The Mother Superior's voice cut through the air. "Marry you? He already is married. His wife just had a child, baptized right here in the sanctuary."

Behind the door, there was a deep silence, heavy with Julia-Berthe's misery.

"No," she said, her voice weak. "No. It can't be true. He wants to marry me. Why would he say he wants to marry me if he's already married?"

I went stiff, the words echoing in my head. A married man. A man who lied to her. A man with a wife and child at home. A *séducteur*. Not unlike our father.

Here at the convent, right under our noses, Julia-Berthe had been tricked by a man.

The door opened, and Gabrielle and I flew back. Julia-Berthe exited, her eyes to the ground, her face glossy with tears, a nun at each side moving her along. Sister Bernadette followed, proclaiming that they must find a priest, they must find one immediately, there was no time to waste.

They disappeared down the hall as more nuns fluttered out of the Mother Superior's office, too distracted to shoo us away. Then came Sister Xavier.

"What are you doing here?" she said. "Go back to the workroom."

"Is Julia-Berthe going to be all right?" I asked.

"What's going to happen to her?" said Gabrielle.

The Mother Superior gave us a stern look. "The eternal rest of her soul is in peril. Your sister has committed a grave sin against modesty." She made the sign of the cross, then rushed off.

I looked to Gabrielle, but she just shook her head and muttered beneath her breath, a perplexed expression on her face. "If you're going to sin against modesty," she said, "you should at least do it with someone who's rich."

We knew from an early age about relations between men and women. We'd lived in small rooms with thin walls or no walls at all. We saw cats in alleys, goats in their pens, livestock in the fields. We knew babies didn't come from cabbages.

Did Julia-Berthe remember what our father did with our mother when he came back from his wanderings? Did she remember his grunts at night, the shadows on the walls? Our mother called it *faire l'amour*. Making love. Julia-Berthe, who saw only the plain meaning of words, must have thought she could "make love" like she could knit a sweater. There would be something afterward, tangible, to keep.

Around the convent, the other orphelines talked about Julia-Berthe's rendezvous with the old blacksmith's son as a great scandal. The nuns often repeated a warning from Saint Jerome: *You carry a large sum of gold about you, take care not to meet any high-waymen.* When they'd said this in the past, I'd wanted to laugh. The nuns knew we had no gold, large sums or small. But now it made sense. Julia-Berthe had met a highwayman. He'd almost gotten her gold.

Poor Julia-Berthe. She was overcome. Not because she almost lost her gold or because at Mass she was forbidden from taking Holy Communion and had to stay seated while the rest of us lined up. Not because at mealtimes and during the day, she was made to fast and spend extra time in prayer or at stations of the cross.

But because whenever she could, she would glance out the window in the direction of the broken gate, looking for the old blacksmith's son in the yard. And he was never there. The nuns had banished him.

"We have to protect her," I said to Gabrielle as we left Mass one morning. Julia-Berthe was older than me, but she was more tenderhearted, more trusting. "She's just turned eighteen. The nuns won't let her stay here much longer. They'll send her to be someone's maid or laundress, with no one to watch over her."

"Look what happened when she was being watched over," Gabrielle said. "How did we not realize she was sneaking out?"

We who knew Julia-Berthe best had had no idea. I'd assumed

she was out feeding bread crumbs to the birds or scraps to the feral cats. I should have been paying more attention.

"But don't worry," Gabrielle said. "The nuns aren't going to send her away yet, not when they can use her as an example of what not to do for the rest of us."

Gabrielle was right. The nuns now spent endless hours catechizing against sins of the flesh. Sister Geneviève had us stand and recite in unison from Galatians: *"The works of the flesh are manifest, which are these: adultery, fornication, uncleanness, lasciviousness…they which do such things shall not inherit the kingdom of God."*

The nuns also used the examples of the martyrs, reading from *Lives of the Saints*, planting the grim acts of those holy ghosts forever in the dark corners of our minds:

"When confronted with temptations of impurity, Saint Benedict threw off his habit and cast himself into a bush of thorns and nettles."

"Saint Bernard of Clairvaux plunged into an icy river in the depths of winter."

"Saint Francis of Assisi rolled unclothed in the snow until he nearly froze to death."

"Do you think it worked?" Julia-Berthe asked Gabrielle and me one afternoon during recreation a few weeks after the incident. She held out her Saint Francis prayer card, the one with the birds flocking around him that she always carried in her pocket. "Do you think the cold snow cleansed him of his impure thoughts?"

"Don't be ridiculous," Gabrielle said. "The saints aren't real. They're stories the church made up to scare us."

"Of course the saints are real," Julia-Berthe said. "They're in a book."

I wasn't sure if they were real or not, but I worried for Julia-Berthe. Another month passed and she still peered out the window whenever she could, always toward the gate. But an old one-armed man with a long gray beard had come and fixed it. It didn't clang anymore.

# TEN

I SHOULD HAVE KNOWN WHEN THE SKY TURNED GRAY. WHEN the air went still and the clouds sank low and heavy over the mountaintops, the first flakes falling, thicker and thicker until the outside world was covered over in white like a sacrament.

But I was warm and dry in class, sure this was just another snowstorm, contemplating the math problem on the blackboard as Pierrette was called up to solve it. On her way, she glanced outside and shrieked. We all ran to the window, even Sister Xavier, who gasped and ordered us back to our desks. "Put your heads down and pray," she said as she flew out the door, her headpiece fluttering like a pair of wings.

We didn't go back to our seats. Instead, we stared at the spectacle of Julia-Berthe, naked and rolling in a drift of snow, her skin so pale she was almost invisible. Nuns rushed out of the building, frosty air coming from their lips in puffs as they tried to get her up, the wind rippling along their skirts.

My heart throbbed in my chest like a pincushion stuck with a thousand sharp-pointed pins.

"What is she doing?" the other girls whispered, not seeing what I saw: Saint Francis. Rolling unclothed in the snow. She was trying to cleanse herself of impure temptation, of her desire for the old blacksmith's son.

Sister Xavier lifted Julia-Berthe in her arms and carried her toward the door, the nuns' black wool shawls piled on top of her. How long had she been out there?

I ran downstairs to the infirmary, but the doors were closed. Gabrielle was already there, and we clung together without a word.

"She's going to be all right," Sister Bernadette told us when they finally let us in. Julia-Berthe was asleep, and I knelt down by her bed and held her hand to feel her pulse, watching her body beneath the blankets for the slow rise of her chest.

Oh, Julia-Berthe. If only wounds and sorrows could be driven away in the freshly fallen snow. If only the longing for love could be numbed by the cold and ice, I would go out there with you.

When the nuns told us a few weeks later that Mémère was on her way to the convent, I wasn't surprised. After her stay in the infirmary, Julia-Berthe had snuck out three more times. She was found wandering in town, searching for the blacksmith's son until someone brought her back.

She couldn't stay in Aubazine.

I overheard the Mother Superior and Sister Xavier talking outside the linen closet one afternoon while I was inside folding pillowcases.

"It's best for Julia-Berthe to be around family," the Mother Superior said in a low voice. "Their grandparents have moved to

Moulins, and Julia-Berthe can go stay with them. But as for Gabrielle and Antoinette, have you spoken to the Mother Abbess?"

"Yes," Sister Xavier said as if to reassure her. "They'll be
under strict supervision at all times. She's assured me that their
virtue will be secure."

"And the doors?" The Mother Superior sounded unconvinced.

"Kept locked at all times. They'll be permitted to leave the
premises only for Mass and other pious purposes."

"But the soldiers' barracks," the Mother Superior said.

"On the other side of town. Far from the Pensionnat."

I dropped the pillowcase.

*Barracks.*

*Pensionnat.*

I couldn't wait to tell Gabrielle. We were going to Moulins, to the Pensionnat Notre Dame. We were going to be with
Adrienne.

# NEW SILHOUETTES

## MOULINS
## 1900–1906

# ELEVEN

"NINETTE," ADRIENNE WHISPERED, LEANING IN BEHIND ME AS I took a seat in the dining room our first day at the Pensionnat Notre Dame. "You're in the wrong place. That's where the *payantes* sit."

The payantes, Adrienne explained, were the rich girls. The girls from paying families. We were the *nécessiteuses*. The charity cases. At the Pensionnat, I quickly learned, everyone had a place. Ours was at the bottom.

"Look how they eat," Gabrielle said, scowling at their table across the room. "Like pigs at the trough."

"And that one," she went on. "Her skin is like the Massif Central, the Puy de Dôme right there on her chin. And yet she's sure she's better than us."

"And there." She nodded toward a dark-haired girl on the end closest to us. "Just because you're rich doesn't mean you don't have to bathe. I can smell her from here."

We charity cases had different tables, different dormitories, different classrooms, different uniforms. We all wore black shirt-waists and skirts, but whereas the payantes' were new and crisp, the fabrics smooth and expensive, ours were ill-fitting and had a thin oily sheen from wear, hand-me-downs faded from too much washing. We wore aprons over them because while the payantes practiced piano or fancy needlework upstairs, we were down-stairs, mopping floors or scrubbing pots. We all wore *pèlerines*, little capes around our shoulders like flower petals, the payantes' made of luxuriant garnet cashmere, ours black wool, rough and knobby, as if the payantes were the roses, and we were the weeds.

In Aubazine, we knew we were poor, but everyone was. We didn't think about it constantly. Here, we were reminded of our lowly station every breathing moment.

Even at high Mass, we nécessiteuses had our place.

At the cathedral, the payantes paraded first into the presti-gious center section with the rest of the congregation, while we tokens of Catholic charity were shuffled off to the side, squirm-ing beneath the soaring vaults and pointed arches, among the sculptures and gargoyles and colorful stained glass that Gabrielle called gauche, so different from the austere simplicity of Au-bazine. The canonesses, dress sleeves buttoned onto their habit bodices, joined the payantes as if they were their rich old aunts, and maybe they were. Only one elderly canoness, Sister Ermen-trud, sat with us as a monitor, drawing, evidently, the short stick.

"It's a wonder they think we're fit for the Body of Christ," Gabrielle said with a sigh one Sunday after we had just finished taking Holy Communion and knelt back in our places for the long stretch of silent prayer.

"They're getting the body," I said. "We're probably just get-ting an arm or a leg."

I hadn't meant to be funny, but next to me Adrienne snorted. Out of the corner of my eye, I saw she was trying to hold in laughter. Her shoulders shook. Her face was pink. The conta-gion spread to Gabrielle and then to me. The more we fought not to laugh, the funnier it all became. The other charity girls nearby eyed us and scowled, afraid we might get everyone in trouble. Laughing during Mass was practically a cardinal sin.

But Sister Ermentrud was hard of hearing, and the rest of the canonesses were far away on the other side of the aisle. They couldn't see us. They couldn't hear us. They couldn't reach us with a stick. The high and mighty, sheltered in their high and mighty world, had no idea what the lowly might be up to.

# TWELVE

"IF WE CAN'T HAVE THE EXPENSIVE FABRICS OF THE PAYANTES," Gabrielle said, "we'll have the best fit. Those sheep aren't any better than us."

When we'd first arrived at the Pensionnat six months earlier, we were each given two sets of the nécessiteuse uniform. Now, in Adrienne's room—a favorite of the canonesses, she had a nun's cell to herself—I stared at Gabrielle's second uniform: cut apart at the seams, the sleeves, the collar, the front, and the back spread out on the bed like pieces of a puzzle along with the parts of her skirt.

I looked at her, alarmed.

"Don't worry," she said. "I'm going to put the pieces back together again so that they fit. These sleeves are ridiculous. We look like clowns. And these skirts. Like we're running a sack race at a fair."

It was true. I moved around all day feeling like a potato with feet. Whereas Adrienne seemed poised in her uniform, her natural grace somehow taming the poor quality, Gabrielle and I, slight of figure, were swallowed up like Jonahs in a whale of cloth. Our overly blousy sleeves dipped into our soup and ink pots and dishwater and when we walked, we tripped over the extra lengths of skirt fabric, the toes of our boots catching in the hems.

I knew the canonesses would punish Gabrielle for destroying property that didn't belong to her, for vanity, for a litany of other sins they would recite like Moses with thunder and lightning and the sound of trumpets. But then I thought of the way the payantes looked at us, always down their noses, and fetched my own spare uniform, tearing out the stitching at the seams. Each time I pulled a thread, I imagined I was pulling the hair of a sneering payante or loosening the pinched expressions of the canonesses.

For two weeks, we worked in secret whenever we had the time, Adrienne helping when she could.

"Ninette, your stitches are too big. Make them smaller," Gabrielle would direct me, a line between her thick black brows as she worked.

"Take that out, Ninette, and do it again. It's crooked."

"No, Ninette, not a blind stitch. Use a catch stitch for the hem. You need the extra hold."

There were times I wanted to stick her with my needle. But this was serious work. We weren't hemming or stitching a cross on a sheet or pillowcase for some stranger's bed as we had in Aubazine. This was different, and she was just as picky with her own handiwork as she was with mine. If she wasn't satisfied with how something came out, she started all over again and made me do the same. Sewing took on a new appeal for her, now that she was sewing for herself. She would try on her refitted uniform and study it in the reflection of the window, then make me try mine, tugging here, tugging there.

"No," she would say, shaking her head. "No. Still not right."

When finally Gabrielle was happy, it was time for our grand début.

In the predawn gray the next morning, I buttoned my altered shirtwaist and smoothed my skirt, straightened my shoulders and lifted my chest. All day, during lessons and at meals, other nécessiteuses threw curious glances our way. I even caught some of the payantes, who normally were oblivious to us, sneaking looks.

The design of the clothes hadn't changed. The alterations we'd made were subtle. It was just that now our uniforms fit, accentuating slim waists that before had been hidden beneath masses of fabric, allowing us to move more easily, which made us appear more dignified.

We didn't look well-off, but we looked like Something Better, and for the first time, we felt that way too.

It wasn't just the other girls who noticed our new silhouettes.

Before dinner that same day, Gabrielle and I were called to the Mother Abbess's office. The Mother Abbess taught natural science, and the walls were covered with butterflies pinned in neat rows in frames and display cases of fossils and bones, everything categorized and labeled, everything in its place, a hint of dead-animal rot lingering in the air. Among these relics stood Sister Gertrude and Sister Immaculata, frowning with disapproval. We curtsied, then folded our hands in front of us and gazed at the floor.

"What have you done to your clothing?" Sister Immaculata asked.

"We've fixed it, Sister," Gabrielle said. "So that it fits."

"So that it fits?" asked Sister Gertrude. "And in what way, may I ask, did your clothing not fit before? Did it not cover your flesh? Did it not protect you from cold? Did it not assure your modesty?"

"It did all of those things, Sister," Gabrielle said, looking up. "But it also got in the way."

"In the way of what?" the Mother Abbess said, a shade of pink creeping up her face. "Your pride?"

Sister Immaculata stepped forward, pulled on a pair of spectacles, and examined Gabrielle's sleeve, the hem at the wrist and the seam at the shoulder. "Hmmm," she said.

Then she came to me, studying the skirt, the side seam, the waistband. "Hmmm," she said again.

She had us raise our arms and turn. Then she handed her spectacles to Sister Gertrude, who, after looking at our stitching up close, passed them to the Mother Abbess.

"Very neat," the Mother Abbess muttered. "No unnecessary adornment. Appears to be excellent work."

"The stitches are precise and nearly invisible," Sister Gertrude said, and Sister Immaculata nodded in agreement.

Gabrielle crossed her arms in front of her. "The payantes' clothes fit. Why shouldn't ours?"

The canonesses stiffened. The air in the room went out. I wanted to reach over and pinch Gabrielle through her perfectly made sleeve.

Sister Gertrude took a step toward Gabrielle, her finger pointing so close to Gabrielle's uplifted chin she almost touched it. "You, Mademoiselle Chanel, are a prideful girl. It was pride that transformed Lucifer into Satan. Pride that led Eve to partake in the forbidden fruit. Pride is the beginning of sin, and he that has it shall pour out abominations and—"

The Mother Abbess put up a hand. "To the chapel, Mademoiselles. You may wear your altered clothing, but right now you will get down on your knees and pray for your souls through dinner. Colossians says you are to be clothed in heartfelt compassion, in generosity and humility. That is what's important."

All the way to the chapel, my face burned. Humility? The payantes weren't clothed in anything but arrogance. I got down on my knees, but instead of praying for humility, I gave thanks. The nuns were always talking about epiphanies, and now, because of Gabrielle's pride, I'd had one of my own. We didn't have to accept the lot we were given. Not ill-fitting uniforms. Not anything else. Not when we had initiative and our own two hands.

This was about more than the fit of a skirt or blouse. This was about the future, about the power I'd never felt before, all because of the cut of cloth and the placement of stitches.

# THIRTEEN

IN MOULINS, THE AIR HUMMED DAY AND NIGHT WITH THE LOW throb of the city outside, the noises and smells of *la vie* seeping in through the walls, up through the floors. The world shifted from fall to winter to spring, but inside the Pensionnat Notre Dame nothing changed.

I wasn't sure which was worse: to be so far away from life, mountains and forests away, or to be so close you could hear it on the other side of locked doors, just out of reach.

Since Mémère and Pépère had moved to Moulins, there were no more trips to Clermont-Ferrand. Our only outings were to Mass on Sundays, when we walked in pairs up the narrow cobblestone street to the nearby cathedral, glancing sideways as we passed the lycée for boys, hoping to catch a glimpse of them in their black smocks and floppy black ties, smoking crapulos in the courtyard out of sight of their teachers. Hoping, better yet, to catch their eye. If we turned our heads as we passed the Hôtel de Ville, the stylish travelers with stacks of trunks and hatboxes and an impression of other places, the canonesses scolded us. "Custody of the eyes!" they would hiss, warning us not to gape.

After more than a year in Moulins, I had grown taller. In June, I would turn sixteen. My skirt length was dropped from boot top to ankle, and I wore a shirtwaist that buttoned in the front instead of the back. My monthly bleeding came, and Gabrielle showed me how to use the rags and the netting. "The English have come ashore," we girls would say when it started, a reference to English soldiers in red coats. Or it was "the moment of the moon." Back in Aubazine, the nuns had called it a curse, proof of our sins and impurity, our penance for Eve's treachery in the Garden of Eden.

"It is a curse," Gabrielle said, for once agreeing with them. "But it also means we're that much closer to leaving. To having our own lives. To being who we want to be."

I knew who I wanted to be, but I didn't ever think about how exactly I would get from here to there. In Decourcelle, the heroines always got their happy endings.

For Adrienne, that happy ending was now suddenly in question.

She had a suitor, a Monsieur Francois Caillot, the village notary of Varennes, the small provincial town where Adrienne often went to see her sister Julia. He wrote letters professing his love, and Adrienne read them with the greatest distress.

"He's old and I'm young and when I think of him, my heart doesn't soar. My pulse doesn't race," she explained to Gabrielle and me one afternoon as we strolled in the small park in front of the Pensionnat, a privilege allowed us only because we were with Adrienne, the canonesses' favorite. In the mélos, soaring hearts and racing pulses were how one knew they were in love. "I don't get lightheaded or feel the least bit faint. Instead, I only feel ill."

Monsieur Caillot wasn't a cavalry officer in scarlet breeches. He wasn't in the society pages of the newspapers or the magazines. There was nothing about him comparable to a hero in Decourcelle. Monsieur Caillot, widowed, fat, almost twice Adrienne's age, was in need of a wife to cook, clean, and scrub the ink from his cuffs.

"At first," Adrienne said, "I didn't think anything would come of it. Whenever I was in Varennes, Julia would invite him to dinner. She kept talking about what a great catch he was. I didn't really pay attention. But now they want me to marry him!"

*They* were Aunt Julia and Mémère, who were thrilled by the match.

"They say it's a stroke of luck for the daughter of traveling peddlers," Adrienne said. "They say I'll never have this chance again." She twisted a handkerchief in her hands. This wasn't the future she'd dreamed of. It wasn't the future *we'd* dreamed of.

"You're not actually considering marrying him, are you?" I asked.

"An old country notary? Of course she's not," Gabrielle said.

Then why was Adrienne so quiet?

She stopped walking and turned to us, a look of pure anguish on her face. "I just don't know how I'm going to tell Julia and Maman. They'll be so disappointed."

"Just tell them you won't do it," I said. "They can't force you. You would never be happy."

"Tell them Marie Antoinette was told to marry Louis XVI and look what happened to her." Gabrielle made a gurgling sound and put a finger to her neck as if slicing it.

Adrienne didn't laugh or even smile. "But what if they're right?" she said. "What if Monsieur Caillot is the best match I can make? I'm the daughter of peddlers. Why should I think I'm more?"

These words, coming from Adrienne, distressed me. "They're not right," I said. "You are more."

It was as simple as that. And besides, I thought but didn't say, the idea making me feel hollow like a reed, if you're not more, then what are we?

Adrienne had convinced Aunt Julia to take all of us back to Varennes for the May first holiday, la fête du muguet. We didn't wear scarlet breeches, but we were ready to do battle with this aunt we'd never met who didn't see Adrienne's true worth.

Aunt Julia, the maker of the mélos. Adrienne said she had stacks of them at her house, along with magazines and baskets of sewing notions from which she made all kinds of embellishments for clothing, curtains, and upholstery. Her favorite pastime was to trim hats. She'd buy the plain forms at a department store in Moulins or Vichy, then cover them over with feathers, cloth flowers, and streamers, sometimes all at once. "Julia is a couturière," Adrienne said. "She sells clothes and hats to the ladies of Varennes."

"The ladies of Varennes?" Gabrielle said. "How many are there? Three?"

"Three dozen," Adrienne said with a laugh. "Maybe."

When Aunt Julia came to get us in Moulins, she wore a cloche, tipped jauntily on her head, overflowing with streamers and an array of feathers.

She waved railway passes in the air, free travel for all Chanels thanks to her stationmaster husband, our Uncle Paul. "Let's go," she said. "Before the train leaves us behind."

Outside the Pensionnat, we passed gleaming black landaus with four-in-hands waiting to take the payantes away for the holiday. The air was warm and smelled of white lilies of the valley, the beautiful bouquets of "muguets" that filled the flower stalls. Lilacs bloomed in purple bunches, and overhead the leaves on the trees shimmered and danced as if they were free, even though like me they weren't, not yet.

Aunt Julia and Adrienne walked ahead, and Gabrielle and I followed, striving to appear as if we were travelers with places to go and not charity cases with limited options. The streets burst with horses, wagons, and carriages, the town going about its business, people in and out of shops and cafés.

At the station, porters pulled trolleys stacked with trunks and suitcases, and I noticed Adrienne walk just a little slower, a sway in her step, and then Gabrielle too. Then I saw why. We were about to pass a group of officers, their mustaches lively, their breeches scarlet. They eyed Adrienne and Gabrielle with interest, like cats eyeing a mouse. A strange but pleasant vibration went through me because they were looking at me too. I started moving with an extra sashay.

But as we reached the platform, Aunt Julia gave Adrienne a stern look. "Gentlemen soldiers don't wed daughters of peddlers," she said, before turning to chat with the ticket collector.

The words hurt. Behind her back, Gabrielle reassured Adrienne, whose eyes were glassy. "It's 1902. A new century. A gentleman soldier would much rather marry you than a flat-faced payante."

In Varennes, Uncle Paul greeted us at the station, unaccompanied, thankfully, by an old, fat gentleman with ink on his cuffs. Uncle Paul wore a pillbox hat decorated with gold braiding and had the bearing of a general directing his troops, in this case railcars. A long, important coat went to his knees, more gold braid at the wrists and rows of brass buttons stamped with "Chemin de Fer" and "Paris Orléans." A whistle hung from his neck. He was, like the gentlemen soldiers, a man in uniform, though he didn't give off the same bold, rakish demeanor. Aunt Julia walked next to him with extra hauteur. Here in Varennes, he was someone, which meant so was she.

But unlike in Moulins, there were no crowds in Varennes for Uncle Paul to preside over. As we made our way down the quiet Avenue de la Gare on the outskirts of the town center, now and then a wagon with a farmer or journeyman would pass by, but there were no carriages or landaus. Houses lined up neatly in a single row, not crammed together with people living on top of each other along narrow, twisting roads like Moulins. There was no bustle, just the sound of our footsteps on the old cobblestones. Varennes was another country village like Aubazine. Fine for old people and those needing country air, but no place for Adrienne to spend the rest of her life.

At least Aunt Julia and Uncle Paul's house was cheerful-looking, with light blue shutters and a window box spilling over with plump red geraniums. The first floor was a sitting room and a kitchen. Upstairs, Adrienne had told us, were three small bedrooms. I gazed around in wonder. Yellow curtains with colorful ribbon and fleurettes framed the windows. Pillows were ruffled and beaded, tablecloths trimmed in tassels and passementerie. Nothing was left unadorned, not even the little boy and girl who came up to greet us. I'd forgotten Aunt Julia had children of her own. They went straight to Adrienne, who embraced them.

"This is Marthe," Aunt Julia said to Gabrielle and me, putting her hand on the shoulder of the girl in a beribboned dress with flounces on flounces. "And this is Albert."

I stiffened. *Albert.* Aunt Julia had named her only son after our father.

They must have been close. But obviously, affection for her brother meant nothing for us. After our mother died, we could have lived here, in this house, with its friendly geraniums and fanciful curtains. There was room for us. We could have worn beribboned dresses with flounces.

I glanced at Gabrielle. There was a cold look in her eyes I understood. No matter where we were, it was always the same. Being around the payantes was a constant reminder that we were nécessiteuses. Being around family, a reminder no one had wanted us.

Except for Adrienne.

She'd helped us when no one else would. Now we would help her.

# FOURTEEN

WE STARTED IN ON THE STACKS OF MÉLOS AS SOON AS WE could, taking turns reading out loud the latest stories of affairs of the heart. But Aunt Julia continually broke in with praise for Monsieur Caillot, who was an "esteemed arbiter of conflicts," a "clever drawer of contracts," and a "trusted holder of family secrets."

"Julia," Adrienne eventually said through a tight smile, desperate to change the subject. "Why don't you show Gabrielle and Antoinette how to make cloth rosettes?"

"Like the ones on the curtains?" I said, trying to help. "I do wish I knew how to make those. They're *so beautiful*."

Gabrielle glared at me. She'd already told me she thought they were vulgar.

We gathered around the kitchen table, and Aunt Julia got out her basket of notions.

"Adrienne," she started again. "You haven't forgotten that Monsieur Caillot has one of the finest houses in Varennes."

I interrupted to change the subject. "You know, at the Pensionnat," I said, "we don't learn anything useful. We aren't going to live in plain, boring clothes when we leave. Learning this is so much more practical." I pulled a string sewn through a square of fabric tight, as Aunt Julia had demonstrated, and the square of fabric turned into a flower. "Voilà!"

But Aunt Julia wasn't listening. She went on about Monsieur Caillot's house as if it were Versailles itself, describing how Monsieur Caillot had "plans for indoor plumbing" and "was considering gas fixtures."

Gabrielle rolled her eyes for the one hundredth time. Adrienne frowned, and I jumped in again. "I do wish I knew how to trim a hat," I said.

"Oh yes," Adrienne said. "Show us, won't you, Julia?"

She took out a different basket, one that almost overflowed with feathers, flowers, and miniature copies of fruit. She went on about placement, how to arrange, how to affix. And about Monsieur Caillot.

"That's it?" Aunt Julia said when Gabrielle held out a straw boater with a single ribbon and pronounced it finished. "Wouldn't you like to add a streamer or two? Or at least a cluster of grapes?"

"No," Gabrielle said.

"I would," I said, attempting to cover for her rudeness. I didn't think we should be too obvious about our feelings for her style.

Aunt Julia turned to Adrienne, clearly unaffected. "When you live here in Varennes, we'll have our own millinery business. Won't that be fun? Everyone will want our creations."

Gabrielle coughed.

"Monsieur Caillot is well respected in town," Aunt Julia said. "He makes a very good living. That's what's important."

Adrienne tried to be firm. "It's not what's important to me."

"Don't be foolish. The Chanels have always been poor. Barely scraping by. Moving from place to place. But you have the chance to be like me. To marry a settled man. To have a home of your own. Come up in the world. It's an honor Monsieur Caillot wants to marry you."

"And I would dishonor him by agreeing to marry him when I don't love him," said Adrienne.

"You would learn to love him."

"Like the priests say, we should learn to love the lepers and the unclean," Gabrielle said in a low voice.

I stifled a laugh.

Aunt Julia snapped her head around. "What did you say?"

Gabrielle's expression was the picture of innocence. "My hands. I need to wash them. They're not *clean*."

Monsieur Caillot was to come for lunch the next day, so Aunt Julia had us dusting and redusting, polishing and repolishing all that afternoon. In the kitchen, she made us clean serving dishes that were already clean.

I kept an eye on Adrienne. Since we'd arrived that morning, her complexion had steadily faded to the lightest shade of pale. I'd always thought being parentless, with no one to care for us, was a burden. But now I saw there was a certain freedom in it. No matter what we did, we had nothing, and no one, to lose.

Whenever she could, Gabrielle tried to show Adrienne she wouldn't be losing much.

"Aunt Julia's hats are vulgar."

"Marthe is a meek little mouse."

"Albert's nose is always running into his mouth. It's disgusting."

"You're too good for the notary, Adrienne. Let him wait a few years and marry Marthe."

But later that night, it seemed Gabrielle finally got through

to her. "Aunt Julia is so nervous," Gabrielle said as she started
unpinning her hair, the dark strands falling to her waist, thick
and lush. "As if the Pope himself is coming. Not a country notary. He'll probably use his napkin as a bib. You'll have to be
brave, Adrienne. Don't let Aunt Julia intimidate you. You're too
young to settle. You have your whole life ahead of you. Right,
Adrienne? Adrienne?"

We both stopped what we were doing when we realized Adrienne wasn't taking the pins out of her chignon or unlacing her
boots or loosening her belt. Instead, she pulled something out
from the pages of the latest mélo she'd been reading and held it
up: her railway pass.

"I've never seen Paris," she said. "Let's go to Paris."

Gabrielle laughed. I almost did too. It wasn't like Adrienne
to propose something so drastic, so risky. "You're not serious,"
Gabrielle said.

"I'm very serious. We can go now. No one will know we're
gone until morning. I checked the schedule. The last train leaves
in fifteen minutes."

We stared at her. She didn't flinch.

"Are you sure you want to do this?" I asked. "Julia will be
furious. She might never forgive you."

Adrienne's usual tranquility had been replaced with resolve.
"All I know is that I can't stay here a minute longer." She gathered her clothes into her bag. "Julia is unbearable. I'm going to
disappoint her. I'm going to disappoint my parents. I'm going to
disappoint poor Monsieur Caillot. I might as well do it in style."
I started relacing my shoes. Gabrielle began repinning her hair.

"I have money," I said. "The coins Sister Xavier gave back
to me when we left Aubazine. I brought them with me. It's not
a lot, but it's a start."

"We can find a room to rent," Gabrielle said, excitement in
her voice. "And we can always find work sewing until we figure out what we're really going to do. Why didn't we think of

this sooner? Goodbye, canonesses. Goodbye, payantes. Goodbye, Aunt Julia and your notary. We're going to Paris!"

Uncle Paul and Aunt Julia always went to bed early. Uncle Paul
woke before sunrise, and Aunt Julia woke before that to make
his breakfast and brush any offensive specks of lint or dust from
his uniform that might have gathered overnight. With Marthe
and Albert in bed too, slipping off unnoticed was easy.

Down the Avenue de la Gare, we looked from side to side as
if we were thieves in the night. At the station, the train grunted
and spewed on the tracks, and I felt a wave of nerves as black
smoke billowed out of the stack. Worse, the air smelled of traces
of coal as if Uncle Paul was not sleeping in his bed but behind
us, watching every move we made, waiting to catch us.

As we walked through the station, I had a strange sensation
of the past closing its doors as we crossed into the future.

In Paris, we would be free.

Along the platform, there were few travelers. We made long
strides toward the second-class carriage, halfway there when
Adrienne took in her breath sharply. A young man in a uniform
similar to Uncle Paul's but with no gold braiding approached.

"Mademoiselle Chanel," he said, smiling at Adrienne.

I saw in his gaze infatuation, but also curiosity. My breathing
went shallow, my boots suddenly heavy on my feet. He would
wonder why we were here. He could keep us from getting on
the train. He could tell Uncle Paul.

But Adrienne quickly composed herself. "Monsieur Dubois,"
she said with a charming nod of her head.

"What are you doing here at this hour? Where is Monsieur
Costier?" he asked, glancing behind Adrienne.

Adrienne pulled out her handkerchief, dabbed delicately at

the corners of her eyes, the most lovely picture of distress I'd ever seen. "We've had terrible news from Paris."

I listened in awe as Adrienne, who never told a lie, explained to Monsieur Dubois that Gabrielle and I were her nieces, that we'd received a telegram from Paris with news of an unexpected death on our side of the family, a treasured uncle. Now Gabrielle reached for her handkerchief, a frown on her face, and I took out mine too for good measure. I even sniffled once or twice.

"His funeral is tomorrow," Adrienne said. "As their aunt, I'm escorting them to pay their last respects." She rested a gloved hand on Monsieur Dubois's arm, her brown eyes latching on to his. "My brother-in-law told me you would be here. He said you could be more than trusted to ensure we make it safely aboard. When we arrive in Paris, relatives will be there to meet us."

Monsieur Dubois stood up taller. He cleared his throat. "Monsieur Costier can count on me."

He led us the rest of the way through the station to the door of the second-class car with solemn formality, as if part of a funeral march. I wanted to fling myself into the carriage, but we boarded as if we were proper ladies, escorted by our proper aunt. Monsieur Dubois closed the door behind us, and we took our seats and flattened our skirts over our knees. Silently we exchanged glances, not daring to look out the windows for fear of seeing Uncle Paul or Aunt Julia bounding through the station to stop us.

*Go*, I thought, willing the train to move. *Go*.

Soon a loud whistle pierced the air. There was a chug, a thrust forward, a jerk back. A vibration came up from the floor, filling the car, filling my bones, as wheels ground on the rails. White steam rose up outside the windows in a long exhale, and the train began its forward progress out of the station.

We were on our way.

# FIFTEEN

IT WAS GABRIELLE'S IDEA TO SNEAK INTO THE FIRST-CLASS carriage.

We'd been traveling for hours. It must have been past midnight. We were hungry. Cold. Maybe they had food there. Surely it was warmer.

"We haven't seen the contrôleur for three stops at least," Gabrielle said, referring to the stern-faced man who went up and down the aisle after every stop: *mesdames, messieurs, tickets s'il vous plaît*. He reminded me of a village rat catcher patrolling the alleys, hunting prey. "He's fast asleep, like everyone else in the world."

We were feeling brave. Too brave.

We removed our bags from the racks and crept through the vestibule. All was quiet but for the rattle of the train, the sound of the wheels rolling over the tracks. As we entered the first-class carriage, we stood still for a moment, taking in the length of the car. Elaborate light fixtures dotted a colorfully painted ceiling. A patterned rug ran up the aisle. One side of the carriage was lined from front to back with plush benches upholstered in opulent fabrics of brown, blue, and gold. Across the aisle were repeating sets of floor-length velvet curtains, some pulled closed, others tied back to reveal an empty made bed.

It reminded me of the payantes' dormitory at the Pensionnat, where they each had a good-sized bed built into a cubby, a thick curtain for privacy, a shelf for their own porcelain basin decorated with blue flowers.

It was the middle of the night. All the passengers were asleep behind curtains. And here, right at the back, was an unoccupied berth, a bed with generous pillows and soft blankets, beckoning us in…

"Mesdames, Messieurs, tickets s'il vous plaît…"

By the time we heard him, it was too late. I opened my eyes just in time to see the contrôleur with his rat-catcher face peering into the berth. When he noticed us, he yanked the curtain open, his expression smug with victory. Just a second previous, I'd been lost in the blissful sleep of an élégante. Now I was a rat. Gabrielle and Adrienne too must have dozed off. We jumped from the bed, attempting to collect ourselves.

"What's this?" the contrôleur barked. "What do you think you're doing here?"

"The berth was empty," Gabrielle said. "What's the harm?"

"You don't have first-class tickets."

"Monsieur," Adrienne said. "Please. We'll go back to the second-class carriage. We made a mistake. Please excuse us." She batted her eyelashes, offered a charming smile. But this was no small-town stationmaster's assistant. This was a contrôleur of the Paris Orléans Railway, charged with ensuring valid passage in and out of the golden city.

"Excuse you?" he said with a sneer. "Not until you hand over the money for three first-class tickets plus penalties."

"But we have no money," Gabrielle said.

"Oh really? We'll arrive in Paris in ten minutes. You can tell that to the prefecture when I have you arrested for theft and trespass."

Adrienne's face went white. Gabrielle's went dark. As I reached into my bag and drew out my money, there was a roar in my ears that wasn't the train.

The contrôleur took every last centime, just enough to cover the penalty.

In Paris, the train idled as passengers got on and off. Back in the second-class car, we waited, shaken, for the train to pull out, the line heading back along the route it had just traveled. Returning to Varennes wasn't an option. Aunt Julia would be furious. Gossip traveled fast, and soon everyone there would know Adrienne had run out on the esteemed town notary. Kind Adrienne, they'd say, was now putting on airs as if Varennes and a notary weren't good enough for her, the daughter of peddlers. They'd blame it on the influence of Gabrielle and me, black sheep just like our lying father. Not only that, the evil-eyed contrôleur could report us. Uncle Paul's job could be in jeopardy. He might lose his important jacket with the fancy buttons and gold braiding.

Our only choice was to ride straight to Moulins and return to the Pensionnat.

Poor Adrienne. I studied her, trying to think of how I might comfort her even though I felt so miserable myself.

But to my surprise, Adrienne didn't seem upset at all. In fact, it looked like she was...laughing? Gabrielle and I stared at her dumbfounded.

"I'm sorry," she said, waving her handkerchief at us. "I just can't...help it... I just..."

I worried the trauma of the confrontation with the contrôleur had made her hysterical. She'd defied her sister, something she'd never done before. Her whole existence had been turned upside down. Ours, unfortunately, was exactly the same.

"Please, don't look so worried," Adrienne said, attempting to compose herself. "It's just that I'm so relieved. Monsieur Caillot will never marry me now. And Julia—she'll never try to make a match for me again. I know you're disappointed we didn't make it to Paris, but I've never felt so free!"

Seeing Adrienne smile, the color back in her face, the sting of going back to Moulins subsided. Maybe great change didn't come with one bold move. We weren't in Paris, but we'd tried. And because we tried, Adrienne was still free. It reminded me of our uniforms, how we adjusted the fit. This was how you get from here to there, from charity case to élégante. You don't accept what you're told you are. You decide for yourself.

# SIXTEEN

"IT'S CALLED THE HOUSE OF GRAMPAYRE," SISTER IMMACULATA said to Gabrielle and Adrienne a few months after our forced return to the Pensionnat, where we retook our places as if nothing had happened. We'd waited for weeks to be called in by the canonesses, for punishments to be doled out. But it seemed Aunt Julia hadn't told them we'd tried to run off. Instead, she sent back Adrienne's letters of apology unopened.

"Maison Grampayre specializes in lace and other fancy accoutrements for the fashionable ladies," Sister Immaculata went on. "It's not far from the Pensionnat, on the corner of rue de l'Horlage where the tall clock tower is. The Desboutins, a good, pious couple, prefer to hire our girls. They know our girls can sew. You two will leave right away. There's an attic room above the shop where you'll sleep."

Gabrielle and Adrienne shared thrilled glances. They couldn't believe their luck. Neither could I.

"What about me, Sister?" I said. "I'm a good seamstress."

"You?" Sister Immaculata said. "You're too young to leave."

"But—" Her scowl silenced me.

A mix of dread and anxiety overtook me. I'd never been apart from Gabrielle in my life. Didn't Sister Immaculata realize that we had to stay together? That was how we'd come to the Pensionnat, that was how we should leave. And I wasn't that young. I was fifteen.

Later, as they packed their things, Adrienne tried to mollify me. "We'll get ourselves established, Ninette. Then come back for you."

"What if you don't?"

Gabrielle stopped what she was doing and looked at me. "I know what it's like to be left behind, Ninette. I would never do that to you."

"It won't be long," said Adrienne with a sympathetic smile. "Don't worry."

But I did worry. I was four years younger than Gabrielle. It could be a very long time before the canonesses saw fit to let me go. My only solace was the other charity cases. Elise the redhead we called *poil de carrotte*. Sylvie who nibbled on chalk because she'd heard it would make her freckles disappear. Full-figured Fifine. Flat-chested Louise-Mathilde.

They weren't my sister and Adrienne, but they were the next best thing.

Behind the Pensionnat walls, we had our small rebellions. Just like with the girls at Aubazine, the usual topic of conversation was boys, a subject that interested me. But here, we were older and impatient, racked with yearnings we didn't understand and that sometimes made us do strange things. One Sunday, on our way back from Mass, Sylvie found a nearly whole crapulo discarded on the street, and that afternoon in the dormitory, we all took turns putting our lips on it, closing our eyes, pretending we were touching the lips of one of the lycée boys we spied on from a dormitory window that overlooked their courtyard.

Sometimes, if they spotted us, they made crude gestures or encouraged us to lift up our chemises. We had something they wanted, and it was an exhilarating feeling.

So was pilfering from the payantes when we had to fill their water pitchers or empty their wastebaskets. Items that seemed as if they'd been discarded or replaced with newer versions, we took for ourselves. We had our own stashes of silver hairbrushes with missing bristles, tortoiseshell combs with broken teeth, and fraying velvet ribbons, remnants from a world so far from ours we were like archaeologists examining relics from another civilization. We took the lotions, creams, and powders the payantes tried to hide—all items they couldn't report missing to the canonesses because they weren't supposed to have them to begin with.

We did what we could to entertain ourselves, to bide our time, praying not so much for our souls as for release from our holy prison.

Each time Gabrielle and Adrienne came back to visit me, they appeared less and less like convent girls. They were young ladies of the monde. They styled their hair differently, pompadours rolled low over their foreheads, and they wore new clothes, blouses with high starched collars that showed off their long necks and straight, tailored skirts. But as time went on they appeared exhausted, their eyes bloodshot. Gabrielle in particular had grown irritable.

"I thought you'd both be swept away by handsome soldiers by now," I said after they'd been gone almost nine months.

"Soldiers don't come into a layette shop," Gabrielle snapped. "Just rich snooty ladies who still wear bustles and have so much powder on their faces they look like flour sacks. As if being born into wealth is an accomplishment. It's luck, that's all it is. That's the only difference between us and them."

"Luck and a grand name and la vie château, among other things," Adrienne said with a wan smile. I was worried to see that even the twinkle in her eyes had dimmed a bit.

"But at least you're free," I said. "You're out in the world. You're *living*."

Gabrielle tightened the scarf around her neck. "All we do is sew. Six days a week. Sometimes seven. My eyes are tired, my back aches, and my fingers are sore. The last thing we are is free."

# SEVENTEEN

THE CANONESSES ALLOWED GIRLS WHO WERE NO LONGER
students at the Pensionnat to be part of the choir. Gabrielle and
Adrienne had never shown much interest in singing, and I was
shocked when, a year after they moved out, they started coming back for evening practice.

"I have to train," Gabrielle said. She seemed possessed by an
enthusiasm I hadn't seen since they had first left the Pensionnat.

"Train?"

"I'm going to be a singer."

She must have seen my confusion. She wasn't known for her
voice.

"It's more about stage presence than anything else," she said,
drawing herself up as if she were on view right then. "Sewing is
only temporary. Once I'm on the stage, I'll never touch a needle and thread again."

Her new preoccupation tempered the strain of working long
hours. I was sure this was just a fleeting whim, but week after

week, they showed up. Gabrielle even began wearing a wool scarf around her neck at all times, though it was June, to protect her voice. "You should too, Ninette. You need to cover your throat to keep from getting sick and ruining your vocal cords if you ever want to have a chance."

Did she actually think I could be a singer? I wasn't known for my voice either, but I started taking choir practice a bit more seriously, just in case.

With summer, another new prospect bloomed for Gabrielle and Adrienne.

"Guess what, Ninette," Gabrielle said after the session ended. "We're going to make extra money working at a tailor shop, on Sundays when the House of Grampayre is closed."

I didn't understand why they both looked so conspiratorial until Adrienne added, "It's where the young cavalry officers go for alterations."

Now when they came for choir practice, I couldn't wait to ask about the tailor shop.

"We work in a back room," Gabrielle said. "But sometimes the owner leaves the door open and the lieutenants peek in."

"We don't dare look up from our work," Adrienne said. "Though we make sure to arrange our best sides toward the door before they get there. Sometimes they're in just their shirttails!"

I laughed at the picture that formed in my mind until a couple of payantes passed by, Eugenie and Margrethe, two of the worst. They peered sideways at Gabrielle and Adrienne and whispered "seamstresses" in a mocking tone.

Adrienne ignored them, but Gabrielle couldn't. "You'll see who gets the last laugh," she said. "We won't be seamstresses for long."

"Oh really?" Margrethe said. "Then what will you be? Laundresses? Maids?"

Gabrielle's chin was lifted, her tone haughty. "You'll just have to wait and find out, won't you?"

The two girls burst into laughter. "Listen to her," Eugenie said as they walked off. "It's as if she really believes it. She really thinks she's going to come up in the world. It would be sad if it weren't so funny."

I looked at Gabrielle, holding in her rage, not wanting them to know they'd affected her. I didn't see my older sister. I saw the little girl who dreamed of Something Better. I hated Eugenie and Margrethe. I wanted to get back at them, hurt them as they'd hurt Gabrielle, but didn't know how until a few days later, when it was my turn to bring the water up to the payantes' dormitory. That time, and every time after, I made sure to spit in their pitchers.

# EIGHTEEN

"THERE YOU ARE," GABRIELLE SAID WITH A HINT OF IMPATIENCE. "Are you ready?"

It was Sunday afternoon, warm for autumn, and I had been called down to the parlor for reasons unknown. I walked in to find Gabrielle and Adrienne waiting, the mood about them so light that for a short moment I didn't recognize them. They wore new hats, belts wrapped tight to accentuate their small waists, and gave off an impression of having someplace important to be.

"Ready? Aren't you supposed to be working at the tailor shop?" I asked.

"We finished early," said Gabrielle.

"Just for an hour or two," Adrienne said to Sister Ermentrud through the nun's ear horn. On Sunday afternoons, the canonesses and payantes went out to visit friends or family, leaving Sister Ermentrud, who napped all afternoon in a parlor chair, in charge. "Some fresh air...it's a lovely day...we'll have her back before dinner, Sister."

"Are we going to see Mémère and Julia-Berthe?" I asked, though I thought I already knew the answer. Where else would we go?

Gabrielle flashed a mysterious smile. "You'll see," she said, tidying up my hair. Then she beckoned me to follow her to the door, and just like that, I stepped from one world into another.

Down the streets of Moulins, Gabrielle and Adrienne moved with the subtle, self-conscious sashay of the élégantes. They glided down the avenues and around corners with a purpose, slowing, finally, when a distance away a red awning jutted out from a building front. It shaded café tables with white cloths and chairs arranged on the sidewalk. One table was crowded with a group of soldiers casually leaning back in chairs, legs sprawled out, and as we neared, their gazes turned toward us. I glanced at Gabrielle and Adrienne, but they stared straight ahead, their expressions glazed, necks long, lips curved up slightly, aware they were on display.

"Officers of the Tenth Light Horse Regiment," Adrienne whispered to me from the side of her mouth, her tone reverent. "The tailor shop lieutenants."

Something unlodged in my chest and fluttered around.

"They keep asking us to meet them," Adrienne said.

"We finally said yes," Gabrielle said, giving me a warning look. "Don't talk too much, Ninette. Custody of the tongue."

Custody of the tongue? She didn't have to worry. The only men I ever spoke to were the priests at confession. I had no idea what to say to cavalry officers.

As we approached the table, the lieutenants stood. "The Three Graces," one of them said with a little bow.

"Elegance, Mirth, and Youth," said another, motioning to Adrienne, Gabrielle, and me in turn.

"And you," Adrienne said, "must be our heroic Argonauts."

The lieutenants made a show of kissing Gabrielle's and Adrienne's hands in greeting. Then they kissed my hand too, their lips brushing the top of my glove, as Adrienne introduced them, the impossibly long last names of aristocrats. These weren't lanky schoolboys from the lycée across the street from the Pensionnat. These were men, real men in their twenties with broad shoulders and mustaches and scruffy cheeks. I tried not to gape.

With sweeping gestures, they motioned for us to sit. Their breeches weren't scarlet but brown, thick stripes running down the side, but the officers were dashing all the same, with a confidence in their eyes and swagger in their movements. Mud splattered their tall black boots and spurs, and their exquisite jackets, with high tab collars and a line of round gold buttons up the front, were rumpled, the top button casually undone. They looked as if they'd just finished a riding competition, which I would soon learn from their casual sparring they had.

A waiter delivered tea and a tray of cookies for us while the officers drank coffee and smoked, my head turning from man to man, trying to follow the slang, the unfinished sentences. They bragged about the height of the obstacles they'd jumped, the quality of their mounts, their bravery and daring, always trying to outdo each other. It was all so confusing and exciting.

A short, stocky officer with a baby face he tried to disguise with a flamboyant waxed mustache was the loudest.

"Don't listen to him," a curly-haired lieutenant said to me with a wink. "He was kicked in the head by a horse."

Another lieutenant, who wore an extravagant gold signet ring, elbowed him. "*You* could use a good kick in the head."

Adrienne's eyes were wide. "It all sounds so dangerous."

"It is dangerous," declared waxed mustache. "Very dangerous." He leaned in toward Adrienne until signet ring knocked him away.

"I think it sounds thrilling," said Gabrielle.

"So do I," I said, picturing a grand spectacle of strong horses and debonair soldiers.

"Next time, you'll have to watch," waxed mustache announced. "All three of you. The winner is certain," he said imperiously, "but you can see the rest of these fellows fight it out for second place."

This led to another vigorous debate, but despite the sparring, the soldiers had a relaxed, casual way about them. They looked like men but acted like boys. They were man-boys, a new kind of species, a fascinating creature.

I was a new kind of species as well. The girl from the convent was no more. I was a butterfly sprung from my cocoon. I sat tall. I tipped my head at an alluring angle. I laughed easily. I played coyly with a loose strand of hair. My eyelashes flitted up and down like hummingbird wings.

And Gabrielle! So bright and funny and quick! I watched as she laughed whenever the lieutenants appeared to say something amusing in their strange language. When she dropped a glove, they pretended to fight over picking it up, making such a scene we all started laughing. Gabrielle was getting the attention she'd always craved, and I almost didn't recognize her.

Too soon Adrienne, shining and self-possessed, the most graceful of the Graces, stood and announced that I had to be returned, that the "dear canonesses" would be waiting for me. The light that glowed inside me went dark.

On our way back, I complained that Sister Ermentrud hadn't set a specific time. I was surprised Gabrielle, who'd been having such fun, wasn't complaining as well.

"It would never do for a lady to linger too long," Adrienne said. "Remember that, Ninette. She should always leave them wanting more. She should always have someplace she must be."

"So that's the reason you brought me along? I'm the excuse?"

"Of course not," Adrienne said. "We wanted you to come."

"And we needed a chaperone," Gabrielle said.

"What? I'm too young to be a chaperone."

"That's the point," she said. "You're still a schoolgirl. You're just as effective as an old widow in black crepe. They have to behave themselves around you."

I wanted to say more but held my tongue, realizing that whether I was an excuse or a chaperone, it didn't matter. They didn't have to include me, but they had.

# NINETEEN

WE DIDN'T MEET THE OFFICERS EVERY WEEK—SOMETIMES THEY had to stay with their regiments; sometimes Gabrielle and Adrienne had too much work to do—making my escapades from the Pensionnat all the more precious.

I did what I could to counteract my drab school uniform. Gabrielle let me borrow a collar and cuffs she'd made with scraps from the House of Grampayre that I could attach to my blouse once we were outside the Pensionnat. I dabbed on powder and rouge I'd pilfered from the payantes, twisted my hair in a sophisticated chignon, slid my golden gypsy ring on my finger.

We'd meet our dashing horse guard officers at La Tentation for sherbet or at the terrace of the Hotel Danguin or whichever establishment was then à la mode. The Grand Café was my favorite. We started going there when the weather turned cold for good. The interior was plush and dramatic, with long tables and banquettes and ornate mirrors reflecting light and laughter, painted landscape scenes hovering on the ceiling over a string orchestra. My gaze didn't know where to rest, there was so much to see, although usually it was on Armand, the lieutenant with the curls, who said he'd never seen hair as shining and golden as mine. He told me I had the face of a Botticelli angel.

I'd come to understand the officers' slang or most of it, adjusting to the rhythm of their repartée, their soldier dialect, aristocratic accents. Horses were the main subject. Now, when waxed mustache, who everyone called Gui, spoke of Lisette, saying "she wants to please but needs the crop now and then," I knew he was speaking of his mare and not of a scene from the boudoir. Or when Mathias, the lieutenant with the signet ring on his pinky, complained that "Ana threw another shoe," I no longer imagined an angry élégante hurling a jewel-encrusted mule across a ballroom.

They argued one minute, then tossed their arms around one another's shoulders and sang a refrain from a sentimental battle song the next. They were bursting with life, with a joie de vivre that was so contagious, it stayed with me even when I was back at the Pensionnat, the freedom of the outside world simmering inside of me, keeping me warm all through the winter.

I couldn't believe it! My sister had performed a song at La Rotonde! We'd been meeting our lieutenants for several months by then, and it was all they could talk about, how they had convinced her to go up on stage.

"You were so charming," Adrienne said, beaming at Gabrielle.

"A breath of fresh air," said Etienne, a dark-haired newcomer with a handsome face offset by a poor mustache, though he carried himself as if he were older than the others, more man than boy.

"It was just one little song," Gabrielle said. But her eyes

flashed. Her face was flushed. I could tell it was so much more than that.

"I wish I could have seen it," I said, feeling left out.

"But you can," said Gui. He motioned to Gabrielle, calling for an encore right there in the Grand Café. The other officers started pounding the table, chanting something strange: co-co, co-co, co-co.

Gabrielle's black eyelashes fluttered. She glanced from side to side, then stood up, quick as a cat, moving just behind her chair. With a coy smile, she put her hands on her hips and began.

I have lost my poor Coco,
Coco my dog who I adore,
Close to Trocadéro…

A dip of the knees here. A turn of the hips there.

I confess, my greatest regret,
In my cruel loss,
The more my man deceived me,
The more faithful Coco was…

A hop and she looked left, hand to her brow. A hop and she looked right.

Eh Coco,
Eh Coco,
Who has seen Coco?

We all burst into applause. "Bravo, bravo!" the officers called out.

Gabrielle glowed, curtsied formally. Patrons at nearby tables glanced over at us. Waiters scowled from a distance.

"I've talked with the manager at La Rotonde," said Etienne

once Gabrielle was back in her seat. "He wants to give you a regular spot."

"Say you'll do it," Gui said.

"You must," said Armand.

"I'll do it," Gabrielle said, exhilarated.

To celebrate, Etienne ordered champagne for the table. To the officers of the Tenth Light Horse, Gabrielle was their discovery. Her triumph was their triumph. It was my triumph too, even though I wouldn't be there to see it. My sister, on stage! Maybe, someday, I would take the stage myself. The lieutenants snapped their fingers and waiters came, filling coupe after coupe. The pop! The fizz! I took a sip and experienced right away why élégantes drank it by the bucketful.

Bubbles danced in my head. A dip of the knees. A turn of the hips.

Gabrielle performed almost every week after that at La Rotonde, through the spring, into the summer, a command performance for all of the officers from the garrison, not just those from the Tenth Light Horse. *Coco! Coco! Coco!* They only stopped when she took the stage and sang about the little lost dog and another she'd added to her repertoire called "Koko Rico," about a rooster.

She loved it. They loved her. So much so that now, instead of Gabrielle, the officers started calling her Coco.

On our way back to the Pensionnat, Gabrielle and Adrienne would sing songs from La Rotonde until I knew them by heart too. They didn't come to choir practice anymore now, Gabrielle working on a new kind of repertoire.

There was the song about the Boudins and Boutons, two married couples who spent so much time together that in the end, Madame Bouton had a little baby Boudin, and Madame Boudin had a little baby Bouton.

There was another song called "Le Fiacre," in which two lovers embraced behind the closed curtains of a carriage. As the woman complained that the man's lorgnette was getting in the way, her husband walked by and heard her voice. Angry, he called out, but slipped and fell, only to be run over by the carriage.

"How awful," I said.

"The officers love it," said Gabrielle. "They say it's a fitting end to anyone who tries to interfere with a *liaison amoureuse*."

If there was time, we'd stop to visit Julia-Berthe, who lived with Mémère and Pépère near the market square at the Place de la Liberté, where they now sold men's things instead of buttons and socks.

"Mémère isn't stupid," Gabrielle said with disapproval after one of our visits. "She sees how men gawk at Julia-Berthe."

My skin prickled. Surely Julia-Berthe had learned her lesson in Aubazine and wouldn't give away her heart—or anything else—so easily again?

I tried not to worry. Mémère would watch over her, I told myself. Mémère would make sure no one took advantage. *Remember, don't give away your gold*, I started warning her before we left, after we sang her the *caf'conc* songs, choreographing gestures, Julia-Berthe laughing and clapping along.

My mind was a music hall. I pictured myself on stage in a red satin dress, trimmed in lace, that showed my arms and shoulders, singing about le fiacre or the Boutons and the Boudins. I made up my own charming gestures, turning to the side, patting my stomach and making a face, miming a pregnant Madame Bouton. I turned the other way, walking in place as Madame Boudin, proudly pushing an imaginary pram.

"I'm going to be a singer too," I'd whispered to Armand one Sunday at the Grand Café.

"The face of a Botticelli angel," he'd said, leaning close to me, "and the voice too."

Later, I pretended to drop my glove in the space between us. When we both reached for it, his lips brushed my cheek. Did it count as my first kiss?

At the Pensionnat, I was so distracted, a song always playing in my head, the feel of Armand's soft lips and rough mustache, that I had to pull out long lines of wayward stitches during needlework. I got most of my math problems wrong. When I was supposed to be writing a composition on "the importance of thrift in the household," I stared out the window at the plain wall of the lycée instead, envisioning myself on a stage in Paris. The canonesses deemed my essays unreadable and rapped my desk with rulers to get my attention. They declared my home-making skills deficient.

I'd bow my head, trying not to smile. What could I do? It was impossible not to be distracted when the world was so full of possibilities.

# TWENTY

IN AUGUST, ARMAND AND GUI ANNOUNCED THEY WERE TO play in a regimental polo match the following Sunday.

"We must have our Three Graces there," Armand said, "for luck."

Gui stuck out his chest. "Polo is the most realistic training for combat."

"Next Sunday?" Gabrielle said as if she were contemplating her schedule.

According to Gui, everyone in Moulins would be there. Armand and Gui would be on a team that would compete against players who'd come all the way from Argentina, men who were horse breeders from the biggest estancias. They were hoping to sell their Argentinian horses—criollos, they were called—to the French cavalry. The polo match was to showcase what these foreign horses could do.

"Those Argentines will be lucky to score a goal," Armand said. "But I'll give them one. I say we win 12-1. Who's in for a bet?"

"I've heard these criollos have extraordinary endurance," Etienne said. "Perfect for a light cavalry."

"Impossible," said Gui. "They're field horses. They should be attached to a plow."

I stopped listening, thinking instead of what I would wear to the polo match if I were wealthy and had more than a convent uniform to choose from. This wasn't a match at the Château de Bagatelle in Paris, but it was a start, a way to learn the rituals and rules of spectating, which, from what I'd read in the magazines, were mainly to be dressed as impressively as possible.

The day of the match, a large field at the barracks had been turned into a polo ground, which just seemed to mean the grass was short and small flags now marked the corners and the goals. Wooden chairs for spectators had been set out along one side, a few yards from what must have been the edge of the playing field, though there was no actual barrier.

Etienne, in civilian clothes, arrived to watch with Gabrielle, Adrienne, and me, and the rest of the onlookers. He'd been discharged, Gabrielle told me, his two years of compulsory military service completed. His parents had recently died, and he'd come into a substantial inheritance from their successful textile company. Having no parents to disapprove of how he spent it, he was scouting for property where he could devote himself to breeding horses for racing and polo.

"And to Émilienne d'Alençon," Gabrielle added in a hushed voice.

"The famous courtesan?"

"Shhhh!" Gabrielle said. She glanced over at Etienne, who was busy talking to a group of strangers nearby.

I knew of Émilienne. Everyone did. She was a celebrated beauty known for ruining royalty and men of great wealth. King Leopold of Belgium had been obsessed with her and gave her so many necklaces and rings she didn't need him anymore and left. He wasn't the only one. The Duchesse d'Uzès sent her son, Jacques, off to Africa just to get him away from Émilienne, but not before he'd gifted her the family jewels. In the Sudan, poor Jacques caught fever and died.

And now the famous seductress was with Etienne? *Our* Etienne?

"It's just an amusement for them both," Gabrielle said. "They won't talk about it in front of us, but Gui told me that's what Etienne says when the other lieutenants tease him." She rolled her eyes. "Men and their amusements. Émilienne's old now, in her thirties, way past her prime. But it doesn't matter because she's rich. She's collected so many rubies and pearls and emeralds, she can do what she wants. Gui says Etienne will only spend money on horses, but Émilienne doesn't even *need* his money."

In her tone, I thought I detected a certain respect for Émilienne. *If you're going to sin against modesty, at least do it with someone who's rich,* Gabrielle had once said about Julia-Berthe.

I wanted to ask more, but Etienne had joined us again and the match was about to begin. On the field, the players and their horses cantered in circles and figure eights, warming up. I should have been admiring our lieutenants atop their French mounts, trying to catch Armand's eye. I'd promised him a quick kiss if they won. "*When* we win," he'd said.

But instead, my gaze was drawn to the Argentines in matching short-sleeve shirts that displayed strong, tanned forearms. Their collars were turned up, and each shirt had a number, one through four, on the back. Their horses were smaller than the French horses, less refined, but they seemed more powerful. Meanwhile, our officers' uniforms were formal, long-sleeved cotton shirts with collars attached with buttons and, over that, vests. They looked like the dandies they were. The Argentines looked like they'd come to play.

Gabrielle also stared at the Argentines, her lip curled, her arms crossed in front of her. "You'd think they'd have dressed a little nicer. Not to mention, their horses are ugly."

"Gabrielle," Adrienne scolded.

Etienne laughed. "Fortunately for them, neither of those criteria has anything to do with winning."

"But who are they?" I said, still in awe.

"They're Anglo-Argentine, descended from wealthy English families that went to South America years ago to build railroads and raise cattle. Their families send them back to England to be educated. They're not quite Argentines, not quite Anglo."

There was one Argentine in particular I couldn't stop watching. When he rode close to my seat, and I saw the muscles of his arms, the solidness of him in the saddle, my breath caught. But it was more than that. It was the way he moved with his horse. It wasn't a fight between them, a master controlling his beast, but a dance, a partnership, as if the two weren't two but one.

"Like half man, half horse," I said.

Etienne nodded. "Centaurian," he said.

"Centaurian," I repeated.

As the player raced about the field, I felt a pull I couldn't explain, a quickening of my pulse.

I silently scolded myself with a laugh. *Custody of the eyes, Mademoiselle.*

A horn blew, and the game started. Riders and horses rushed this way and that, the two teams going after each other, galloping to win the ball or edge each other out, horse bashing against horse, sticks slashing through the air. The experience was terrifying and exhilarating all at once, especially when the play was so close, sometimes only a few arm-lengths of space separating us from the action. It quickly became too exciting to sit.

The Argentines called out to each other in words and inflections I didn't recognize, making them all the more mysterious. "What language are they speaking?" I asked Etienne.

"Spanish. But they speak French and English too."

"You know a lot about them," I said.

"We've been corresponding. I might buy some of their horses, if they're everything I've heard they are. When it comes to horses, I like to win. These criollos aren't for the racecourse. But they're perfect for the polo field. Just look at them."

He didn't have to tell me to look. Our centaur turned and twisted with his horse, chasing the ball at a full gallop as if nothing else mattered, then coming to a quick stop, then back into a gallop. He was magnificent. He swung his stick and soon the score was 1 to 0, then 5 to 0, then 10, 11, 12 to 0. This was war. And the Argentines were winning.

The crowd had quieted. Out on the field, Gui and Armand cursed, whacked at the ball wildly in frustration. Gabrielle proclaimed the Argentines rude for scoring so many times. Adrienne seemed distressed that everyone was so upset. Everyone but Etienne. And me.

When the match was over, the players from both sides handed their horses over to their grooms. Our lieutenants stormed into the barracks, embarrassed. Armand wouldn't get his kiss, but it didn't matter. I'd forgotten all about Armand.

The Argentines mixed with the remaining spectators, mostly gentleman riders like Etienne who wanted to know more about the South American horses. While Adrienne and Gabrielle critiqued fashion choices, I followed Etienne toward the players. My heart pitched at the sight of the handsome Argentine. I guessed he was in his midtwenties. His eyes were a golden, mesmerizing brown, his tousled hair black. He was clean-shaven, his fine face not hidden behind the distraction of a mustache. It had a sensitive quality I hadn't expected.

"Juan Luis Harrington," Etienne said, shaking hands with him. "It's good to finally meet you in person."

"Call me Lucho," Monsieur Harrington said.

"Where did you learn to play like that, Lucho?"

"On the pampas, we play polo before we can walk."

I listened as the horse talk continued. What did the nickname Lucho mean? What was the pampas? I had a strange desire to know everything about him. Then I noticed the scrape on his arm, blood dripping, on the verge of staining his white jodhpurs.

I pulled out my handkerchief, one of the many I'd had to practice stitching my initials on, and without thinking put it directly on his arm to stanch the blood.

"You're bleeding," I said and felt my face go pink. I'd just touched a man I didn't know.

He looked at me, caught off guard, his fingers brushing mine as he took the handkerchief. "Merci," he said, turning his arm and blotting at the blood.

"May I present Mademoiselle Antoinette Chanel," Etienne said with an amused smile. "With her sister and her aunt, one of the famous Three Graces of Moulins."

Lucho's eyes met mine and lingered. "But how could she be just one when she qualifies for all three, Beauty, Mirth, and Youth?"

I tried to behave naturally, as if I were complimented like this by handsome men all of the time. "You're kind," I said, "but as the youngest, I've been designated 'Youth.'"

"To Youth," Lucho said with a gentlemanly bow. "A valuable quality some like myself have squandered. I owe you a hand-kerchief, Antonieta." His eyes held mine for an extra moment before he left to rejoin his teammates, still pressing my hand-kerchief to his arm.

As he walked off, Etienne shook his head and laughed. "Smooth, isn't he?" He paused for a beat, then added in a teasing tone, "*Antonieta.*"

I might have retorted, but my heart had taken flight inside me. I could barely speak.

As we headed back to our group, I mulled over something Lucho Harrington had said that confused me. I turned to Etienne. "Why did he say his youth is squandered? He still looks young enough to me."

"I suspect it has to do with his marriage," Etienne said, my heart's new wings suddenly clipped. "If you can call it a marriage."

"What do you mean?" I said.

"According to the gossip, it was one of those arrangements where one powerful Argentine family merged with another for the sake of land. Lucho's bride insisted on a trip to England and then refused to return to Argentina. So now she has a house in Mayfield, where she lives independently, lovers coming and going, or so they say. The family expects children, of course, but Lucho will have nothing to do with her. Yet there's nothing to be done. Besides the usual complications, under Argentine law, divorce is illegal. The only way to put a marriage asunder, biblically speaking, is for one of the parties to die."

So that was it. I'd met my Decourcelle hero at last, but he could never be mine. I'd lived an entire mélo in a single afternoon.

# TWENTY-ONE

A FEW WEEKS AFTER THE POLO MATCH, AS I PASSED THROUGH the foyer on my way to the kitchen humming "Le Fiacre," I was surprised to spot Mémère and Aunt Julia, a cluster of turkey feathers dyed blue bobbing atop her hat.

I froze. What were they doing here?

Aunt Julia looked disgusted. Mémère dabbed at tears and acknowledged me with a weak smile as the Mother Abbess ushered them out the front door.

Before I could disappear, the Mother Abbess grabbed my arm. "Come," she said and led me to her office, shutting the door behind us.

I stared demurely at the floor while she stood over me, arms crossed amidst her jars of specimens, the butterflies pinned in their display cases on the wall like miniature crucifixions.

Outside, church bells rang the hour.

Finally, she spoke. "All we do is try to protect you. We warn, over and over and over again. Men have inclinations. They're driven by instincts you can't underestimate. And yet you girls flaunt yourselves. You tempt men to sin against purity like Eve in the Garden with your smiling, making eyes instead of following the example of our Holy Virgin Mother, of purity and chastity."

A sick feeling rose in my stomach. Someone must have seen us with the lieutenants.

"It's our duty as canonesses to teach the poor how to be clean and virtuous. To be industrious. To overcome the character defect of poverty. All we ask is that you don't disgrace this institution as your sister has done."

My sister? This wasn't just about Sundays at the Grand Café. Had the Mother Abbess somehow found out about Gabrielle performing at La Rotonde too? I dug my fingernails in my arm as she went on and on about morals, good sense, how my sister was an embarrassment, a loose woman, her reputation ruined, her virtue stained, on and on and on until I couldn't bear it anymore.

I met her glare, my hands in fists at my sides. "Gabrielle is just trying to make something of herself. The officers are always perfect gentlemen when we meet them. And as for singing in a music hall, it's only a song about a little lost dog."

The Mother Abbess's eyes suddenly grew wide. "Officers?" she said. "Music hall? You Chanels! Will you never learn? Your grandmother and aunt were here begging for our help. A place must be found to take the infant. Your sister Julia-Berthe is with child."

I couldn't visit Julia-Berthe. I wasn't even to mention her name. The canonesses looked at me now as if it was only a matter of time before I followed in her footsteps.

I wasn't allowed to leave the Pensionnat at all, and only Adrienne was permitted to see me.

In November, she arrived with the news that Julia-Berthe had given birth to a boy she'd named André. In the visiting room, Sister Ermentrud dozing across from us in her chair, Adrienne told me that Mémère and the canonesses made Julia-Berthe give the baby away to the priest at a local parish and that Gabrielle was furious. My heart broke. Another Chanel sent away to be raised by strangers.

"Who is the father?" I asked. "He won't marry her?"

Adrienne shook her head. "She'd been living with a man for a couple months. His last name is Palasse. He's gone now. He's disappeared."

A highwayman, I thought. A thief.

Adrienne glanced at Sister Ermentrud to make sure she was still asleep. Then she slipped something small in my hand. A package.

"Tuck it away," she said in a whisper. "So no one will see it. It's from Etienne."

"Etienne? What is it?" I said.

"He didn't say. All he said was that you would know when you opened it."

She eyed me as if I had a glorious secret to tell. But my perplexed expression must have made clear I didn't.

After she left, I snuck into the chapel. No one would be there on a Sunday afternoon. I kneeled as if I were praying, bowed my head, and slipped the package from under my sweater. I pulled out something wrapped in tissue paper, opened the folds to find a square of linen cloth, white and pristine. A scent tickled my nose, lavender and bergamot. It was a man's handkerchief with the initials JLH embroidered in the corner.

At first I thought it was a mistake, a handkerchief meant for someone else. And then I remembered. *I owe you a handkerchief.*

JLH.

Juan Luis Harrington.

Lucho.

It was the handkerchief that would get me through the next year at the Pensionnat, the longest one yet. I was eighteen and life was still an endless conspiracy of traps, from the walls and rules of the Pensionnat to my place in society. The very air I moved in was dense and stifling.

Had it all been just a dream? The horse guards, the Sunday afternoons at the cafés, the polo match? *Lucho?* No. That moment between us—that was real. I had a small square of linen tucked in my pillowcase, nestled beneath my head every night as I slept, to prove it.

# TWENTY-TWO

IN MAY, JUST BEFORE I WAS TO TURN NINETEEN, ADRIENNE came to the Pensionnat and announced she and Gabrielle were moving to Vichy.

"Moving?" I said. "But why?"

"The music halls are grander there. A step up, Gabrielle says. It's a real city, with real theater for la haute who go there to take the cure for the season. She's going to audition."

I was quiet, trying to take this news in.

Adrienne's excitement turned to concern. "Don't worry Ninette," she said, putting a hand on my arm. "Vichy's not far. It's just a short train ride away. And we'll be back to visit."

*I'll be back,* our father had said, but he didn't come back, those words always haunting me. But Adrienne's eyes sparkled with a new sense of possibility, a contagious one. I noticed that her clothes and her hat were new too, and she smelled of rosewater.

"Your jacket," I said. "It's so beautiful." I ran my hand along the smooth fabric of her sleeve. Gold trim was stitched in a pattern along the wrist. A matching theme decorated her collar.

"Surah," she said. "That's what the fabric's called. A kind of silk."

"It looks expensive."

"Etienne's helping us, giving us a leg up, as the lieutenants say in their horse talk. He said we need to start with a quality wardrobe. We went to the House of Grampayre but as customers this time. You should have seen Gabrielle lording over the Desboutins."

Etienne gave them money? I didn't think Adrienne would ever do anything untoward, and she was usually a check on Gabrielle. But I'd observed the way Etienne looked at Gabrielle, interest and amusement in his eye. And the two of them had an easy way with each other. Thinking of Émilienne d'Alençon, I couldn't help but ask, my voice low as if the idea might wake Sister Ermentrud asleep in the corner. "Etienne is helping...in exchange for favors?"

"No!" Adrienne said, so appalled I was embarrassed I'd asked. "He finds Gabrielle entertaining, that's all. He says she has no voice, but she has determination and you can't teach that. He's going to pay for singing lessons. Gabrielle insists it's a loan, that she'll repay him after she makes a name for herself. He says it's a good thing he can afford to lose it."

"If he thinks she can't sing, why would he help her?"

"You know how these men are. They like to bet, and his bet is on her. He says he has a soft spot for the underdog. Personally, I think he has a soft spot for *Gabrielle*. Either way"—she twirled—"I have a new ensemble. And here," she said, picking up a small package wrapped in decorative paper I hadn't noticed. "There's something for you too."

"Me?"

"Of course. The Third Grace. From Etienne. He told us to pick out something for you." I opened the package, revealing a set of tortoiseshell combs inside.

"They're beautiful," I said. I was touched. Etienne was like an older brother we never had. First Saint Etienne of Aubazine. Now, Saint Etienne of Moulins.

"What about the rest of the lieutenants?" I asked as Adrienne helped me put the combs in. Up close, they were exquisite. But tucked in the folds of my hair, they wouldn't draw much notice from the canonesses.

"They're all gone. Their commissions were up. It's not the same without them but especially without you."

Time marched forward outside of the Pensionnat. But inside, it gathered dust, the hands turning at a frustrating crawl.

"Oh, and Ninette, I haven't told you about Maud."

"Maud?"

"Madame Mazuel. Gabrielle and I went to a horse race with Gui, and he introduced us to her there. She's a salonnière."

"A what?"

"A hostess. She's refined in an old-fashioned kind of way. She invited us to tea at her villa in Souvigny, just outside Moulins. And the people! You should have seen them. Handsome officers and gentlemen with titles longer than the plume on her hat. And she only invites women who are beautiful, women with potential, she says. And she thinks *I* have potential." Adrienne leaned in closer. "She thinks she can find me a husband. A real aristocrat. Once I help Gabrielle get settled in Vichy and she finds a role, I'll move to Souvigny and live with Maud."

"An aristocrat? Just what you've always wished for," I said. "Oh, Adrienne, what if you'd listened to Aunt Julia and married the notary?"

"Thank goodness you and Gabrielle didn't let me. Soon, Ninette, you'll be nineteen. You'll leave the Pensionnat and have so many choices. By then Gabrielle will be a famous singer and can help you find a place on the stage if that's what you want. Or Maud can help find a match for you. She'll see that you have potential too. It won't be much longer."

# TWENTY-THREE

*May 15, 1906, Vichy*
*Chérie Ninette,*
*Our adventure has begun! Vichy is a fairyland, everyone rich and*
*exotic. We've seen Russian princesses, Italian ambassadors, Leba-*
*nese emirs. Even colonialists from L'Afrique to recover their health*
*from the hot climate.*

*We've found a dreary room to rent in old Vichy but we won't be*
*there for long. We stare at the grand hotels and dream... Tomor-*
*row Gabrielle auditions at the Grand Casino. She's floating on air!*
*Bisous,*
*Adrienne*
*(Gabrielle asked me to tell you she will write as soon as she has*
*time.)*

I COULDN'T KEEP THE LETTER TO MYSELF. IN THE DORMITORY
that night, I read it to the other charity cases. Elise, Sylvie, Fifine.
Louise-Mathilde. We all sighed with longing. How lovely to be
in such a magical place, where just the water could cure ills and

ailments. There was so much to wonder about, what Russian princesses wore, what they might look like. Were there princes too? And what was an emir? Thanks to Adrienne's letter, we were far away, free from the Pensionnat, at least for one night.

> *May 25, 1906, Vichy*
> *Chérie Ninette,*
> *The Grand Casino wouldn't let Gabrielle audition! Neither would the Éden. They said they only hire performers from Paris. They looked at us like we were country bumpkins just come from milking the cows!*
>
> *When the Alcazar let her audition, they said she has charm but no voice. But the pianist told her she has promise. For a small fee, he's giving her singing lessons and helping her with her gestures. He thinks she can become a "gommeuse," a backup singer. He says with just a little work, she'll be ready to audition again. Gabrielle is thrilled!*
> *Bisous,*
> *Adrienne*

Excitement filled the dormitory like never before.

"What kind of songs does she sing?" Sylvie the chalk-eater asked, scratching at a freckle.

By candlelight, in a hushed voice so we wouldn't get caught, I taught them the songs I'd learned from Gabrielle and Adrienne. "Coco at the Trocadero." "Le Fiacre." "The Boutons and the Boudins." I showed them the gestures. A dip here, a twirl there.

We were living inside a mélo, Gabrielle the heroine. We waited for Adrienne's next letter as if it was the latest installment of a series printed in the newspaper.

> *June 3, 1906, Vichy*
> *Chérie Ninette,*
> *M. Dumas the pianist told Gabrielle she had to find a better costume for the next audition. He says that's why she still hasn't got-*

*ten a role. He has a friend who has costumes, more expensive,
but he says they're worth it. She's going to look at them tomorrow.*

*Just think. By the time you get this letter, she could be a gom-
meuse, performing on the stage of the Alcazar for international
society!*
*Bisous,*
*Adrienne*
*(Gabrielle sends greetings. She is too busy to write.)*

*June 29, 1906, Vichy*
*Chérie Ninette,*
*Gabrielle is still not a gommeuse!*

*Just a few more lessons, M. Dumas says. But our money is run-
ning low. The costumes she has to rent are so expensive. Short
dresses—almost up to the knee!—covered in sequins with low décolletage. Red sequins were the fashion two weeks ago. Last week
it was mauve. Now it's black. Gabrielle says they're vulgar, but
what can she do?*

*We make a few francs doing alterations for some clients of the
Desboutins here for the waters—but we're skipping lunch. And
owe our last rent.*

*Say prayers, Ninette. Light candles. Gabrielle is more deter-
mined than ever. She just has to become a gommeuse before we
run out of money!*
*Bisous,*
*Adrienne*

"Surely the next audition," Sylvie said.

"Maybe because she's flat-chested," said Louise-Mathilde,
shaking her head.

"She can stuff handkerchiefs in her bodice," Elise said. "Everyone does."

"Not everyone," said Fifine, annoying us all as her large
breasts stretched the top of her chemise to its limits. It didn't
help that she had a habit of holding them in her palms like a
peasant weighing melons at market.

I told them not to worry. I knew my sister. I knew she wouldn't leave Vichy until she'd succeeded. We were all counting on Gabrielle. Her success would mean that we could be successful too. Say prayers, Adrienne had written, and every time church bells rang the hour, I knew all the charity cases were silently chanting the same words. *Oh holy ange, let Gabrielle become a gommeuse. Oh holy ange...*

In the chapel, I'd never seen so many candles alight in the votive stands, flames burning for Gabrielle, for us, for our hopes and dreams.

But then too many weeks went by without another letter from Adrienne. As Sister Ermentrud handed out the mail in the refectory, I'd sit on the edge of my seat, waiting for her quiet presence to draw near. But day after day, there was nothing for me. The other charity cases and I would exchange questioning glances, then look down at our soup.

I wasn't sure what to think. I tried to stay optimistic, for their sake and my own. I hoped the fact that Adrienne hadn't written might be a good sign. Gabrielle was a gommeuse at last. They were busy being fêted, wearing chic new clothes, eating at expensive restaurants, celebrated by the haute monde of Vichy.

All I needed was the letter to confirm it, but instead Adrienne wrote of more ominous events.

*July 30, 1906, Vichy*
*Chérie Ninette,*
*We are desperate for money. I'm working now in a hat shop. And Gabrielle's a donneuse d'eau at the Grande Grille. I wish you could see it. All of la haute wait around a kiosk. Girls like Gabrielle in long aprons hand them glasses of mineral water for their gout.*

*M. Dumas keeps saying the next audition will be the one. Gabrielle puts all her faith in him. But he's always wearing a new lorgnette or cravat around his neck. And your sister's still not a gommeuse.*

*Ninette, I don't know what to do. Maud says it's time for me to come live with her in Souvigny. But I'm afraid to tell Gabrielle.*

*Maud could find a husband for her too, but she refuses to give up.*
*There are so few options as the curtain goes down on our youth.*
*Bisous,*
*Adrienne*

The silence in the dormitory after I finished reading took all the air out of me. "In the mélos," I said, my voice hard, "the heroine is always at her lowest before her dream comes true. That's how it works."

Still no one spoke, until Elise broke the silence. "Who is Maud?"

"A salonnière," I said.

"What's a salonnière?" Fifine asked.

"A grand lady who hosts teas that everyone hopes to get an invitation to."

"But what does it mean that she's invited Adrienne to live with her?" Sylvie asked.

"It means nothing," I said, turning out my light, pretending to go to sleep.

Instead, I was remembering what Adrienne had told me: she would stay with Gabrielle in Vichy until she got a role and, after that, would spend most of her time in Souvigny, where Maud would introduce her to society and help her find a husband from the gentilhommes of the local château aristocracy. But becoming a singer wasn't supposed to take this long. And Adrienne was already twenty-four.

*I'm afraid to tell Gabrielle…she refuses to give up.*

But was Adrienne giving up on Gabrielle?

Sometimes the other girls asked if it bothered me that Gabrielle didn't write. But I didn't need her to. I knew what was in her heart, felt her pain as if it were my own. I knew why she couldn't give up.

I'd noticed the way Gabrielle had brightened when she'd performed for the lieutenants that time at the Grand Café, the way she absorbed their admiration like drops of water on a dry sponge. Her desire to be a singer was about more than never touching a needle and thread again, as she'd claimed. It was about that recognition.

Our father said he'd return, and maybe if she were a famous singer, he would. He'd hear about her, how people loved her and called her Coco, and he'd realize he'd made a mistake.

*You see, Papa,* I imagined her thinking, *you were wrong. Everyone else can see what you didn't: I am someone worth loving.*

# TWENTY-FOUR

A BAD FEELING WEIGHED ON ME AS THE MOTHER ABBESS SAT at her desk, her eyes half-closed, the picture of religious contemplation. Sister Immaculata stood to one side of her, Sister Gertrude to the other. Old Sister Ermentrud was in a chair nearby, holding her ear trumpet close. The room smelled as usual of dead-animal rot, making my stomach heave, but I curtsied and forced myself to assume a posture of humility.

The canonesses looked at me as if examining one of the Mother Abbess's specimens.

"She's always been an unexceptional student," Sister Immaculata said.

"And her piety," said Sister Gertrude, peering at me over her spectacles. "Unimpressive."

The Mother Abbess shook her head. "It seems she's squandered her years here, the opportunities for improving herself."

Sister Immaculata nodded. "Squandered. Just like her sisters."

I waited for Sister Ermentrud, listening intently through her ear trumpet, to join in, to add that I wasn't reverent during Mass, that I was vain, that I didn't meditate as I should on Sunday afternoons.

"The Desboutins won't hire another Chanel," the Mother Abbess interjected, "not after they found out Gabrielle was performing at a place of ill-repute."

"What about her grandparents?" Sister Immaculata asked as I realized they were trying to figure out what to do with me. I was nineteen. It was past time. "The old peddlers. She can be with them at the market."

The Mother Abbess inhaled sharply. "Sister! Look at what happened to Julia-Berthe." She shook her head again, then picked up an envelope from the top of her desk and turned it in her hand as if contemplating its contents.

I leaned forward. The handwriting on the letter looked like Adrienne's, yet it was addressed to the Mother Abbess, not to me.

"A position in Vichy," the Mother Abbess said with a frown, "...a hat shop..."

I sucked in my breath. There was a place for me at the hat shop.

Unless the canonesses wouldn't let me take it.

"We can't have her soil the good name of this institution the way her sisters have," the Mother Abbess continued. "Especially in a city like Vichy, for all of the *beau monde* to see, the families of paying students, those who keep this school going. We have our reputation to uphold, we have—"

"But, Mother," I said, speaking out of turn, desperate not to let this opportunity slip away. "I would never soil the name of the Pensionnat. I would never do anything to harm its reputation. And I'm good with sums. I—"

"Custody of the tongue, mademoiselle!" the Mother Abbess said, her eyes wide with indignation.

Just then, Sister Ermentrud stood suddenly, her ear trumpet falling to the floor with a bang, startling us all. I braced myself for more criticism. But instead she waved a finger at the Mother Abbess.

"So she can't work at the House of Grampayre. You don't want her to go with her grandparents. What do you expect to do with the girl? Stick her in a closet for eternity so as not to shame the Pensionnat? Ridiculous! She has a pleasant disposition. She's competent with sums. What is the problem, Henriette?"

I'd never heard anyone address the Mother Abbess by her first name. I'd heard rumors that Sister Ermentrud had once been the Mother Abbess, that all of the canonesses had once been under her supervision. But she was so old, prone to napping, hard of hearing, none of us had believed it.

Now I did.

"Antoinette isn't as strong-willed as her sister Gabrielle," Sister Ermentrud continued. "If she works hard, she can make a place for herself. She might even find a young clerk to marry. Now let the girl go, Henriette. It's time."

She spoke so loudly the words seemed to reverberate off the walls.

*Let the girl go, Henriette.*

Sister Ermentrud walked out, and that was that.

# WORKING GIRL

VICHY
1906–1910

# TWENTY-FIVE

THE DAY I ARRIVED IN VICHY, ADRIENNE LEFT FOR MAUD'S, BUT I wasn't upset. We hugged and cried and laughed because soon she would be engaged. Soon, she would find her gentilhomme, and her dreams would come true.

I took her place in the dingy room she shared with Gabrielle and at the hat shop on the rue de Nimes, where I swept floors and dusted hat stands. I watched through the picture windows as people passed by, élégantes and gentilhommes from foreign lands who'd come to take the waters. The world unfurled right there before me, everything I'd been anticipating for so long, and I couldn't wait to get out into it. But for now, I was preoccupied with Gabrielle.

I'd tried to hide my alarm when I first saw her. She was wan and too thin. She had a restless energy, always tapping her foot to a refrain playing in her head. Each day, she put on her long apron and went to her job handing out glasses of water and tried to get auditions during her breaks. At night, she stayed up late and sewed sequins back onto her rented gommeuse dresses, a deep furrow between her brows. I wanted to ask her to show me the new songs and gestures she must have learned, but I didn't dare. Once, I started singing "Le Fiacre," hoping she'd join in. Instead, she snapped at me to hush.

She would get a role, I told myself, and everything would be better. These things took time. There were famous singers who came from nothing and nowhere. Mistinguett. Yvette Guilbert. If they could do it, so could Gabrielle.

But by late September, just a few weeks after I'd arrived, I came home from the hat shop to find her in just her nightdress. Her hair hung past her waist, thick and black and unbrushed like a woman of the woods. Her eyes were flat, a contrast to the bright gommeuse dresses tossed haphazardly on the bed. Loose sequins were scattered across the floor.

"It's over," she said.

"What do you mean?" I could see she'd been crying, though there were no tears now. She was so pallid she looked cried out, her face almost translucent.

"I've auditioned everywhere they would let me. No one will give me a role. Monsieur Dumas has another pupil now to pay for his lorgnettes and cravats, which is just as well because my money has run out. I'm not going to be a gommeuse."

She looked as if she'd been dumped at the doorstep of the orphanage in Aubazine all over again. The heavy weight of helplessness filled me. I had to do something. I wanted her to be a singer as much as she did. I wanted her to prove to our father he was wrong to leave us. He might never know, but we would.

"You can't give up," I said. "Think of the lieutenants in Moulins, how they loved you. And all the officers at La Rotonde. They pounded on the tables for you. You can find a new instructor. A better one. You'll get a role next season, I'm sure of it."

"There's no more money, Ninette. I can't pay for dresses. I can't pay for lessons. I can barely eat."

She seemed intent on withering away in our rented room, staring at the ceiling in the dark, mourning the death of her dream. She'd never been one to do nothing. She always had a plan. Now she didn't, and it frightened me. I wasn't sure how to help her until the sight of my tortoiseshell combs lying on top of the small bureau gave me an idea.

Etienne.

I tried bringing him up. If he'd supported her once, he'd support her again, wouldn't he? If he could pay for just a few more voice lessons...

Gabrielle refused to hear of it. "I don't want him to know I haven't gotten a part. I don't want him to know I'm out of money. It's humiliating. He was right, I have no voice. I should have listened to him all along. Now I can't even pay him back. In which case, it's good that he seems to have forgotten all about me."

Before she left, Adrienne had told me Etienne had been busy and they hadn't heard much from him. All they knew was that he had purchased an estate in Compiègne to breed horses, that he named it Royallieu and men were invited there with their mistresses. There were rumors he was still having an affair with Émilienne d'Alençon.

But I couldn't stop thinking of how Etienne had bought champagne after Gabrielle's first successful performance, the way he always looked at her with amusement but admiration too, how he was one of the first to call her Coco, how kind he was to me, how all the other lieutenants had left, but Etienne had stayed. He'd given her money to try to make her dream come true, knowing he would likely lose it.

I found paper and an envelope, and without telling Gabrielle, I sent a letter to Monsieur Etienne Balsan, Royallieu, Compiègne, France, hoping, praying, it would reach him.

One evening in October, I was pleased to return home from the hat shop to find Gabrielle properly dressed, fixing her hair before a small mirror. She was even humming to herself. She still seemed fragile, like a porcelain doll, but at least she was moving.

"A letter came from Etienne this morning," she said, adjusting a hair pin.

In my mind, I crossed myself. My prayer had been answered. "What did it say?"

"He's bought an estate near Compiègne where a monastery used to be. He's going to breed horses." She paused for a moment. "I'm going to go live there with him."

I clapped my hands together. This was more than I'd hoped for. "You're going to be married!"

She laughed, looking at me as if I'd said she was going to China.

"Ninette, Etienne is already married."

He was? How could that be? There was never mention of a wife.

"It was a matter of necessity," Gabrielle continued. "There's a daughter, conceived before the vows. It's a marriage in name only."

Slowly, the realization sunk in. *Going to go live with him.* "But… but you can't just live with him. You can't…"

"He's offered, and I'm going. What else can I do? I'm out of choices. I won't be a seamstress from dawn until dusk for two francs a day. I won't marry some pig farmer or vinegar maker just to spend all my time mending his shirts and washing his underthings, an unpaid femme de ménage."

I shook my head as if that would help me absorb this news. "But…you could go to Souvigny and live with Maud and Adrienne."

"Souvigny is boring," she said. "The teas are awful. The

ladies do nothing but pose and bat their eyelashes while the men talk about who should or shouldn't be let in the Jockey Club. I'm not some galette on a baker's shelf, hoping to be picked before I go stale."

"But Maud could find you a husband."

"Maud finds lovers, not husbands."

I bristled. "That's not what Adrienne says."

"Maud has her convinced she's different. Maybe she is. But I'm not. At least I know Etienne. I trust him. It's not love. But we understand each other."

"What about Émilienne d'Alençon? Doesn't Etienne already have a…"

Horizontale. Irrégulière. Kept woman. Mistress. I couldn't even say the words out loud.

Gabrielle lifted her chin. "What about her? She'll probably be there too. I don't care. It's Etienne's house, he can do what he wants."

This was all my fault. I was the one who wrote to Etienne. What did I expect, that he'd give her more money for nothing? That he had connections that would get her a role as the lieutenants had in Moulins? Yes, that was exactly what I'd expected.

She reached for a suitcase on the bed. "I've got to go. My train leaves in twenty minutes."

"You're really going to do this? What about Something Better?" I felt desperate to stop her. A career on the stage did not necessarily make a woman unvirtuous. But a kept woman's options were limited. "You'll never be welcome in society. You'll never have a husband. You'll never have your wedding announcement in the newspaper. You'll never sit inside the enclosure at the races. You'll never—"

"Ninette," she said, her voice calm. "That's *your* Something Better. Not mine. I don't care about convention. Convention has done nothing for people like us. I'm tired. I'm just so tired.

At Royallieu, I can do nothing. I can sleep all day if I want. I need rest. Then I'll figure out what comes next."

She tried to embrace me, but I turned away. By the time I regretted it, wanting to hold on to her one last time before everything changed for good and she became a person of the demimondaine, an irrégulière, she was gone.

# TWENTY-SIX

OUTSIDE, THE TREES FLUNG OFF THEIR LEAFY FROCKS. THE ONCE sparkling city dimmed to a low glimmer. La haute were off to the next fashionable spot, scattered about like the sequins on Gabrielle's gommeuse dresses. I thought I'd cleaned all of them up, but there was always one more wedged in a crevice of the floor, catching my eye like a taunt.

Gabrielle wrote, telling me she'd arrived safely at Royallieu. I knew by now that she hated writing letters—it was a chore, reminiscent of composition class, penmanship, hovering nuns—so I appreciated the gesture, however brief her note. After that, I made myself push worries about her new arrangement away. She had a roof over her head. She was with Etienne, a man I trusted.

For the first time, I was alone, but for the first time, I could also come and go as I pleased. There was no one to tell me what to do or when to do it. There were no walls holding me in. I felt taken over by a strange kind of hope. It was like a vine, shooting up, wrapping itself around me, reaching wildly for the sun without nuns or canonesses to cut it back.

During the lunch hour or in the evenings when I wasn't needed at the shop, I explored the city. With the fashionable set gone, now Vichy belonged to the native Vichyssois and shoppers from the provinces coming in for the winter sales, looking for a bargain. There was a market here too, and I thought of Julia-Berthe and how someday I would convince her to move to Vichy. The bath establishments, open year round, drew a genteel if less showy crowd, *curistes* who ambled through the park to and from their treatments alone or with their caretakers, a crystal glass of mineral water clutched in one hand.

Still, I had to get out of that dreary room. I moved into the attic over the shop, a bright, cheerful slope-ceilinged space with a bird's-eye view of the busy rue de Nimes. From there, I could see the rooftops of the mansions, villas, and chalets, the summer homes of the crème de la crème, the most splendid of which faced the park. I strolled by them when I could, studying the styles, the sizes, the shapes, as if one day I would get to choose. I wanted a home of my own, to live in a great house. I wanted to be a woman who had married well, a woman people would have to acknowledge.

It startled me to realize I was more like Gabrielle than I'd thought. Our Something Betters were different, but the end was the same: to be admired, noticed, *seen*. Everything we'd never been.

Vichy was full of wonders, and Pygmalion, a store just down the street, was one of them. The first time I walked through its doors on an errand for the Girards, an electricity zigzagged through me as I beheld the most tantalizing displays—dresses, gloves, shoes, the space seeming to go on forever. It was a new sort of place, what people called a "department store." There was a silk department, a fancies department, a shoe department, a ready-to-wear department, a curtain department, a furniture department, and on and on and on.

Pygmalion sold blouses and skirts that had never been worn by anyone else and "dresses fully made," no patterns or sewing required. It had pretty unscuffed shoes that didn't carry the odor and imprint of someone else's foot and shelves of perfumes and powders that hadn't already been opened by a payante. I floated from department to department, floor to floor, sales clerks bustling about, smiling, holding out items for customers, ringing cash registers, and memorized what I would buy once I saved enough money. A blouse with a high collar. A belt made of soft kid leather with a brass buckle. And though completely impractical, white sealskin walking shoes with buttons up the sides. I was a working girl now, not a charity case—I earned a respectable wage—and if you had enough money, it was entirely possible to go in Pygmalion as one person and come out another. For me, of course, change would have to be gradual.

My favorite area was the trousseau department, with everything and more to set up a new household. Nightdresses, chemises, handkerchiefs. Tablecloths, napkins, doilies. Sheets, pillowcases, bedspreads. I ran my hands along them all, a dream I could touch. Once Adrienne was engaged, I told myself, we'd shop here for her trousseau, and I'd help her embroider her initials on the linens. Then, one day, we'd come back for mine.

For the moment, that seemed like pure bliss. A husband, a house, a *home*.

# TWENTY-SEVEN

IN VICHY, ALL THE SALESCLERKS KNEW EACH OTHER. OFTEN, a group of us met for *la pause de midi* and ate lunch at the park, where we'd gossip about customers and other salesclerks. On cold or rainy days, we gathered at a small café for tea and hard-boiled eggs.

There were two girls in particular I grew close to. Delphine worked in the fabric department at Pygmalion and had the gloss and polish of experience handling customers, a way of carrying herself with an efficient self-assurance that I tried to emulate at the hat shop. Sophie worked at a florist and always smelled like roses. Wherever they went, young men eventually followed. Garçons, packagers, and cashiers from Pygmalion. Busboys and bellhops from the hotels.

On Wednesday nights, we went to a brasserie with a low prix fixe. On Saturday nights, to a dance hall where admission was free. We girls usually danced together, the boys off to the side drinking pinard. Every now and then, when a slow song played, they would cut in and dance with us. But then the music would pick up again, and we would spin off, laughing and clutching at each other as they watched.

It was usually Alain, the grocer's son, who danced with me during the slow songs. At one of our lunches, Delphine and Sophie wondered what I thought of him.

"He's nice," I said. "He has a self-assured way about him."

"Do you think he's handsome?" Sophie asked.

He had broad shoulders and strong arms from lifting heavy crates all day. And soft brown eyes, the kind that always had a warm smile in them.

"I suppose I do," I said, realizing by the way they were studying me, waiting for my reply, that they weren't asking for themselves but for him.

When the season opened in May, Adrienne came to Vichy in the company of suitors with expensive carriages and lavish mustaches. Maud chaperoned, the leisurely appearance of their outings to the races and theater belying the serious business of matchmaking.

I visited Adrienne in the small hotel where she and Maud stayed, and she modeled her latest outfit for me, a corselet skirt, a blouse of delicate, embroidered chiffon, a short bolero that accentuated her waist and set off her natural grace, all in shades of gray that were almost violet.

"What do you think, Ninette?" she said, the usual serenity of her expression dissolving into something I didn't usually hear in her voice: worry. "Do I look like I could be the wife of a gentilhomme?"

"Adrienne," I said, truly admiring her. "You look better than a wife of a gentilhomme. You have a light inside you that even the élégantes don't have. Money can't buy it. A dressmaker can't make it."

As she tried on other ensembles, preparing for an evening at the theater, we talked about Gabrielle. I wished we could visit her at Royallieu, but Maud said it could ruin our reputations and any chance of a proper marriage. We'd had only a few letters from Gabrielle since she'd left in October.

*I can sleep as long as I like here*, she'd written. *Such luxury! Already I'm feeling better. Etienne thinks it's funny that I stay in bed until noon reading mélos.*

I tried to picture her lying in bed all day. That, we'd always been told, was a sin, and anyway, Gabrielle could never sit still. It wasn't like her to lie around.

"Do you think Gabrielle's all right?" I asked Adrienne.

"I'm sure she's enjoying *la vie château*," Adrienne said, always trying to see the bright side. "Who wouldn't?"

I couldn't imagine having nothing to do. At the hat shop, I was busy all the time, dusting, sweeping, straightening, running errands.

In another letter, Gabrielle had written about Émilienne d'Alençon.

*Émilienne wears her hair down with a fringe of curls across her forehead to bring out her eyes. Her clothes are covered over in rosettes and other fluff impossible to properly wash. It's a wonder she smells so clean.*

At least Gabrielle sounded like herself. That, Adrienne and I agreed, meant she was at ease. And she wasn't just lying around doing nothing. Her letters were short and infrequent, but they contained pointed observations of the mannerisms of Etienne's friends, the gentlemen and their mistresses. My sister was busy soaking it all up, quietly deciding what, and what not, to mimic, just as she had, as we all had, from the magazines, trying to bring ourselves up in the world.

"Tell me about your suitors," I asked Adrienne. "Are they handsome? Do they make your heart soar and your pulse race?"

"So far," she said, "my heart soars only from nerves. I'm afraid I'll call someone by the wrong name. The count of who? The marquis of what? I'm having trouble keeping track. What if I unknowingly offend my one true love before I have a chance to even know him? Thank goodness for dear Maud. She keeps everything straight."

# TWENTY-EIGHT

IT WAS STRANGE TO THINK WE WERE ALL LEADING SUCH separate lives.

Gabrielle riding horses at Royallieu. *When you ride a thoroughbred*, she'd written, *you feel like you can fly, like you can do anything.* Etienne was teaching her.

Julia-Berthe working in the marketplace in Moulins, separated from her little boy.

Me at the hat shop or with my Vichyssois friends.

And Adrienne on the cusp of society amidst her suitors. She had narrowed the field down to three—the comte de Beynac, the marquis de Jumilhac, and the baron de Nexon. These were sons of families of the highest echelon, the gratin of the gratin, members of the old, French titled aristocracy. They were a notch above even Etienne, who was of the newer, moneyed aristocracy of entrepreneurs thanks to his family textile business.

Best of all, each made her heart soar. Sometimes, I was invited to join them at one of the restaurants or cafés of la haute, worlds away from the places I went with my friends. There, I was to "watch and listen," Maud said, observe for when my time came, as soon as Adrienne was married. The outings were almost like the old days in Moulins with the cavalry officers, though these men were much more serious. One, trying to outdo the others, had presented Adrienne with a little brown-and-white spaniel she named Bijou. The pet was usually on her lap or at her feet, and together they made a charming tableau.

I liked to think I did too. Their competition over Adrienne included a competition to see who could best spoil me, and I now had a new pair of gloves thanks to the comte de Beynac, a new hat thanks to the marquis de Jumilhac, and a jabot of Valenciennes lace thanks to the baron de Nexon. The only problem was I couldn't wear any of it unless I was with them. Not to the brasserie. Not to the dance hall. What would Delphine and Sophie think if I turned up in such luxuries? They would assume I was giving favors. In Vichy, there were plenty of working class girls who did.

The more the season progressed, the more I lived in two worlds, hovering over both, not truly a part of either.

In the world of Adrienne, Maud, and the suitors, I was an observer, waiting to be brought into the fold, with no guarantee Maud would find a husband for me. Adrienne had suitors, but were they the marrying kind? Behind her regal exterior, she still fretted about it night and day.

In the world of the prix-fixe brasserie, the shop girls and boys, Alain pulled his chair closer to mine. He talked of improvements in refrigeration, his father's plans to move to the countryside and leave the store to him once Alain was "settled." There was a look in his eye of expectation, of hope.

Soaring hearts, racing pulses, I wasn't sure I felt that for Alain. I remembered Aunt Julia telling Adrienne she could "learn to love" the notary, but the notary was old and fat, and Alain was young and handsome. Most of all, he was there while the gentilhomme Maud might or might not find for me was still a figment of my imagination.

Alain never drank too much or acted unreasonably possessive or tried to put his hands on places I didn't want him to when we danced, as others had. He did have nice eyes, and he almost always brought me some small gift from the store. Chocolates or a jar of confiture or a tin of mints.

Once, at a café, as the young men talked about boxing and the girls about the latest products for la toilette at Pygmalion, I became fixated on his left arm resting casually on the table, watching for a twitch of the wrist or for his fingers to mindlessly play with a wine cork. Or maybe he might crack his knuckles like Jacques always did.

But his arm stayed still, that strong grocer's forearm never moving as if it were a sign of his true nature. Solid. Steady.

The opposite of my father.

The only place I felt sure of myself was at the hat shop.

Instead of just dusting and sweeping, the Girards let me take on greater responsibilities, demonstrating how to sew on the frippery and make repairs, more fun than work, and how to record sales in the ledger.

When they were too busy or out on errands, I assisted with customers. I was learning quickly how to match complexions with colors, builds—tall, short, thin, heavy—with hat sizes. I'd choose a hat for a customer, smile, adjust it ever so slightly as they tried it on. "*Parfait!*" I would say. Or, "You look like you should be receiving the Empress Eugenie in that chapeau." Or "You have such an eye for fashion, madame—the princess de Metternich wore a hat just like this to take the waters last season."

"I believe you have a knack for sales," Madame Girard had said one day, studying me from behind the counter.

For a second I was stunned. Had I just been praised? At the convent and the Pensionnat, I'd been so used to being told I didn't do anything well, it was a surprise to be complimented. Sister Gertrude. Sister Immaculata. The Mother Abbess. What would they think of that? Not only had I not soiled the name of the esteemed Pensionnat, but I had a *knack for sales*. I was good at something.

"The customers like you," Madame Girard said. I liked them too. It satisfied me to see the pleased look on their faces beneath new, more flattering chapeaux. But what satisfied me most was to earn a wage and take care of myself. I was saving for the blouse with the high collar at Pygmalion. Soon, I'd have enough.

I asked the Girards if they could teach me how to make a hat from scratch, how to shape a wire frame or raw buckram, how to put all of the pieces together just as Gabrielle had with my uniform at the Pensionnat. They showed me how the head size of the brim had to be smaller than the head size of the crown. How to make allowances for the thickness of the braid or the fabric. The tie stitch for trimming. The stab stitch for heavy fabric. The slip stitch to lay a flat hem. The buttonhole stitch to finish edges.

When élégantes visited the store, their hats from the most expensive milliners in Paris in need of a fix, in the back room the Girards always examined how the hat was made, snipping away at a few threads to reveal the "bones" beneath, then stitching it carefully back up. Now I did the same.

I was good at something, and I intended to get even better.

# TWENTY-NINE

EVERYONE WAS TALKING ABOUT MARRIAGE. NOT JUST MAUD and Adrienne, but Sophie and Delphine. Sophie would marry David, Delphine would marry Jacques, and I would marry Alain, they said, as if it were all settled. It was a natural assumption that a girl from the lower classes like me would be privileged to marry a man in Alain's position, the most fortuitous way, everyone knew, out of poverty and out of trouble. Sometimes I let myself relax into the idea of a future with Alain, the comfort of knowing I wouldn't be alone ever again. I would be loved and cared for.

And I liked talking with Alain. We discussed work, trading stories of demanding customers, of the struggle to keep supplies stocked, of the satisfaction we both got from pleasing clients.

"What do you think will be the best part of being married?" Sophie asked one afternoon as we ate our hard-boiled eggs in the park during la pause de midi, just the three of us girls.

"Quitting my job," Delphine said without hesitation. "I'll

never set foot in Pygmalion again. Always on my feet, pretending to like customers when I don't."

"Me too," Sophie said. "David and I will start a family and then after that, if we need extra money, I can take in sewing or laundry."

Delphine turned to me. "What about you, Antoinette?"

Quit my job? It hadn't occurred to me. I'd thought about asking Alain if there might be a place for Julia-Berthe at the grocery, still hoping she might someday come to Vichy. But I didn't want to work there. "I like working at the hat shop," I said. "The ladies of la haute bring the latest fashions from Paris. I like seeing what they're wearing, listening to them talk. And I've gotten used to having money of my own, even if it's not much."

Delphine snorted. "The wife of a grocer can't work at a hat shop. She has to help her husband. Besides, you have all the qualities Alain needs. Hardworking. Good with sums. And a way with customers."

Sophie clasped her hands to her chest, eyelashes flapping. "It's as if you were meant to be!"

After that, I started having strange dreams of whole cabbages as cloches, of asparagus aigrettes, of peaches and plums as little round chignons, of myself fussing around the customers. "This cluster of grapes, madame, if you pin it in your hair just so— ravishing! And then if you're hungry, voilà, a snack!" And, "This season in Paris radishes are the rage. All of la haute are wearing them."

One morning, well before dawn, one of these dreams jarred me awake. I didn't need to go down to the hat shop for hours, but I dressed, wrapped a shawl around myself, and went out onto the street. The city was barely beginning to stir with the earliest of workers, the milkman's cart, the wagons of the farmers with their produce jostling down the road. In the dark, I walked the few blocks to the grocery store.

I stayed back, just close enough to observe Alain unloading crates, heavy-looking boxes he picked up with ease as if they were filled with air, carrying them from a wagon into the store. I could see Alain's mother, arranging the day's produce in the bins that lined the sidewalk, her apron tied tightly around her waist, the shadow of his father inside, the three of them moving as if synchronized. They'd done it so many times before there was no need to speak. The sun would come up, easing itself over the apples, the tomatoes, the lettuce, the cabbages, gentle brush strokes of light until pastels of pink and green turned fiery red, brilliant emerald, the striped awning overhead flapping in the breeze just as it did day after day, season after season, year after year.

A life of endless repetition. The only change the rotation in the bins, rhubarb in April, eggplant in May, endive in the winter.

This was the life I'd just escaped.

Order. Routine. Rise at five thirty. The Angelus at six. The hours, days, and months, partitioned like convent walls.

The nuns, Aunt Julia, it was as if they were whispering in my ear from afar. *You, Antoinette Chanel, would be lucky to be the wife of a grocer.* I could hear Delphine and Sophie even when they weren't there. *Those brown eyes, a hard worker.*

I watched Alain and his family like I was a ghost from another world, one of dreamers and seekers never staying in one place. It frightened me to realize I was the daughter of Albert Chanel more than I knew.

I skipped lunch. When I wasn't at the occasional dinner with Adrienne and her suitors, expensive restaurants far from the brasserie and other places my working-class friends went, I worked late into the evenings. I had to tell Alain we weren't meant to be, but I didn't know how. He would be upset with me. Everyone would be upset with me.

There was always so much to do at the hat shop anyway, orders to fill, damaged chapeaux to be repaired, those costly, elaborate concoctions that came from Maison Alphonsine or Madame Virot in Paris. Hats were always prone to flying off in a swift breeze, ending up crushed or run over. Or they were the target of squirrels or birds who stalked the ladies at the parks in order to fortify their nests with a lovely piece of tulle or a long, silky streamer.

One day a lady of la haute stormed into the shop with her husband and another man who turned out to be a carriage driver. The entire back of madame's chapeau—the season's latest from Caroline Reboux in Paris—looked as if some enormous creature had taken a bite out of it! Which was exactly what had happened. Madame had been lingering on the sidewalk near a carriage when the horse, mistaking the cornucopia of silk flowers just under his nose for real ones, couldn't resist. The husband and the driver argued over who was responsible while madame broke down in tears.

Madame Girard sent me to Pygmalion to see if they had similar flowers in stock. There, Delphine spotted me and stalked me down the aisle, asking where I'd been.

"I'm just so busy," I said.

"Poor Alain feels like a third wheel," she said.

"You know how it is during the season," I said, pangs of guilt running through me. "It can't be helped."

I avoided the grocery store too. But one afternoon, I ran into Alain crossing the street near the hat shop.

"I waited for you last Friday at the dance hall," he said, a hint of hurt in his voice.

*Tell him*, a voice whispered in my head. *Tell him the truth now.* But I couldn't. Not out there on the street. "I'm sorry. I just haven't had time for anything but work these days. The Girards really need me."

His eyes held mine and wouldn't let go. "I'm busy too. I've taken another job, at night. Just for the season." He paused. "To make extra money."

A feeling of nausea stirred at the base of my throat. "Alain, I—"

He broke in before I could finish. "I know, you have to go. You're busy. It's all right," he said, turning to leave. As he headed to the grocery, he turned back to me one last time. "The season will be over soon, Antoinette. We'll have time then."

# THIRTY

"IT'S CALLED *RIGOLETTO*," ADRIENNE SAID WHEN SHE CAME BY the hat shop the next day, her expression serious. "It's an Italian opera. Monsieur de Nexon has a box for tonight, and you're going too. It's a box for six."

She'd said this as if going to the opera was a regular occasion, and we stared at each other for a moment before bursting out laughing.

It felt good to laugh. All day I'd been thinking about Alain. It was cruel to keep avoiding him. The sooner I let him go, the sooner he would find someone else. But the right words were a jumble in my head. I was a coward and a fool, and I wasn't sure which I was the most: a coward for not telling him, or a fool for giving him up. But my greatest fear wasn't that I wouldn't learn to love him. It was that I'd learn to hate him.

Tomorrow, I decided, I would talk to him. Tonight, I would go to the opera. After all, I might never get the chance again.

But what would I wear?

After closing the shop, I rushed to the hotel where Maud and Adrienne had rooms. There, patient Maud explained how it all worked. "Opera, my dears, is a sacred affair. A pageant of the most exquisite gowns. Of opera cloaks and opera glasses trained more often on the crowd than the stage."

Thanks to Maud, Adrienne had all of that and more, an extensive wardrobe a necessary expense in matchmaking that would be reimbursed eventually by a "thank-you gift" from whomever won Adrienne's hand. Adrienne chose a gown of white satin with a lace overlay, hinting, as was the intent, at a bride, and a wide belt of blush pink taffeta to accentuate her small waist. They dressed me in one of Adrienne's silk gowns the color of daffodils that matched the gypsy ring now proudly displayed on my finger. For added effect, Adrienne draped a fichu of tulle around my shoulders. She had a never-ending supply of fichus, inserts, medallions, and more so that gowns and tea dresses could be worn again and again yet still seem new.

I studied myself in the mirror but didn't recognize the reflection. The hat shop girl was gone. I looked like someone people would notice. Or at least I looked like someone I would notice.

"Lovely," Adrienne said, smiling at me. "Simply lovely."

"Remember," Maud said to us. "You must appear highly serious at all times. You won't understand a word of the opera, but you must pretend that you do." She explained the difference between bravo, brava, and bravi. She explained the types of operas, the types of singers, the types of songs using exotic designations like aria, cadenza, prima donna, coloratura.

"What is *Rigoletto* about?" I asked. If I had the general idea, it would help me act as if I understood. I did not want to give myself away as someone who didn't belong there.

"Oh my," Maud said. "It's quite dark. A curse is put on a philandering duke and his jester, a hunchback called Rigoletto. The duke seduces Rigoletto's modest yet beautiful daughter

Gilda. Rigoletto wants revenge only to find that poor Gilda has sacrificed herself to save the duke."

And then she laughed. "But none of that really matters. The entire purpose of going to the opera is not to *see* the opera but to be seen *at* the opera."

How many times had I admired from afar the casino opera house with its ethereal glass and metal canopy. Now I was on the inside, and it was better than I'd imagined, a life-sized jewel box, the spectators the gems, glimmering in summer gowns the colors of rubies and emeralds and other precious stones. Everyone glowed, even the theater itself, a plush gold-and-ivory temple of sophistication.

Monsieur de Nexon sat between Adrienne and me in the front row of a balcony that seemed made for a royal party, swooping out over the audience. Maud sat between the comte and the marquis in the row behind us, her opera glasses pressed to her face as she scanned the crowd.

The performance began. This *Rigoletto*. Maud was right. I didn't grasp a word.

Still, it caused a vibration in some unearthly part of me. I leaned forward slightly in my seat, my eyes fixed on the stage, emotions alternating between degrees of joy, sadness, wonderment. How did one sing like that? These performers—they must have been inhabited by angels. I was completely absorbed when too soon the music stopped. The curtain dropped down. The lights came up.

I turned back to Maud. "It's over already?"

"No, chérie. It's just the first intermission. Time," she said with a wink, "for champagne."

Now the spectacle of people moved to the vestibule, spreading out onto the terrace, stars glistening in the sky as if they too were part of the soirée. Ladies in diamonds, men in tails, smoking, talking loudly, laughing, reaching for coupes of champagne.

Through the magnificent blur, I heard monsieur de Beynac call to a waiter and then a tray of coupes, golden and fizzy, bubbles going up and up, materialized. Monsieur de Beynac reached toward them and offered a glass to Maud, then to Adrienne, then to me.

"Mademoiselle?" he said, holding a delicate crystal out with a gentlemanly manner.

"Merci," I said, my eyes going from him to the waiter holding the tray, coming to rest amidst the sparkle and shine upon a familiar face. It was Alain, his normally ruddy complexion white, his lips tight, his words echoing in my head. *I've taken another job, at night.* His usually soft eyes were hard, holding mine just long enough so I could register the scorn. Monseiur de Beynac took the last coupe for himself and tossed a few coins on the empty tray. Then Alain was gone.

I saw myself as he must have, wearing clothes I couldn't afford, in the company of men of a higher class than me. To Alain, that could only mean one thing. I had been "busy" giving myself away.

I went to the grocer's the next day. I would explain to Alain that Maud was a proper chaperone, that Adrienne was going to be engaged. She wasn't giving favors and neither was I. But he would still feel betrayed, especially when I told him, finally, I couldn't be his wife. It was my fault for going along with the idea for so long.

I waited for almost twenty minutes, lingering outside near the produce until I had to go back to work. Every day that week, I went by again and again, but he never appeared. At Pygmalion, Delphine avoided me too, talking longer than she had to with customers, not meeting my eye, walking in a different direction and pretending not to hear when I called her name. At the florist, as soon as Sophie noticed me come through the door, she dashed into a back room and didn't return. At the bench where we used to meet in the park for lunch, I ate by myself.

Alain must have told everyone what he'd seen at the opera. Or what he thought he'd seen. I couldn't let them think that was true, false rumors that could jeopardize my position with the Girards. And if they'd just give me a chance to explain I wasn't someone who gave favors, we could all be friends again. We might even laugh about it.

The next morning at the hat shop, I told Madame Girard we were running low on millinery thread and offered to go to Pygmalion for more. This time, I wouldn't let Delphine get away.

"What are you doing here?" she hissed after I'd cornered her in the corset department. "I can't have people seeing me with you."

"Why not? I haven't done anything wrong. I was with my aunt and a chaperone—"

"A chaperone? Is that what you call it? You mean a lady who gets paid to introduce young, willing women to men looking for a tryst? You always did put on airs," she said. "Always talking about hats and fashion as if you were too good to be just a shop girl or the wife of a grocer. I had my suspicions. Well, now everyone knows who you really are. And that aunt of yours too. Irrégulières. Prostitutes. Whores."

So that was it. A week ago, we'd been friends. Now we weren't, all because I hadn't followed what she thought were the rules. I stared at her smug face, her chin lifted in the air, the corsets around us, the whalebone, the ties and straps, the horn and wood and steel. Some were perched upright on shelves. Others were worn by mannequins that stared out at nothing, their eyes dead.

Poor Delphine. I almost felt sorry for her. She had no idea. We lived in cages, both of us, of what the world thought we should be.

At least I was trying to get out of mine.

# THIRTY-ONE

DELPHINE'S ACCUSATIONS SIMMERED IN MY HEAD FOR DAYS. I went from caring what she and the rest thought to being insulted. They were supposed to be my friends, and yet they wouldn't listen to me, they wouldn't give me a chance. Deep down, I didn't blame them. From their point of view, it looked as if I'd rejected them and all they aspired to. But in a way, I envied them. They were satisfied with what they had, with what the world told them they would be.

*They're not like us*, Gabrielle would always say about the other orphelines in Aubazine and the nécessiteuses in Moulins, her nose wrinkled. Yes, I thought now. Their feet were on the ground while our heads were always in the clouds.

That's why Gabrielle was at Royallieu, her latest letter reporting that she was traveling to various racecourses around France with Etienne and his turf society friends to watch Etienne's thoroughbreds compete. Her life, if not respectable, was interesting, and that was what she wanted.

And my life went on at the hat shop, where I was determined to succeed. If I couldn't have company, I could at least make money to buy myself that high-collared blouse.

One afternoon in late September, Adrienne glided in, Bijou in her arms, and I could tell she had news. I had to wait until two customers left and Madame Girard went into the back room before we could talk.

"Oh, Ninette," Adrienne said, her expression a mix of excitement and worry. "You won't believe it—I'm going to Egypt!"

"Egypt?"

"Maud says I have to choose who will be my husband. She says it's time. But how can I? I always thought I'd fall in love at first sight. I always thought I would know right away. And I don't."

"But what does that have to do with Egypt?"

She set Bijou down. "Maud says nothing shows the true character of a person like traveling with them, especially in a hot climate. I hope she's right. It was monsieur de Jumilhac—he's an Egyptologist—who came up with the idea. And monsieur de Beynac is all for going too because he's convinced monsieur de Jumilhac will bore me so much with his talk of hieroglyphics that I'll fall right into monsieur de Beynac's arms."

"What about monsieur de Nexon? Is he going?"

"Oh yes. But monsieur de Beynac doesn't worry at all about monsieur de Nexon either. He says monsieur de Nexon is too young to be taken seriously. I don't mind that he's young, but he's so quiet. I don't know what's behind those impenetrable eyes of his. He's like the Sphinx! They say I have to choose a husband by the end of the trip!"

"Surely you have a favorite by now?"

She shook her head, ostrich plumes fluttering. "One day, I feel sure it's monsieur de Beynac. The next, I'm convinced it's monsieur de Jumilhac. The day after that, I'm positively giddy over monsieur de Nexon. But then it all goes round and round again. Maud is afraid they're losing patience, and I don't blame them."

A comte, a marquis, and a baron. A tour of Egypt, the place to be during the winter season. This was straight out of a Decourcelle mélo. All I could do was swoon.

Adrienne adjusted her hat, pinched her cheeks for color. "And now, I need to hurry. I've got to meet Maud at the dressmaker's. She says we need traveling clothes. Outfits for heat and sun. Veils to protect from dust and insects. We're going in a boat down the Nile. I'm afraid we'll need a separate one just for all of our clothes and accoutrements!"

We hugged, and then she left just as quickly as she'd come, Bijou padding along at her heels. I watched her go, a warm feeling radiating inside me, wondering who she would be when she returned.

Adrienne was on the precipice of her dreams. In Egypt, she would fall in love. Before the backdrop of the Pyramids, of natives in exotic clothing, of all the splendors of an ancient land, she would be proposed to, undying devotion declared. She would come back to Vichy, and there would be a grand, romantic wedding with a photograph of the bride and groom in the magazine *Femina* and an announcement in *Le Figaro* listing all of the lavish gifts they would receive.

Proof in black-and-white type that no one was giving favors.

Take that, Delphine and Sophie! You too, Alain! They were the past. Adrienne was the future. And I was somewhere in between, teaching myself to be an élégante so that when my time came, I would be ready. It was good I had no distractions.

The day after Adrienne left for Egypt, I overheard the Girards talking in the back room when they thought I was out. I crept as close as I could, hiding behind an enormous tuft of egret feathers decorating a *chapeau de chinchilla* on a nearby hat stand.

"Egypt," I heard Madame Girard say, "...fashionable with the rich or the scholarly types."

"But Adrienne..." Monsieur Girard said, "...not rich...not a scholar."

"...other reasons people go..." Madame Girard said. "...lovers... liaisons amoureux. For the gentlemen of the *haute monde*...they take their mistresses. Away from the constraints of society."

A bell rang over the door. A customer. I tried to compose myself, but the Girards' words echoed in my head. What if Gabrielle had been right? Lovers, not husbands. Would the man who won Adrienne's heart really marry her? Or would he expect favors *away from the constraints of society*? She'd told me her suitors came from families that were old friends. Their fathers and their father's fathers hunted together, raced horses together, and gambled together just as their sons did now. They were used to making gentlemanly wagers, to winning and losing to each other for sport.

It was how they entertained themselves.

They were also raised to marry women of means and society, women from old families with long names. They were raised to understand any other kind of woman would never be acceptable to their families.

I didn't know how to reconcile this. All I knew was that Adrienne was different. She was special. She was more beautiful and poised than any élégante who entered the shop or swished along the avenues of Vichy with a parasol and a gentleman on her arm. Not only that, she had the kindest, most generous soul. She wanted love. Not their name. Not money. They had to see that. Adrienne had to be more than a *game du jour* of a trio of wealthy, titled bachelors. Surely they were in this for marriage.

Suddenly Vichy felt too lonely. I had a strange longing for Aubazine, for the days when my sisters and I were all together. A holiday was coming up, and for a few days all the shops would be closed. I could go to Moulins to see Julia-Berthe, but

I would have no place to stay. I wrote to Gabrielle, telling her I wanted to visit Royallieu. Maud had warned not to go there, it could give me a reputation as a woman of loose morals, but now even the idea of my "reputation" angered me. What did it matter when people would make assumptions whatever I did? All these upper-class men, Etienne and his friends, Adrienne's suitors, they could do as they pleased, with no consequence. I didn't want anything to do with them. I just wanted to see Gabrielle. It had been two years, and I missed her.

She sent a telegram back right away. "Come."

# THIRTY-TWO

WHEN I FIRST SAW GABRIELLE I WAS SO RELIEVED AT THE SIGHT of her, I almost didn't notice how she was dressed. A chauffeur in a red motorcar picked me up from the train station, and at the entrance to Royallieu, I rushed to embrace her. I felt like my lungs had opened, and I hadn't even known they were closed. She hugged me back, healthy and not as thin as she'd been when she left Vichy. But what was she wearing? She smelled like hay and leather oil.

"Has Etienne made you the stable boy?" I said, only half joking. I'd expected fluff and frills, bows and lace, the typical costume of a kept woman. Or at least the riding habit of an élégante. Instead, she wore a pair of what looked like a man's riding breeches, which fit her perfectly, a starched white blouse, and a little black tie.

She laughed, hooking an arm through mine and leading me into the house. "I told you, didn't I? Etienne's taught me to ride. I'm a horsewoman now. An equestrienne."

What else had he taught her? The answer hung in the air like the ivy dripping off the sides of the château. To *faire l'amour.*

"You look more like a horse *man*," I said, eyeing her outfit. "An equestrian."

She shrugged. "The men have so much more fun. They can move with the horse, not weighed down with heavy skirts and corsets. Sidesaddle is dignified, but dignified is boring."

Inside Royallieu, I tried not to gape. Everything was money, comfort, and luxury like I'd never seen before, the furnishings so plush I imagined sitting down and never getting up. The draperies were long and grand, like ball gowns, framing every window with sweeping trains, pooling on chevron-patterned floors. Enormous portraits of horses or important-looking men covered the paneled walls, making me feel important just being among them.

"Where's Etienne?" I said.

"Where he always is. With the horses. And there's a houseful of guests, his Jockey Club friends and their liaisons amoureux. They're all off on a hack."

"A what?"

"Out riding. I came back early for you. You'll see everyone later."

Everyone? I didn't expect there'd be others here, with one exception. "Émilienne too?" I asked.

"No," Gabrielle said, and I knew I should have been relieved for the sake of reputation that I wasn't in the same company as the famous courtesan, but I was disappointed. I had been curious to observe for myself what it was about her that would cause a king or duke to ruin himself.

"She's taken up with an English jockey," Gabrielle went on. "He has no money, but he's handsome. And when I say handsome, ooh la la. She's brought him here a couple of times. But it doesn't matter that he's poor. She can do what she wants. She's not beholden to a man anymore. She wears her freedom around her neck. Layers and layers of pearls."

Now that I earned my own wages, I recognized the allure of

freedom. But no matter how "free" Émilienne was, there were still places she could never go. The drawing rooms of la haute, for instance.

We went upstairs to what would be my bedroom, my valise already delivered by a servant. The bed, wide and soft with sheets of crêpe de chine, mounds of pillows, and a draping canopy, was fit for a queen.

"Do you remember Sarah Bernhardt's *salle de bain* from the magazine?" Gabrielle said. "Here the bathrooms are almost as luxurious."

We settled onto the bed, curling up as if we were back in Aubazine or Moulins gossiping in the dormitory. I shared my concerns about Adrienne and her suitors. "What if you're right? What if Maud finds lovers, not husbands?"

But Gabrielle wasn't worried. "No matter how gentle Adrienne seems on the outside, on the inside she's still a Chanel, born with the shrewd sense of a market trader. She can watch out for herself."

I hesitated a moment. "And you?" I said. "Can you watch out for yourself?"

She laughed. "Look around. I think you can see I'm managing."

"But...what is it like?"

"What do you mean?"

"Etienne and you," I said, my voice low. "Tell me. What's it like to faire l'amour?"

A secretive smile curved her lips. "It's something you have to experience. I can't explain."

"But how do you know what to do?"

"Émilienne gave me advice. She saw I was just a country girl, unsophisticated, a hayseed in a drawing room. Her advice was simple. Don't think. Never think. Just feel. That's all you have to do. And then she gave me all the practical advice, how not to end up like Julia-Berthe."

"It's strange to think we have a nephew, and we don't even

know him," I said. All we knew was he still lived with a curate somewhere near Moulins. The canonesses gave little information, and there wasn't a thing we could do about it, having no real means of our own.

"Do you hear anything of Julia-Berthe?" Gabrielle asked.

"Just from Adrienne. Last time she went to Moulins to visit Mémère and Pépère, Julia-Berthe had a terrible cold. It's not good for her to always be outdoors in the marketplace."

Gabrielle frowned. "She's not as hardy as Mémère. Ever since what happened in Aubazine."

The episode in the snow. That was what Gabrielle was referring to, sure it had ruined Julia-Berthe's constitution. The whole affair with the blacksmith's son, I thought, had ruined her constitution.

"I hope she'll move to Vichy one day," I said. "But Adrienne says she's happy. She says she always has a basket of puppies or kittens she's taking care of next to her at market."

We moved downstairs to the salon, where Gabrielle had us take our places in the room like ladies of the manor. She ordered tea from a servant, her expression and tone haughty even for her.

"The servants hate me," she whispered after the maid left. "They're snootier than the old ladies in bustles who used to come in the House of Grampayre. They think I should be like them, in an apron, serving, not served."

Just like Delphine and Sophie, I thought.

When the maid returned with a tea tray, I sat up taller. We sipped our tea, and Gabrielle told me about life with Etienne. When she first arrived at Royallieu, she said, she was intimidated by Etienne's friends, by a lifestyle she had no idea how to lead. That was why in the beginning she spent her days reading in bed. "I was afraid to see anyone. Afraid they'd think I didn't belong here. I lurked about feeling sorry for myself, until one morning I got out of bed, put on some of Etienne's old riding clothes, went down to the stables and devoted myself to learning to ride."

She became good at it, and soon she was riding with his Jockey Club friends and their mistresses who admired her for her fearlessness. During the racing season, as she'd written me, they'd all travel together to watch Etienne's horses compete at places like Saint Cloud, Auteuil, Vincennes, Longchamp. Sometimes Etienne himself rode as a gentleman jockey, hurtling over shrubs in a point-to-point. When they weren't on the road, they were at Royallieu entertaining themselves, playing practical jokes.

"Last month," Gabrielle said, "Etienne had all of us wear our most refined clothes and hats, then ride donkeyback to the local track to watch the races. We ladies were in sidesaddle. You should have seen the looks people gave us. Etienne loves the ridiculous. He pokes fun at the well-to-do even though he's one of them."

No wonder he and Gabrielle were compatible. She was always eager to take the pretentious down a peg or two.

We reminisced about Moulins, about our lieutenants, until we were up on our feet singing "Coco at the Trocadero," the gleaming studs in the oil paintings our audience. We sang and danced "Le Fiacre" and "Les Boudin et Les Bouton," pantomiming the characters, our backs to each other, our stomachs pushed out like we were with child, lost in the performance when suddenly—

"Bravo, bravo!"

We turned, and there in the doorway was Etienne, a twinkle in his eye. With him were men I didn't recognize but who were the same type as he, well dressed in the kind of sporting clothes for the kinds of sports that only the affluent could afford. But there was another man I did recognize, just the sight of him giving me a thrill. He had one eyebrow raised, a smooth mustache-less face. Our eyes met, and the divining rod in my chest lurched.

Juan Luis Harrington.

Lucho.

# THIRTY-THREE

THERE WAS NO CHANCE TO TALK. I GREETED ETIENNE, AND then Gabrielle said we needed to change for dinner. I wore a dress with flounces and fringe that Adrienne had given me, my gypsy ring, and had Gabrielle fix my hair in a style she'd learned from Émilienne. I had yet to lay eyes on the other ladies, the mysterious mistresses and demimondaines. What if one of them was Lucho's?

Downstairs, everyone gathered in the salon, smoking, flirting, drinking champagne. Gabrielle nodded at a man who reminded me of a lizard with a head shaped like an egg. He looked at her and winked. "That's Leon," she said. "He's a comte. It was his little red coupe you rode in from the train station. And there's Henri. He's a baron, and his mistress with the big theatrical eyes, that's Suzanne. And over there, that's Juan Luis Harrington." She tipped her head toward Lucho, who studied a leather-bound book he'd pulled from a shelf across the room, handsome in an evening jacket. "He's one of the polo players who beat our lieutenants all those years ago in Moulins. Do you remember? His family owns the largest estancia in Argentina."

An Englishman with a patched eye was a horse trainer. A Frenchman who smelled like menthol ointment was a jockey. "And that one over there," Gabrielle said, "is an actress. But she's not famous yet. If she acts as poorly as she dresses, she never will be."

The actress had drawn a mole on her face to emulate the beauty Geneviève Lantelme and wore a corset so tight and a bodice so low I expected her bosom to pop out at any moment. Over that she wore a strange wrap-around gown in the style of a *negligée mandarin* and on her head a towering dramatic aigrette. I couldn't decide if she was glamourous or gauche or maybe a mixture of both. Either way, she had a strange allure that came from her own certainty she should be noticed.

"Is she here with the polo player?" I dared to ask. I tried to sound as disinterested as possible.

"No. He's alone."

Why did every part of me come alive? He was still a married man. I took a glass of champagne from a passing waiter to calm my nerves.

Gabrielle clucked her tongue like Mémère. "Not too much, Ninette," she said. "Some of the people here, they lose their wits. I've learned it's best to keep mine."

Dinner brought more champagne, and I made a point to sip it. I listened, wondering at this world, the underside of la haute. Talk was of horses, society gossip, similar to the back-and-forth of the lieutenants in Moulins, except here every conversation hinted at matters of the boudoir. Gabrielle sat next to Etienne like the lady of the manor, and I observed they still had a natural way between them. Lucho sat at the other end of the table, and I wished I was near him. Through furtive glances, I saw that his mouth curved up slightly at the ends even when he wasn't smiling, a feature I liked. Bits of the conversation floated my way:

"A polo pony's training isn't complete until it's worked among cattle," Lucho said.

"Lucho knows more about breeding horses than anyone," Etienne announced to the group.

And then Leon, loudly, "Breeding? You mean what goes where? I don't think you need any assistance in that area, Etienne."

The table erupted in snickers, but Lucho wasn't laughing. He looked toward my end, his expression serious, maybe curious. I wasn't sure. Most likely, he didn't remember me.

But after dinner in the drawing room, he approached with a smile. "Youth," he said, and it took me a moment to recall this was how Etienne had introduced us back in Moulins. "One of the Three Graces."

"Did Etienne buy some of your horses?" I said, regretting it immediately. I should have been more coy, acting as if I didn't remember him when in fact I remembered everything. In Vichy, I still slept with his handkerchief in my pillowcase. I hadn't expected to see him again, but that handkerchief represented more than the pull I'd felt between us: it was an acknowledgment that Something Better might really be ahead.

"He has. I'm helping him get them settled. I go home at the end of next week."

"Back to the pampas?" I said.

He seemed surprised, but pleasantly. "You remember. Yes, by way of Paris. I have some family business there. Then back to the pampas. I don't like to be away from the estancia for too long."

So he wasn't part of the regular Royallieu crowd. That was a relief.

We were interrupted by cheers and laughter. Leon had entered the room dressed as a woman, his lips smeared with lipstick, and was now attempting to perform "Coco at the Trocadero" in falsetto. I glanced at Gabrielle, standing near the fireplace talking with Suzanne, so at ease here at Royallieu. She started laughing with everyone else, clearly delighted. I laughed too.

Etienne put an arm around Lucho's shoulders and pulled him away.

I swallowed the rest of my champagne, the bubbles burning my throat, and leaned against a divan in the middle of the room. On my left, the English horse trainer motioned to a servant to bring me another glass. On my right, the French jockey moved closer. I flirted with them like I had with the lieutenants in Moulins. I wasn't interested in them at all, but it was safer this way, I told myself, because sometimes I caught Lucho looking at me from across the room, and it took everything I had to look away.

A Victrola played a ragtime song, and my feet tapped along with it. Drinks were refilled, corks popped, amber floated in cut crystal glasses, more laughter and shouts. Now, the baron, Henri, had stuffed a pillow under his shirt and stood arm-in-arm with Gabrielle, who had disappeared and come back dressed as a man. Leon too had a pillow under his dress, and Suzanne wore a man's hat perched on her pretty head while she strutted like a squire. Gabrielle was directing them in a bawdy version of "Les Boudin et Les Bouton."

It was all so strange. Beside me, the French jockey whispered in my ear, his face too close to mine, pointing out the shape of the champagne coupe in my hand, that it was designed from a mold of Marie Antoinette's left breast, his gaze sliding down my own décolletage. When he offered another glass, I hesitated. Everything already glowed with rings of light like halos. I glimpsed a face in the gilt mirror over the mantelpiece, a false smile, dazed expression. It was my own, flush, on edge, unsure of this place, these people.

I glanced over at Lucho, hoping his presence might steady me. He rested casually against the bookcase in the corner with Etienne, the two of them talking, I guessed, about horses. If his eyes met mine, this time I wouldn't look away. The world was turning upside down. Was it the champagne or was it Lucho? Watching him now, all I wanted was to be with him. What I thought was important—my reputation—maybe wasn't. What I didn't think was important—passion, the moment— maybe was.

My head had gone light.

I needed air.

I excused myself, shouldering past the French jockey, moving down a long hallway toward a room I'd seen earlier with French doors that led out to a terrace. There, I stood looking out over the wide lawn toward the stables, the winter air, crisp with the clean scent of the countryside, calming me. I closed my eyes and breathed it in.

I smelled him before I saw him, menthol, whiskey, and sweat. The French jockey must have tiptoed behind me. Despite the cold, his face was damp with perspiration. "How clever of you to come out here where we can be alone," he said, his words slurring. "Are you cold? Let me warm you up."

He drew near, and I tried to go back inside but was cornered against the side of the house.

"Get away from me," I said, but he took another step forward so that we were almost touching.

"You don't really want me to do that. You wouldn't be here at Royallieu if you did." He tried to kiss me, and I turned my head, repulsed, just in time to see Lucho.

"Get out of here, you fool," Lucho said.

The jockey appeared as if he might protest, wobbling on his feet, then must have thought better of it and slunk away.

"Are you all right?" Lucho said. "I saw him follow you out."

I was shaking. "I don't know."

He led me to a nearby bench and took off his jacket. "Here," he said, putting it over my shoulders, lavender and bergamot, the scent of his handkerchief—of him, I now knew—dappling the air.

He gazed off toward the stables on a nearby rise. "Do you hear that?" he said, sitting forward.

I shook my head, not sure what he meant.

He smiled. "The horses. Listen. It's never quiet in a barn. They're shuffling around, knocking at the walls, whinnying at each other, plotting."

"Plotting what?"

"Their freedom. How to get out of the boxes they live in and set themselves free."

My heart caught. I thought of what Etienne had told me, how Lucho was trapped in a marriage he could do nothing about.

He sat back and turned to me. "Why are you here?"

"I was just trying to get some air—"

"I mean here, Royallieu. You don't belong in a place like this. Even Etienne said..." He hesitated.

"That I should be left alone?"

"Yes."

"I came to see my sister, that's all." I considered stopping there, but I wanted him to know the truth about me too. He had opened a door, and I didn't want it to close, not yet, anyhow. "Sometimes I'm convinced I'll lose everyone I love. They'll all disappear into the distance, and I'll never see them again."

He looked straight into my eyes. "I would think you would draw people to you," he said. "Not make them disappear."

I longed to move closer to him, to brush back the renegade strand of glossy black hair that had fallen across his smooth forehead. There were only centimeters between us but still so much distance.

Instead, I stood. I had to, before I actually did brush back that strand of hair. "Thank you," I said.

"For what?"

"For saving me."

He insisted on escorting me up to my room to make sure the jockey wasn't loitering about, waiting in the wings. "I'll tell Etienne to send that drunkard and his horse trainer friend back to where they came from. They won't bother you again."

We found a back stairway, the strains of the Victrola drifting past, a slow song this time. I paused with my hand on the railing. It felt scandalous to be going upstairs with a man.

"Don't worry," he said. "I won't do anything untoward."

At my door, we stopped, and I gave him back his jacket. Could he see in my eyes that I was conflicted? That I *wanted* him to do something untoward? That if he asked to come in, I wasn't sure I could say no?

He took my hand and kissed it. "Antonieta," he said, his voice suddenly tired and hoarse. "Everyone here is ruined. Haven't you noticed? Everyone except you."

He let my hand go and turned away.

"*Dulces sueños,*" he whispered as he disappeared into the dark.

# THIRTY-FOUR

HOW WOULD I EVER FALL ASLEEP? ALONE IN MY ROOM, THE memory of what happened with the jockey faded away. All I could think of was Lucho, his smooth, open face, his eyes that seemed to see not just the outside of me but the inside as well. Did he know how perfectly he was put together? The way he looked, the way he moved and breathed. I wanted to memorize the way he walked, the intonation of his voice, the way he spoke French with an accent. *Antonieta*. The feel of his lips brushing my hand. *Dulces sueños*.

The way he so easily handled that jockey with just an intimidating glare.

Lucho made me feel safe, even—as he'd vanished down the hall—when I wasn't sure I wanted to be.

The next morning, I didn't wake until nearly eleven. Eleven! I'd never slept that late in my life. At the convent, half the day would have already been over.

Gabrielle came into my room, appearing as if she'd just woken

up herself, and handed me a plush white robe identical to the
one she was wearing. At Royallieu, she informed me, everyone gathered for breakfast in their pajamas. Formalities were
frowned upon. "It's la vie château," she said.

"But...it's not right. I can't go down there like this." When
la noblesse française met for country weekends, did they breakfast in their pajamas? I didn't think so.

"Ninette, it's different here. No one cares. It's just the baron,
Suzanne, and Leon. That actress is still asleep. Etienne and Lucho
are out at the stable." She put her hands on her hips. "Don't embarrass me."

Reluctantly, I put the robe on over my nightdress. I didn't
understand it, but this was the life my sister had chosen. I was
just a visitor.

"Can I at least put my hair up?" I said, trying to smooth the
long strands with my hands.

"No." Gabrielle's own thick locks hung down to her waist
in waves. "And stop giving me that disapproving nun look. We
don't always sleep late here. It's different on race days. Or if we're
riding, which is almost every day. Then we all get up early, rain
or shine. But today's Sunday, a day of rest."

Sunday. I crossed myself and followed Gabrielle down the
stairs. The breakfast table was covered with newspapers and
coffee cups. The baron wore a silk kimono, Suzanne a dressing gown with a white ribbon tied around her long, dark hair.
Leon sat very properly in a matching shorts pajama set, his legs
like sticks of celery. I tried not to smile at the sight.

As I sat and tightened my robe, the actress nearly stumbled
down the steps, her beauty mark smeared. She took a seat next
to me, then dropped her head on the table theatrically.

"Too much champagne, my dear?" Leon said, not looking
up from the racing results.

She didn't respond. A servant brought her a cup of coffee and
she lifted her head and gulped as if the liquid were life itself.

I was on the verge of relaxing, acclimating to this strange display, when more footsteps approached, and to my horror, Etienne and Lucho strode into the room in their riding clothes, a sense of vigor and the crisp outdoors about them. I knew I should have insisted on dressing. I avoided Lucho's eye as he joined us at the table, wishing I could sink into my chair, fade into the paneled walls.

A warm fire crackled in the hearth. Light-footed servants re-filled cups of coffee. I gave all my attention to a croissant while the others studied the newspapers, discussing these new machines that flew in the air, the death of some old war hero, problems in the Balkans, the racing pages, la vie sportif, the usual debate among the men as to the best kind of horse for polo: the thor-oughbred, the criollo, a cross between the two.

"What about donkeys?" said Suzanne. "Always carting things here and there. Doing all the heavy lifting. Why do they always get left out of the fun?"

"Donkeys?" Leon said. "For polo? What a mockery!"

"They're sure-footed," Lucho said. "But stubborn. A polo mount has to be willing to do anything for its rider. There's a sacred trust between the two. But burros don't trust anyone ex-cept themselves."

"Smart creatures," said Gabrielle, stirring her coffee.

"I wonder how exactly one would play on donkey-back?" the baron said. "Would there be different rules?"

"Different rules?" Etienne said. "I should think so." He was silent for a moment, seeming to be in deep thought, until he pushed his chair away from the table suddenly and stood up, a mischievous smile on his face. "We'll have to make them up as we go along. But rule number one is, as always, to be dressed appropriately for the occasion."

Leon scoffed. "Etienne, don't be absurd."

Etienne picked up a napkin and put it on his head. "Exactly. Absurd. Thank you, Leon. That is the dress code." Then he told us all to hurry and get ready. He was off to the stable to tell the grooms to saddle the donkeys.

The match would begin on the back lawn in twenty minutes.

A mad frenzy took over as everyone rushed upstairs. Gabrielle dug through Etienne's dressing room in a flurry until we were both costumed in men's jodhpurs and velvet jackets, silk cravats for head wraps with scarf pins for jewels. "Something's missing," she said, staring at me with a critical eye before pulling the sashes off the curtains and tying them around our waists as sarongs.

At Royallieu, evidently, the outfit was as serious as the game.

The usually quiet back lawn was now a circus of people, donkeys, and grooms. There was Lucho wearing the baron's silk kimono over his clothes, already astride, his long legs nearly brushing the ground. The actress, dressed in a man's raccoon coat and her own towering aigrette. Suzanne, looking mysterious wrapped in a full-length white hooded cloak, a burnoose, someone called it. The baron, with a woman's scarf around his head so one could only see his eyes. And Leon, a robe over his pajama shorts, his egg-shaped head topped with an old red-plumed dragoon helmet I'd seen displayed in one of Royallieu's cabinets.

From donkeyback, Etienne directed the setup in a cape made of a fringed oriental tablecloth. He even brandished a sword.

"You're not going to play with that thing, are you, Etienne?" Leon asked, sticking a foot through the stirrup of his mount and swinging his other leg over the top. "I'd hate for you to fall on it."

"You know very well I'm not honorable enough to fall on a sword," Etienne said.

As we milled about what was to be the playing field, he divided the group into sides. He, Lucho, the actress, and Suzanne, he declared, were Team Ridiculous. Gabrielle, Leon, the baron, and I were Team Absurd.

Me? I'd planned to watch from the sidelines. I tried to protest, but before I could blink, Gabrielle, already mounted, motioned to a groom, who lifted me up and set me in the saddle of a white donkey named Lucille.

"Don't worry, Ninette. It's not like riding a horse," Gabrielle said before trotting off. "If you fall, it's not as far. It won't hurt as much."

Thankfully, Lucho rode up. "Like this," he said, showing me with his own reins how they were to be held. "If you feel unsteady, just grab the mane." He winked and was gone.

The match had begun. I plunged my fingers into Lucille's mane as she ambled toward the mêlée, a swirl of donkeys going in all directions, players swinging croquet mallets because polo sticks were too long. My plan was to stay out of it, but Lucille had other ideas, moving, no matter what I did, straight for the fray.

She was determined to skirmish. My little donkey put herself in the way of others so effectively everyone thought I knew what I was doing, adding to the farce. Lucille had a particular affinity for Etienne's mount, perhaps a barnyard grudge or crush, it was hard to tell. Several times she cornered him, letting Gabrielle swoop in and steal the ball from her paramour, a triumphant smile on her face.

After one of these blocks, Lucho cantered past. "You're a natural," he said with an admiring look that made me woozy, his presence commanding even on a donkey.

My nerves soon turned to giddiness. The baron's head scarf kept unraveling and falling in his eyes so he couldn't see. As he tried to adjust it, his donkey turned aimless circles. And already Etienne had fallen off twice trying to get his mount to make a sharp turn toward the ball, Etienne's body flying one way, the donkey staying put. When Leon's donkey, running at full speed, stopped suddenly, pitching him over the front in a heap, it was impossible not to laugh. Leon jumped up quickly and saluted the creature as if it were Napoleon himself, then climbed back on for another go.

Meanwhile, the actress made her usual scene. Despite Etienne's warnings, she kicked at her mount, pulling on its reins, shouting unanswered orders until the donkey had enough. It lowered its large head, shot its legs out behind, and bucked all the way back to the stable, the actress cursing, her arms wrapped around the creature's neck for dear life, the feathers of her headdress bouncing like a poor trapped bird trying to fly away. When Leon suggested she might be better suited for comedy than drama, I was nearly helpless with laughter.

Eventually Lucho's mount decided the game was over. The animal stopped in the middle of the field, refusing to move, impervious to Lucho's coaxing. When the other donkeys noticed, they stopped too, offering a fantastic round of brays to make sure we all got the message. Lucho laughed, patting his burro on the neck, talking into its enormous ear. "Don't worry, *mi hijo*, I'm sticking with horses."

We dismounted, left the animals with the stable boys, and headed for the house. I felt aired out, a pleasant sensation that took me by surprise.

I'd expected to find sordidness at Royallieu, the seven deadly sins under one roof: pride, covetousness, lust, anger, gluttony, envy, sloth. The incident with the jockey had confirmed my fears. But now I saw it was more complicated than that. There was something almost childlike at Royallieu, a place for pleasure, yes, but with an underlying innocent longing for simplicity. Royallieu was Etienne's creation, a haven from society and judgment, a place where rules didn't matter, or if they did, you could make them up. Of course Gabrielle was at home here.

Life as a demimonde wasn't as tragic as I'd expected it would be.

Before disappearing into the house, Etienne waved his sword. "As is tradition here at Royallieu whenever there is a competition, the losers must dance for the winners. The Absurd will perform for the Ridiculous after dinner."

# THIRTY-FIVE

IT WAS THE BARON WHO CAME UP WITH THE IDEA FOR THE dance. "The key," he said as we assembled in the salon after dinner, "is to pretend as if you're flying a kite."

"Do show us, Baron," said Etienne, comfortably seated on a divan with a glass of whiskey as we dancers stood in the middle of the floor, the furniture pushed away to make a stage. Lucho, next to him, leaned forward, an expectant look on his face that made me feel warm inside, a good kind of jittery.

The baron stretched an arm out as if holding a taut string and gazed toward the heavens. "There should be a sort of swaying, you see, as the kite is drawn leeward, then windward, then leeward again, a dance, if you will, with a kite caught in the vagaries of the winds."

Suzanne sat prettily at the piano in the corner, gently toying with the keys. To find the appropriate mood for our dance, the baron had Suzanne play the beginnings of one piece of music after another, rejecting each until Lucho made a suggestion.

"How about Wagner?" he said. "'The Flight of the Valkyries'?"

Suzanne's fingers batted the keys in a rapid staccato, a pretty fluttering that sounded like a chorus of a thousand humming-bird wings.

The baron's face lit up. "Yes. Yes. Of course! A song of flight. Perfect."

"Now you, my dears," the baron said to Gabrielle and me, waving an arm dramatically, "are the kites. Leon, you and I the kite flyers."

Leon shook his head. "No, no, no. Do I seem like the type to keep my feet on the ground? I'm a hawk, an eagle, soaring over my kingdom."

"It's true," Etienne said. "We all saw you soaring earlier today. Right over your mount's head."

"Fine," the baron said to Leon as the song picked up. "Now fly, all of you, fly! And remember, it's a struggle, you must find the right current, one that will lift you up, not play with you, tease you, only to plunge you down heartlessly toward earth."

We didn't need instruction. Gabrielle was practically a professional. The actress, who actually was a professional, watched, clearly perturbed to be left out of the performance as Gabrielle and I twirled and spun, graceful poetic kites. The baron held his imaginary strings, letting us out, reeling us back in as we fought the current and tried to avoid colliding with the eagle who circled and wheeled between us.

It was silly, of course. That was the point.

But the music. Oh the music. It filled me. That joyous sound of wings, of flights of hummingbirds and butterflies, bees and action. And in the midst of it a melody, what could only be the gallop of some kind of glorious creatures bounding toward an epic adventure, a great struggle to be won or lost. This was life and longing, the sweetness, the tragedy, captured in a crescendo of notes. I'd never heard this music before, but a piece of my soul already seemed to know it.

I glanced at Lucho, and he was looking right at me, serious.

The tempo darkened, a battle, a pounding of the keys, good versus evil. We kites floundered. Leon dove here and there, nearly knocking a marble bust from the mantelpiece.

Then at last a denouement, a resolution, the drama of the clash collapsing to a tender simplicity of notes, too simple. Where there had been many, now there were just a few. Who had won? Who had lost? The performance was over.

"Bravo!" Etienne called out, he and Lucho standing, applauding, as Gabrielle, Leon, and I drifted to earth with one last flutter and crumpled onto the floor.

I lifted my head to see Lucho reaching toward me, helping me to my feet, his hand steadying me for a moment as I wobbled, flustered from the emotion of the music, from his warmth.

"The composition," he said. "Did you like it? It's one of my favorites."

"It was beautiful," I said, now fully upright. "It swept me away."

From across the room, a ragtime song blared from the Victrola. Next to it, the actress danced by herself. It was her turn now, the evening heading in a different direction.

Lucho leaned closer. "When I was young, I used to imagine the Valkyries, those beautiful goddesses descending from the heavens on their flying horses. How they swooped over the battlefields pointing with their swords, deciding which soldiers should live, which should die. How they carried the souls of their chosen back up through the clouds to Valhalla, their heavenly palace. They only took the bravest soldiers, the most worthy, and I was sure I'd be one of them."

"But deciding who should die? I don't envy the Valkyries," I said. "To have to make such a choice."

"But it's a noble choice, a noble act," Lucho said, so close now we were almost touching. "To take a brave soldier from an imperfect world, a world of suffering, and carry him to the afterlife and a life of bliss. That's how I think of it now. Although as a boy, my real idea of bliss was riding through the clouds on a flying horse."

I smiled. "I suspect it still is."

He laughed softly. "You see right through me. The truth is, all men are just boys inside. Dreaming of a goddess who will recognize their bravery, swoop them up, and take them to Valhalla on the back of a flying horse."

"Valhalla," I said. "Is it real? The happy ending?"

I could feel his breath on my cheek. "Yes," he whispered. "I believe so."

I put a hand on his forearm. I couldn't help myself. Words weren't enough. There was so much I didn't know about Lucho. The day in, day out Lucho. And yet still I knew him. I understood him, and I felt sure he understood me.

"Valhalla?" Etienne said, and I quickly pulled my hand away. "Literally, 'house of the fallen.' Reminds me of Royallieu. Both places of fun and games. Including cards. Come, Lucho, we need you. Leon and the baron have broken out a deck in the billiards room. We can't play without a fourth."

"Come back with me," I said to Gabrielle the next morning as Leon's chauffeur waited at the wheel of his red coupe to take me to the station.

The sun had only just begun to rise, a faint light behind a curtain of gray. The house was still. Even the horses hadn't yet been turned out from their stalls. The pastures around Royallieu were empty, carpets of emerald green with a silver glaze of frost. Gabrielle burrowed into her white robe against the cold, her hair down, tousled by the bitter wind. She'd told me last evening, while the men played cards downstairs, that she still had dreams of being a performer.

"You can audition again," I said now. Why not? She was rested. She could take lessons from a different teacher, a better teacher. It was a desperate thought, but leaving her felt like I was losing her again. I didn't trust the separation.

"Vichy was a bad dream, Ninette. A nightmare. I like it here. It won't last forever. But for now, I'm happy."

She was. I'd seen that. This was her life, and now it was time for me to go back to Vichy to figure out what mine would be. Lucho was married. Adrienne soon would be. And I was Maud's next protégée. In the meantime, the Girards and their customers were waiting. I had regulars now, ladies who trusted my opinion, who said they never got more compliments than when they wore a hat I'd chosen.

I kissed Gabrielle on the cheek and took my seat, a part of me wishing I could run back inside and up the stairs to say goodbye to Lucho, to glimpse him one last time. As the motorcar rumbled and shook down the drive, I looked back at the house for as long as I could, until Gabrielle and Royallieu, Lucho and all the rest, dissolved into specks.

# THIRTY-SIX

WHEN ADRIENNE CAME BACK FROM HER TRIP, IT WAS A NEW
year, 1909. She breezed into the hat shop with her usual air of
serenity, but there was something else, something new and ra-
diant and—

"You're in love!" I said. "The trip to Egypt. It worked!"

She nodded, her face lighting up. "I am. It did!"

I hurried to the door and turned the sign from *ouvert* to *fermé*.
The Girards were out of town at a relative's funeral, and I didn't
want to be interrupted by customers, not until I'd heard everything.

"But with who?" I said. "Who did you choose?"

She sat down on a silk divan meant for customers, for husbands waiting while their wives tried on hats.

"Monsieur de Jumilhac," she said, "cared only about seeing as
many temples as possible. And monsieur de Beynac cared only
about being treated like a prince by the natives. But Maurice—
monsieur de Nexon, I mean—" She suddenly seemed overcome with emotion, unable to speak, until it all came out in a

burst. "There we were, amidst the Pyramids, the Sphinx, the beauty of the Nile and its people, everything new and unusual and magnificent—and he only had eyes for me."

My legs felt weak, my heart pulsed. I sank onto the divan beside her. Decourcelle couldn't have written it better.

Monsieur de Nexon, she went on, didn't spoil the romantic panoramas of the Nile by speaking incessantly of mummification techniques as monsieur de Jumilhac did. He didn't proclaim within the hearing of the staff that "The only way to deal with Arabs is with sticks," as monsieur de Beynac had. When the little children called out for "baksheesh," he didn't shoo them away with a look of disgust.

No.

Monsieur de Nexon would quietly pull a coin or a piece of sugar cane from his pocket. Every time. And he didn't try to pay the water-carriers or the donkey-boys less than the agreed-upon fee after the fact, complaining about the taste of the water or the quality of the donkeys.

"I saw monsieur de Nexon's soul in Egypt," she said, "and I think he saw mine."

Her words stopped me like a revelation. That was how it had felt with Lucho at Royallieu.

"Now, he just needs to tell his parents," she continued. "He's sure they'll fall in love with me just as he has." She paused and looked up at me. "But what if they don't?"

"They will," I said. "How could they not? Once they meet you, they won't be able to help but love you. Just like everyone else."

She shared more about the trip, and then I told her about my visit to Royallieu, that Gabrielle was, as Adrienne had once said, enjoying la vie château. I'd never seen Gabrielle so content.

"Like you, Adrienne," I said.

I didn't tell her about Lucho. He was my secret. It was the only way I could keep him all to myself.

Now that Adrienne was officially engaged, I was determined to inform Delphine and Sophie, to let them know they were wrong about all they'd accused me of. I stopped at the florist the next morning. Sophie was more reasonable, and if I could just get through to her, she might smooth everything over with Delphine. I missed talking to them. A part of me wanted to be friends again. I didn't have anyone else. Gabrielle wasn't leaving Royallieu any time soon. I didn't know where life would take her next, but I didn't expect she'd come back to Vichy. And Adrienne would be married soon, devoted to monsieur de Nexon, with less time for me.

I caught Sophie on the street just as she was coming back from a delivery.

"Antoinette?" she said, truly surprised. "What are you doing here?"

"My aunt is engaged," I said. "To a baron. One of the men we were with at the opera. You see, I told you. No one has been giving favors." Then I told her that I missed her and Delphine.

"Do you miss Alain?" she said, not returning the sentiment.

I hesitated. There was challenge in her voice. Why was she asking? "I miss his friendship."

"Well, he doesn't miss yours. You know Camille? The tall girl who works in the shoe department at Pygmalion? He's seeing her now. She has a talent for arranging the merchandise in appealing displays. A hard worker."

"I'm glad for him," I said with a smile, though her words stung, the implication that he'd been interested in me only because he needed a wife to help with the store, to wash the stains from his apron, to arrange the fruits and vegetables in *appealing displays*.

"Yes," she said. "He's forgotten all about you. We all have."

She turned on her heel and went into the shop.

I stopped at a patisserie a block away, pretending to browse the pastries in the window while I collected myself, willing the tears away. I couldn't greet customers with red-rimmed eyes.

Why was I crying? Her coldness wasn't totally unexpected. I already knew how quickly these people I'd once called friends could turn on me for doing nothing but trying to better myself. The working classes, I saw now, could be just as judgmental as the upper classes.

I wasn't upset that Alain had someone else. It was a relief. Marrying Alain would have been a kind of arrangement, affection but no passion. I couldn't settle for that, not now, not after seeing Lucho again.

And that, I grasped finally, was the real source of my tears, emotions I'd been holding in since leaving Royallieu. What if that was it, the weekend there with Lucho?

What if that was the closest I would ever get to that feeling— seeing someone else's soul as they saw into your own?

# THIRTY-SEVEN

FOR THE LAST FEW WEEKS OF WINTER, I DEVOTED MYSELF, AS I'd been doing, to the hat shop, preparing for the new season, increasing our stock of hats and trimmings, the kind that appealed to élégantes and not our winter customers from the provinces. In May, the season arrived at last and so, to my delight, did Gabrielle.

Adrienne and I met her at the hippodrome where Etienne's horses were racing. She stood on the grass outside the enclosure with him and his entourage of Royallieu bon vivants—the baron, Suzanne, Leon, and other turf society aristocrats and their mistresses. The sky lost a bit of its brightness when I saw that Lucho wasn't among them.

Gabrielle moved away from them to greet us because it wouldn't do for Adrienne or me to be seen in public with the Royallieu crowd. Especially Adrienne. Months had passed and no invitation had come to meet Maurice's parents, the baron and baroness Auguste de Nexon.

"They're probably traveling," Maud had said earlier that week in the apartment she and Adrienne had taken to plan the wedding. She'd glanced up hopefully at Maurice from the writing table, reading glasses perched on her nose, surrounded by to-do lists. "Or they're tied up with social obligations or..."

Adrienne dissolved into tears. Maurice's face was pink as he admitted that his parents were refusing to receive Adrienne. They expected him to marry from their circle, to choose a bride from one of the oldest families of the Sud-Ouest.

"Once they realize I won't give Adrienne up," he said, pulling Adrienne to him to comfort her, "they'll come around, I'm certain."

Now at the hippodrome, poor Adrienne was so distracted. She stood to the side with Maud, checking the crowds, ready to move off to avoid an awkward encounter with one of monsieur de Nexon's family members. She wanted to avoid them but also to catch their attention all at the same time. Her posture was demure, her clothes tasteful, so that if they did see her, they would recognize she meant no harm, that she was respectable, that she was fit to be the wife of a gentilhomme.

I played the same role, wearing the expected attire, blending in with the great sea of white gauzy dresses and plumed hats beneath frothy parasols, a regatta of sails waving gracefully in the breeze. Gabrielle, on the other hand, was an island in the middle of it, so plain she was almost flamboyant. She wore a simple dark skirt, a fitted blouse, and a tailored jacket cut like a jockey's. Around her neck, she'd tied a floppy little bowtie like the boys from the lycée.

She caught me staring and laughed. "You know very well, Ninette, that if I smothered myself in ruffles like the ladies of la haute with their hips and their bosoms and their double-chins, I'd look like a little pin lost in an enormous pincushion."

"Are those Etienne's clothes you've altered?" I asked.

She shrugged. "What else can I do? Compiègne is nothing

but horses and fields and more horses after that. You've seen it. I have to wear something. Besides, his clothes are comfortable. And practical. I can move in them."

She took in my ensemble, from the tips of my delicate little boots to the blouse I'd finally been able to buy myself at Pygmalion to the puffs of tulle and graceful streamers adorning my hat. There, her gaze came to a lengthy, uncomfortable rest.

"That hat," she said. "It doesn't suit you. It's overdone. It hides your prettiness. And you look so much like everyone else that no one can see you."

Over the years, I'd recognized that Gabrielle's aversion to excess stemmed from the fact that our lives were so lacking in it. She hated it because she couldn't have it.

"But I want to look like everyone else," I said. Even if I'd had to skimp for months before, purchasing my outfit from Pygmalion had been a moment of great pride. My work at the hat shop was bringing me one step closer to that better life I aspired to, and I didn't need Gabrielle to like it. "And you should too," I added.

"Why would I want to look like them?" She waved a hand toward the panorama of ladies in white. "They look like sheep. You can't tell one from the other. They should want to look like me."

"Suzanne looks like you," I said. "At least, her hat does. Did you get them at the same place?" They were of an unusual shape, pulled down over the ears, more masculine than feminine. I'd never seen anything quite like them. Not at the Girards' hat shop. Not in the magazines.

"I made them," she said, explaining she'd grown bored, isolated at Royallieu with Etienne's friends and their mistresses. She needed something of her own, and whenever she passed through Paris with Etienne on the way to or from the next horse race or polo match, she bought as many plain hat forms from the Galeries Lafayette department store as she could carry. Then she did them up with single ribbons or bows back at Royallieu.

"Making hats like Aunt Julia?" I said.

She frowned. "No. Not at all like Aunt Julia."

She said the actresses and mistresses who visited Royallieu thought her plain-cut clothes were funny, the way she dressed like a schoolboy in a skirt, and liked to come up to her room and try on her understated boaters for fun. "They think they're amusing," Gabrielle said.

But the unexpected drew attention, and these ladies, Gabrielle explained, were always looking for attention. The month before, Émilienne d'Alençon had even worn one of Gabrielle's hats to the races at Longchamp in the Bois de Boulogne for all la haute to see.

"*The* Émilienne?" I said. I could hardly believe it. The famous courtesan had worn one of Gabrielle's odd little hats? In public? But Gabrielle's success with hats, evidently, wasn't the biggest news. As she spoke, Gabrielle's eyes kept going to a figure along the rail with black hair swooping away from an intense face, piercing eyes, a thick mustache. With lingering glances and hidden smiles, they seemed to be keeping watch over each other. There was an unusual quality about him, the way he dressed, his manner, but I wasn't sure what it was.

"He's English," Gabrielle said. "His name is Arthur Capel, but everyone calls him 'Boy.'"

"Boy? Like *garçon*?" I said.

"No. Not like *garçon*." She said this as if everything English were better, even an odd nickname.

"Is he married?" I said.

"No," Gabrielle said. "He's not married. He's one of Etienne's friends from the Jockey Club. He's handsome, thoughtful, a champion polo player, and a ladies' man, just look at him. He owns coal mines and shipping companies and works even though he doesn't have to because he likes it."

I leaned in, my voice low. "But Etienne?"

Gabrielle rolled her eyes. "He cares more for horses than any-thing else. He's going away on horse business. He'll be gone for months. It's the perfect time for me to try something of my own."

And she meant Boy?

"I've convinced Etienne to let me use his apartment in Paris while he's gone as a place to sell hats," Gabrielle said. "He says Paris has too many milliners already, and why would I want to make hats and sell them when he'll take care of me? He says it's not proper. But Boy helped me talk him into it. Boy understands that I need something to do, that I can't sit around and paint my fingernails all day. So Etienne's letting me use his garçonnière, and Boy's lending me the money to get started."

Jealousy pinched at me, not because of Boy, but because of *an apartment in Paris. I* was the one who knew about selling hats, not Gabrielle. The hat she wore was distinctive, artistically done, but I could see small imperfections in the way it was finished. There were tricks I'd learned from the Girards. I'd worked three and a half years in a hat shop, yet *she* was going to Paris to sell hats?

"It's not a real hat shop," Gabrielle continued. "It's just some-thing to keep me busy until I decide what I'm really going to do. I'm thinking of taking up singing again. Or maybe dancing. Did I tell you Etienne's actress friend, Gabrielle Dorziat, says I have a talent for mimicry? She says I was meant for the stage."

# THIRTY-EIGHT

"IN OUR HEARTS WE'RE MARRIED," ADRIENNE SAID WHEN SHE gave me the distressing news that she and Maurice were taking an apartment together, just the two of them, in a discreet part of Vichy. Maurice's parents had threatened to withhold his inheritance if he married Adrienne. "He says he doesn't care. He wants to marry me anyway. He's practically insisting. But I told him no. I won't become his wife without his parents' consent. You and I know what it's like to be poor, Ninette. We know how to live with nothing. He doesn't. He has no idea what it would mean. He has no idea how it might drive us apart. I'm afraid—I'm terrified—he would resent me. I would live in constant fear of it. There's nothing else to do."

She was resigned, her heart lanced but not broken. The light inside of her had dimmed slightly, replaced with something else. Acceptance. They had given up.

Maud packed her things to go back to Souvigny. She mentioned I should come in the spring, but she didn't look me in the eye. We all knew the truth. If she couldn't marry Adrienne off, she would have no chance with me.

I'd thought Adrienne cared about marriage as much as I did. But she cared more about love.

What would become of me now?

I was already twenty-two. I cared about love, but I wanted legitimacy. If I married well, then maybe we would all be lifted up. It would make up for Gabrielle not becoming a singer, for Maurice's parents not accepting Adrienne. That was how it seemed to me. But right then, what I wanted most was to get away from Vichy, from Delphine and Sophie and Alain, who would gloat if they knew how everything had turned out. I'd been here four years, long enough to realize the city I once thought was so big wasn't that big after all, that I'd never find the happiness I was looking for in this town.

*You, Antoinette Chanel, would be lucky to marry the son of a grocer.* I wrote to Gabrielle.

*I can help you. I know everything there is to know about selling hats. I can move to Paris and be your assistant.*

I expected her to tell me once again it wasn't a real hat shop, that she was spending most of her time auditioning or with this man called Boy Capel. Instead, at the end of December, a cable came. Gabrielle's hat shop that wasn't a hat shop was busier than she could keep up with. "Come," she said. "I need you."

I said goodbye to the Girards, hugged and kissed Adrienne, and was on a train for Paris the very next day.

# ÉLÉGANTES

## PARIS DEAUVILLE BIARRITZ
### 1910–1919

# THIRTY-NINE

PARIS!

It wasn't a city. It was a lady, the grandest élégante of all, done up in a gown of spun gold, everything shimmering and light. Avenues broad and regal stretched out like long, graceful limbs. Allées of trees, branches knobby, stood en guarde, her protectors. Her streets glittered with life, cafés, brasseries, carriages, motorcars, people, young, old, rich, poor.

Not just people. *Parisians*. And now I was one of them.

I wanted to see everything I'd read about in the magazines. The Moulin Rouge. The Bois de Boulogne. The Folies Bergère. The Champs-Élysées.

But Gabrielle, who met me at the station, said there was no time. "Who would have thought so many people would be interested in my hats?" she said. "I have so many orders to finish. I can't keep up."

She hired a taxi to take us straight to the Boulevard Malesherbes and Etienne's garçonnière, a first-floor apartment on a quiet street lined with handsome buildings. Inside, I looked for clues into the ways of the male mind, studying Etienne's mysterious den of masculinity that smelled faintly of cigar smoke, a place to stay when he was in Paris, a place for trysts, for pleasure.

Now, a place to display ladies' hats. Decorated with my sister's feminine, feathered creations, the dark-paneled drawing room, with its equestrian oil paintings and cigar boxes and leather-bound books, looked more like a misdirected ladies' auxiliary meeting.

Gabrielle showed me the rest of the love nest, everything modern and magical. The heat was gas, the lighting electric. There was a telephone and plumbing. I pressed a handle on the commode and *voilà*, clear water rushed in. A gold clock that worked on its own presided over the mantel. Connected to Paris's pneumatic air system, it didn't need to be wound.

"You'll sleep here," Gabrielle said, patting a comfortable-looking bed in a room in the back, a servant's room, but still nicer than any place I'd ever lived.

"Where do you sleep?" I said. "Etienne's room, I suppose?"

A mischievous smile lit her face. "I sleep at Boy's. His place is just down the street."

Of course. "Does Etienne know?"

"He knows. Now that someone else wants me, he seems to think he loves me. Funny how that happens. But Boy and I were meant for each other. Even Etienne sees that. He's a gentleman. He'll bow out gracefully."

"But he lets you use his apartment, knowing...?"

"He doesn't need it. And remember, we never made any promises to each other."

"What if while I'm here he comes by with one of his old lovers to help him forget you?" I said.

"He won't. He's away in Argentina visiting that Lucho Harrington, learning all about polo strategies and one thousand ways to breed a horse—"

*That* Lucho Harrington.

"—Argentina is Etienne's idea of heaven. He won't be thinking of me or the Boulevard Malesherbes."

It all sounded so far away, another world. A pang of longing pierced me, but Gabrielle brought me back to this one, pulling out a new ledger in the drawing room.

"A new year," she said. "A new ledger. Write your name here."

She pointed to the first line and handed me a fountain pen. I wrote "Mademoiselle Chanel, Antoinette," then "January 1, 1910," in my finest convent girl handwriting.

"*Vendeuse*," she said, nodding toward the page. "Antoinette Chanel, *vendeuse*. You'll work for commission. Ten percent of every sale. The more you sell, the more money you'll make."

I wrote "vendeuse" next to my name with an extra flourish. I was no longer just a shop girl. I was a vendeuse!

In *Paris*!

She led me to the kitchen, or at least what had once been a kitchen. There was no cooking taking place here, no meals being prepared. Instead, the room was overtaken by an explosion of scissors, spools of millinery thread, pins, pliers, bottles of glue and shellac, and rolls and rolls of string. There were scraps here, there and everywhere of buckram, velvet, muslin, and silk. Feathers seemed to have fallen from the sky as if a steady stream of exotic birds had flown overhead.

"What happened?" I said.

"What do you mean?"

"This looks like the laboratory of a mad scientist. A mad hat scientist."

She looked miffed. "I'm not mad. I'm teaching myself. There's only so much a person can do with plain straw boaters from a department store. I want to do more. I have ideas. I just have to figure out how to turn my ideas into hats."

I saw right off how I could help. I pointed to different hats in various stages of completion. "Well, this brim needs extra wiring if you want it to hold its shape. And there, you can still see the seams. That's because you're using the wrong fabric. And that one, the bindings aren't properly stretched."

I thought she'd appreciate the advice. Instead, her face had turned red.

"What do you know about making hats?" she said.

"What kind of question is that? You know I worked in a hat shop."

"*Selling* hats."

"And making them. And repairing them. Sometimes hats from the most famous milliners in Paris."

She gestured to the hat on my head with obvious disapproval. "Did you make that?"

"No, I bought it."

"Hmmm," she said, and not in a good way. "You paid money for it?"

"Actually, Adrienne bought it for me," I said. "As a farewell present." But I'd picked it out myself. It was black velvet with crisp white heron feathers artfully arranged at the crown, and I felt chic and Parisian in it, or at least I had.

"It looks like you've run headfirst into a pigeon."

I drew in my breath. I was here to help her, and she was insulting me.

"You should take at least five of those feathers off," she said. "It would look much better with just one or two. Overdone is vulgar. The most important part of making a hat is ensuring it's not too fussy, that it doesn't draw attention away from the beauty of the woman wearing it. After you think you've finished trimming it, you should always remove at least one thing. In your case, five."

I was not about to be lectured by Gabrielle, who was clearly annoyed that her little sister knew more about constructing a hat than she did. While she'd been playing games at Royallieu, I'd been learning the art of millinery.

I picked up another hat. "Put your finger there. Do you feel that? Wire. Poking your potential customer's scalp. You need more padding. More binding. And all of these seams. The perfect hat has to look effortless. The most important part of making a hat is the construction."

We faced each other, glaring, until her scowl cracked, and she started laughing.

"What's so funny?" I said.

"Listen to us. We sound as if we think we could put Maison Lewis and all of the rest of the great Paris milliners out of business. You're right. I need help. A lot of help. Let's go get something to eat. I'm famished. Then when it's dark, we'll take a taxi around Paris so you can see the monuments lit up at night. Oh, Ninette. I'm so glad you're here. We'll get to work first thing tomorrow morning."

# FORTY

"BUT WHO ARE YOUR CUSTOMERS?" I ASKED GABRIELLE A COU-
ple of days later as we arranged the displays in Etienne's drawing
room, moving around for best effect the slim rosewood stands
called "champignons" because with hats on top, they resembled
exotic-looking mushrooms.

"The Boulevard Malesherbes," I continued when she didn't
respond, "this part of it, at least, isn't a street of merchants. You
have no sign advertising a hat shop. How do people know to
come here?"

"They don't need a sign," Gabrielle said, studying a brown
felt hat with a wide moiré ribbon. "Some of the customers are
Etienne's old friends from la haute. They've been here before,
if you know what I mean."

She gave me a look so that I did know what she meant. Affairs. Liaisons. The whole purpose of having a garçonnière.

"Some of Boy's old flames come by too," Gabrielle said. "I
suppose they have to see with their own eyes the little peasant

Etienne humored and Boy stole away, the nobody from nowhere who made the hat Émilienne d'Alençon wore to the races at Longchamp. I'm sure they expect to find me clomping about in wooden clogs."

She took the brown felt hat off a short champignon, exchanging it with a navy cloche on a taller stand and considering the impact.

"But now that you're here," she said, "I'm staying in the back. I won't give them the pleasure of gawking at me. Besides, Adrienne says you have a way with customers."

At that moment, the bell rang, startling us both. Gabrielle scurried to the kitchen, leaving me to face my first Parisian customers alone. Nervous, I smoothed my skirt, checked my hair in the mirror. Did I look like a bumpkin, a plouc from the provinces?

*You know what to do*, I reminded myself as I opened the door to two very distinguished ladies of la haute. I stood as tall as I could, greeting them, welcoming them into the foyer, my eyes grazing over their expensive ensembles and hats, their suede gloves, their fur-trimmed coats.

In the drawing room, their eyes darted about. It seemed odd, until finally the taller one blurted out, "Are you Coco?"

They stared at me as if I were an animal at the zoo. A freak at a sideshow. Some sort of spectacle.

"I'm her sister," I said as disappointment flashed across their pretty faces. "Coco's out right now. But I can help you. What sort of chapeau are you looking for? A cloche, perhaps? Or maybe a picture hat?"

They seemed flustered, as if they'd forgotten where they were, why'd they come. I put on a smile, feeling defensive of my sister in the face of these voyeurs. I said, in my sweetest, firmest voice, enunciating every syllable, "You *did* come for a hat, didn't you?"

From the kitchen, I heard a small, almost imperceptible snort.

Gabrielle, eavesdropping through the door.

In the end, they bought hats. They all bought hats, these ladies who came to the Boulevard Malesherbes. I was surprised to find that every day the bell rang, bringing more curiosity seekers, and I employed my usual flattery and charm to sell them. But I didn't need to. The customers appeared truly taken by my sister's rebellious little chapeaux, adorned with just a single dramatic feather or a ribbon perfectly placed. Was it their simplicity that made them daring? Or was it simply daring to wear a hat made by the woman who'd been "kept" by Etienne Balsan, who was now the mistress of the dashing English polo player Boy Capel?

Maybe it was both.

When Gabrielle's friends from Royallieu visited, the actresses and demimondaines, she would leave her kitchen hiding place and saunter into the drawing room. There were hugs, greetings, laughter, lively exchanges of gossip. The atmosphere in the garçonnière changed completely, and Gabrielle wasn't shy about giving out advice.

One time, to Gabrielle Dorziat, she bemoaned, "No one can even see you in that concoction!"

"But how could they not see me?" Gabrielle Dorziat said, sincerely confused. "It's enormous!"

"Exactly! Like the Arc de Triomphe right there on your head. It's appalling. Oh darling, please take it off. You're too beautiful, too stunning for that. You do want to be noticed, don't you? Then you have to be different. You have to stand out, not disappear beneath an enormous pile of fluff."

I reached for a wide-brimmed navy hat. For trimming, Gabrielle had used a white ostrich plume nearly eighteen inches long, an *amazone* it was called because of its size. "Here," I said to Gabrielle Dorziat. "Try this on. The color, the shape—it's perfect for you. Just enough, but not too much."

I showed her exactly how the hat should be placed on the head and where to insert the pins, adjusting her chignon just so, freeing a few strategically placed curls. She stood back and studied herself in the mirror with a pleased look, tilting her head from side to side.

"It's magnificent," she said.

"As if it were made just for you," I agreed.

My sister nodded. "Ravishing."

"I adore it," Gabrielle Dorziat said, but then her smile turned to a pout. "But I'm sure I can't afford it. The play I'm in now, we won't get paid until it's over, a few weeks away. It's all I can do to eat."

Of course. And she must have spent quite a lot already on the "Arc de Triomphe." It was funny. Once I would have coveted such a headpiece for myself. But I was gradually getting used to Gabrielle's pared-down style, observing how the overdone could overwhelm, how perhaps Gabrielle didn't hate excess because she couldn't have it but because it really was too much. Excess didn't equate to flattering. Money didn't equate to taste. Although the ladies of la haute thought so, and it felt powerful knowing something they did not. I'd even been letting Gabrielle dress me. We wore sweaters from Etienne's closet that were cut up the middle. She sewed on ribbon and buttons and we wrapped ourselves in belts. We didn't wear corsets, not that we had anything to squeeze in or push up anyway.

Poor Gabrielle Dorziat. Perhaps we would still have the picture hat after her play concluded. Or when the time came, we could make another just like it.

"It's yours," Gabrielle said to her friend. "A gift. You must have it."

I stared at my sister, shocked.

"But are you sure?" Gabrielle Dorziat said.

"Of course! Chérie, it's just a hat. Pieces of felt. A feather."

Just a hat? That feather alone, she'd told me proudly, had

cost twenty-four francs at the Bon Marché's counter for *plumes et fleurs*! And did Gabrielle not recall the time it took? I'd demonstrated how to craft the hat from scratch so she could go beyond the basic department store form. How to trace a pattern and cut it out and sew the millinery wire to the brim to hold the shape. How to cover the wire with muslin. How to sew all the pieces together into one sumptuous whole. The brim to the side band to the crown tip. That was just the beginning. And the fact that she changed her mind all the time, and we had to start over! *No, no, Ninette. That's not right.* She was bossy even when she didn't know what she was doing. For the final overlay, she'd tried eight different colors and fabrics before deciding on navy velvet, various arrangements of ribbon and feathers before finally selecting the single amazone, turning it this way and that until the feathers fell at just the right angle.

We'd spent hours on that hat. Days. It was a masterpiece.

And now she was giving it away?

I looked down, busying myself with another hat so Gabrielle Dorziat wouldn't see my anger. After she sashayed out the door, picture hat perched prettily on her head, I confronted Gabrielle.

"You can't just give hats away," I said. "This is a business. Not a charity ward."

She laughed, only making me madder. "Just because she has no money doesn't mean she doesn't deserve a beautiful hat. Besides, it's not like we're on the rue de la Paix alongside Madame Alphonsine. I don't mind one bit taking money from Etienne's and Boy's old lovers, but I feel strange asking my friends to pay for my hats, especially as they're more a hobby than anything else."

"It's not a hobby for me," I said. "Gabrielle Dorziat isn't the only one who has to eat."

For the rest of the day, I fumed. She had Boy, Etienne. I had only myself. Had I made the wrong decision leaving a good job in Vichy to help Gabrielle with what might be no more than a passing whim?

Every morning Gabrielle traipsed up to Montmartre and took lessons in a strange kind of dance called Eurythmics, and it was in one of those instances, as I sat in Etienne's apartment, eating breakfast alone, that an uncomfortable realization dawned on me. Could it be that she considered hats a pastime because she thought *dance* was her future? That had to be it. Her dreams of the stage still lived on, of the applause and cheering crowds that would prove once and for all to our father that he never should have left her.

Back at Etienne's after class, when she'd show me some of the movements, I would bite my tongue. I didn't want her to resent me, and it was unlikely she would listen to me anyway. She would have to see on her own that she wasn't meant to be a dancer. Especially when she clearly had a passion for hats. How could she not see it? We worked on them constantly, rarely resting. She was a quick learner and so full of ideas, animated with possibility whenever she had a new one.

Maybe I couldn't make her face the truth, but there was something I could do about her casual attitude toward sales, and the next time a lady of la haute wanted to buy a hat, I blurted that it cost twenty francs more than it actually did. I panicked inside that I'd ruined the sale, waiting for her to laugh, to hand the hat back and say in a voice full of condescension, "My dear, this isn't the rue de la Paix."

But she didn't blink.

For her and all the ladies of la haute, twenty more francs meant nothing. But to me, and to Gabrielle, whether she admitted it or not, they could mean our future, our very survival.

# FORTY-ONE

THOSE FIRST FEW WEEKS SINCE I'D COME TO PARIS, AS GABRIELLE and I worked on the hats, we'd sing the old caf'conc songs from Moulins at the top of our lungs. The femme de ménage who came with the apartment would look up from waxing the floor as if we were crazy, which only made us sing louder. As part of our performance, we often wore kitchen pots or bowls on our heads to test out the shapes for possible new hat styles. If Gabrielle decided she liked one, I'd use it as a form to mold buckram, dampening it, then securing it tightly with a string until it dried. The hat form makers had recently gone on strike. She was lucky to have me.

Gabrielle also loved to talk about Boy.

"Boy says idleness weighs on intelligent women, and that's why it's important I have something to do," Gabrielle told me as we cut ribbons and fluffed feathers in the dining room.

I'd never heard my sister refer to herself as intelligent before. Usually, an "intelligent" woman was considered a *bas bleu*, a bluestocking, frumpy, unattractive. "I thought men don't like intelligent women."

"Boy does. The strangest thing is he listens to me, Ninette, as if he thinks I have something to say."

I'd heard he was a playboy. He traveled often to manage his shipping business and was said to be a man who had mistresses in every port. But Gabrielle seemed to like the challenge. I knew her thinking. Why would any woman want to be with a man no one else wanted?

"When I first saw him," she continued, "I knew. I knew I would love him, and he'd love me. He doesn't think of me as a pet, like Etienne. Etienne cares only about horses. But Boy is an intellectual. He cares about so many things. He studies mathematics and art and Hinduism. He believes in humanism and making the world a better place. And I embarrass him because all I know is Decourcelle. He wants to teach me, to show me things. He gives me books to read by philosophers like Nietzsche and Voltaire and poets like Baudelaire."

My sister didn't take direction from anyone, but it appeared Boy Capel was the one person she'd listen to. Boy was making her into Something Better. I'd only seen him that one time at the hippodrome in Vichy, and I was eager to meet him. When he came by the garçonnière, and I did, I saw right away: Gabrielle, who worshipped elegance above all else, had found the male epitome. Boy was smooth, handsome, a perfect dresser, with manners, kindness, a man who gave the impression of having important things to do but time to listen as well.

I too wanted to be Something Better. But when Gabrielle lent me one of Boy's books on something called Free Masons, I couldn't read more than half a page. It was so dull.

Luckily I had Celestine, an artist Gabrielle Dorziat had taken under her wing and brought along on her visits to the Boulevard Malesherbes. Celestine knew Gabrielle Dorziat from painting set designs for theater productions. She was my age, and she floated about with dried paint on her hands and clothes but in a charming way, as if she'd walked out of a canvas herself, a painting of a fairy with calm, wide-set brown eyes that made her look wise and dark hair that curled in perfect spirals. She was tall and lanky and moved like a colt that hadn't yet gotten its legs.

As my sister's group of Royallieu theater friends talked about the roles they were trying for, or gave us parts to help them rehearse, Celestine would sit at Etienne's desk and draw clever little sketches of the hats on their champignons.

But sketching was the only time Celestine could sit still.

"Antoinette," she said to me in an accusing tone one day as I sewed the lining on a hat. "Do you do anything else but work?"

"Well..." I was embarrassed to admit that the answer was no. I was so caught up in helping Gabrielle. After all that had happened in Vichy, with Alain, with Adrienne and Maurice's parents, I had needed to lose myself in something. The placing of one stitch after another had its medicinal effects, was soothing, the mind too occupied to think of anything else.

Celestine, who wore long, interesting tunics she found in flea markets, took pride in the fact that she was a native-born Parisienne and decided she would be my guide, since Gabrielle usually spent all her free time with Boy. We started out ice-skating at the Bois de Boulogne on Sunday, where we rented skates for two francs and glided around to the strands of an orchestra, avoiding falling children and young men who veered in and out with reckless abandon. We ate warm roasted chestnuts at the cinema on the Boulevard des Italiens even though we'd heard the moving pictures could hurt your eyes. We went to the circus in Montmartre, laughing at the clowns, gasping at the acrobats performing tricks on horseback, and met her friends at small indoor cafés, where businessmen bought all our drinks— Vermouth Cassis because that was what all the girls drank.

There was no shortage of potential love interests. Students from Germany who were very serious. Jugglers from Spain who weren't. Tourists from America who were earnest and naive and whose French made us giggle hysterically. Artists who asked if we'd pose for them—at first we agreed, but in the end I couldn't go through with it. A stranger looking at me so intently, studying me inch by inch, seemed so intimate, more for a husband or a lover.

Celestine laughed when I told her this. "It's not like that. Artists look at models the same way you look at a hat. They see the parts, how everything is put together."

"Do you want to get married someday?" I asked her, curious. "Do you ever think about that?"

"I'm not meant to settle down," she said. "I want to be a famous artist. I want to travel. I want to see everything. And right now, I enjoy life as it is. I'm Creole, you know. My great-grandfather was a sailor from West Africa. He met my great-grandmother in Normandy. Moving about is in my blood."

I worried it was in mine too. My father, my grandparents. But I still craved the idea of a husband, a home of my own, a place in society that meant people had to acknowledge me, confirmation that I was more than an orphan or charity case or unwanted daughter.

I could have had that with Alain. Not high society but a step up from a family of itinerant peddlers. But the grocery store was Alain's place. And here I was in Paris now, one step closer to finding my own.

# FORTY-TWO

I HADN'T BEEN IN PARIS EVEN A MONTH WHEN IT STARTED TO
rain day and night. "Comme les vaches qui pissent," Gabrielle
said one morning, mimicking Pépère as she walked in from a
downpour, shaking water from her coat. We thought the weather
would keep customers away, that it would give us time to catch
our breath, to relax, but it didn't.

Parisians went about in the rain that sometimes turned to
snow, paying visits, shopping. How to bring a ray of sunshine
to a dreary day? A new chapeau. And if they were out, they
might as well stop by Etienne Balsan's garçonnière for a look
at this Coco's hats, for a look at Coco herself if she'd show her
face. Customers arrived, bottoms of skirts soaked, shoes waterlogged, hats ruined, drooping and spotted from the rain. Which
meant they needed new ones, ordering two or three at a time.

But the rain turned out to be more than just rain.

On Saturday, Boy came into the garçonnière talking about
how high the river was around the giant Zouave sculpture near

the Pont de l'Alma, which was used as an informal marker for the height of the Seine when it rained. I went with Celestine to see for myself. Crowds were gathered on the bridge near the stone soldier that was supposed to protect the city. When I was finally able to get to the front, I looked down and there he was, rising up from the water and gazing out with a stern expression, the usually calm river thrashing and churning around his knees.

"The last time it rained this much," Celestine said, "the water only came up over the Zouave's feet. I've never seen it higher."

The footpaths and boathouses along the river were underwater. The barges, laundry boats, fishermen and groomers who bathed and clipped dogs along the banks were gone, and in their place, a mad rush of water, wooden barrels and furniture and debris flying by from upriver, crashing into splinters against the base of the bridge while onlookers cried out.

The next few days brought a barrage of more news as the Seine steadily rose. Customers told us that the streets near the river were now flooding, water invading homes and shops, gushing up through the sewers. Some of the ladies of the nouveau riche stopped by before the matinees, élégantes in their usual finery despite all the rain. Theaters on higher ground, they told me, were still open. Dinner parties went on as planned.

When the waterlogged rue Saint Honoré and rue Royale were blocked off after they buckled in on themselves and left dangerous, gaping holes, the fancy boutiques closed and even more customers came our way, calling out reports like newspaper boys, the water rising hour by hour:

"The Seine is up to the Zouave's thighs."

"The Metro is flooded."

"The Hotel de Ville and the Grand Palais are flooded too."

"There are no lights on the Champs-Élysées."

"Hotels on the rue de Rivoli have no heat or light."

"Maxim's is closed. Water has filled the cellar."

"My dears, did you hear? A bear escaped from the zoo. It swam right out."

Mon Dieu. A bear on the loose.

Wednesday, the concierge left for the countryside. The femme de ménage didn't show up. Churches held special masses. Parisians went to confession in case this was the end, the coming of the Last Judgment.

I had no time for confession. The city was running short on coal, but thanks to Boy and his coal shipping business, the garçonnière was warm and dry. Ladies still came to try on picture hats, gossiping about who had flooded, who would organize the next Charity Bazaar for the displaced, how they'd sent their maids to deliver food and blankets to those sheltering at the Pantheon and the Saint Sulpice seminary.

At night, I dreamed it was raining ribbons, pins, scissors, and felt. I was the Zouave, up to my ankles, my knees, my thighs in hats.

On Thursday, the Seine was up to the Zouave's shoulders.

On Friday, it was at his neck, and all around the city, the lights went out.

The city of light was in the dark.

When we heard that afternoon that the Louvre was flooded, Celestine was distraught.

"I have to go," she said, her voice urgent. "Maybe there's something I can do to help. Imagine all those paintings and statues drowned! The Mona Lisa, Venus de Milo, the Odalisque, carried away in the current." In her free time, Celestine liked to spend hours at the Louvre sketching works of the great masters. Then she'd sell her sketches on the streets to tourists for a few francs.

We went together, sloshing through the rain and high water in the freezing cold. As we drew closer to the river, we saw people being rowed out of neighborhoods in boats, the streets turned into canals, enterprising fellows providing transport as if they were gondoliers in Venice. On some flooded streets, we had to pick our way along with everyone else on café chairs that had been lined up one after the other in chains. In other places, we could only get through by balancing like tightrope walkers on *passerelles*, raised walkways made of narrow wooden boards that workers had put up. It was all very precarious. I tried not to look down. One wrong step, and I'd plunge into icy water.

We crossed the rue de Rivoli and there was the Louvre, that noble palace, but on the quay side, the police had it cordoned off. We watched men, sweating despite the January chill, slicing into mounds of sand with shovels and filling small bags as fast as they could. Others took the bags and piled them against the buckling quay walls or mixed cement to plug the spaces in between. Driftwood hauled up from the river and pavers pulled out of the streets were added as fortifications. Water had gotten into the Louvre's basements, someone said, and they were doing all they could to keep it from rising any higher. Inside, someone else said, museum workers were moving art to higher floors.

Hearing this, Celestine seemed satisfied. The Louvre was in good hands, its treasures safe.

And so, at last, were we. The next Saturday, after a week that had felt like a month, the sun edged through the clouds. The muddy water of the Seine began to slip back into its banks like a snake into its lair. The lights turned back on, and so did the clocks.

*Le cru de le Seine* was over.

During the flood, Gabrielle had continued to attend her Eurythmics class every morning. Montmartre, built up on a hill, had stayed dry. In the garçonnière, she still liked to show me some of the movements she'd learned.

I turned away, rolled my eyes. Paris had flooded. It had nearly washed away. And still people had come for her chic little hats. But here she was still focused on the dancing.

When I mentioned the idea of opening a real boutique, a store in a business district, on a fashionable street, Gabrielle snorted. "A boutique? Ninette, you're still so naive. I'm just the *curiosité du jour*. The ladies of the monde and the demimonde will lose interest soon enough."

I shook my head. It wasn't me who was naive.

# FORTY-THREE

OH THE STENCH! OF MUST AND MOLD, DAMPNESS FESTERING.
Rotting piles on the sidewalks, the ruins of peoples' lives. Soggy
mattresses. Stinking rugs. Mildewed clothing, photos, books,
and papers in soaking clumps of pulp. The river had enveloped
everything in its path, churning it into a fetid soup of manure,
mud, debris, and sewage. It had lapped over the low parts of the
city, sinking in, destroying, leaving its mark before slowly easing away. Finally, the Seine was back in its banks, but the deluge of water had turned into a deluge of smells that lodged in
my chest and made me cough until I was sick in bed for a week,
Gabrielle scolding me for having ventured out in the rain and
floodwaters with Celestine.

It took months of cleanup, people shoveling silt, mopping,
scrubbing, sprinkling quicklime over everything, men repairing
roads and shoring up buildings. Then the first signs of spring
came. The bad smells thinned and drifted off as the pink blooms
opened on the chestnut trees along the avenues and in the parks
where, with the change in temperature, orchestras played on

certain days. By May, we'd almost forgotten all about le cru de la Seine, the ruin, and the stench.

When a telegram from Adrienne arrived at the garçonnière one afternoon, Gabrielle tore it open, the two of us thinking this was it: Maurice's parents had approved of the engagement. But as Gabrielle read the telegram out loud, her voice went from excited to distressed.

MY DEARESTS, JULIA-BERTHE IS ILL. WE ARE BRINGING
HER TO THE HOSPITAL IN PARIS. THE MAISON MUNICIPALE
DE SANTÉ ON RUE DU FAUBOURG ST. DENIS. WE ARRIVE
TOMORROW. PRAYERS.

A cold wind blew through me, and I sat down in a chair in a daze, the world narrowing to one thing: Julia-Berthe.

"Hospital?" I said. We hadn't even known she was ill. And now they were taking her to a hospital? "That's where people go to die."

Gabrielle snapped at me. "Don't be a peasant. You sound like Mémère. What Chanel has ever been in a hospital that isn't a charity hospital? The Maison Municipale de Santé is for people *with means*. It's completely different."

All this time, I'd had an image of Julia-Berthe in my mind, sitting at the market with a basket of puppies, bread crumbs in her pocket for the birds, smiling as she always had. Adrienne went to Moulins often to check on Mémère and Pépère, and she'd check on Julia-Berthe too. That must have been how Adrienne found out she was sick.

But Julia-Berthe didn't like change. She wouldn't have come to Paris unless the situation was dire.

There was a church just down the street from the garçonnière, the Église Saint-Augustin, with its towering gray dome. A statue of Jean d'Arc on horseback guarded the front, her sword raised in defiance, her gaze fierce. Gabrielle and I swept past her, climbing the front steps of the church beneath a frieze of Christ and the twelve apostles.

In a side chapel, we lit a candle, then knelt. The first thing I did was ask for forgiveness. I hadn't been to church since Moulins. Then I appealed to the figures in the paintings and stained glass, the carvings of angels and saints, martyrs and bishops, anyone who would listen.

*Oh holy ange, please don't take Julia-Berthe.*

That night, I didn't want to be alone. Gabrielle's presence was reassuring, a link to Julia-Berthe, but I could see she wanted to be with Boy. "You understand, don't you, Ninette?" she said.

We were grown now, not girls in a dormitory who only had each other. But still I wished she would stay.

She gave me a powder called Veronal she sometimes used to help her sleep. "I won't leave until you fall asleep," she said, and she sat beside me until the drug took effect, closing off my thoughts, pulling me into the darkness where there were no fears, no dreams of our mother, cold and gray and dying on a cot. Just sleep.

At the hospital the next day, the sight of Julia-Berthe in that bed, head on a stack of pillows, took the breath out of me. Our beautiful, voluptuous sister had wasted away, her cheekbones sharp beneath yellowish skin, thicker, rougher than I remembered. Her lips were dry and cracked, her breath coming in shallow, rattling gasps. Her eyes, opening for a moment, had a strange, delirious glitter. She didn't seem to see us. I fought to stay composed, a lump swelling in my throat.

Adrienne told us Julia-Berthe had a fever, had been in and out of consciousness. She was coughing blood. "She has been for years," Adrienne said. "But she's been hiding it. She didn't want anyone to know. Even Maman. Until a few weeks ago at the market." She shook her head, her voice catching.

"What do you mean? What happened?" Gabrielle said.

"She coughed up so much blood. There was blood everywhere in one big gush, Maman said. After that, they couldn't... she couldn't be out at the market anymore. People were afraid to be near her. They were afraid they'd catch it."

"Catch what?" I said.

"Consumption."

The disease that had killed our mother.

I felt like my insides were made of glass, shattered and broken into shards. Poor, poor Julia-Berthe.

"When I found out, I took her right away to a doctor in Moulins," Adrienne said. "He said she needs to go to a sanatorium. There's one in Switzerland he recommended. Maurice so kindly offered to pay for it. But Julia-Berthe refused to go. I could only convince her to come here, to Paris where the doctors are better. She only agreed because you two live here."

"But what does the doctor here say?" Gabrielle said. "Can they cure her?"

Adrienne choked back a sob. "He told Maurice...he told Maurice it's too late."

Too late? I looked at Gabrielle, hoping for one of her eye rolls or smirks, a statement that this doctor must be no good, we had to find another. But she was quiet. Her eyes were closed as if trying to grasp what Adrienne had just said.

"No," I said, shaking my head. "No. Now that she's here with us, she'll get better. We're together. That's what matters." I thought of Jean d'Arc outside the Église Saint-Augustin, the determination on her face. Julia-Berthe would recover. She was in a real hospital in Paris, an advantage our mother hadn't had.

The nurses, their faces like stone, said we had to leave. Visiting hours were over.

We would come back the next morning.

"It won't matter," one nurse said. "She doesn't even know you're here."

Maurice took Adrienne to a friend's garçonnière on the rue Saussier-Leroy, where they'd stay the next couple of days, and Gabrielle and I went back to the Boulevard Malesherbes. When someone knocked on the door, we didn't answer. We just sat in the dining room, working on hats in silence. They seemed so trivial now, but at least this was something we could do, something we could fix.

Was Gabrielle thinking what I was thinking? If the worst happened, what would become of Julia-Berthe? The nuns would say she would go to hell. She was a fornicator. A sinner. What if the nuns were right? Gabrielle, Adrienne, they were sinners too. The whole world was going to hell.

Later that night, after Gabrielle went to Boy's, as I started to take the Veronal, Julia-Berthe's words from our childhood, from Aubazine, rang in my head: *There are ghosts here.*

I put on my hat and went back to the hospital. I couldn't leave her alone with the ghosts.

It was easy to sneak in. The halls were dark and empty, and so was her room, quiet but for the sound of her labored breathing. I crept up to her bed. Her eyes were closed, and I smoothed strands of hair from her damp forehead, wiped blood from the corner of her mouth. I tried not to look at the blood on her pillow.

Quietly, I dragged a chair closer to her bed, pushing away a wave of helplessness, of overwhelming despair.

"Julia-Berthe." My voice was a whisper, as light as I could make it. "It's me, Ninette. I'm here. Don't worry. I'm not leaving you."

She didn't open her eyes, but she made a sound. Maybe she was trying to speak. Maybe deep inside her unconscious world, she was trying to tell me she knew I was there. Or maybe it was a groan or a whimper of pain. But it seemed to me, as I kept talking, her breathing came just a little bit easier.

"You don't have to say anything. You know me. I can do all the talking. You remember how the nuns always scolded me. 'Custody of the tongue, Mademoiselle Chanel.' Now, I talk all day to Gabrielle's customers. She makes hats, Julia-Berthe. Chic hats, and la haute come to buy them, élégantes from the monde and the demimonde. You'll come work with us, as soon as you're able. We're all together now, Julia-Berthe, finally. I'm so glad you came to Paris."

I told her Gabrielle's hats were selling faster than we could make them, that we needed a boutique with more room and more helpers, like the great Paris milliners, with advertisements in all the magazines. When Julia-Berthe coughed, I cleaned the blood with a towel, then shared more about the customers, the way they dressed, the way they carried themselves. I told her about Boy Capel, that he was making Gabrielle into Something Better, that he was handsome and rich and loved her, and about Lucho Harrington, how he had made my heart beat out of my chest.

"I haven't told anyone about Lucho," I said. "You're the only one who knows. It's our secret."

When I ran out of things to say about our lives, I recounted stories from *The Dancing Girl of the Convent* just as I had back in Aubazine, when I'd climb into bed with her in the dormitory. I removed my hat and shoes and eased myself into the small hospital bed next to her. I closed my eyes, felt her heat, the dampness of her skin, her shallow, pained breathing, and put my arms around her. I went on about ballerinas and handsome counts and love at first sight, to comfort her and to comfort myself as old memories hit me in flashes.

*An early death.* That was the gypsy's prophecy from long ago. I had been so sure it meant our mother. I could feel her now, our mother, her shadowy presence, all of the ghosts of the past, the holy and the unholy, here, in the Maison Municipale de Santé, waiting until I fell asleep…

That's when they took Julia-Berthe.

"She's gone," a nurse said, light spilling in from the window. I was groggy, confused. I lifted my head. "No, she's right here," I said, feeling her beside me.

But her skin was cool. She wasn't struggling to breathe. She wasn't moving at all. I started to panic, but as they began to pull her from my arms, I swore I heard a voice—her voice—so clearly in my head, free and untroubled.

*Don't worry, Ninette. Something Better. I've found my Something Better.*

A few days later, Gabrielle, Adrienne, and I, along with Boy and Maurice, buried Julia-Berthe at the Cimetière de La Chapelle amidst the flowers of spring, new birth among all the death and rot. Moss the color of emeralds covered the older stone tombs as if they were dressed in ball gowns for some morbid fête.

We were adamant that Mémère and Pépère not be informed until later. We didn't want to see them. We blamed them, in part, for Julia-Berthe's death, for not properly watching over her, for using her and her figure in the marketplace to draw customers for their own ends, a hard life that now had done her in, just like our mother.

When the ceremony was over, Adrienne and Maurice left for Vichy. Boy offered to take us back to the garçonnière, but Gabrielle and I needed to be alone. We lingered at the gravesite, sprinkling bread crumbs over the freshly turned earth to attract the birds Julia-Berthe so loved. I didn't want to leave her alone.

"It's our fault," I said. "We left her behind. We should have visited her more often. Maybe we would have seen the blood. Maybe we could have noticed that she was ill earlier, in time to do something about it, maybe—"

"Stop!" Gabrielle said with a force that startled me. I raised my head and noticed her eyes were blacker than I'd ever seen them. Her nostrils flared like a bull's. "It's over. It's finished. We'll never talk of it again."

"Of Julia-Berthe?" Surely she didn't mean that.

"No. The past. Our past. Aubazine. The orphanage. Moulins. It never happened, none of it."

"Gabrielle, you're tired, distraught—" Her expression was so severe it frightened me.

"All that darkness," she said. "Can't you feel it? It pulls at us night and day. It wants to drown us, to smother us, just like it did to our mother, to Julia-Berthe. We can't let it."

She leaned forward, her face so close to mine, her voice low.

"It wasn't consumption that killed Julia-Berthe. It was the curse of our birth. Our past is a weight. A rope around our necks. Telling us, telling the world, what and who we're supposed to be."

Her eyes conveyed a cross between mad and genius. "You think I'm crazy," she said. "But I'm not. This is the only way to go on. It's the only way we'll ever be free. We're burying the past in that grave right there with Julia-Berthe. We're smothering it before it smothers us."

"But how? What does that even mean?"

"It means we choose our own past. The past doesn't control us. We control it. Our mother died, but she wasn't a fool for love. Our father went to America. We were raised by aunts in the countryside. Well-to-do aunts who owned land and had horses. They were strict but took care of us. There was always food, an abundance of hearty country-style food. We were always warm. We were clean and had good, comfortable clothing."

Her words flabbergasted me. How long had she been imagining this? She was like a girl again, a girl desperate with loneliness who made up stories to escape the truth. I remembered how she'd lied about our father being in America back in Aubazine.

Pride helped her cover it up, but Gabrielle's pain was real, buried so deep inside her, the only way she could survive was through denial. Delusion.

She and I were different, but I understood.

"Promise me, Ninette. Tell me you promise. We'll never speak of where we really came from. Not to anyone. Not ever."

I looked down at Julia-Berthe's grave again, where a few birds had gathered, pecking at the crumbs. It felt disloyal, but Julia-Berthe was gone and Gabrielle was here, and more than anything, I wanted her pain to go away. I would go along with it, but I wouldn't forget. I turned back to Gabrielle and told her what she needed to hear. "I promise."

# FORTY-FOUR

IT SEEMED CRUEL, BUT THE WORLD WENT ON WITHOUT JULIA-Berthe. The sun rose and set in its usual pattern, nature undisturbed. I suppose that was its role. To nudge those left behind along, to remind us we were still here.

Hats once again were my comfort, and I threw myself into work. Gabrielle did too. With my help, she experimented with shape, hats that curved like an "S" with the brim turned up in the front, swooping down in the middle, then coming up again in the back, a difficult design to create. She experimented also, as she never had before, with types of feathers, their placement, sticking, always, with a single type of feather per hat, but varying how many. In the midst of this process, she would have me model the hat-in-progress, then study me from all angles for what seemed like hours as she crafted a waterfall of curled ostrich feathers or a sunburst of heron.

"No. That's too many, Ninette. Take some off."

"That's not enough, Ninette. Put more on."

She could be frustrating. Maddening. But it'd all be worth it when the two of us, splayed out on chairs after, exhausted, fabric, needles, feathers, and pins everywhere, would gaze proudly at our jewel, resplendent on its champignon throne. The hat in its final form was a release of all that was inside us, an ordering of the inner chaos.

For me, seeing our hat on the right customer was the greatest reward. That was what brought it to life, the glint in the wearer's eye, the pleased look on her face, the extra spring in her step, the total transformation in mood and spirit. That I could do this for someone gave me immense satisfaction, a sense of usefulness and power I'd never had before.

I started to dream more and more of a real boutique, with space to work and for storing all our supplies. I could picture it in my mind. In the back, Gabrielle would design her hats. We'd have a workroom with girls who did the stitching and steaming, making everything to Gabrielle's specifications. And I would be out front, presiding over the showroom where customers were indulged with mirrors and lights and comfortable feminine seating, everything glamorous, elegant, *riche*.

That summer, Celestine spent most of her time in a part of Paris called Montparnasse, and sometimes I accompanied her to the Dôme, a café where the poor artists who used to live in Montmartre now met. Montmartre had gotten too expensive, too touristy thanks to the artists of a generation before whose famous canvases had painted this new generation right out of a home.

In Montparnasse, the rents were cheap and so were the restaurants. This was a working-class neighborhood, and on nice nights sympathetic proprietors would let those who gathered sit outside for hours without buying anything. It was the same at the Closerie des Lilas on the Boulevard Saint Michel (the "Boul' Mich'," as Celestine called it), another *café-térrasse* where artistic types, painters, poets, models, muses, vagabonds and down-and-outs congregated beneath shade trees and arbors covered in lilacs.

There was always a sight to see, always someone curious to talk to. Bohemians, people called them. There were all nationalities. Long hair. Shabby clothes. Affectations like pipes and ragged beards and strange outfits. In my ready-to-wear blouse and skirt from the Bon Marché, *I* was the one who stood out. Still, I felt I belonged. There was an air of underlying sadness here, a longing to explain the unseen, a sense of quiet suffering that with the loss of Julia-Berthe made me feel at home.

Celestine came for a different reason: to watch the artists at work. They sketched all the time, on napkins or scraps of paper. If they sold a drawing for a few francs, they immediately spent the money on drinks. They lived on credit at restaurants and art supply stores. Around the café tables, they argued about theory and expression, color and light. For Celestine, the terraces were one large classroom.

Mixed in among the artists were well-dressed men who strolled about, surreptitiously looking over shoulders with appraising glances.

"Who are they?" I asked Celestine the first time she took me there.

"The art dealers," she whispered. "They try to buy up all that they can from the artists they think might have talent for as cheaply as possible. In case the artist should become famous."

"And have any of the ones here become famous?"

"Not yet. There's one called Picasso who people talk about. The art dealers are always hovering near him. He carries a pistol, and sometimes when there are too many people clustered around, he fires it into the air. There's another named Modigliani. We call him Modi for short. They say he's one to watch."

Everyone did watch Modi, I'd noticed, not in the way she'd

meant, but because he usually made a spectacle of himself after he drank too much. He was tall and rakishly handsome, with a vulnerable quality and charisma that drew people to him despite his antics. Sometimes he would sit with us as we chatted and draw furiously for hours, sketching whatever was on the table, a carafe, a hand, a package of cigarettes, a flower in a vase, as if he was trying to pull the soul out of it.

He would drink glass after glass because earlier he'd sold a few sketches to one of the art dealers and had money in his pocket. Then he would fall asleep, sometimes with his head on Celestine's shoulder, sometimes on mine, and we would try desperately not to move and wake him, this large man-child who seemed like he needed to be protected.

Until he did wake and drank more, too much, and the proprietors kicked him out for causing trouble.

There was another man who would join us too, a poet who was always scrawling words in a notebook, who had the most poetic name: Guillaume Apollinaire.

"It's not his real name," Modi said once with his Italian accent after Guillaume left to join a table of his literary friends. "He made it up."

"Well," I said. "If I were to make up a name, it would be one like that."

A war-like name, the name of a god, to shield the fragile being underneath from all that was hard and cold in the world.

Gabrielle didn't understand why we went to Montparnasse. She thought people would mistake us for prostitutes. "It's the slums," she said one afternoon at the Boulevard Malesherbes.

I was steaming the brim of a hat form to curl it up on one edge, a new style Gabrielle was trying out. Celestine was sketching her in profile in one of her picture hats with a dramatic ostrich amazone.

"Decrepit. Shabby," Gabrielle went on, and it occurred to me that maybe she didn't like Montparnasse because it reminded her of all she insisted we forget. "I can't think of why you would want to go there. Especially you, Ninette. I thought you were looking for a husband, not a charity case."

"But it's so romantic," Celestine said. "The artists there are poor because they *choose* to be poor."

Gabrielle huffed. "That makes no sense. Why on earth would anyone choose to be poor?"

"Because it's pure and noble and lets them focus on nothing but their art," Celestine said as she continued sketching. "They aren't beholden to anyone. They have something inside of them, Coco, something bursting to get out, an expression of some deep truth. They can't rest until they figure out what it is and how to show it to the world. It's a grand, epic battle."

I laughed. "Like you, Gabrielle, when you're making a hat. A grand, epic battle. You won't rest, or let me rest, until it's perfect."

Celestine nodded. "You see? Antoinette understands," she said. "Paul Poiret got his start in Montmartre, you know. And now he's the King of Fashion!"

"The King of Costumes," Gabrielle said with a roll of the eyes. "Of the impractical."

"He's an artist in his own way, it's just that clothing is his medium," Celestine said.

A couturiere as an artist? I had been joking before, but it was an intriguing idea. Both worked with their hands. Both took raw materials and turned them into a creation that started in the imagination.

And there was an energy on those terraces, a mania laced with demons and euphoria alike. An ever-present desire, like a pulse, a driving need for expression that reminded me of Gabrielle, how she threw herself into singing and dancing. And hats.

Gabrielle was more like these people than she knew. And I was like the dealers, the go-between for the artist and the world.

I picked up one of the finished hats and held it out toward Gabrielle. "Why shouldn't this be art? It's an expression of the soul. Just as much as brushstrokes of paint on a canvas."

I waited for her to laugh and say, "It's just a hat," as she usually did. But she didn't. She stayed still, presumably for the sake of Celestine's drawing, a small smile on her face.

# FORTY-FIVE

WHEN BOY TOLD GABRIELLE THAT SHE NEEDED TO MOVE TO a real boutique to sell her hats, I thought I'd misheard. Boy Capel, shipping magnate, coal exporter, had the same thought as I, a mere vendeuse from the provinces? He saw too that there was more to her hats than just a hobby, more to their appeal than a *curiosité du jour*.

I wasn't naive. I was vindicated.

"I think you have something here, Coco," he said, leaning casually against a bookcase and studying the ledger, his jet-black hair combed so flawlessly to the side you could see the lines from the comb's teeth. "You shouldn't let it go to waste."

He wore a tweed single-breasted blazer with turn-back cuffs, his perfectly tailored trousers pressed and loose-fitting, his tie knotted with a flair. The ends of his thick black mustache were trimmed to align with the edges of his lips, balancing his thick black eyebrows in a pleasing symmetry. Boy gave an air of authority, of being able to go anywhere, in any milieu, and the way would part for him. He wasn't brash but quietly confident, mysterious with those all-seeing green eyes that wouldn't betray what he was thinking.

I wondered if Gabrielle ever showed him her dance steps. She still went to class religiously. Surely he saw, as I did, there was no future in that.

"I think you have the raw qualities of a businesswoman," he said to Gabrielle. "You ought to be able to make something of this. Especially with Ninette, who has the charm and intuition of a natural saleswoman."

Gabrielle's eyelashes fluttered. Around Boy, my hard-edged sister turned soft and pliant, her straight lines and pointed angles bending into curves. "You're just saying that," she said. Did she mean the part about her or me or both? I, for one, was happy to take the compliment. "You just want to keep me busy," she went on, playing with a strand of hair that had come loose from her chignon. "You don't like it when I'm bored."

Boy walked up to her, taking her chin in his hand and lifting it, looking directly into her eyes. "You know very well, Coco, I'm not a person who just 'says' things."

She didn't bat her eyelashes or say anything coy. She gazed back, and I felt a current pass between them. Maybe he knew her better than she knew herself. He took her seriously, her instincts, her vision, her intelligence, and he was trying to teach her to do the same.

A few weeks later, Gabrielle returned from her dance class in a dark mood. Her instructor had told her she didn't have enough talent for the stage.

"What does she know?" I said, feeling defensive, wanting to protect Gabrielle from the kind of trauma she'd suffered after the gommeuse auditions, though of course the instructor was right.

"She knows," Gabrielle said, her face pinched.

I hoped she would say something about a boutique. Surely she saw by now making hats was her future? But she kept going to the lessons, to "stay in shape," she claimed.

My poor sister. How discouraging to be able to see the beauty in something, to feel it in your essence, but not be able to create that beauty yourself. You try to move in a certain way, but the grace you'd hoped for isn't there. You open your mouth to sing, but the melody doesn't come out the way it sounds in your head.

I shared the frustration. I still held on to my own dreams, as frivolous as they were. A wedding announcement in the newspaper. A seat in the enclosure at the races. All the years living behind convent walls, I still sometimes felt like a shadow instead of a person. I needed proof that I was more.

In September, Celestine rushed in to the garçonnière with news. Good news. Gabrielle Dorziat had taken Celestine's sketch of Gabrielle to a popular theater magazine, *Comoedia Illustré*, to see if they would buy it for their next edition. They liked it so much, they wanted Gabrielle herself to pose for a photograph.

"Me?" Gabrielle said, and I could hear astonishment in the way her voice went up.

"Yes," Celestine said. "Usually they ask the actresses to model the hats. But they think my drawing of you is so charming, they want you to do it yourself. Two o'clock next Monday, Coco, at their offices. The photographer will be waiting. And they told me they want to start using some of my drawings. Even though they aren't going to use this one, they gave me an advance!"

We were thrilled. All the years of collecting magazines, all the hours admiring the photographs, and Gabrielle was about to be in one.

"But what will I wear?" she said.

We spent days trying to decide on the perfect look, clothing that wouldn't overshadow the hat but that would complement it. We studied photos of actresses in older magazines. Should Gabrielle face the camera or turn in profile? Should she appear serious or smile?

The day of the appointment, Celestine and I accompanied an anxious Gabrielle to the studio and waited in the reception room. When she found us afterward, she was excited but the nerves were still there. What if none of the photographs turned out right? What if she looked foolish? What if they chose one that didn't show her or her hat in their best light?

But at the end of the month, it was Gabrielle Dorziat's turn to come rushing into Etienne's, waving a copy of the soon-to-be-released October edition of *Comoedia Illustré*. "Coco, Ninette, look!"

They'd given her an early copy, and we flipped through the pages until we landed on Gabrielle in profile, wearing the picture hat with the dramatic white plume and a blouse with a feminine collar. In the photograph, she gazed downward, that small smile on her lips.

"It's perfect," I said, breathless, in awe. It hadn't been just a dream. "You look like a star of the stage."

Except she wasn't. All the time she'd spent trying to sing, trying to dance. Longing for recognition. Now, she finally had it, and it was because of her hats.

"Boy's found a place," Gabrielle said, walking in the garçonnière one brisk morning in October and slipping off her coat. "It's on the rue Cambon."

"A place?" I said. "For what?"

"A boutique."

I wanted to hug her or cry or both, but I held myself back. I sensed it had been hard for her to tell me this. It meant she was officially giving up on the stage. But the more she talked about it, how it was right in the heart of Paris, just steps from the rue du Faubourg Saint Honoré and the Place Vendome, how the rue de la Paix, with Madame Alphonsine and premier couturières Paquin, Worth, and Doucet, wasn't far away, the more enthusiastic she became.

"Boy was leaving the Ritz one day last week after lunch when he saw it," she said. "It's just across the street."

I felt a great wash of relief. The idea of having to return to small, provincial Vichy, and its bad memories, because Gabrielle had grown bored with hats always lingered in my mind. But a boutique meant something permanent, not just for me but for her as well. Now I did hug her. She laughed and put her arms around me too.

"There's so much to do," I said, standing back suddenly. "We have to set up a showroom, a workroom, order supplies." My head was spinning with joy, exhilaration, fear, panic, but in a good way.

And the next few weeks were a whirlwind. Adrienne moved from Vichy with Maurice, who'd bought a large apartment at the Parc Monceau, a fashionable but discreet area of Paris where they could live as a couple more freely. When we vacated Etienne's, I would live there with them.

Gabrielle, Adrienne, and I went around to all of the top modistes. We pretended to be customers while we took in the showrooms, how they were arranged, what we might emulate or do differently.

"Redfern's showroom is so fussy. It's gauche," Gabrielle said.

"There weren't enough chairs," I said. "You want customers to stay, not leave because their feet are tired and there's nowhere to sit."

"You should have fresh flowers every day," Adrienne said. "Like they do at Alphonsine."

"They need flowers because their salesgirls don't wash," Gabrielle said. "I could smell them before we walked in the door."

On the Chanel Modes account Boy set up for us at the bank, we shopped at the antiques stores on the rue de Seine and the rue Bonaparte, where furniture spilled out onto the sidewalks.

"I want the showroom to be unfussy," Gabrielle said. "But expensive-looking."

"There," I said, pointing to a pair of enormous gilt mirrors in the corner of one store.

"And these," Gabrielle said, testing the drawers of a pair of matching chests with black marble tops, perfect for displaying champignons.

We went to the rug dealer on the rue des Saints Pères. We found chairs and settees at the Hotel Druout auction house. Chandeliers too. Boy hired a carpenter to make shelves and tables for the workroom.

Finally, after a month, everything was new, sparkling, and chic at 21 rue Cambon. Gabrielle placed an ad in the newspapers, and we filled a workroom upstairs with seamstresses who were to make and trim hats as we instructed. For once, I was the one overseeing the construction instead of doing the actual labor.

I was the *première vendeuse*.

The day before we opened, as we put on all the finishing touches, I heard a pop and a fizz and turned to find Gabrielle laughing, foam running down the neck of a champagne bottle in her hands. "I have something to show you," she said. She handed me a coupe and led me to a spot out front where men had been working all morning.

"Do you see what it says, Ninette? Chanel Modes. That's the name. The boutique was your idea first. I haven't forgotten." She clinked her glass against mine. "Chanel Modes. For me and for you."

At the sight of our name, my throat felt tight with emotion. This was our piece of the world, at last we had staked our claim, and I would do anything to hold on to it.

# FORTY-SIX

MY BOUTIQUE. OUR BOUTIQUE. THE NAME CHANEL HAD officially come a long way from selling old socks and women's underthings in an open stall. I thought of Julia-Berthe, all of those years working outside in the elements, and now she would never get to see it. Chanel Modes was for her too.

The boutique was a swirl of élégantes in fashionable ensembles, bobbing about in hobble skirts—Poiret's latest infliction, as Gabrielle liked to say—laughing about how their coachmen had to lift them into carriages because it was impossible to climb up with bound knees. Soon enough, I knew all of the Parisian gossip, who had taken a new lover, who had left an old one, who had been slighted, who had done the slighting.

At Boy's insistence, just after we opened Gabrielle hired a woman named Lucienne to help. She was just a year older than me but had formal fashion training and had worked at the prestigious hat shop Maison Lewis on the rue Royale, where she made her way from workroom apprentice to *petite première* who greeted clients and supervised their fittings.

"You must understand, Coco, that you don't know everything," Boy said. "You think you do, but you don't."

I hid a smile. Only Boy could talk to her like this.

"You're a quick learner," he went on, "but first you have to be willing to learn."

The day Lucienne arrived, the boutique immediately took on a more serious tone. To her, hat-making was a solemn affair. She wore well-fitting but unremarkable clothes, and told us that we should as well. "One mustn't compete with the customers," she said. "One must let them shine."

I glanced at Gabrielle, who I knew was fighting to bite her tongue. People were interested in her hats because they saw how appealing *she* looked wearing them. If she didn't shine, why would they come to her in the first place?

When Lucienne asked about our procedures for running the showroom, for ordering supplies, for organizing the workroom, we stared at her. Procedures?

"It's hard to believe she's just one year older than you, Ninette," Gabrielle said out of Lucienne's earshot. "She acts like she's a hundred and five."

I knew Gabrielle felt encroached upon, but I trusted Boy, who said we could learn from her. So I listened as Lucienne revealed where to get the best quality feathers, quills, fabrics, and ribbons, the kind that wouldn't fade in the sun or wilt in the rain. "Not," she said, "at the counter for plumes et fleurs at the Bon Marché. By the time they get there, the best have been picked over at the wholesalers."

"The ones I've been using don't fade or wilt," Gabrielle said, her arms crossed in front of her.

I listened as Lucienne described how to run the workroom and supplies for maximum efficiency.

"That's where she belongs," Gabrielle said under her breath. "The workroom."

Gabrielle herself refused to go in the workroom, always sending me or Lucienne. It was too similar to the fate the nuns had laid out for her: *You, Gabrielle, must hope to make an adequate living as a seamstress.* If she set foot in the workroom, the nuns would win.

Once, when Lucienne lectured us on the blending of colors, which colors went together, which didn't, Gabrielle grew bored and simply walked out.

"A good milliner always studies the styles of the season," Lucienne said another time.

Gabrielle laughed. "A good milliner *invents* the styles of the season."

Lucienne followed the rules, Gabrielle followed her instincts.

One sticking point in particular was that according to Lucienne, the appointment times of the demimondaines and the ladies of la haute should be carefully divided.

Gabrielle treated her Royallieu friends the same way she treated the society ladies, if not better, and it was clear to me why. The demimondaines had accepted her. The ladies of la haute had not. But when making appointments, I wasn't always sure who was who, and Gabrielle didn't care. To her, the juxta-positions were amusing. She got to hide in the back and watch as each lady pretended the other wasn't there, casting veiled, sideways glances across the room. It reminded me of the Pen-sionnat, the payantes and nécessiteuses living in two parallel worlds, trying hard not to intersect. Except in Chanel Modes, Gabrielle liked to send them crashing into each other.

"Why can't your sister understand," an exasperated Lucienne said one afternoon when Gabrielle was out, "what a terrible faux pas it would be to have the wife and the mistress of the same man here at the same time?"

I tried to explain Gabrielle's way of thinking. "It may be a faux pas," I said. "But it would also be the talk of the town. People would flock to Chanel Modes in case it might happen again, and they could be there to witness it. In the meantime, they'd buy hats."

Lucienne snorted. "The mondaines would stop coming. They'd be too afraid of being humiliated. And if the mondaines don't come, poof, there goes your Chanel Modes."

"Yes, but Émilienne d'Alençon wore one of my sister's chapeaux to Longchamp and voilà, everyone wanted one," I said. "No one copies the hat of a dowdy grande mondaine from the Faubourg. The fashionable set look to the stage, to people like Émilienne. They all want to wear what the actresses and irrégulières are wearing. That's what sells hats."

Lucienne shook her head and drifted away, muttering under her breath. "Four years in a plouc shop in Vichy, and she thinks she knows it all."

I didn't think I knew it all, but my confidence *had* grown. I'd learned my lessons. Giving away a hat to Gabrielle Dorziat when she was struggling turned out to be the best thing we'd done, even if the benefits had been unintentional. She had become famous and was still a loyal customer who regularly wore our hats. Now, I often gave away hats to up-and-coming actresses who seemed to have potential.

Still, I could see Lucienne's point. We needed the money to continue coming in.

For Chanel Modes to succeed, we had to accommodate both types of customers, and that meant keeping the appointment times separate. It was my job, and I promised to do better.

Some afternoons during the lunch break, to escape Lucienne's lectures for a little while, I visited the Galeries Lafayette. It was Pygmalion but on a more sophisticated level, with display after display of the most glorious shoes, exquisite clothing, sweet-smelling powders and creams and perfumes. To be the première vendeuse of a boutique near the rue de la Paix, it seemed to me that I had to dress and smell the part, which meant I needed new everything. With an account charged back to Chanel Modes, I didn't worry about cost. Gabrielle helped me choose, insisting on outfits with clean lines, with defined shapes and subtle adornments, and I saw how one well-placed ruffle could be more effective in enhancing the face and figure than cascades of them.

"You're so pretty, Ninette," she would say. "You don't want people to pay more attention to billows of lace and fleurettes than they do to you."

She still favored a boyish way of dressing, stealing now from Boy's closet or making her own jackets using his as a pattern. Boy even took her to an English tailor so she could see how it was properly done.

Other times, Gabrielle and I spent our lunch break in the shops on the Faubourg Saint Honoré that sold objets d'art, bibelots of all kinds, antiques, tapestries, pillows, electric lamps, all the necessities of la haute way of living. Or we'd go back to the auction house at the Hotel Druout and the nearby furniture shops. She and Boy had moved out of his garçonnière and into a new apartment on the Avenue Gabriel that she was intent on decorating in her own style. I watched her select items with a tinge of jealousy, wishing I had a place of my own to decorate, but still the news that she and Boy were living together like this thrilled me. Most men didn't live with their mistresses. Maybe this meant he was giving up his bachelor ways for good. Maybe this was the prelude to a marriage proposal. I was elated for Gabrielle. And, selfishly, for myself. If she and Boy were married, that might mean a step up for me, vistas of potential gentilhomme suitors spreading before me. Because if she was marriageable, so was I.

A year before, when I'd first moved to Paris and told Gabrielle that Maurice's parents wouldn't approve of the match with Adrienne, she'd been furious but not surprised.

"They expect him to do what their ancestors have done for centuries," she'd said. "Take Adrienne as a mistress while he marries some ugly, fish-eyed dolt from the Faubourg who'll get fat as a pig and smell like stale rice powder. It's a tradition as old as the Puy de Dôme."

But Boy was different. He had a fortune he'd made himself and wasn't beholden to his parents. He had modern ideas about equality and class. If a respected man like Boy Capel married his mistress for love, a woman not from the upper classes, perhaps that would open a door through which others would follow.

Like a new bride, Gabrielle was focused on furnishing their shared apartment, choosing muted but luxurious fabrics and hints of crystal and gilt. Nothing too flowery. Nothing overdone. While I found everything in the antiques stores lovely, the vases, the painted boxes, the tapestries, she had a way of honing in on just what she wanted, usually in tones of brown, black and white. She paid for everything herself on the account of Chanel Modes. "How easy it is to make money," she'd laugh, enjoying the feeling of freedom that she'd longed for since Aubazine.

This was her new life. The life she'd created from nothing. Boy's shipping interests meant he traveled often, but when in town, he took Gabrielle and sometimes me to the theater or the opera, to art galleries and exhibitions and lectures. But mostly they stayed in their apartment, where the Coromandel screens Boy had introduced her to, the shiny panels layered with mysterious scenes of Asian designs, now lined the walls. The effect was magical, a world within a world, a cocoon of black lacquer and inlaid swans and pheasants. She hid the bare walls behind false ones, embellishing them, just as she'd embellished our past.

For me, the only missing piece was a gentilhomme.

I knew Gabrielle was behind it when Boy's friends would stop by the boutique, claiming to want a chapeau for their mother or sister. I could see them eyeing me in the mirrors instead of the hats on the champignons. There were nights she insisted I go out to dinner with her and Boy and more friends, and I flirted and smiled, went along with the game. Gabrielle said the men were interested, and I was flattered, but I didn't feel anything more than that. No one spoke to me as if they wanted to know me. Not like Lucho had. At Royallieu, he and I had shared something between us, an understanding.

It was another kind of understanding these men were looking for. They'd tell me I should drop by their apartment some time so they could show me their amazing view of the Eiffel Tower or the Place de la Concorde or their amazing collection of such-and-such. I knew how they were "interested." As a lover. A Parisian mistress they could brag about back home in London, someone to meet in the afternoons at their garçonnière.

But eventually I started to doubt myself. What was I waiting for? A fantasy? A dream? Celestine was spending all her time in Montparnasse now, but I'd stopped going, Gabrielle's chastising wearing me down. She was right. I wouldn't find anyone there. I was no bohemian. I still mourned Julia-Berthe, but it wasn't as fresh, and sometimes the poverty, the desperation, struck too close to home. So many of the struggling artists, especially Modi, walked about with a pallor, a lethargy, a deep tight cough I recognized from childhood, the sound of my mother and more recently of Julia-Berthe. At first Montparnasse had soothed me. Now it was filled with ghosts.

One evening in early October, Gabrielle insisted I go to the Salon d'Automne, the annual art exhibit, with her, Boy, and a friend of Boy's, a man called Algernon.

"He's nice-looking in that tweedy, Anglo-Saxon kind of way," she'd told me the day before. "He and Boy went to boarding school together. He's well-to-do, of course, keeps an apartment in Paris, not married yet, and best of all, Boy vouches for him. Either way, if you don't try, you'll never find anyone."

At the Grand Palais, room after room was filled with art, and the four of us wandered through, commenting on this and that. Algy, as Boy called him, was the kind of Englishman who was of a fair complexion, his cheeks pink as if lightly rouged. He had pale blue eyes, and his eyelashes were so blond it was as if he didn't have any.

While he and Boy lingered over a painting of an equestrian scene, Gabrielle and I walked ahead into a room where the works were not portraits or landscapes or scenes from antiquity but paintings of shapes, layers of circles and squares, kaleidoscope-like, people or things seemingly taken apart. Thinking of Celestine, I wondered what deep truth these works were meant to express. Around us, people talked of geometry, of painting in cubes.

"Look at that one," I said to Gabrielle, pointing to a confusing painting of what looked to be a woman, or parts of a woman, or maybe not a woman at all, hidden amidst overlapping fragments of rectangles. "It reminds me of the time you took your convent uniform apart and spread the pieces all over the bed. Except instead of putting it together the right way, they've put everything in the wrong places."

"It's strange, isn't it?" she said. She leaned closer to the canvas, squinting. "Is that a nose floating about?"

Just then, Algy and Boy joined us, Algy scowling at the painting in question. "Good God, what is that? It looks like a child got a hold of some scissors and paste. That can't possibly be art."

Something about his reaction made Gabrielle and me laugh. I was glad to hear him laugh with us.

"It's from a new school of French painters," Boy said. "I've been reading about them. They experiment with shape, as you can see. Show more than one perspective all at the same time."

"I like that," Gabrielle said, still soaking in whatever Boy had to say. "The world has operated for too long under just one point of view, don't you think? It's time others are taken into account."

"You mean yours?" Boy said.

She smiled. "Of course. Why not?"

Boy laughed. "I couldn't agree more."

"You see?" she said, tilting her head flirtatiously. "You're teaching me well."

"I suppose," Algy said, "that makes me the bore. I much prefer a good still life." He looked at me. "What do you think? Surely you agree? Something with flowers or fruit? Or better yet, both. Perhaps even with a pheasant or two."

I liked that he'd asked my opinion. That he'd called himself a bore. Self-deprecation was rare among Boy's friends. And I agreed with him. There was so much ugliness in the world. What was wrong with a lovely rendering of a bowl of fruit or bouquet of flowers or a colorful bird? But deep down I was also still insecure around Boy's crowd. I wanted to seem worldly. "There's an artist called Picasso," I said. "I hear he's doing great things."

"Picasso?" said Algy. "Italian? Then he must paint religious scenes. I haven't heard of him."

Boy glanced at me, surprised, I was sure, that I knew about happenings in the art world. "Picasso is Spanish," he said. "He only shows at Kahnweiler's gallery. Definitely not religious scenes."

Later at dinner, instead of talking about himself, I was astonished when Algy asked if I was interested in art, that he wanted to know something about me.

"I do prefer paintings of flowers," I confessed, feeling a little looser that night. Maybe it was the extra glass of wine that warmed me. Maybe it was the art, everything shuffled around. "And lovely scenes of dancers or bathers or classic figures around fountains. I like art that's pretty. I suppose I'm a bore too."

"I don't think it's boring. I think it's important to surround yourself with lovely things. Especially what is lovely to you."

His blue eyes held mine, his lashes unblinking. His shyness

was endearing. For a moment I wished I might actually be able
to feel more for him.

But then he kept speaking. "You know," he said, and I
braced myself. "I have some very nice still lifes at my apartment
on the rue de Rennes. Do you think...would you perhaps be
interested...in possibly seeing them...sometime?"

Over the next couple of weeks, Gabrielle and I had our usual
back-and-forth after these outings. Algy was still on the scene,
accompanying me to dinner or the theater with Boy and Gabrielle. We even went to Kahnweiler's to view the Picassos, of
which Algy did not approve. Of all of Boy's friends, he was the
most persistent, and I was afraid I was getting used to him. It
was nice to have a companion. In his awkward way, he always
made it clear the offer to see his "still lifes" stood.

"You're so stubborn," Gabrielle would say. "What are you
waiting for? Why don't you just let someone take care of you?
Algy, for instance."

"You know I don't want to be just 'taken care of,'" I would
say. "I want more than that."

Usually she would scoff at me, tell me to give up on marriage,
remind me that poor girls don't get to marry wealthy men, that
our fate was as demimondaines or to die poor in a workhouse.

But as time wore on, she stopped.

I wondered if her silence had something to do with Boy, their
relationship growing closer. I wondered if now she had her own
thoughts of marriage.

# FORTY-SEVEN

AFTER RUNNING ERRANDS ONE COLD AFTERNOON IN DECEMBER, I entered Chanel Modes to the sound of deep voices, the distinct smell of saddle soap, and three men in riding clothes ambling around, examining hats.

Etienne. Leon.

And Lucho.

Three years had passed since I saw him at Royallieu, and still my heart flipped and fluttered and flipped again. There was a way he had of just looking at me, a quality to his gaze, that made me feel he was glad to see me too.

They greeted me with the customary kisses on the cheek.

"Antonieta," Lucho said, his lips brushing my skin so that my knees wanted to buckle.

Etienne continued the argument he'd apparently been having with Gabrielle, playfully trying to convince her, and now me, to have dinner with them later that night.

"Boy's out of town on business, and when he's gone, I catch

up on work," Gabrielle said, being coy. Did it bother Etienne that she'd mentioned Boy? If it did, he didn't show it. He was, as Gabrielle had pointed out, a gentleman, a graceful loser. Somehow, they were still good friends. "You know, Etienne," she went on, "it turns out Paris actually *does* have room for another milliner. We have so many customers we can hardly keep up."

"But, Coco," said Leon, wearing one of Gabrielle's hats on his egg-shaped head. "I don't understand. You used to be so much fun."

"Youth is still Youth," Etienne said, winking at me before turning back to Gabrielle. "But something has happened to Mirth."

"Mirth is busy," she said.

"Well, then, Ninette, you'll go with us, won't you?" Etienne asked, turning my way.

Dinner with Lucho? My head said no. The rest of me said yes. But I didn't have the chance to answer.

"Over my dead body would I leave my little sister alone with you," Gabrielle said.

"Then it's settled," said Etienne. "You're coming, both of you. Now, where should we go? You choose, Ninette."

Me? It felt odd to make a decision for these worldly men.

Gabrielle pouted. "Why does Ninette get to choose?"

"Because the rest of us are old and jaded. She sees things through fresh eyes. And I have a feeling you, Coco, are always telling her what to do. Now she can tell you. Go ahead, Ninette."

I glanced at Lucho, wishing I knew where he'd like to go. It was just dinner, after all. We'd be in a crowded restaurant. Nothing could happen, even if I wanted it to. It'd be a harmless night of good fun while I waited to cross paths with my own gentilhomme, the man I would one day marry.

"Maxim's?" I said. It was the first place that came to mind. Gabrielle and Boy went there all the time. Boy said it was the only place in France you could get a real English-style whiskey and soda. Maybe Lucho would like that, being Anglo-Argentine. And Gabrielle said they always saw famous actresses, personalities, aristocrats.

"Youth has spoken," Etienne said. "Maxim's it is."

We met at ten o'clock on the rue Royale near the swirling Place de la Concorde, fine motorcars and carriages lining the boulevard. Maxim's *grande salle* glowed with a warm hue from the plush red velvet seats and red carpet. Small, pink-shaded table lamps reflected off beveled mirrors and dark-paneled walls with art nouveau murals of half-clothed nymphs amidst pastoral scenes. The ceiling was stained glass. Tall floor lamps were made to look like bunches of drooping calla lilies.

We were greeted by Hugo, the famous maître d'. "Monsieur Balsan," he said to Etienne with a smile.

The room was a whirl of gentilhommes and élégantes in dazzling array, tables packed in tight, laughter, music, loud conversation. The comte de Castellane entered with a blonde beauty who wasn't his wife. I recognized him from the gossip pages. Across from them, André de Fouquières, the famous dandy and another gossip page regular, dined with an entourage of dandies-in-waiting.

We were seated right in the center of the room, Lucho next to me. Even though I hadn't seen Lucho since Royallieu, I felt comfortable with him, glad he was the one at my side.

Just when we'd settled in, the restaurant came to a momentary stop, heads turning, conversations pausing as Hugo led a striking élégante to a table near the window. She wore a black picture hat with cascading ostrich feathers in luxuriant shades of sable gray, diamonds glittering around her neck. Liane de Pougy, people whispered, the notorious courtesan, the woman who'd performed with the Folies Bergère, who'd seduced the Prince of Wales. At a nearby table, the artist called Sem, known for his society drawings, took out a pen and began to work, his gaze alternating between Liane de Pougy and the napkin he scribbled on.

I was still getting my bearings, trying not to be intimidated by the women sparkling in jewels, velvets, ribbons, lace, when Lucho turned to me. "Beware of the gentleman over there," he said, nodding toward a nearby banquet. "He's been looking at you. And that fellow beneath the mirror too. You have admirers, Antonieta."

I felt my face color. I was wearing an embroidered dinner gown of Gabrielle's, black lace over green silk that I hoped brought out my eyes.

"Don't worry," he said protectively, "I've checked, and there are no rogue, drunken jockeys lurking about."

"That seems like a lifetime ago," I said. "So much has changed."

"Has it?"

"I live in Paris now instead of Vichy, thank goodness."

And Gabrielle was with Boy, not Etienne. And we had a boutique. She made hats, I helped her sell them. When I last saw Lucho, I'd thought Adrienne was about to be married, that I would be next.

"There are things that have happened," I said earnestly. "And things that haven't happened."

"Things that haven't happened," he said thoughtfully, looking off into the pastoral scenes on the walls. "Yes. There are those."

Maybe he was thinking of his wife and until death do us part. I didn't dare ask.

Etienne and Leon debated the wine list, asking Lucho his opinion. Château Latour? Madeira? Pouilly-Fuissé?

"Champagne," Gabrielle said. "What could be better than champagne?"

Waiters delivered the first course, a melon glacé with lobster and smoked salmon, and then the second, tartelettes with Parmesan, but I could hardly eat. Lucho, just his presence next to me, was too much of a distraction. Though I liked to watch him eat. He was strong, solid, a man with appetites. He ate as if he hadn't all day, which he soon explained was the case.

"We've been out with the horses," he said.

I sipped my champagne under Gabrielle's watchful eye, tempted to gulp it down. "The horses," I said, "is that why you're here in Paris?"

"Partly. We were just fooling around today, playing a little polo for fun. Mainly I'm here because my family—Harrington & Sons, to be exact—exports beef to Europe and someone had to come meet with the lawyers. There are contracts to negotiate. Documents to sign. My father's dream is for everyone in the world to know that Argentine beef is the best. That's his passion."

The way he said "his" made me wonder. "But not yours?"

"Horses are my passion," he said between bites of carpe braise á la chambord. "I want everyone in the world to know that Argentine horses are the best, to appreciate them as I do. They're the most selfless creatures. Strong, hearty, trustworthy. I've convinced the French cavalry to take several hundred. I'm going back to Argentina tomorrow to make sure they're being properly trained."

Tomorrow. My heart fell, though it had no reason to. Lucho Harrington had a wife.

"What about you?" he said. He set down his fork, his eyes meeting mine so that a shiver ran up my spine. "Tell me. What's your passion? You have to have at least one."

I'd never thought about it before. Not in that way. No one had ever asked. But the answer came to me immediately.

"Chanel Modes. Our boutique. I want everyone in the world to come for our hats, to appreciate them, just like your horses."

"Well then," he said. "To world domination." He lifted his glass and tipped it toward me. "You'll make women feel beautiful. I'll make men feel brave."

Our glasses touched, champagne flashing in the candlelight, as if we were co-conspirators, as if we could do anything.

"What is Argentina like?" I asked. I wanted to picture him there, imagine him in his own milieu.

"Some people say Buenos Aires is like Paris, the buildings, the architecture. I prefer the countryside. The pampas are the real Argentina. Horses and cattle as far as the eye can see. So much unspoiled land, the most peaceful place on earth." He laughed. "The only thing spoiling it is my father's house."

He told me his father had it built to replicate a castle on a moor and insisted that only English was to be spoken there. "The servants are English. The butler is English. The food is English. The furnishings are English. The ivy covering the house is English. All in the middle of the pampas."

I could tell from his tone he didn't approve.

"My father's heritage is English," he said, "and my mother's Argentine. I got most of the Argentine blood. I was meant to be a gaucho. Instead, I was born a Harrington. With Harrington... responsibilities."

"A gaucho? What's that?"

He took a long drink of his champagne then looked at me, sadness hidden in the depths of his eyes. "A man who is free."

His sorrow touched me, and I stared at my plate, not sure how to respond.

Suddenly, the room filled with applause. The orchestra, which had been playing quietly, announced a waltz, the "Merry Widow," popular because it was from an operetta with a scene set at Maxim's. Couples swarmed the dance floor, Gabrielle and Leon among them and Etienne with a lady friend from another table who practically draped herself around him.

Lucho held out a hand to me. The spark in his eyes was back. "Shall we?"

I didn't know how to waltz, but it didn't matter. He led me around the dance floor, a rhythm I easily fell into, my breath shallow from the nearness of him. He went so smoothly, gliding me here and there, a steadying hand on my back. "Breathe," he said with a smile. "Don't forget to breathe."

The orchestra played another waltz and then another, and we moved together until I'd memorized the feel of his shoulder, until his hand on my back felt like a part of me. I let my body listen to his until I could anticipate his movements and knew which way he would take me next.

Once, he whispered in my ear. "I think I've found a new passion."

"What is it?" I said.

"This."

That long-ago night at Royallieu, he'd said he wouldn't do anything untoward. But if he had, I wouldn't have said no. And now—

I felt a tap on my shoulder. Gabrielle.

"Ninette," she said, "it's late. It's almost two in the morning."

My feet went flat. I'd lost track of time. The spell was broken.

Lucho bowed slightly, giving me up to Gabrielle, letting her pull me away. The men saw us into a cab, Lucho taking my hand, helping me step in, the smell of bergamot, lavender. "Dulces sueños, Antonieta," he said just before he shut the door and the cab drove off.

The next morning at the boutique, elation from the night before faded into a dreary melancholy. I imagined Lucho on a ship crossing the Atlantic, on a sea of unending blue, unreachable, a dream.

When a small package arrived later that day, I barely paid attention. It was probably for Lucienne. She had a new suitor who was always sending her little gifts. And it couldn't be for Gabrielle. Boy didn't give presents. He found them superfluous. Once, after she complained he never sent her flowers, he had flowers delivered every thirty minutes for two days to make the point.

"It's for you, Ninette," Gabrielle said, a teasing singsong in her voice.

The package was from a business called E. Flajoulot on the rue Charlot, a "fabricant," the card said, of "objets d'art." I opened it and inside found an exquisite mahogany box with a design on the top in a contrasting wood: two horns entwined in a flowing ribbon. I lifted the lid, and as I did, a song began to play.

The "Merry Widow."

A rush of emotion came over me, the ache of longing, of wishing things could be different. But mixed in was a certain quiet happiness. He'd been thinking of me.

A small card peeked out of the packaging. "To Antonieta," it said in handwritten script, and beneath that a single, elegant "L."

"You have an admirer, Ninette," Gabrielle said.

"Yes. One who's *married*."

"I saw the way he looked at you last night. And the way you looked at him."

"He lives in Argentina," I said. "An ocean away."

"He'll be back. And if he isn't, there are plenty of men in Paris just like him."

But there weren't. There was no one like him. That night at the Parc Monceau, I took out the music box and wound it. I closed my eyes and waltzed as if I were still in Lucho's arms, as if I could go back and live in that moment forever.

# FORTY-EIGHT

ONE GRAY SATURDAY MORNING IN JANUARY, JUST A MONTH after the evening at Maxim's, I arrived early at the boutique, surprised to find Gabrielle in a cloud of cigarette smoke, bent over a ledger book, tears streaming down her face.

"What is it?" I said, alarmed to see her in such a state. Gabrielle rarely cried.

Her voice was hoarse. "Boy Capel is a liar." She looked up at me, her eyes rimmed in red. "He kept it from me. All this time."

"Kept what?" My mind immediately went to the rumors of Boy having lovers in every port.

"I have no money," Gabrielle said. "All the money I've spent on furnishing the apartment, on the boutique, I thought it was mine. I thought I'd made it selling hats. But it was his money. Not mine. His."

I was confused. "But you have money." I was the one who took the deposits to the bank every day. I didn't check the balances, but whenever Gabrielle or I charged to the Chanel Modes account, the bank always covered it. "Look at all the things you've bought. All the things we've bought." The trips to the Galeries Lafayette, the antiques stores.

"Last night we were on our way to dinner," she said. "I was talking about how well Chanel Modes was doing, how much money we were making, bragging like a little fool, and he laughed. He laughed! He told me Chanel Modes is in debt. A lot of it. He said the bank only gives me money because he's given them a guarantee. Oh, Ninette! I threw my handbag at him as hard as I could and ran all the way back to the Avenue Gabriel."

I glanced down at my shoes, my new shoes, and felt queasy.

"Everything I bought for the apartment—everything here—" She motioned around the room at the chandeliers and the gilt mirrors and marble-topped commodes. "I thought I'd bought it all with money earned from my hats!"

The hand holding her cigarette trembled. Despite the turmoil, she was still dressed impeccably in one of the simple blouses and belted sweaters she made for herself, "presentable," as always.

"You have to go to the bank for me, Ninette," she said. "Boy said I should go so I can see the books and understand, but I'm too embarrassed. And you've always been good with numbers. I've never checked the bank statements. I've just thrown them out. The bills got paid. I bought what I wanted. Why should I look at them? I know why now. I could kill Boy. He tricked me! He's keeping me, just like Etienne. No, he's worse than Etienne. At least with Etienne, I knew where I stood. Will you go for me, Ninette? Please? You have more experience running a boutique than I do. You'll know what to do."

She was in no state to go herself, so I had to gather my courage. The bank was solemn, intimidating, a place for men and people of wealth, not the daughter of a traveling peddler. To steady my nerves, I reminded myself that I'd been around enough ladies of the mondaine to know how to act. Inside, I pushed back my shoulders and didn't ask but *told* a young clerk in horn-rim glasses behind a desk that I wanted to go over the Chanel Modes account. He hesitated. Though my name was on the business, he clearly wasn't accustomed to dealing with women. I considered turning and running out, but I was doing this for Gabrielle and for myself. I smiled and looked him directly in the eyes. "Monsieur Arthur Capel, the financier behind Chanel Modes, sent me."

It wasn't a total lie.

Monsieur Arthur Capel. The magic words. The mere mention of the man's name opened doors. The clerk motioned for me to sit. Then he brought out the books.

"Here are the deposits from Chanel Modes," he said, pointing to a series of numbers in a column. "And here are the withdrawals."

I tried to hide my shock when I saw that the withdrawals were more than twice the deposits.

"What is this?" I said, gesturing toward another column where money was added back into the account. Maybe there was hope yet. Maybe Gabrielle *had* misunderstood.

"Those are funds drawn from the line of credit," he said, pushing his glasses up the bridge of his nose.

"The line of credit," I repeated, as if I knew what he was talking about.

"Yes, from the bank," he said. "For when the account is overdrawn. Backed by Monsieur Capel's guarantee."

*He tricked me,* Gabrielle had said. Boy should have known she wouldn't understand how it worked. He should have seen how proud she felt. She thought she'd finally had her own money. She thought she was free. And so had I. We had so many customers, sold so many hats, I'd just assumed we were making more than enough money. I hadn't paid enough attention to the ledger.

I didn't think Boy meant to hurt her. But it was the worst feeling of all, that sensation of not being able to breathe, of the world turning a deepening shade of gray, of realizing that what happened to our mother could happen to her. Men came, and they left with no warning. Boy might write a guarantee now, but that didn't mean he would later. He was an attractive, sought-after man, generous enough to give Gabrielle a start, to keep the business going. But that didn't mean he would stay, that he would marry her.

The only way to survive was to rely on ourselves, totally and completely.

At the bank, I'd seen all I needed to. By the time I got back to Chanel Modes, I knew it was time to listen to Lucienne, who was always trying to give us advice on how to be more economical. We thought she was patronizing us, that she was a snob, but this, I recognized, was what Boy meant when he'd said Gabrielle could learn from Lucienne. This was what he meant about being a "businesswoman."

By that evening, Gabrielle and Boy had made up. She was still in love, but there was an edge to her devotion now, an awareness that hadn't been present before. "Yesterday was the end of my unconscious youth," she said, sounding like one of Boy's books on philosophy, her tears all dried up.

She was determined to pay Boy back, no matter how long it took. At Chanel Modes, she cut wages. She argued with suppliers of fabrics and notions until they lowered their prices. She stopped buying decorations for her apartment and the boutique. "Every centime must be accounted for," she said.

I stopped buying shoes and gloves every time I went to the Galeries Lafayette. In fact, I didn't go there at all. Lucienne knew sources that were just as good, but less expensive, for hat forms.

"I think we should raise prices," I said a month later, after I'd visited other millinery shops to see what they charged. I'd studied our books. Cutting costs wouldn't be enough to repay Boy and free us from the debt.

Gabrielle was unsure. Somehow, a part of her still thought

of herself at Royallieu, decorating hats as a hobby and giving them away.

"You don't have to tell them how much it costs," I said. "I will. Most of the time they don't even ask because they're all rich or someone rich is paying for it. Besides, the higher the price, the more they'll think it's worth."

Lucienne laughed. "But this isn't Maison Virot on the rue Saint Honoré."

"No," I said. "It's Chanel Modes. New, young, not stale."

"A high price for a modest hat and a feather?" Lucienne said.

"For elegance," I said. "That's what they're buying."

Lucienne shook her head.

"We won't raise them by much," I said as a compromise. "Just a little at first, to see how it goes."

Despite Lucienne's misgivings, Gabrielle agreed to my plan, and the customers kept coming, even as we raised the prices more and more. Eventually Lucienne quit, moving on to a more prestigious salon. That was fine by us. We'd learned all we could from her. Now she was just another expense we could take off the books.

# FORTY-NINE

DESPITE HER AND MAURICE'S SITUATION, ADRIENNE STILL HAD a way of making life more fun. She liked to go out, especially when Maurice was away at his family's estate in Haute-Vienne, where he ran the stud farm with his father. She was comfortable in the world of the monde, never questioning that she deserved to be there as well.

During the lunch hour, we would shop and eat at fashionable cafés, Adrienne with Bijou and a new spaniel Maurice had given her called Babette, one of Gabrielle's hats always gracing our heads. Sometimes, people would stop to ask where we got them, Adrienne's natural charm attracting even more customers to Chanel Modes.

"I'm nearly twenty-five," I complained to her one day as we lunched at a café near the boutique. "And still I'm alone." I was so busy that time passed quickly, a blessing and a curse.

"Your Maurice is out there, I know it," Adrienne said. "Don't give up hope. We'll find him together."

I still slept with Lucho's handkerchief under my pillow, remembering how it had made me feel back in Moulins—the promise it had held of a future where I would be acknowledged. I confided to Adrienne that I was waiting for someone like him, but someone *available*. She didn't tell me to compromise. But I knew she was a romantic like me, and I would fret that Gabrielle was right. Some nights my mind went to terrible places: my lack of romantic prospects, then to Lucho, then his wife. It was always possible something could happen to her, illness, an accident, my imagination working until I had to forcefully shut it down. It was a despicable, selfish thing to wish death on anyone, especially as I knew what loss was like. No matter how terrible Lucho's wife might be, she was someone's sister or daughter.

Those nights, I'd wake up in a cold sweat, reeling from old dreams of my mother, unloved, alone. I'd get out of bed and take a dose of Veronal so I could sleep again. Sometimes, I'd listen to the music box.

Then one cold March day at the boutique, after a customer came in with her nanny and a young boy with black curls, a realization struck me. There were times I still agonized over whether I should have done more to get Julia-Berthe away from the market, to look after André, her little boy the nuns stole from her at birth. Had she even gotten to kiss him goodbye? Tell him she loved him? Gabrielle and I hadn't had the means to help her back then, struggling as we'd been to take care of ourselves. But now, with Chanel Modes, we were more settled. The business was doing well, so much so that recently I'd had to hire more employees for the workroom. We weren't able to save Julia-Berthe, but we could save André. He would be eight years old now, just a little boy.

"We have to find André," I said to Gabrielle in the back room, where she was working on a sweater for a friend who'd admired hers. Sometimes she gifted those now too, as she had her hats.

She looked up at me with surprise, as if in burying her past, she'd forgotten all about André.

"I know you don't like to think about the past, but we're his aunts," I went on. "He should be with us, not with strangers, believing no one cares for him." The idea sent an ache through me. Did he have a place inside him, like we'd had, that told him he wasn't worthy of love?

"But what can we possibly do for him?" she said.

"Julia-Berthe's gone but her child isn't. We can give him a future."

She was quiet.

"He's young. He doesn't know anything about his mother and her family. And he should."

"The canonesses will never approve of him living with us," Gabrielle said. "They'll never tell us where he is."

"Adrienne," I said. "She can talk to them. They'll tell her."

Gabrielle frowned. "I'm sure they know about Maurice, that she's been living in sin all these years with the Baron de Nexon. Vichy is right around the corner from Moulins. That kind of gossip must have traveled there, even to the Pensionnat."

"What about Boy?" I said. Paris was far enough away from Moulins that the canonesses wouldn't know about Boy and Gabrielle. And he was a respected, wealthy businessman. Better than that, Boy was Catholic.

Gabrielle nodded slowly. "Yes. They would have to listen to Boy. He was educated by Jesuits, you know. He went to boarding school. He has all the credentials. Maybe André could...it could be a place for him...we'll have to meet him first."

"So you'll talk to Boy?"

"I'll talk to him tonight."

Already I was thinking about having André in Paris with us. I pictured him, small and dark, like Julia-Berthe and Gabrielle, big, round eyes. He could live at the Parc Monceau with me and Adrienne and Maurice. There was plenty of room.

I imagined him attending school, me helping him with his schoolwork. On Saturdays, I'd take him to the puppet show in the Champ de Mars and the carousel ride in the Jardin du Luxembourg. I'd take him ice skating in the Bois de Boulogne in winter and to the circus in Montmartre whenever he wanted. Gabrielle and I could give him the childhood we'd never had and maybe, in the process, it might help fill the hole that still lived in our own hearts.

Boy agreed to help and wrote to the Mother Abbess right away for the priest's address.

For a few months after that, Boy and the priest went back and forth. The priest told Boy that André didn't want to leave him. André didn't know us at all. He didn't even know his mother. The priest was the only "parent" he'd ever had.

I felt guilty taking him away from the only life he knew, but I wanted desperately to see him, to look for signs of Julia-Berthe in his eyes.

Finally, Boy and the priest came to an agreement. André would visit Paris over the Easter break. He'd stay with us, then go on to Beaumont College, the Jesuit school Boy had attended in England.

The idea of sending André to boarding school bothered me. "Aren't we doing the same thing to André that was done to us?" I asked Gabrielle. "Sending him off to be raised by strangers?"

"These aren't strangers," Gabrielle said. "These are the gatekeepers to the world of the elite, the gratin of the gratin. Just think, Ninette. André won't turn out like the rest of the Chanels, a poor marchand selling old shoes and belts at market. André will be a real gentilhomme. He'll know important people. Maybe someday he'll work with Boy. Maybe he'll take over Boy's business."

Now, I prayed Julia-Berthe was looking down on us from heaven. Maybe she even had a part in this. I felt a deep satisfaction to think of what was happening, to realize that Julia-Berthe's son would grow up to be a real gentilhomme.

André came to Paris at Easter as planned. At first, he was shy. There was a frightened look in his eye, but it didn't remain for long. Gabrielle and I practically smothered him with candies and treats. We bought him new clothes and toys, including a sailboat to push around the Grand Bassin duck pond in the Jardin du Luxembourg like the other little boys. Some nights he stayed with me, some he stayed with Gabrielle.

We held his hand and hugged him and looked for Julia-Berthe in his face. I thought I saw it there in the wide-eyed expression.

"It's a good thing he's going off to boarding school," Boy said, tousling André's mop of hair. "You two would spoil him rotten."

He was right. We would have.

But he needed taming. He ate with his hands, wiped his nose with his sleeve. Gabrielle and I were mortified when once, at a nearby tea room to which we'd taken him for ice cream, he belched loudly. He was behind in his schooling. When the day came for him to leave for England, our sadness was tempered with the certainty that we were doing the right thing.

He would be back in Paris for the summer break. We would see him again then. In the meantime, the idea that there was still a part of Julia-Berthe in this world comforted us. She wasn't all gone. We saw André, his innocence. And we saw our sister. We saw ourselves.

# FIFTY

THE DAYS GREW LONGER AND WARMER, THE BLOOMS ONCE
again on the chestnut trees, and one day, like a miracle, he was
back. Lucho. He walked into the boutique, the sight of him, so
handsome, so vital. Just his presence had a way of making me feel
that the world was on course, that everything would be all right.

He was in Paris to represent Harrington & Sons, exporters of
beef, and to play polo, to show off his criollos to the world. He
introduced himself to Adrienne. He knew Maurice. Everyone
in the horse world knew each other.

He was staying at the Ritz, just across the street. "I'll be in
France most of the summer," he said. It was winter in Argentina, in the other half of the world. He looked at me. "I'm following the sun."

A warm, shimmery feeling enveloped me. Then he had to
go. He'd been on his way to a meeting.

That night I went to a restaurant on the rue Boissy d'Anglas with Gabrielle, Boy, and Boy's friends, including Algy. Lucho was there too, dining with another group.

Our eyes met throughout the meal, and eventually Lucho made his way to our table.

"Antonieta," he said in his way that made me shiver. "I'm not interrupting anything?" He glanced at Algy across the table. Poor Algy. His face had gone from pink to white with splotches of crimson.

"Not at all," I said, and he slid in next to me, his hand so close to mine on the banquette seat.

We spent the rest of the evening talking, Algy eventually turning to the others in the group, then slipping off. I asked Lucho about Argentina, the place he called the pampas. I wanted to know what it was like, where he came from, what he loved. He told me to imagine a landscape of brown and gold, an endless sky, plains that stretched beyond the horizon, fertile earth, new grass, streams cold and clear, herds of horses living by instinct, not kept in barns and pastures, their senses numbed.

"You're different," he said. "Most women talk about their latest hairstyle or social triumph. Not you. Somehow you get me to talk about parts of my life I don't usually share."

"You don't mind?" I said.

"I like it."

He asked about me too. I couldn't lie and tell him the stories Gabrielle made up, that we were raised by old-maid aunts in the countryside. Not to him. So I explained about our mother, about Albert abandoning us, about Aubazine, the orphanage, and the nuns. The Pensionnat in Moulins.

And Vichy. "Sometimes it seems like I don't belong anywhere. The class I was born in won't have me. They think I'm too high and mighty simply because I've tried to better myself. And the high and mighty won't have me simply because of the class I was born in. I'm an in-between."

He thought about this for a moment. "Like a man born in

Argentina, born of the pampas, the horses, the horizon, sent to England to be educated where he was seen as a South American, an outsider. Then sent back to Argentina where he was seen as an Englishman, an outsider. Not really belonging anywhere. You see, Antonieta, you're not alone. We're both in-betweens."

And there was another sort of in-between he hadn't named: being married on paper but not in the heart, a kind of purgatory, stuck between heaven and hell.

We talked about our ghosts. My ghosts. His ghosts. His father. His wife. And always there was that tension between us, a thread that seemed to pull us together. At one point in our conversation, he tucked a piece of loose hair behind my ear, making me lose my train of thought. When I told him about Julia-Berthe, he put his hand on mine, briefly, and squeezed it. I willed the glassiness in my eyes to go away.

The night ended as it had before with a kiss on the cheek, with me going off once again to where I belonged, with the space between us still there, impulses in check.

# FIFTY-ONE

THE NEXT SATURDAY, I SAW LUCHO AT THE POLO MATCHES AT THE Bois de Boulogne. Gabrielle, Adrienne, and I had gone to see and be seen in Gabrielle's hats.

When Lucho played, everyone took notice, conversations quieting as he guided his mount, dashing downfield and beating the others to the ball. After the matches were over, trophies awarded, the players mingled with the crowd. Lucho had his ponies to talk up, and I saw him conversing with groups of men. But women approached him too. Beautiful women who batted their eyelashes, tilted their heads, and smiled. My stomach tied up with knots. Of course, Lucho had lovers. He wasn't a priest. He was an attractive man. I told myself it wasn't my place to care.

Still, relief washed over me when finally, I felt a hand on my arm, heard a whisper in my ear: "Antonieta."

He was mine again, for the moment.

It seemed I saw him everywhere. On Sunday afternoon he was at the hippodrome, where Adrienne, Gabrielle, and I watched Etienne's and Maurice's horses compete. Between races, Lucho left the gentlemen's box and joined us outside of the enclosure, his eyes lingering on mine before he leaned in to greet me.

"They're fast, but they're delicate," he said as the thoroughbreds passed, their stampede drowning out the beating of my heart. "Criollos aren't fast like that. But they have stamina. I think the French army is warming to them."

"People are seeing that Argentine horses are the best in the world," I said, smiling.

"They're coming around. And your hats?"

I gazed up at the bandstand, at the Tribune des Dames where the Jockey Club wives sat—the men had a separate section where they could bring their mistresses—it looked like an explosion of fruits and flowers. But among them, a few of the more daring women wore hats that stood out for their austerity, straw boaters with a single ribbon, picture hats with one dramatic bow. "There are some Chanels here," I said with pride.

Just then, a Jockey Club wife strolled past. Earlier that week, she'd been in the boutique, chatting with me about the tea she was hosting to raise money for the poor. She was complaining about a certain other society woman, Madame F, who had scheduled a charity tea at the same exact time. I'd listened to her go on and on, worried her invitees would choose the other event, her social cachet at stake. I'd reassured her that everyone who came into the boutique was talking about going to her tea, and she seemed relieved, grateful. I shouldn't have been surprised that here, at the hippodrome, her eyes looked right past me, as if she had no idea who I was.

Lucho saw my frown. "What is it?" he said.

I nodded discreetly toward the woman. "She's wearing a Chanel Modes chapeau, one that I helped her pick out. When she passed me just now, she didn't acknowledge me at all. It happens to Gabrielle too. These ladies of the monde. They come to the boutique, confide in us, but in the world, they'll have nothing to do with us. They walk by us as if we're invisible."

"Invisible?" he said. "Is that what you think?"

I was suddenly self-conscious. I nodded. "Yes."

He motioned toward the Tribune des Dames. "The women in the bandstand, the lady who passed by. They may act as if they don't see you. But the proof is on their heads. They're wearing what you told them to wear. You have influence over them. Power. They just don't want to admit it." He chuckled. "I think the joke is on them." He tipped his head toward me, his expression serious now, his voice sincere. "I admire you, Antonieta."

I was astonished. "You admire me?"

He took a step toward me, placing his hands on each of my shoulders, his face close to mine. "Yes," he said, so definitively I was even further taken aback. "There's a fearlessness in not letting the world tell you no. In putting yourself in front of those inclined to dismiss you. It's difficult, convincing others to appreciate something so close to your heart that might be new or different for them. It takes determination, persistence, verve."

His horses, I thought.

A moment passed, and he took his hands from my shoulders, but I felt them for the rest of the day.

The next morning at the boutique, I pulled Gabrielle aside.

"I want to ask you something," I said. "About Lucho."

"Yes?" she said, eyebrows raised with interest.

"Our stars keep crossing. There has to be a reason, don't you think?"

"I think you worry too much about reasons. You're waiting for someone who may not exist. Lucho is here. Why not live now, Ninette, in the present? No one knows what the future will hold. Well, no one except the gypsies."

During the lunch hour, I convinced her to take me to a fortune teller, an old woman who read cards just on the outskirts of the Marais. When she laid out my cards, it was clear. There it was, the heart card. There was passion, love. And a ship.

"If you don't follow your heart," she said. "It will pass you by."

"You see, Ninette," Gabrielle said. "I told you so."

The fortune teller turned more cards, eventually showing the combination we'd seen before, the one that meant an early death. Our mother. Julia-Berthe.

Or...could it mean, perhaps, possibly, Lucho's wife?

"Will I ever be married?" I asked.

She shuffled the cards and spread them again. I held my breath, and then it was there, the card with the ring. It could mean marriage, but it could mean other things. A commitment. A broken commitment. A business partnership. It was up to the fortuneteller to discern the true meaning.

"Yes," she said. "It's in the cards. One day, you will be married."

I looked at Gabrielle, my eyes wide, and she nodded.

It could only mean one thing.

Lucho would be free.

And then, at last, we would marry.

# FIFTY-TWO

LUCHO HAD A PLACE FOR HIMSELF, A SIMPLE HOUSE OUT ON the pampas, where he was most at peace.

"I want to take you there, Antonieta," he said one night at dinner, his voice low and husky, the kind of voice that could smooth out nerves and sharp edges, warm you from the inside. "It's almost as beautiful as you," he went on. "The sunrise, the sunset. The scent of eucalyptus, the lowing of the cattle, the singing of the cow birds. And the horses grazing in the fields. Around them, I have no cares in the world. They live in the moment. That's all that matters."

I wanted to live in the moment. I was ready, Gabrielle's words playing in my mind. *Lucho is here. Why not live now, Ninette, in the present?*

Before with Lucho at Royallieu, at Maxim's, I'd had only glimpses, the tug of a deep, primal connection, but then he was gone, years or months passing. Now, in Paris, spending time together, seeing him so often over the period of a month,

I couldn't pretend that the pull between us didn't matter. And I didn't have to ignore it anymore. I'd thought being accepted by society would satiate the void that had opened when our father left us. But quietly, gradually, through Chanel Modes, it had filled on its own. I was making something of myself on my terms. Lucho had shown me that.

How ironic. Our hats had infiltrated the drawing rooms of la haute, and now their acceptance no longer mattered to me. With Lucho, I always felt I was where I was supposed to be. I'd started to forget that he was married. Or when I remembered, I didn't care. I didn't know if the fortune teller's prophecy was right or wrong. Either way, it didn't seem important anymore.

What was important was being with him. All I had to do was tell him. I wasn't sure how he'd react. *Everyone here is ruined,* he'd said at Royallieu, *everyone except you.* He might be too much of a gentleman to accept my proposal. I prayed that he wasn't.

He stopped by the boutique the next morning on his way to a meeting with Harrington & Sons' bankers. Just the sight of him, his face tan from the outdoors, how he carried himself, casual but in command—a current always ran through me when he walked into a room. I knew his face better than I knew my own, his expressions, how his eyes danced when he looked at me.

Now was my chance.

Thankfully, there were no customers. Our appointments were usually later in the day.

"Will you walk with me?" I said. I didn't want Gabrielle or any of the seamstresses to overhear. "It's such a nice morning."

He glanced at his watch, then back at me, and smiled. "Of course. I never have a problem keeping bankers waiting."

It was just a few blocks to the Tuileries, and there we sat on two empty garden chairs in the shade, away from the gravel path, from the people strolling about or picnicking in the grass.

I took a deep breath. "Lucho," I said. "I've made a decision."

He had a way of folding in toward me, listening with his body.

"I'm ready," I said.

"Ready?"

"I don't want to wait any longer. I've been waiting for a future that's never going to come while all this time, you've been right here. I want to live in the moment. I want to live in the moment with you."

He moved closer, so close I thought he might kiss me right then. But he didn't. His voice, his eyes, were serious.

"Antonieta. Are you sure of what you're saying? I can't give you what you want. I can't give you respectability."

"What I want has changed. I don't care about respectability in the way that I used to. I'm twenty-five, and I'm only half-alive. I didn't realize it until you came back this summer. I want to feel. I want to love. I want to be loved. By you. It's all I want."

"I want that too," he said. "But for you, everything would change. For an unmarried woman to take a lover—you can't go back from that."

"I know, and I don't care. I've been around men who would take me in an instant if I said yes. But I always thought of you. I always thought that if I were to give myself away like that, it wouldn't be to anyone but to you. You've been so considerate of my...position. But I don't need you to be considerate anymore. I don't want you to be."

He studied me as if waiting for me to blink or flinch or give him some signal that meant I had doubts. "I don't want you to have regrets," he said.

"My only regret is that I've waited so long."

He took my hand in both of his, covering it, pressing on it, thinking, until finally he spoke. "I've wanted this. I've wanted you from the first time I saw you. But there's one condition." Now it was his turn to take a deep breath. "You know I'm not free. I can't be yours. But someday you might find someone who can be. When you find that person, go. You have to promise me, you'll go."

"That won't—"

"Promise me."

"If that happens, I promise." But it wouldn't. I couldn't imagine ever finding someone I wanted as much as Lucho.

We decided to meet at his suite at the Ritz later that evening. He thought I should go to him. That way, I could still change my mind. "If you don't show up," he'd said, "I'll understand." But I could see it in his face, a longing that he hoped I would, and it gave me a thrill.

That night, the entrance hall was bustling. My wide-brimmed hat was pulled low so my face was in shadow as I walked through. I was self-conscious—ladies weren't seen at the Ritz on their own—until I realized that no one noticed me. The crowd of gentilhommes in evening dress, women in expensive gowns, all of them were concerned only about themselves. Even the elevator attendant seemed disinterested, though part of his job was to be discreet.

Meanwhile, every part of me was awake, my senses sharp, anticipation thrumming through me.

Lucho said he'd leave the door unlocked. When I found the door to his suite, I knocked lightly, pushed it open, but he was already there on the other side, waiting.

"Antonieta," he said, pulling me right into his arms, my hat falling to the floor.

*Don't think,* Gabrielle had said, but I wanted to think. I wanted to think of him and me in a place where nothing else mattered, just the two of us.

"Tell me about the pampas," I whispered as he kissed my neck and removed the pins from my hair. "What does it smell like, what does it sound like, what does it feel like?"

I closed my eyes as he slipped off my jacket. I felt his hands undoing the buttons at the back of my dress.

"Take me there," I whispered into his shoulder, and he did, our bodies pressed together, a sunset orange and pink and red, the sweet smell of eucalyptus, the plains that went on forever, and a sky dark like the most luxuriant velvet, wrapping me up in explosions of stars that took my breath away.

"Breathe," he said, as he held me in his arms and kissed my face. "Don't forget to breathe."

# FIFTY-THREE

WHEN I WASN'T PHYSICALLY WITH LUCHO, I WAS WITH HIM IN my mind, reliving how he'd touched me, what we'd done, in such detail that it made me flush even hours later.

"You seem different, Ninette," Gabrielle said one morning with a knowing smile, and I remembered how she'd looked at Royallieu, after she'd been with Etienne. There was a certain glow about her. Did I look like that now? Certainly, I felt that way.

Sometimes, late in the evening, afterward, Lucho and I would become restless and explore parts of the city I'd always wanted to visit, just as we'd explored each other. Paris was magical at that hour.

One night we went up to Montmartre. I'd expected sophistication, glamour, only to find a whole live underbelly of smut and intrigue, opulence and desperation, the butte filled with wealthy tourists who just wanted to say they'd been there, prostitutes on the street corners who had no place else to go. At the Moulin Rouge and the Folies Bergère, the waitresses were bare-chested.

Onstage, lines of dancers raised their skirts in unison and kicked their legs impossibly high, giving glimpses of parts one wasn't normally supposed to see. The show moved from one act to the next quickly, from *tableaux vivants* of scenes of Egypt, to comics making vulgar jokes, to skits with bawdy themes.

Next to me, Lucho was quiet, glancing at me from time to time to gauge my reaction.

When a pair of women strutted out in nothing but artfully placed garlands of flowers, bosoms and bottoms proudly flaunted, I laughed out loud at the idea of what Gabrielle might think. She always said women shouldn't be overdone, but they shouldn't be underdone either. Elegance was somewhere in between.

"Is it smutty or sensual?" I said to Lucho. "I just can't tell."

"I know what's sensual," he said, his finger tracing my bare arm suggestively, "and it's not that. Should we go?"

He'd seen all this before. And I'd already seen enough. Montmartre, it turned out, wasn't for us.

Which meant, I thought with a sense of wonder, there was an "us."

After that, if we wanted to go out, we headed to Maxim's just in time for the "Merry Widow," because it felt like our place, our dance. Other times, when he stayed with me at the Parc Monceau, we went to a quiet café nearby, candles in empty wine bottles in the middle of the tables, wax dripping down the sides like a warm embrace. There, we talked about the smallest of things—our favorite colors, favorite foods—as if they were life-changing revelations.

"I'll be back," he said one night as we strolled along the Canal Saint Martin. The summer was halfway over, and we both knew eventually he'd have to return to Argentina. "For a few weeks in

November. And then most of March. Then the summer again. I'll be here for the whole summer, Antonieta."

I looked up at him. Would he? Sometimes people left, and they didn't come back. He drew me close, and I made a point of memorizing the scent of him, the feel. I held his hand up to mine, strong and capable, not too hard, not too soft.

From then on, every day he'd give me something he'd seen that reminded him of me. "I see you everywhere," he said.

First it was a pink rose with no thorns, then a small rock that had caught his eye as it sparkled in the sun. He brought me a strawberry. "Taste it," he said. "It's not too tart. Sweet, but not too sweet."

A bouquet of apricot-colored dahlias. "So pretty," he said. "So vibrant, so alive. Look at the colors. The way the little petals open up to the world."

A leaf in the shape of a star. "We're all pieces of stars. Fragments fallen to earth. And you and I, Antonieta, we're from the same one. I'm sure of it."

In my youth, I'd thought the Decourcelle mélos were the epitome of romance. I'd had no idea real life could be even better.

In late July, André came back from school, and Lucho took him to the stables to teach him to ride.

In August, when I watched André leave with Boy and Gabrielle for Deauville, a resort town on the Normandy coast for the wealthy and titled, they looked like the perfect family, a married couple and their son with his little dog. I wondered if strangers thought that about Lucho and me when we were with André, a bittersweet feeling.

Mistress. Irrégulière. For so long, I'd been afraid of those words. Now I saw them for what they were: condemning labels with no room for nuance. Technically, I was one, but I didn't think of myself that way. I simply thought of myself as in love and loved back and that was all that mattered.

We spent time alone in Lucho's suite at the Ritz whenever we could. The inevitable was coming, and there was a new urgency to be as close as possible. From the bed, he would order room service, whatever I wanted, like a queen, and all kinds of entrées I'd never tried before just so I could taste them.

When the hour did arrive, he took my face in his hands and asked me to come with him. There in his suite, I could see the sorrow back in his eyes, a steady strength mixed with sadness.

"I will," I said. "One day, I will."

He didn't press it. We each had our place. His was with the horses in Argentina. Mine was here with Gabrielle and Chanel Modes. We'd talked about Julia-Berthe's death, how it had affected my sister and me, how our entire lives, we'd had no one to rely on but each other. Sometimes my bond with Gabrielle felt almost physical, like a sharing of flesh and blood. Lucho understood.

"If you find someone when I'm gone—" He looked away, the muscles in his face tightening.

"I won't." I couldn't.

"If you do, it's all right," he whispered. "I'll just want to know, that's all."

And your wife, I wanted to say, if something happens to her...

But he would tell me. I wouldn't have to ask. That I knew for sure.

That night, neither of us could sleep. It seemed as if by staying awake, the next day wouldn't come and he wouldn't have to leave. But, as always, the sun rose, and together we went to the train station. He waited until the last moment to board, and when the train slowly began to move, I stood alone on the platform, thinking of my father fading into the distance without even a look back. But Lucho stayed in the doorway, leaning out, watching me, until the train had picked up too much speed and he was gone.

# FIFTY-FOUR

*BREATHE*, LUCHO HAD SAID, AND I TRIED. BUT HIS LEAVING HIT me like one of those cold winds from Aubazine that howled and rushed through the gorges. The space around me seemed so empty without him. The first day, I cried until my eyes were swollen and Gabrielle said I had to stop. No one would buy hats from a bawling vendeuse, and she needed my help.

At Chanel Modes, the showroom teemed with clients. Gabrielle Dorziat had become famous, and she wore one of Gabrielle's hats, a wide-brimmed straw hat with one side upturned and a velvet tricorn, in the popular play *Bel Ami*. Not only that, *Les Modes* had recently published photographs of another actress, Geneviève Vix, in Chanel Modes hats. I'd been right when I told Lucienne that it was the actresses who set the trends.

Our sales doubled. We were paying down the letter of credit.

As I got back into the routine of hats, hats and nothing but hats, the lonesomeness subsided. I busied myself hiring more girls for the workroom, a task Gabrielle shunned. In September, a letter came from Lucho informing me he'd arrived in Argentina. Another in October said that in a few weeks he would be on his way back to Paris. Lucho returned in November as he said he would and then again in March.

"I remember this," he said, kissing my earlobe when we were alone at the Ritz. "And this," he said, moving down my neck. "Oh yes, and this…"

When he gave me a gold bracelet from Cartier, I couldn't stop staring at it. I'd never had anything so nice. "It's the color of your hair," he said. "And the little shimmering flecks in your eyes."

We had our interludes, the glorious coming together, the painful cleaving apart. "Come with me," he'd say when it was time to go back to Argentina.

"Stay here," I'd say. "You don't have to leave."

But he did have to leave, and I understood, as heartrending as it was.

Summer couldn't come soon enough.

At the boutique one day in late April, before the rush of afternoon appointments, Gabrielle put her finger over her upper lip as if it were a mustache and said in a deep, masculine voice, "I think you have something here, Coco." She was imitating Boy.

"He wants me to open a boutique in Deauville," she said, her voice back to normal. "He thinks I should sell clothes." Because of city regulations, in Paris she hadn't been allowed to. People stopped her on the street to ask where she got her outfits, always surprised when she said she made them, but the number of licenses issued in different areas of the city was limited, and there was already a dressmaker nearby. But was Deauville ready for Gabrielle's style?

I knew that when she was there with Boy, she wore clothing she'd made, uncomplicated dresses, no corset, loose-fitting sweaters, ankle-length skirts, the complete opposite of la haute, the élégantes who could barely stroll down the promenade in their enormous hats and stiff, constricting dresses. Gabrielle frolicked on the beach, even swam in the sea in a bathing costume she'd devised herself. "You should see the old ladies," she told me. "When I come out of the ocean, they stare at me behind their lorgnettes as if the world is ending."

In her comfortable clothes, she learned how to play croquet. Boy was teaching her tennis.

"You're giving women their freedom, Coco," I'd once overheard him say when he'd stopped by the boutique after one of their trips. "How will we keep you in your place?"

"You won't," she said, and he'd beamed with pride.

Now, she was the one who beamed. "I'm going to do it, Ninette. There's a place on the rue Gontaut-Biron, between the Hotel Normandy, the casino and the beach, right in the middle of everything. Boy's already put up the rent."

"But I thought you wanted to pay him back what you already owe him?" I said, treading carefully. I was especially wary about opening a new store when she still depended on Boy. Didn't she remember how upset she'd been when she found out about the guarantee? How she'd felt she'd been tricked?

"I do. But this is an opportunity to do more than just hats."

I went over the bank statements every week. We weren't drawing anything off the line of credit anymore. Slowly, we were paying Boy back. But when I reminded her, her face took on that look it sometimes did that reminded me of an angry bull about to charge.

"Well, I've already decided. You've never been to Deauville. You don't know what it's like. You have no say."

Now I was annoyed. "I know what the ledger is like. When's the last time you checked it?"

"Boy says to be successful in business you have to take risks."

"And that's why they call them risks," I said. "Because you can lose everything."

The truth was, I wasn't sure about these clothes of hers either. I saw their appeal, but would others? What if the boutique failed? I couldn't stand the possibility of it. Not just for my sake, but for hers.

It was our first business argument. We barely spoke to each other for days.

Before she returned to Deauville, Gabrielle told me she needed me more than ever, that I was in charge of the Paris boutique now. But I still wasn't convinced. I thought we should concentrate on Paris. Chanel Modes was growing. More magazines had featured Gabrielle's hats, and already, we'd had to open another workroom and hire a matronly woman named Angèle as head seamstress to oversee the rest.

And now she wanted to sell frumpy sweaters?

Paris was the center of fashion, not some small resort town on the Normandy coast.

# FIFTY-FIVE

I WAS WRONG. I COULDN'T HAVE BEEN MORE WRONG.

The new boutique was a success from the moment it opened, Gabrielle wrote, telling me not to worry.

Adrienne and Maurice had gone to Deauville to help, and Adrienne returned with a full report: "You should have been there, Ninette. One afternoon, Gabrielle and I dressed in the same outfit, even the same shoes!" They stood just outside the door to the boutique, waving people in. Boy and Maurice sat on a bench out front, and, before they knew it, a crowd of friends from the Jockey Club, catching up on the news, had gathered. That made other people stop to find out what was happening, sportsmen, nobility, aristocrats with nothing better to do.

"It was like a fête," Adrienne explained. "Like the Bois de Boulogne on a Sunday afternoon. Ladies strolling by all went in the boutique, examining the chapeaux and the cardigans until there were practically none left."

Not long after, I got to witness it with my own eyes, the

Deauville shop another place on this earth we could call our own. Lucho was back for the summer, and in addition to our interludes in Paris, we spent as much time as we could in Deauville, leaving Angèle in charge of the rue Cambon shop for a few days at a time.

We stayed at the fashionable Hotel Normandy, and in the mornings, while the men were with the horses, Adrienne and I would walk along the pier in Gabrielle's creations, those soft, belted cardigans she loved so much, matching soft skirts, our chins lifted, our eyes forward, a slight smile on our lips, while people stared and wondered who we were.

André, who was out of school, joined us. Gabrielle and I had gotten him a dog he named Bruno and often took the two of them for picnics on the beach. He was nine years old now, his face thinning, his legs getting longer, and we marveled as he spoke perfect English with Boy.

We spent afternoons at the polo club. I would never tire of watching Lucho play. With him, polo was more than a sport. It was something heavenly, a merging of spirits, human and animal. When he was with his horses, there was a contentment about him, that peace he said he had only on the pampas.

In the evenings, we would all dress and meet for dinner. Sometimes there would be dancing. The tango was the rage in Paris, so much so that people had started calling the city "Tangoland," and it had carried over to Deauville. There was even a train, the Tango Special, from which the seats were taken out so people could dance during the ride from Paris to Deauville and back again.

"That's not a tango," Lucho said one night as we observed the couples on the dance floor at the Normandy, an appalled expression animating his handsome face. "That is a crime. An insult to Argentina. A blasphemy. Look at them, they're thinking too much about their next step."

He led me out among them, drawing me closer than usual,

pressing me to him as he moved, turning his hips this way and that so mine did the same.

"El tango está entre paso y paso," he said. "It's not the steps. It's what happens in between. It's about longing and desire. Passion, feeling, instincts."

Suddenly he took a backward step, the momentum spinning me away, one hand still holding mine, then pulled me back, wrapping me into him, his hands now on my waist.

"It's supposed to be exciting, sensual," he said, his breath on my neck. "Later, when we're alone, I'll teach you the real tango."

Soon enough, all of Deauville knew of Gabrielle Chanel. Lucho and I preferred to spend time alone at the hotel when we could. So did Maurice and Adrienne. But Gabrielle liked the attention. She wanted people to see her with the dashing Boy Capel, the champion English polo player who stood out wherever he went with his dark good looks, his courtly English mannerisms. Gabrielle wanted people to see how in love they were, that of all the women, he'd chosen her.

And people did take notice. The artist Sem was in Deauville and drew a caricature of Gabrielle and Boy dancing, Boy half horse, half man, my sister like a femme fatale in his arms, in the clothing she'd designed herself. He published it in a collection he titled *Tangoville sur Mer*. Passion, feeling, instinct. He'd captured it perfectly.

There were those in society who dreaded being the object of Sem's pencil. Not Gabrielle.

*You see, Papa*, I imagined her thinking, even after all these years. *Look at me. I am worth loving.*

# FIFTY-SIX

BACK IN PARIS, THE TANGO SHOWED NO SIGNS OF FADING OUT. Parisians flocked to the *tango-thé*, events hosted by hotels for four francs a person with sandwiches and tea for refreshment. Later, there were tango parties, charity tangos, tango balls, tango dinners. *La Vie Heureuse* published an article debating the proper style of tango. Ladies of the monde hired professional instructors. There were tango shoes, tango trouserettes, special loose tango corsets. Skirts had to be raised to keep from tripping. Hobble skirts, at last, were done for. Even hats were different, with one aigrette straight up at attention in the front rather than a plume meandering off to the side, which could leave a dancer unbalanced.

Everything was tango, tango, tango. The color orange was no longer the color orange. It was the *couleur tango*.

"Antonieta," I heard someone call out one afternoon at the rue Cambon boutique in a voice that couldn't be Lucho's. It was September, which meant he was already back in Argentina.

I looked up from the orders Gabrielle and I were going

through to see a young man with a dazzling smile standing in the doorway. His thick black hair was combed back with brilliantine. He wore white spats, flamboyant clothing, a fresh carnation in his lapel, and carried a large, unusual case.

"Who is that?" Gabrielle, sitting next to me, whispered under her breath as Adrienne, trying on hats in front of the mirror, exclaimed, "What in the world?"

"Arturo!" I stood to greet him. "You must be Lucho's cousin. From Buenos Aires."

Arturo bowed formally. "Arturo de Alba de Vallado de Irujo de Harrington," he said as if he were at the court of Versailles.

I hid a smile. I hadn't met Arturo before, but Lucho had said he was a character, a bon vivant, the family black sheep because he preferred the nightclubs to the estancia. He was a charmer. A dandy. He was five years younger than Lucho, and his parents had cut him off until he became more serious. He had a glittering smile, intense eyes, a joie de vivre mixed with a Latin swagger that was irresistible.

"He's here to give tango lessons," I explained to Gabrielle and Adrienne. Young men from Argentina had been flocking to Paris as instructors to take advantage of the craze.

"Here?" said Gabrielle with a confused look, motioning to the boutique.

"Not here in the boutique," I said. "Paris."

Adrienne smiled. "Well, since he's here in the boutique, Senor de Harrington, show us what you can do, s'il vous plaît. We all love the tango."

"That," he said, eyes flashing, "would be my pleasure. But first…" He opened his case and, to our astonishment, pulled out a portable gramophone. He put on a recording, then swept me around the boutique, tango-walking very intensely this direction and then that with sudden dips and turns. With Lucho, it was passion. With Arturo, pure fun.

Adrienne had a turn and then Gabrielle, after which we noticed a trio of ladies had gathered inside near the door, our next appointments, staring. "Mesdames," Arturo said, turning to them with a flourish.

I hurried to greet them, but they didn't want to speak to me. They wanted Arturo. "Do you give lessons, monsieur?" one asked.

He drew out a card and handed it to her, entrancing her with his grin, his exuberance contagious. "Arturo de Alba de Vallado de Irujo de Harrington. At your service, madame," he said and then held out a hand. "Shall we?"

Who could refuse? Everyone wanted a turn.

That afternoon, we didn't sell a single hat. All anyone cared about was Arturo. Customers asked when he'd be back.

"You have to come every afternoon," I told him. "You can hand out your card to our customers. They'll want to take lessons from you and soon enough you'll be teaching all of Paris to tango."

He did return, with his gramophone, sometimes taking even Angèle around in a lusty tango that made her blush. His client list grew, and so did ours. All the ladies wanted to be around Arturo, but I had my own reasons. He reminded me that Lucho, so far away, was real. I wanted to ask Arturo about Lucho's wife. Did he know her? What was she like? But I didn't let myself. Once I started thinking about her, I'd never stop.

Before long, Arturo became the most sought-after instructor in the city. A group of society ladies led by the Princess Murat rented a lavish mansion on the Champs-Élysées and set him up there for lessons, issuing tickets in order of priority. Blue tickets for ladies of the gratin, pink tickets for ladies of the next tier of the monde.

It was 1913, and the world was practically unrecognizable. There were more motorcars on the streets than horses. Brave men attempted to conquer the sky in flying machines or drove at death-defying speeds in cross-country motor races. The globe seemed to be expanding and shrinking at the same time, and all everyone wanted to do was dance, to cling to each other and move about in preordained patterns on the floor—this direction, then that direction, then this direction again. It was the only way to know exactly where you would end up.

Deauville that next summer, the summer of '14, was more dazzling than before, like a theater tableau, a stage setting that would
remain in my memory forever. Lucho was back, and we often
slipped away from Paris.

Around us, everyone was rich. Everyone was beautiful. Everything was easy. In the mornings, the boutique filled with the
most stylish élégantes who bought hats and clothing like they
were candy. The men meanwhile convened outside to discuss
the racing pages, the latest news. In the evenings, everyone
danced. We drank champagne. We ate oysters, not because we
liked them but because we could. Chanel Modes was making a
profit, expanding from hats to resort wear, a new kind of clothing that women could move freely in on tennis courts and golf
courses. Gabrielle had been losing interest in hats, and I'd been
surprised to find that I was too. There was only so much one
could do with felt and feathers.

After dinner, Lucho and I didn't last long in the crowd. Alone
on the pier, we'd look up at the sky, a million stars blinking,
and search for the one that was ours, the one we came from. "I
think it might be that one," he said, pointing.

"No," I said, gesturing toward the brightest I could find.
"That one."

Back in our room, orchestra music from the restaurant floated
up on the salt-heavy air and in through the open windows,
and we danced, a sultry swaying. When the music stopped, we
moved to the rhythm of the tide, the crescendo of waves crashing on the sand, their smooth retreat like the soft rustling of silk.

While somewhere, far away, an archduke was assassinated.

# FIFTY-SEVEN

"WAR?"

Back at the Paris boutique, I stared at Angèle, trying to understand. It was late afternoon. I'd sent her out on an errand, and she'd just returned, empty-handed and out of breath. Sweat dotted her temples. It was hot, even for August.

"That's what they're saying," she said. "They're saying Germany's declared war on Russia, and France is next. They're putting mobilization orders on all the post office doors as we speak."

My heart stopped. In France, once they turned twenty, every man spent the next several years in the army. After that, they were considered reserves. Now, according to Angèle, the reserves were being ordered to report for duty starting the next day. There was no time to waste. The Germans were massing at the border.

Thank God Lucho wasn't French.

I glanced out the window at the sound of automobiles honking all the way from the rue Saint Honoré. I stepped outside and, near the corner, found people streaming toward the Place de la Concorde. Some of the workroom girls were leaning out the upstairs windows, calling out to passersby to learn what was happening.

I closed the boutique early. The season in Deauville would be cut short, and Gabrielle would return. André was still there with her, but soon he'd go back to England, where he'd be safe, far from the war.

War—what did that mean?

Inside the boutique, I waited for Lucho. He came as soon as he heard the news. "What's going to happen?" I asked, but he didn't answer, just pulled me to him.

It seemed all of Paris had taken to the streets. We joined the crowds walking along the boulevards, gathering in parks and at monuments singing the Marseillaise. *Vive la France*, they called out, or *Vive l'Armée*, waving flags or straw hats in the air. Someone handed me a flag, and I found myself singing as if I were Marianne herself. It was impossible not to get caught up in the fervor. The Germans, people said, didn't know what they were in for.

Eventually it grew dark, and the streetlights didn't come on. A government-ordered blackout, Lucho said, typical in a time of war to make it harder for the enemy to spot you. A frightening thought, but still no one wanted to go home, too afraid of missing some important piece of news. More voices rang out. *To liberté! Égalité! Fraternité! Down with Kaiser Wilhelm! À bàs Guillaume!*

"The war will be over by December," a young man said.

"I'll give it eight weeks," said another. "It's as if the Germans have forgotten who we are."

References were made to Napoleon, Charlemagne, William the Conqueror, old glories recounted, defeats ignored. Rumors spread that in other parts of town, German-owned businesses were being looted, and already French ones were pasting signs in their windows that said "maison française" to keep the raiders away.

But on the main boulevards, the café terraces were packed, small orchestras playing "La Marseillaise" over and over again, glasses clinking to endless patriotic toasts. To drink champagne was no doubt an act of patriotism, and Lucho and I joined in. He seemed distracted, his mind working. Now, the army would really need his beef, his horses. But it wouldn't take him.

We huddled close as above us searchlights crisscrossed the sky, one direction then the other, their own kind of dance. I thought of the tango, of how it was all about angles and sharp, sudden turns.

Over the next several days, men who'd been mobilized walked with resolved expressions and knapsacks over their shoulders toward the train station, dotting the avenues like pearls on a string. There, trains would take them east, to the front.

Lucho was especially busy, arranging shipping for Harrington beef, frozen in tins, to feed the troops, for Harrington criollos for the cavalry. His work took on increasing urgency.

"Your criollos will help us win this war," I said with pride.

"They'll do their part," he said, and I could tell by the tone of his voice he was proud too. His strong, brave, steady horses. Now the world would see what they were made of.

I opened the boutique because I didn't know what else to do, but no customers came. In Paris, no one was thinking about hats, not even me. I sent Angèle and the workroom girls home. They had brothers, fathers, lovers to bid farewell.

I fidgeted about, anxious, not sure what to do with myself, until one day Celestine showed up. She earned money selling sketches of our hats to the magazines.

"Apollinaire volunteered for the army and they took him," Celestine said, distraught. "Modi tried to but they didn't want him. His health is too poor. It's terrible in Montparnasse now, Antoinette. No one is going to spend any money on art now. Or drawings of hats and sweaters. I don't know what's going to happen."

When Gabrielle arrived from Deauville a week later, she seemed flustered. The train station, she said, was mobbed with soldiers, with mothers and wives trying not to cry, sons and husbands looking stern but determined.

Everywhere else, the city was practically shut down. So many stores and restaurants were closed "pour cause de mobilisation," signs on the doors explaining that its employees were off at war. The rue de la Paix, the fashion district, was deserted too, all of the great dressmakers and milliners shuttered: Poiret. Pacquin. Redfern. We observed the changing mood in Paris, a new fear rising within us. What would happen to Chanel Modes, to all that we'd worked for? We had bills to pay. A line of credit gathering interest. How did you sell hats in Paris and sportswear in Deauville during a war?

That summer, everything had been going so well. Better than well. Between Deauville and Paris, we had over one hundred employees. Gabrielle's name and reputation had been spreading. *Women's Wear Daily*, the "bible of fashion," had published a glowing article about her belted tunics. The true *coup de grace* came when the Baroness Kitty de Rothschild, a real member of the gratin, the *crème-de-la-crème*, with a flair for fashion, started wearing Gabrielle Chanel. Usually, she went to Monsieur Poiret for her ensembles, but according to rumor, they'd had a falling out. Everyone wanted to wear what the Baroness de Rothschild was wearing, and so now it wasn't just actresses and daring society ladies who were customers but members of the true French aristocracy.

Poor Monsieur Poiret. He couldn't open his salon if he wanted to. He'd been mobilized.

But those old Aubazine winds, they found us again, moving, rearranging, sweeping up life as we'd known it.

At the end of August, Maurice was mobilized. Adrienne was inconsolable. She cried all the time, refusing to leave the Parc Monceau in case Maurice came back.

"He's an officer," I said. "In a distinguished regiment. He won't be right on the front lines."

"He'll be close enough," she said. "What would I do if something happened to him?"

I held her hand, but I didn't know what else to say.

Boy was mobilized on the British side as a liaison for a high-ranking officer. Gabrielle was stoic as usual. She worried for his safety but was used to his absences. Over the past year, he'd been away a lot.

"He's always with that Clemenceau," she'd been complaining since winter. She'd told me that the former French premier and Boy had become allies, on a mission to convince the French government that the Germans wouldn't be satisfied unless there was a war and that they had to prepare. Part of that preparation was signing contracts for Boy's ships and coal, always, for Boy, a business angle.

"But does Boy really believe there will be a war?" I'd asked back then, before the declaration.

"Boy says the best way to prevent a war is to prepare for one. I'm not worried. It's a whole new century. We're all much more sophisticated now. Surely war has gone the way of arsenic soap, bloodletting, and leg-of-mutton sleeves. It's all just talk."

With Boy gone so often, this summer in Deauville hadn't been like the last. I knew Gabrielle tried not to complain, but sometimes she couldn't help it.

"My dear Coco," Boy once said. "If it were up to me, I'd have you come along. You'd make a better general in the army than most of the ones we have. When you want something, you have a way of getting it."

"Not always," she'd said with a pout.

But the truth was the way they were together had changed. I sensed a shift between them, one that had been forming slowly for months. As Boy prepared for the front and they had their last days together, he was passionate one minute, more ardent than I'd ever seen him, but distracted the next. And Gabrielle looked at him not with tenderness but as if keeping watch.

It had to be the war. War set everyone off balance.

# FIFTY-EIGHT

IN EARLY SEPTEMBER, A BUZZING SOUND COULD BE HEARD over Paris. People on the streets stopped and searched the sky for its source: an aeroplane. Everyone gasped. What a thrill! What a wonderful distraction to glimpse one of those brave aviators, defying the laws of nature, as we read about in the newspaper stories.

But that afternoon, we learned the horrifying truth. It had been a German aeroplane, dropping bombs over the city. There was a crater on the rue des Recollets and another on the rue des Vinaigriers. An elderly woman had been killed.

When, days later, another aeroplane flew right over the rue Cambon, Gabrielle and I ran out the door like moths to a flame at the sound of the motor, Angèle and the seamstresses right behind us. Everyone came out of the stores nearby, transfixed, watching as the aeroplane veered off toward the Eiffel Tower, circled back to the Tuileries, and then faded out of sight. We were shaking for the rest of the day, completely unnerved. We should have taken cover. After, we heard this one had dropped its bombs on the Avenue du Maine. This time, a young woman was killed.

The war should have been almost over. It had already been a month. Instead, the Germans were turning village after village to rubble, drawing closer and closer to Paris. We heard they were just thirty kilometers away. It seemed impossible. But on quiet nights, we thought we could hear the boom of guns. I was thankful for Lucho beside me.

The city began emptying out, people on the move everywhere with suitcases and trunks. From the front, Boy telegrammed Gabrielle: *Go to Deauville.* Lucho agreed. Adrienne wanted to stay in Paris in case something happened to Maurice, who was also at the front, but we convinced her it wasn't safe.

Lucho was still working on arrangements for a shipment of his horses and needed to stay in Paris.

"When I'm done," he said before I departed for Deauville, "I want you to come to Argentina with me. I want you as far as possible from this war."

It sounded so simple. The two of us together, away from everything. Already we'd been faced with the horror. The wounded were coming in, their eyes distant, having seen terrors the rest of us couldn't fathom. And the refugees from Belgium, with no place to go, lost and confused.

But it wasn't simple at all. I imagined myself in a strange country, waiting every day for Lucho to return from the stables or business meetings, or visits with his family, who wouldn't accept me. The idea panicked me. Here, I had my position at Chanel Modes. I took care of myself financially. In Argentina, I'd be far from the Germans, but also from Gabrielle and Adrienne. I couldn't leave them. Not in the middle of a war when everything was so uncertain.

When I didn't respond, he tried again. "Antonieta," he said, his eyes locked on mine. "Promise you'll come with me. It's important to me that you're safe."

I looked down at the floor. "Lucho, I..."

He sighed, reaching for me. He knew my answer.

In Deauville, the crowds were gone. The casino, the Hotel Normandy, the beaches—deserted. In a back room of the boutique, we sewed, Gabrielle, me, Adrienne. Just outside of Paris, a battle was raging, a horrible one, and we had to do *something*. So we made straight, plain skirts, unadorned ivory silk blouses with a sailor collar, cinched at the waist, stacks and stacks of them. Our thumbs were sore, our fingers stiff. We hadn't sewn in ages. That was for the workroom girls. But now, we couldn't stop. We sewed as if we were back at the Pensionnat in Moulins altering our uniforms, a time we never thought we'd long for.

There were no customers. There might never be again. But we weren't sewing for them. We sewed for our mother, for Julia-Berthe, for ourselves. We sewed for what once was, what we hoped would be. We should have been at Mass, praying. *Oh holy ange, don't let the world end.* But the needle and thread were our church, sewing our confession, our sacrament, our salvation.

It had been Boy's idea to keep the boutique open when all the other shops in Deauville were closing. "Wait," he'd said to Gabrielle. "Let's see what happens."

It seemed ridiculous. But after a few weeks, they all came back. The wealthy. The titled. Those who could afford to live indefinitely at the Normandy or in their villas along the coast, a safe distance from the ugliness of war. They returned even though there was no polo, no horse races, no promenades on the pier. Instead, the Hotel Royal was converted into a hospital, and the ladies of the monde formed a volunteer nursing society.

But one couldn't wrap bandages and spoon soup in tea dresses, Valenciennes lace, and crêpe de chine. The wounded needed nurses, and the nurses needed uniforms. I could practically hear Gabrielle plotting in her mind.

The doctors insisted the nurse volunteers wear white, and someone had handed out old hotel maids' uniforms, shapeless, boring sacks the ladies couldn't possibly be seen in. They might be volunteering at a hospital, but they still needed to look chic. Clothes defined them just as a cashmere pèlerine defined a payante and a wool pèlerine was the mark of a nécessiteuse. So they brought their uniforms to Gabrielle, who knew how to make something from nothing, turn the inelegant into the elegant through a strange alchemy of design, fit, proportion. When they weren't in their nurse uniforms, la haute needed clothing that was stylish but not overdone. They needed the clothing of Gabrielle "Coco" Chanel.

The same was true, we hoped, in Paris. The Germans had been pushed back from the outskirts of the city, the front stabilized farther to the east where fighting, we heard, was in trenches dug into the earth. Paris was safe again, for the moment. Leaving a saleswoman in charge in Deauville, we returned to reopen Chanel Modes, bringing with us Gabrielle's sporty knit sweater-coats and belted tunics, items that didn't violate the licensing requirements, resort-wear now transformed into the much gloomier category of war-wear.

Simplicity was the order of the day. The era of being decorative was over. And Gabrielle "Coco" Chanel seemed to be one step ahead.

# FIFTY-NINE

LIKE EVERYONE ELSE, PARIS HAD TAKEN OFF HER BALL GOWN
and jewels. She'd put away her dancing shoes.

On the Western Front, the armies dug in while here the government prepared for a long fight. The race track at Auteuil, the scene of so many twirling parasols and top hats, was converted into a cow pasture. Sheep were herded through the Place de la Concorde. People still remembered the Siege of 1870, when Parisians had been forced to live on rats, cats, dogs and, when those were all gone, animals from the zoo, an elephant feeding a whole arrondissement. The government was hoping to prevent that. Now, to save butter, flour, and milk, it decreed that the only breads bakeries could make were boulot and demi-fendu. The croissant was outlawed.

Most of France's coal mines were behind German lines, which meant that coal was regulated too. Staying warm was a feat but indirectly brought more sales to Chanel Modes. The tea room at the Ritz, its back entrance just across the

street, was heated, and the old rules of propriety dictating
that ladies weren't to be seen unaccompanied at a hotel had
left with the men. To beckon them as they made their way
to and from the tea room, Celestine painted fanciful window
displays, like stage backdrops of parlors with cozy fires. And
it worked. The élégantes always stopped in to see what was
new. They never left empty-handed.

It felt almost like a sin for Chanel Modes to be doing well
when the war was so cruel to everyone else.

But we couldn't shield ourselves from the casualties. The newspapers carried lists of the deceased. There were names we knew.
First Gui, one of our tailor shop lieutenants in Moulins. Then a
suitor of Adrienne's from her days with Maud. Then a friend of
Boy's who'd invited me to his garçonnière to see his collection of
ivory carvings. Every death pulled at me; even unfamiliar names
left me agonizing over who they were and who they would have
been, about the hole now in the lives of those who had to live
without them. I remembered the faces of the young men during
the mobilization, ready to prove themselves. There were ghosts
everywhere, injured men hobbling about on crutches, a pants leg
pinned up, others with vacant, emotionless stares.

When there was a cloth shortage, Gabrielle found a textile
manufacturer who had a surplus of jersey and was willing to sell
it cheap. She bought all of it.

"Jersey?" I said. No one would wear jersey!

She made me stand still, arms outstretched while she draped
the cloth over me, once again turning nothing into something.
She made dresses, slim and loose, comfortable yet refined. Everyone wanted them. The absurdity of what she was doing made
me laugh. These snobs of the monde. Now Gabrielle had them
wearing the fabric of men's underthings!

"It's brilliant, Coco," Boy said when he was in Paris on leave.
"Genius. You're making jersey fashionable."

She gave him a smile that was all tenderness. They seemed to be content with one another again, and I was relieved.

In the evenings, I'd cross the street to the Ritz. The great Harrington criollos would soon help save France, and Lucho was invigorated by this new sense of purpose. "Horses are the backbone of an army. Men can't win wars without good horses," he said. "They're strong. They're brave. Thanks to them, men will come home who might not otherwise."

In his room, I loved seeing his things scattered about. The newspaper, creased from reading, on a side table, along with loose coins from his pockets. A discarded tie. A jacket flung over a chair. Sugar cubes from a restaurant in a napkin for horses not yet requisitioned. When I was with him, I lived in the moment, savoring every fragile second, every minute, every hour. It was impossible to know what would happen next.

But the state of his horses also made him tense. Just shipping them over from Argentina was dangerous. So much could go wrong. There was the potential for attack from German submarines. And onboard, unable to move about, the horses were at risk for shipping fever, a type of pneumonia. They would arrive at Le Havre, a French port on the Channel with a huge supply station for the army. Once on land, it could take weeks for them to recuperate before they were ready for active service, and many of the soldiers in charge had no idea how to handle horses or train them. That winter, Lucho had discovered the British troops were shaving some of their horses on the front to protect them from mange. "Fools," he said. "They could die of exposure without their coats."

When the ship was due, Lucho left for Le Havre to help settle the animals in. A few weeks later, he returned, quiet, brooding. His criollos were war horses now.

One morning I woke to the sun streaming in through the window of his room at the Ritz. I sat up to stretch, pulling my hair back, turning my face toward the light like a flower, wanting to feel its warmth on my skin.

Lucho was standing at the foot of the bed, fixing his tie, ready to go off to the work of selling horses to the army. "Don't move," he said.

I wasn't dressed and suddenly felt self-conscious, laughing and reaching for a sheet to cover my chest, always the modest convent girl.

"No," he said. "Stay just like that."

I went still, letting him take me in, his eyes brushing over me so that my skin tingled.

"I want to remember this moment. Your smile, the spark in your eyes, the sun's glow on your hair and skin. Antonieta, you remind me that there's still beauty in the world. Lately, it's so easy to forget."

Not long after, I visited a studio in Place Pigalle to commission a portrait from a Polish painter named Tadé Styka, who I'd overheard customers praising in the boutique. During the afternoon hours, I'd slip away to pose, shoulders and chest bare. The painting was a surprise for Lucho, to lift his spirits. Still I couldn't imagine what Gabrielle might say if she were to see the portrait, so I made sure to wear a gold-colored shawl, strategically placed to ensure she wasn't scandalized.

In the studio, the artist's brush working the canvas was the only sound, no armies, no cavalries, no men and horses marching off to war. The world, for a little while, stopped. I sat as still as I could, my head turned over my shoulder toward an imaginary window and a golden sun shining in as if I were looking to the future, to me and Lucho and everything that would surely come to be.

# SIXTY

AT THE END OF APRIL, ANOTHER SHIPMENT OF CRIOLLOS WAS due to arrive in Le Havre. As the time drew near, Lucho grew more and more agitated. He read *Le Figaro* cover to cover, folding it back up and staring off at nothing, his jaw tightening, silent. He knew the newspapers were censored. The government told us only what they wanted us to know, calling the war a mechanical war, a modern war, our army's old tactics struggling to adjust to the German's new weapons. Armored tanks. Submarines. Aeroplanes, those daring young airmen who flew them for adventure before the war, now having to take sides.

Lucho started going for long walks along the Seine, and when I could, I joined him, the city around us gray and cheerless, the river calming but for the armored tugboats tied up along the side gently nudging each other. Barges carrying war supplies floated past until it grew dark, but still we walked.

"They're leading cavalry charges against machine guns," he said one evening.

"But that's insanity."

"Yes. And..."

I waited.

"The Germans are using shells with poisonous gas in them. The cowards are killing men with chemicals."

Killing men, I thought. And horses. I looked up at him. His face was strained.

"The men have gas masks, if they can get them on. The horses have gas masks too. But there's never enough time."

I felt sick to my stomach.

"They're not waging war," he said, revulsion in his voice. "They're waging destruction."

After meeting the second shipment of horses in Le Havre, Lucho was even more unsettled. He seemed lost, absent, his mind elsewhere. He didn't sleep. Sometimes at night, I'd wake to find him sitting in a chair, watching me.

"Close your eyes, Antonieta," he'd say, coming to my side and stroking my hair. "I like to watch you sleep. It calms me."

All I could do was be there for him.

In the evenings, we resumed our walks along the Seine. The days were getting longer, warmer, and I wondered if flowers still bloomed in wartime or if the chestnut trees would stay bare. Would the daffodils pop up in the Jardin du Palais Royal? It seemed heartless that they would.

Though he was silent I could hear the changes stirring inside him.

"I went to the front," he finally admitted one time. "Straight from Le Havre. With the horses. This time, I wanted to see for myself."

He told me about men living in mud-filled trenches, rats

everywhere, lice. No-man's-land, a vast, desolate expanse of horror that used to be a forest, trees blown apart so that they looked like arms with gnarled hands rising up out of the earth as if begging for reprieve. Dead bodies left where they'd fallen, slowly disintegrating because it wasn't safe to run out and retrieve them. There were dead horses too, bloated, shot up, swallowed in giant muddy craters left by shells.

Even the living horses were covered in mud, impossible to groom, endless muck breeding diseases of hoof and coat. They had no shelter, were wet and cold all the time without enough food, choking on their empty hay bags, nibbling at each other's tails. Some horses collapsed from exhaustion trying to pull guns through the sludge. He'd seen a horse with both of its front legs blown off struggling to get up, panicking, not sure why it couldn't. No one could reach it to put it out of its misery.

The anguish in his voice. I thought it was for what he had done to his horses, not realizing it was also for what he was about to do.

The next morning, he said he was leaving. He was going back to the front.

I tried to stop him. "We'll go to Argentina," I said. "Right now. We'll live on the pampas and forget all about the war." I started throwing things into a case. I was frantic. "Let's go. You and I. I'm ready. I want to smell the eucalyptus. I want to hear the cattle, the singing of the cow birds. We'll live in the moment there, like the horses in the fields. Please, Lucho, please—"

"Antonieta."

The torment in his tone quieted me.

"You don't understand. I can never go back to the pampas.

They trusted me. My horses trusted me, and I sent them to the slaughterhouse."

He was gone that day.

I didn't find his note until that night, lying on the side table where his loose coins used to be:

*I ruin what I love most in the world, Antonieta. The innocent. The pure. Always making sacrifices, for me. But it's not too late for you. You can still find someone who can give you the life you've always hoped for, the life you deserve. This is what I want for you, with all my heart. It's the only thought that comforts me. When you find him, go. Do it for me.*

My hand shook. The note fell to the floor. He didn't expect to come back alive.

# SIXTY-ONE

AT THE PARC MONCEAU, I DIDN'T GET OUT OF BED FOR DAYS.

It was as if I'd been cut in two, half of me missing, a physical pain and loss.

I cried more than I didn't, my head aching, chest tight, appetite gone. A fever soon came on and with it a cough. I lived on doses of Veronal, often staring into space for hours, twisting the gypsy ring on my finger, wishing I'd slipped it into Lucho's pocket before he left. It could have kept him safe.

Adrienne brought me cod liver oil, saying it was good for a cough, but I refused to take it.

"Maurice says most of the time nothing really happens at all on the front. The men wait, taking turns in the trenches, holding the line."

They weren't always waiting. I knew that. Sometimes they were charging across no-man's-land, men and horses against machine guns. I saw the old fortune teller's face, her lips moving. *An early death.* What if she'd meant Lucho? I considered trying to locate her, but I was too afraid of what she might reveal. Besides, she'd also said I would be married, and she had clearly been wrong about that.

A calming thought occurred to me. Lucho was at the front to do what he could for the horses. If he were dead, he couldn't help them. He had to realize that. He wouldn't risk his life carelessly. I tried to take some comfort in that.

Still, more often than not, the panic rose up inside me in waves, pushing on my chest so my breath became short and shallow. For three weeks, I lived in a fog of fear and loss and Veronal, not caring about anything, not even Chanel Modes, until one morning Gabrielle swept into my room. She'd visited before, offering kind words, a warm hand. But this time was different. She thrust open the curtains and stared at me, her expression anxious, angry.

"Antoinette Chanel," she said, hands on her hips. "Do you know what I see right now?"

I put up an arm to shield my eyes from the light, from her judgment.

"I see our mother. Weak. Ashen. Unmoving in a bed, killing herself with grief."

If I had any energy at all, I would have slapped her. How could she be so cruel? She knew what the nuns used to say to me, that I'd end up like my mother. She knew how I hated that.

"I feel for you, Ninette. You know I do. But you can't keep on like this. You remember Aubazine. How when we first got there, we cried all the time. Our mother was dead. Our father had left us. The nuns had no pity. They made us get up. Every single day. And it was for the best. 'Awake up, my glory! Awake, psaltery and harp!' Do you remember?"

"Stop," I said, wanting her just to go away, but she went on.

"They made us bathe and comb our hair. They organized our days, one activity right after another, to tame our thoughts and worst inclinations. Work. Staying busy. That was what kept us from falling into despair."

She sat on the edge of the bed, took my hand, and made me look at her, her gaze as piercing as it had been that day at the cemetery, just after Julia-Berthe had died. "Ninette, you're all I have. I can't lose you. I need you. Especially now."

I turned my head away from her.

"We're going to Biarritz, Ninette," she said, smoothing my matted hair. "In Biarritz, everything's better."

She explained about the resort town on the Spanish border, the Côte Basque, where the gratin of Europe was waiting out the war. She'd just returned from a short *vacances* there with Boy.

"We're opening a new boutique there," she said. "You and I. A house of couture, like Monsieur Worth but without all the fussiness. The most expensive clothing, exquisitely made. Which means, of course, the wealthiest clientele."

Boy had given her the money to rent a place on the rue Gardères called the Villa Larralde, a distinguished, romantic-looking building that, she said, "even has two turrets." The rue Gardères was a busy, popular street, just across from a casino and on the way to the beach.

"In Biarritz, they still dine. They still dance. They play tennis and golf. They gamble. People still dress there. They still wear evening gowns to dinner. I want to make evening gowns, Ninette. I want them to wear what I make."

She said there were teas and galas. Opera. Orchestras playing on terraces. And wealthy women from Barcelona and Madrid, where society went on unimpeded by the war plaguing the rest of Europe.

"It's like going back in time. To before this horrible war. Back when everything was lovely."

There was a wistfulness in her voice, and through my own pain, I sensed that it was about more than the change in scenery. I wondered if the tension between her and Boy was back.

Then her voice turned urgent again. "You have to get up, Ninette," she said. "I need you. I need you to help me in Biarritz. You're the only one I trust. Chanel Modes is our legacy. It's for us, for all the people who said we wouldn't be anything, for the memory of Julia-Berthe, for André's future. Now please, please, you have to get up."

We departed for Biarritz the next week with a trunk of my things from the Parc Monceau. In the back of a cupboard, I left the music box, the Cartier bracelet, the monogrammed handkerchief that still smelled faintly of bergamot and lavender, other trinkets and reminders of Lucho. To see them rubbed me raw inside, each one like a small promise that had been broken.

There were the beautiful dahlias he'd given me, once so fresh and colorful, now pressed in the pages of a book, brown, dry, and crumbling. And the portrait I'd commissioned, still in its wrapping. It had been delivered to the Parc Monceau the day after Lucho left.

My cough lingered, but in the warmth of Biarritz, it eventually went away. The ocean placated me, drowning out my frantic thoughts. Men might kill each other a hundred times over, yet the tide would still come in. The tide would still go out.

*Breathe*, I said to myself and to Lucho as if he could hear me. *Don't forget to breathe.*

I threw myself into opening the new boutique. Interviewing seamstresses, buying furniture, mirrors, chandeliers, making arrangements with suppliers, greeting customers, overseeing fittings, setting up the books. When a familiar face with auburn hair came to interview, I hired her on the spot. It was Elise, the redhead from the Pensionnat we called poil de carrotte. She was all grown up and, as Gabrielle would say, "presentable." She'd worked at the House of Grampayre in Moulins and at another maison in Vichy. I trusted her almost like a sister.

The Biarritz boutique was an instant success. We were overwhelmed with orders, working night and day, hiring seamstresses until we had over three hundred employees between the three boutiques. Everything Gabrielle made, people wanted. Gowns for evening, for formal dinners and balls. Three-quarter-length coats of jersey embroidered with metallic gold and silver threads. Russian blouse coats with loose sleeves, fastened with leather belts. She added fur trim and collars. In wartime, chinchilla from South America and sable from Russia were in short supply, so she used common rabbit without a second thought and charged an exorbitant price. That was always her trick. Taking the not-precious and making it precious. Like us.

There was so much to worry about I didn't have time to dwell on the war. Making sure we had enough supplies. Fulfilling orders. Difficult customers, the prima donnas, the complainers, the eternally indecisive. And then there was Gabrielle. A perfectionist. There could be no mistakes. I slept at night from exhaustion.

In the evenings, I went to the casino with Arturo, who had come to Biarritz to give dancing lessons. He hadn't heard from Lucho. No one in the family had. Whenever he said my name, "Antonieta," a charge thrummed through me, warm then cold.

Arturo still glittered. He still moved with swagger, a carnation in his buttonhole, a smile, still took his gramophone wherever he went. But he was suffering too. In Paris he'd fallen in love with a violin player "with the most supple hands, Antonieta. If only you could hear him play." The violinist had been mobilized just like everyone else. He too was at the front.

At the Biarritz casinos, Arturo taught me how to gamble, to play baccarat.

"When you get the cards, Antonieta, you have to blow on them right away to ward off bad luck."

To occupy our minds, we danced and then smoked cigarettes in long white holders on the balcony. I wore Gabrielle's couture evening gowns, and to those around me, I looked sophisticated. There was no sign of the naive plouc from the provinces.

But on the inside, I was still hollow.

I worked hard to keep busy. It was the only way not to notice the emptiness, not to hear Lucho in my head. *Horses starving, swallowed up in the mud, blown up by shells.* I traveled from boutique to boutique, overseeing everything, posting notices in *Le Figaro* for clients so they would know where I was and could make appointments. There were those who preferred dealing only with me.

```
MLLE ANTOINETTE CHANEL Á PARIS.
MLLE ANTOINETTE CHANEL Á DEAUVILLE.
MLLE ANTOINETTE CHANEL Á BIARRITZ.
```

As the months went on and the days I'd been with Lucho drifted farther away, I could finally admit to myself that the notices were meant for him. I couldn't write to him. I didn't know where he was. I refused to chase after him as my mother had with Albert.

All I had to give was a line in small black type on the back page of a newspaper, hoping that maybe one of the millions of copies, distributed to far-flung places around the globe, might find its way into his hands.

By the end of 1915, Lucho had been gone for over six months. When I'd first arrived in Biarritz, the pain of missing him was so strong it would ricochet through me out of the blue, almost doubling me over. But loss was cruel. The pain had lessened into an ache, the sharpness fading until I wasn't sure if he was real or a figure in a dream. And that to me was worse.

# SIXTY-TWO

THE BIARRITZ BOUTIQUE WAS EVEN MORE SUCCESSFUL THAN Deauville. On a short trip to Paris, after everyone had left the rue Cambon boutique for the evening, I handed a piece of paper to Gabrielle. It was a check, payable to Arthur Capel.

"This is it?" she said, not glancing up from the paper in her hands.

"This is it."

"After this, I don't owe him anymore?"

"Not a single centime." I expected her face to light up. I expected a smile, some joyous outcry, a call for celebration. Perhaps even a thank-you. *Ninette, I couldn't have done this without you.* Instead, she was quiet, pensive.

"Do you know what this means?" she said.

"That you're free?"

For a moment she seemed lost, as if the realization was still dawning on her. Then she lifted her head and looked me right in the eye with a sadness I hadn't foreseen. "That I don't need him anymore."

# SIXTY-THREE

BOY HAD GIVEN HER WINGS. BUT SHE WASN'T READY TO USE them.

When Boy was in Paris, she'd hurry back from her regular visits to Biarritz, leaving her evening gowns and other designs unfinished, afraid she'd miss him. She even bought a Rolls Royce and hired a chauffeur. "This way, it's faster to get from one place to the next. I'm not always waiting on a train."

Meanwhile, Gabrielle's daytime jersey suit had taken off, clients buying them in several colors at a time, especially after the actress Geneviève Vix was spotted at the Hôtel de Paris in a blue jersey sports coat. We'd celebrated in May and again in July when *Les Élégances Parisiennes* featured her jersey seaside suits in drawings sketched by Celestine. Gabrielle was wealthy, independent. The American magazine *Women's Wear Daily* wrote that "Chanel has become the craze and jersey the rage," and still her happiness turned on Boy. She was afraid of something, but I didn't know what. I could tell by the jittery way she moved about, smoking cigarette after cigarette. Her temper was short with the seamstresses, and she had no tolerance for the mannequins who complained about their wages.

"They're pretty girls," she said with an annoyed wave of her hand. "They can find a man to take care of them."

I worried for Gabrielle. She always held her troubles so close.

One weekend, on a visit from Paris, Gabrielle took André and his little dog Bruno to the beach, and Adrienne stayed back to fill me in. Gabrielle had looked sallow, tired.

"When Boy comes back from wherever he is, the world stops," Adrienne said. "They don't leave their apartment for days. Then he's off again, and after that she's either shouting at someone or barely speaks."

"Yes," I said. "She's that way here too. She'll snap at one of our best seamstresses and make her cry. Then I have to smooth everything over. We can't afford to lose a good seamstress, especially since Gabrielle won't agree to pay them more."

"It's just that Boy's away now more than before," Adrienne said. "He's always in England. Clemenceau's given him some kind of diplomatic post, something about forming alliances. The rumor is he's been spending a lot of time in aristocratic circles."

"In England, almost everyone's an aristocrat, aren't they?"

"Not Boy," she'd said, unsmiling.

An alarm went off inside me. "What do you mean?"

"I mean that he might *like to be*," Adrienne said, concern in her voice. "An aristocrat, that is. I'm afraid Boy's looking to make a strategic marriage."

I put a hand to my chest in disbelief. "Did Gabrielle tell you that?"

"No, not in so many words."

"But he would never do that," I said. Not Boy. Boy, who was so open-minded. Boy, the socialist, the humanist who believed in equality for all, who didn't care about class, who treated André as if he were his own, who gave Gabrielle a start because he thought women should have a chance too, because he saw something in her, a talent to nurture. All this time, I still assumed he'd marry Gabrielle in the end. I'd thought he was different.

No. I wouldn't believe it. Boy had his liaisons. Gabrielle knew about them. Sometimes, she said, they discussed them. To me, she'd shrug and act as if it didn't matter. "He always comes back to me." And he did.

"What about you, Ninette? Have you heard from dear Lucho?" Adrienne asked.

A lump gathered in my throat.

"Gabrielle hopes you'll find someone here. She says Biarritz is full of wealthy Spaniards and exiled Russian aristocrats. She says you'd have your pick if you wanted."

I shook my head. On the other side of France, good men like Lucho were giving their lives while here, they still dressed in tails and top hats, doing nothing except waiting, with the women, for the war to end. I still wanted only him.

I couldn't stay in one place, or all that I didn't want to think about would slowly descend upon me. I had a new strange sympathy for my father and grandparents. There was comfort in moving about. An illusion of progress. It crowded your head with logistics so your thoughts couldn't roam.

Gabrielle's name had spread to the south of France, and now I was traveling there too, in demand by la crème of society for private fittings at their villas, customers who preferred me over her because she told some of them they were too fat for her clothing and needed to lose weight, whereas I complimented them as I always had, highlighting their best qualities.

MLLE ANTOINETTE CHANEL Á MONTE CARLO.
MLLE ANTOINETTE CHANEL Á ROYAL-CANADEL-SUR-MER.
MLLE ANTOINETTE CHANEL Á SAN SALVADOUR.

I traveled first class. I stayed in the nicest hotels. Men would look at me in lobbies and restaurants, but I didn't return their gaze. The thought of being with another man made me feel like I could crack apart, splinter into a thousand tiny pieces.

I marked time by collections, cuts and trims, embroideries and sashes, the gradual lowering of waists and raising of hemlines. I counted battles and death. Verdun. The Somme. As the endless savagery continued, I turned twenty-nine. I'd always thought that by twenty-nine, all lessons would be learned, the future sure, struggles over, demons vanquished. Instead, everything seemed all the more uncertain.

Over a year now, and not a word. But if Lucho were dead, he would be on a list somewhere, someone would have seen his name. Maurice. Boy. Arturo. His family. That's what I told myself, putting all images of war, of bodies lying where they fell, out of my mind.

There was a no-man's-land in western France, and there was a no-man's-land in my head, a place I couldn't go.

# SIXTY-FOUR

THE YEAR 1917 WAS A BAD ONE, EVEN THOUGH IN APRIL, THE Americans joined the war. Everyone thought it would be over soon now, but the Americans had to get here. They were green. They had to train. Somehow it all got worse first, the Germans pushing with everything they had before the Americans could make a difference.

From Biarritz, I followed it all in the newspapers. In Russia, there was a revolution. In France, on the front, mutinies. In London and Paris, strikes. Food was rationed, bread and sugar cards handed out. The government ordered restaurants to limit their menus to two dishes. In Belgium, the battle of Passchendaele raged, one of the bloodiest yet. Everyone was in mourning. In Vichy, Adrienne buried Mémère and Pépère, who had died within a few months of each other. Gabrielle and I didn't go. We still blamed them for Julia-Berthe's death.

André came to Biarritz for his school breaks, living with me there because it was safer than Paris, his boyish energy invigorating me. We'd go on excursions to nearby ruins, and he'd ask all kinds of questions I couldn't answer. When I asked if he'd teach me English, he took his job very seriously, coming up with lesson plans, trying not to laugh at my mispronunciations. Already he was almost thirteen, growing so fast.

Meanwhile, the seasons went by, and with them more collections. Jersey suits were still all the rage, some plain, some embroidered. Patch pockets. Slim silhouettes. Clean-lined chemise-style dresses, dresses with turn-back cuffs, but underneath, open-neck blouses, V-necks, deep sailor collars. There were cape coats trimmed in economical fur, squirrel and skunk, Gabrielle's version of the old payante pèlerines. Anything to keep warm.

It wasn't just the fashions that were changing. Gabrielle still traveled to Biarritz every couple of weeks to work on her couture designs, but when she showed up that next January, I gasped when I saw her. "Your hair!" It was cut to her ears. She looked like a schoolboy.

She tipped her head. "Do you like it?"

"But...why?"

"I got tired of it. Too much trouble. I feel so light now. Like I can move."

The cloud in her eyes didn't match her carefree tone. Such a great, dramatic change. It seemed like a sign, a statement of something.

Finally, she told me. "Boy's engaged."

# SIXTY-FIVE

BOY'S FIANCÉE WAS AN ENGLISHWOMAN. HE'D BEEN WITH
Gabrielle eight years. He'd known this woman a few months.
But she was the daughter of a lord.

"Are you sure he'll go through with it?" I'd asked Gabrielle.
"Surely he won't."

Her eyes were moist, but she didn't cry. "He's planning for
after the war. He has political aspirations. He's already made a
fortune with ships and coal. Boy has his eye on a different kind
of power now."

She said that in addition to everything else, he'd just finished
a book called *Reflections on Victory*, in which he proposed theo-
ries for how to achieve world peace. And thanks to his continuing friendship with Clemenceau, he'd been appointed to various
prestigious war commissions and councils. He'd become an active participant in Anglo-French diplomacy.

"You can't be a politician without a wife," Gabrielle said. "If
you're unmarried, people will suspect there's something wrong
with you. You need a wife with pedigree, a wife who won't

embarrass you because she sells clothes, because she's the daughter of a peddler."

"But he loves you," I said. "He couldn't ever love anyone else as much as he loves you."

"Love has nothing to do with it," she said, and then she laughed, a dry, bitter laugh. "It's funny. One of the qualities I've always loved best about Boy is his ambition."

Gabrielle was Something Better, but she still wasn't good enough.

Once again, she became the defiant little girl, angry at everyone, taut with frustration, unable to understand how her father could betray her. Now, it was Boy betraying her. Genuine or not, to the world, he was declaring his love for someone else.

Even I felt betrayed. He'd become like a brother to me. To André, he was like a father.

I hurt for Gabrielle, but a new feeling crept in too, a hardness. Men left. That was what they did. Fathers. Lovers. Men you trusted. Men you gave your whole heart to. They told you they loved you, and then for one reason or another they left. In love and war, the only guarantee was heartache.

I went about Biarritz in a daze. Only the sight of American and Canadian soldiers drew my attention. They came to the seaside on leave in groups of two or three and swam in the ocean, far out into the waves. They jumped off the tallest cliffs. There was an openness about them, an exuberance, an unawareness I wished I could imitate. They were confident, fearless.

It had been a few days since Gabrielle had gone back to Paris when I pulled out a pair of our sharpest shears and handed them to Elise.

I wanted to know what it was like to feel light, to feel like I could move.

The news from Paris grew worse. The stalemate had ended but not in our favor. The Germans were again gaining ground closer and closer to the city. German aeroplanes once again terrorized from overhead, but this was 1918, and now they were faster. They carried more bombs. They were better at destruction.

The horrors only continued for the men at the front. For the horses.

The Germans attacked civilians now too. They fired on the city from long-range guns stationed one hundred twenty kilometers away, at least twenty shells per day, shells that seemed to come out of nowhere, destroying buildings, roads, and parks, murdering innocent Parisians.

Cowards, Lucho had called them long ago, and he was right. In March, on Good Friday, a shell came down on Saint-Gervais-et-Saint-Protais during Mass. Over ninety people were killed as they prayed.

I sent telegrams to Gabrielle and Adrienne, pleading with them to leave Paris and seek shelter in Biarritz, but they refused. Adrienne still insisted on being near the front in case anything should happen to Maurice. And Gabrielle wanted to be close to Boy. He wasn't married, not yet, and still came to her on his leaves.

Ignoring the bombs from the sky, the shelling, the assault all around, Gabrielle went on as she always had. For the new season, she lined her jersey coats with patterned foulard to match the dress or blouse that went underneath. Her mind was focused on pairs, matching sets, and in the midst of the storm, she turned bombs into profits. The female guests at the Ritz needed to be presentable in the air raid shelters. In the middle of the night when the sirens went off, there was no time to properly dress. So she made outfits that could be slept in or thrown on at the last minute from a supply of men's red jersey pajamas she'd found, loose-fitting tops and bottoms, expertly tailored. Everyone wanted them.

"It's brilliant, Coco," I imagined Boy saying with an approving smile. "You've brought fashion to the bomb shelters."

# SIXTY-SIX

SPRING TURNED TO SUMMER AND THE NEWSPAPER BOYS'
voices carried a different tune as they called out the latest head-
lines. It was the sound of victory, one after another: Belleau
Wood. The Marne. The Battle of Amiens.

The Americans had finally arrived at the front in full force,
trained fighters who weren't exhausted from years of war, and
with the British and the French, they were pushing the Germans back at last. There was hope again. At first in whispers,
then louder and louder. The war would be over soon.

It was time to move back to Paris. Elise was capable of directing the Biarritz boutique on her own, and I wanted to be in
the city when the war ended. I wanted to be there to celebrate.

And Lucho. Maybe he'd finally come back.

It had been a year since I'd been to Paris, and the city had
changed. Windows were broken or boarded up from the shelling.
Those still intact had pieces of paper taped over them to prevent
shattering, some in whimsical patterns and designs. Sandbags

were layered around monuments, not in heaps but artfully, almost tenderly, reminding me how much Parisians cared about their city. In some cases, there were piles of rubble where entire buildings once stood. But most shocking was the giant shell crater in the Tuileries where Lucho and I used to walk. And the beautiful chestnut trees... In the cold of winter, with the shortage of coal, they'd been cut down in places for firewood, though still with a sense for aesthetics, gaps here and there, not total desecration.

I'd missed Paris.

And Gabrielle, who worked with a fever pitch. "The war is going to end, Ninette, and people are going to want new clothes. They're going to need sports clothes and day clothes and eveningwear. We have to be ready."

We needed more space and put a deposit on a whole building down the street at number 31, without consulting Boy. It was our money now. Because of the war, new licenses were available. Gabrielle could bring her couture creations from Biarritz to Paris. We could finally sell luxury fashion, not just knitwear, in Paris, the most expensive garments, sewn by hand, made to order for private clients. The orphan who was told she'd be lucky to be a seamstress would be at the helm of a house of haute couture in the fashion capital of the world.

"There's so much to do," she was always saying, never resting for a minute, as if to drive away what was coming.

In August, the announcement was in *Le Gaulois*.

Boy had married the Honorable Diana Wyndham.

Gabrielle had known the day was nearing, but still it was a shock. Boy had wavered back and forth, she said, but in the end, he went through with it. She'd moved out of the apartment on the

Avenue Gabriel weeks before. Her new friend, the exotic salonnière Misia Sert, a woman Adrienne considered pushy, helped
her find an apartment with a view of the Seine and the Trocadéro, along with a butler and a maid and a room for André for
when he was home from school.

Gabrielle rearranged her Coromandel smoke screens, her crys-
tals and good luck charms, her leather-bound books, and her
soft beige furniture to fill the new space. But even among her
old things she seemed lost, out of place.

One Sunday afternoon, I brought her an omelet from her
favorite brasserie. "You should eat," I said to her back, but she
just shrugged, not facing me.

She sat on a divan in the drawing room, staring out the window at the river curving below, the sun reflecting off the barges
as they quietly slipped by. The terriers Boy had given her not
long before, Pita and Poppée, were curled up at her feet.

"There was a time I thought I'd actually be Mrs. Arthur
Capel," she admitted. "Then I convinced myself he wouldn't
marry anyone at all. Our love was different. We were together
because we chose to be together and that was better than marriage, more sacred." She turned to me, tears running down her
face, silent tears. "Ninette," she said. "I don't know who I am
anymore."

Her words surprised me. I knew exactly who she was.

"Look at you," I said, sitting next to her, taking her hands in
mine. "Can't you see? The whole world knows who you are.
You're not the poor little orpheline anymore."

Did Boy miss the young Gabrielle who looked up to him?
Who hung on his every word? Who needed to be taken care
of? She'd told me what he'd said when she'd given him the final
check, paying him back. *I thought I'd given you a plaything. Instead, I gave you freedom.* His tone, she'd said, had been wistful.

Maybe that was what he saw in the former Miss Wyndham. Someone bound by tradition and the rules of society who couldn't easily fly away.

But we could. There were no rules holding us back. Suddenly, I had the urge to shake her, to shake myself. A feeling of overwhelming pride came over me. The war against Germany was still going on, but our war was over, the one she and I had been fighting since the day we were born, since the nuns had decreed I would be lucky to marry a plowman, that she'd be lucky to make a decent living as a seamstress. We'd won. We'd been so busy, we hadn't had the time to notice. We'd become who we wanted to be. Not who the world told us we were supposed to be.

Think of the élégantes, I told her, the ladies of the monde and the gratin, the actresses and demimondaines who sought her out and wore her clothes and even cut their hair like her. No one wanted to look like Paul Poiret or Madame Vionnet or Charles Worth. They all wanted to look like Gabrielle. She was her own best creation.

"Men can come and go, Gabrielle. Boy can marry and marry again. But you, you're Coco Chanel and that will never change."

By the time I was done talking, she'd stopped crying. Her jaw was set.

"Thank you," she said. "I don't think I've ever said that to you. Thank you, Ninette. I would never be here, none of this would ever have happened, without you."

We were sisters. This was how we cared for each other.

# SIXTY-SEVEN

IN NOVEMBER, THE GERMANS SURRENDERED. THE KAISER ABdicated. The guns, at last, were silent. The war with Germany was over.

In Paris, the boulevards teemed with people just as they had when the mobilization was announced four years earlier. But instead of patriotic resolve, the mood was jubilant. Soldiers couldn't take two steps without being kissed by the French girls mobbing them. I watched from a distance. The last time the world had taken to the streets, I'd been with Lucho.

For days, as the parades and festivities continued, I searched the crowds. Every time I saw a group of soldiers, every time a soldier walked past, every time a door opened and a man came through...

He was nowhere and everywhere. Leaving the Ritz. On a bench in the Tuileries. Walking along the Seine. On a terrace at the Café de la Paix, his face concealed behind the latest issue of *Le Figaro*. Only it wasn't his face. It was never his face. I tried to wrap the memory of him in brown paper, tie it up with twine, hide it in the back of the cupboard at the Parc Monceau with everything else. But I couldn't.

In the quiet of the apartment, Adrienne and Maurice made up for lost time, spending every moment together. Meanwhile, I went out every night. I went out to forget Lucho. I went out to find Lucho. Maybe he was there at the Café des Ambassadeurs or Maxim's or La Rotonde in Montparnasse. In every restaurant, bar, and café, people were drinking champagne, dancing, taking lovers. Ragtime that was so popular before the war had given way to something called jazz.

Soldiers took over the city. There were so few Frenchmen, a generation lost in the trenches, but Americans and Canadians, with their forthright joie de vivre, were everywhere, celebrating the end of the war with abandon. Evidently, they had nothing else to do. It was impossible to send them home all at once. There were so many of them and not enough ships. They had to leave in shifts.

Gabrielle went out too. She had friends to help her heal, Misia Sert and an entourage of others. Paul Iribe, the illustrator. Eduardo Martinez de Hoz, a wealthy South American.

One evening, at a dance at the Hotel Majestic on the Avenue Kléber, Gabrielle whispered in my ear. "This is where the well-to-do British officers stay." She didn't say it outright, but I knew what she was thinking. Lucho had been killed in the war. It was time to move on.

I didn't want to believe Lucho wasn't coming back. But I needed to believe it. It was the only way to keep going.

I was an expert dancer now, thanks to Arturo and our days in Biarritz, and I danced and danced with American and British soldiers. *You can still find someone*, Lucho had said so long ago. *Do it for me.* So I did. I forced myself to dance with whoever asked, for him. I looked in their faces, hoping a light inside me would ignite, but so far it'd been just embers.

Then I noticed a man watching me from a distance, interest on his face that made a spark run through me, a sensation I'd almost forgotten. *Handsome*, that was my first thought. Then, *debonair*. The crowd shifted, and I saw the wings on his uniform. An aviator. So that was why the ladies had clustered around him. But still he was looking at me.

Another dance and then another, the one-step, le fox, the quick-step. No one waltzed anymore. The tango, too, was out of fashion. I tried to be discreet with my gaze, wanting a better view. Blond, wavy hair. Tall. Broad shoulders. My eyes met his whenever I was spun in his direction, and I felt flush as I hadn't in years.

The next time I looked for him he was gone, and the flutter in my heart stilled. My feet suddenly felt filled with sand.

Then a hand tapped the shoulder of my dance partner, and the aviator cut in. He was even more handsome up close, but younger than I'd expected. A smooth, precise dancer. The bearing of a prince.

He smiled. "What's your name, mademoiselle?" he said in very good French. His eyes were soft, like velvet.

"Antoinette," I said.

"Antoinette," he repeated, his eyes still on mine, so calm, so gently self-assured. And then, with that smile again: "I'm going to marry you, Antoinette."

# SIXTY-EIGHT

HIS NAME WAS OSCAR. OSCAR FLEMING. A STRONG NAME. A gallant name. The syllables rolled off my tongue. Unnecessarily, he apologized for his dancing. "Years of lessons at the country club," he said. I had no idea what that meant, but it seemed important.

We went out on a terrace where it was quiet and we could talk. He put his aviator's jacket over my shoulders to keep me warm. I shivered, but not from the cold.

There was an underlying ease about him, a confidence that must have come from having lived knowing he could die the next day. He was so open, so straightforward. And romantic. Every day, he sent the most beautiful bouquets to the boutique. In the evenings, he took me to dine at the most expensive restaurants, to dance at the nicest hotels. He was an aviator and an officer, so we were always given the best tables. We stayed out late, often until sunrise.

"Windsor," I repeated when he told me the name of the city he was from in Canada. It sounded so genteel.

"Like the city in England," he said. "The home of Windsor Castle."

"Is there a castle in your Windsor?" I asked.

"There will be. How do you like your castles, Queen Antoinette? With or without a moat?"

Canada. I'd never thought about it before. He said there were mineral springs near Windsor where people went to take the cure. There was a beach on a lake as well as a hippodrome. It was Vichy, Biarritz, and Deauville all wrapped into one, though when I said that out loud, he laughed. "It will be," he said, "once you're there."

Detroit was across the river, the birthplace of the automobile just a ferry ride away. "People call it the Paris of the Midwest," he said.

His father was a barrister, a leader in Windsor, a former mayor who'd presided over the town when it was given city status by Queen Victoria. Oscar, one of eleven children, was to follow in his footsteps. He had attended the Royal Military College in Ontario, trained to be a pilot with the Royal Flying Corps. Once back in Canada, he'd go to Osgoode Hall to study law. Clearly, the Fleming family was one of means and privilege.

And he wanted to marry me.

When he asked about my past, I wavered. The war was over. It was a time of celebration, not a time to recall sad stories from long ago. I blurted out the version of our lives Gabrielle had made up, that we were raised by aunts in the countryside. I didn't want to disappoint him. The war years had been lonely, and I didn't want to run him off. He might not understand. He wasn't damaged like me. Like Lucho. And that was what attracted me to him. Lucho and I saw the shadows. Oscar saw the light.

When he told me he was only twenty-one, I nearly fainted.

I'd had no idea he was that young. I was ten years older. "But how can that be?" I said. "You seem so sensible. So urbane."

"War is the best cure for youth and foolishness," he said. "I'm officially ageless." He took my hand. "Darling Antoinette, don't judge me by the year of my birth, a fact over which I had no control. Judge me by the adoration in my eyes."

I couldn't help but laugh. "As long as you don't judge me by the year of *my* birth," I said.

He gave my hand a squeeze and looked at me with the most earnest expression. "I judge you to be absolutely perfect."

He came by the boutique often. Gabrielle said he was dashing. Adrienne said he was soigné. "An aviator, Ninette," she said. "And so handsome. Those eyes!"

In Paris, there were marriage ceremonies practically every hour, every day, a steady stream of newlyweds coming out of the doors of the registry offices.

By March, just one month later, we were engaged.

"But…Canada?" Gabrielle removed the scissors that hung on a ribbon around her neck. "It's so far away."

"Oscar's going to be my husband. It's his home." I turned the sign on the front door from ouvert to fermé. I didn't want to have this conversation, but I couldn't avoid it forever.

"That doesn't mean he has to go back there," she said. "He can work for Chanel Modes. He's presentable. I'll find something for him to do."

I looked at her, and in that moment, I didn't see what she'd become, but who she'd been. Who *we'd* been. Little girls in peasant rags who for so long had only each other.

I pushed away any apprehension. We were older now. Separation was a natural progression. Sisters went off with lovers, husbands, but the bond was still there. It was just different. And Chanel Modes was established as a couture house, settled in finally at 31 rue Cambon with more room, more glamour, more glitz. She had employees she could trust, Angèle, Elise, and others. Thanks to Misia, she had a large group of friends. And she still saw Boy. Despite his marriage, he spent a great deal of time with her. He hadn't been able to give her up. She was Coco Chanel. Famous. Admired. Sought after. She didn't need me in the same way that she used to.

"In Canada, he'll be studying to become a barrister." I liked saying that word. It sounded noble. "Meanwhile, I've been thinking. Canada is the perfect place for a new boutique. There are mineral springs near Windsor. And a hippodrome. And Detroit, where all the automobiles are made so everyone is rich, right across the river. Oscar says people call it the Paris of the Midwest. Once I get settled, I can find the perfect location for our first North American boutique!"

The doubt on her face when I first started talking had faded, and the more we discussed it, the more she warmed to the idea. Her clothing had been praised by American magazines like *Women's Wear Daily* and *Harper's Bazaar*. Of course there would be a market there for Chanel Modes. Americans were always copying French styles.

"And Canada's not really that far away," I said. "Just three days by ocean liner. I'll come back to Paris at least twice a year. And you and Adrienne will come visit me. We'll go to New York City. André can visit too on school breaks. Maybe one day he'll even attend the Royal Military College like Oscar."

"But, Ninette," Gabrielle said, her expression now serious. "It's such a big change. Are you sure this is what you want? You haven't known Oscar very long."

Yes, Canada would be a big change. But that was part of the appeal. I didn't care about prestige, about who Oscar's family was and who he would be. All I cared about was that I loved him, and the war was over and it was time to live.

"I'm sure," I said. "I love him. This is what I want."

She sighed, then hugged me, so tight and so long I didn't think she'd let go. Finally, she did, stepping back to appraise me.

"What do you think, Ninette? Satin? Lace? We have to get started right away." She clapped her hands together and smiled her wide smile, her eyes lighting up. "We have a wedding gown to make!"

At Chanel Modes, in addition to a wedding gown, Gabrielle had the seamstresses working on my trousseau.

It was my turn to be fitted.

# SIXTY-NINE

OSCAR TRAVELED BETWEEN PARIS AND ENGLAND, STILL OFFI-
cially on duty with the RAF for a few more months. Soon I
would be Mrs. Oscar Fleming, the wife of the soon-to-be barrister son of one of Windsor's most prominent families. Oscar
said there would be teas, dances, at-homes, parties at country
clubs and boat clubs, trips to Detroit, tennis tournaments, a game
called bridge. His family had a yacht and a country house. How
strange to think that all I'd dreamed of when I was younger—a
place in society—was suddenly before me, and I didn't need it
anymore. Now, all I wanted was Oscar, a companion, a lover,
a husband.

"I'll teach you," Oscar said when I told him I didn't know
how to play bridge.

"But I do know to blow on the cards," I said, "to ward away
bad luck."

"Bad luck," he said with a smile. "There's been enough of

that." He kissed me on the cheek. "It's only good luck from here on out."

It was 1919, and in Paris, everyone was in love. Everyone was in love with love. Romance rippled the surface of the Seine. It rustled the leaves in the chestnut trees. It poured out of ballrooms and cabarets, the sounds of jazz, of a new kind of music and new way of living.

Women were ready to dress again, really dress, and Gabrielle's new collection was sophisticated, tunic-style gowns made of the finest materials, adorned with the most enchanting details, gold or black net, delicate embroidery, subtle beadwork in grapevine patterns, velvet capes trimmed with ostrich feathers. I imagined wearing them in Windsor to the country clubs, though I still wasn't sure what a country club was. All that really mattered to me now was that I would be on Oscar's arm, my brave, handsome aviator.

Gabrielle was herself again, the drama of Boy's marriage continuing to fade. She rented a villa in Saint Cloud, outside of the city, where they could be together more discreetly. "He's married to her," Gabrielle said of Diana Wyndham, "but he loves me." It wasn't the ideal situation, but she loved him back. She couldn't turn him away, not even out of pride, which she had so much of. "It's funny the things you never thought you could live with, and you do," she said.

I planned to bring one of everything in the collection to Windsor. How I loved saying that word. *Windsor.* As if I were the Queen of England herself! I was even taking one of the young seamstresses, Jeanne, along as a maid and to help me set up the new boutique. Every day, I practiced my English. I knew a little bit, in part thanks to Boy and to André, who still gave me lessons when he came back from school. *Windsor. Mrs. Oscar Fleming. How do you do? So pleased to meet you.*

It was all so exhilarating, everything moving so quickly.

But sometimes, especially when Oscar was on duty in England, doubts still crept in. Not about Oscar, but about all I was leaving behind: Gabrielle, Adrienne, André. Paris. Everything I'd ever known.

And of course there was still Lucho, lodged somewhere deep in my heart.

Oscar and I never spoke of past loves. He never asked why I didn't have anyone. It wasn't unusual. So many Frenchmen had been killed over the long years of war.

It was best not to dredge up old memories. That's what I told myself. There was no need to talk about what had been. Only of what would be. One night at the Majestic, as Oscar and I danced, I savored his warmth, the rhythmic movement of his body, his hand firmly over mine as he led me across the floor. It was an aviator's hand, strong, deft at levers and switches and complicated maneuvers. I let myself relax, my eyes seeing and not seeing other couples gliding about or sitting at tables all around. But as we drifted past the ballroom entrance, a face I recognized took form.

Lucho?

It was a split second, that was all, but in that moment, I was sure it was him.

I broke away, leaving Oscar in the middle of the dance floor, pushing my way through the crowd to the ballroom doors, my heart thumping, my pulse in my ears.

I looked everywhere, the lobby, the dining room, the parlor. Outside, my eyes searched beneath the streetlights, scanned the dark places, trying to make out a figure from the shadows. "Lucho," I called out, but there was no answer. My voice echoed down the Avenue Kléber.

Finally, I sat down on the steps, shaking. Maybe it wasn't him. Maybe it was my imagination. Maybe it was a ghost.

What was I doing? I loved Oscar.

I didn't know how long I'd been there when a warm arm wrapped itself around me.

"Antoinette," Oscar said, alarmed. "What happened? Did I do something?"

"No," I said, my mind racing, a queasy feeling in my stomach. "No. I…" I took a deep breath. "I thought I saw my sister, Julia-Berthe, the one who died. André's mother. I thought I saw her face in the crowd, but…it wasn't her."

I didn't want to lie. I'd never lied to Lucho, not once. But Oscar's expression was so innocent. How could I tell him the truth? He was so concerned, attempting to comfort me as I cried, not knowing who I was truly crying for, not knowing that as I sat there, I was sure the air carried a hint of bergamot and lavender.

The next day, I told Gabrielle.

"It wasn't Lucho. I know that now," I said.

Her voice was soft. "Ninette, he's not coming back."

The war had been over for nearly a year. He would have returned by now. So many men were still missing. So many lost in the mud of no-man's-land who might never be found.

An early death, the gypsy said. I would be married. It all made sense now.

My voice was a whisper. "Do you see why I have to go to Canada?"

"No," she said. "Not really. You can both stay here."

How could she not understand? In Canada, I wouldn't be looking for Lucho every time a man walked by or a door opened.

Oscar loved me, and I loved him. Lucho was the past. Oscar the future.

*When you find him, go. Do it for me.*

We were married on November 11, 1919, at the Registry Office of the eighth arrondissement. It was the anniversary of the Armistice. Celebration was in the air.

Boy Capel was a witness, Gabrielle and Adrienne my attendants. I wore the gown Gabrielle made for me, white satin with the loveliest white Chantilly lace, a fashionably low waistline of white satin ribbon. Oscar's older sister, Augusta, who he called Gussie, was there too, a charming girl who'd just arrived in Paris to study art.

"They're going to love you in Windsor," she said.

# A KEPT WIFE

## WINDSOR, ONTARIO
### 1919–1920

# SEVENTY

"WHEN DO WE GET TO WINDSOR?" I ASKED, LEANING IN TO OSCAR, my *husband* Oscar, as the train lurched to a stop. We'd been traveling for days, first from Biarritz, where we'd honeymooned for two weeks at the Villa Larralde, then to Liverpool, where we'd boarded the Empress of France, and crossed the Atlantic to Newfoundland, my first sight of Canada a cold, rocky, blustery expanse with winds stronger than Aubazine. There, we'd boarded a train for several hours, until out the window I spotted a collection of houses and buildings, brown and short and square.

"Sweetheart," Oscar said with a smile. He stood and put out a hand for me. "We're here. This is Windsor."

Oscar's parents' house was a solid, imposing home where we were all to live together. It was touching to watch his family welcome him.

I stood to the side as his siblings crowded around him.

"This," he then said, pulling me in, "is Antoinette. My wife."

I observed the wariness in Oscar's parents' eyes, a couple in their fifties, conservatively dressed, proper. How had I not realized? Oscar always said his brothers and sisters would adore me. But never his *parents*. There was never any mention of what they might think.

"How do you do?" Oscar's mother said formally, putting out a small gloved hand.

"So pleased to meet you," I said.

I felt out of place immediately, mistrusted, suspected. I was an older woman. A French woman. What a sight I must have been with my maid, seventeen trunks of clothes, and a crate containing a silver tea service with an exquisite Russian samovar Gabrielle had given us as a wedding present. My clothes that were so fashionable in Paris seemed frivolous here, ostentatious or worse.

Behind the parents, little eyes blinked, the sisters and brothers. What curiosity our arrival must have stirred up.

Our room was his old room, a boy's room, decorated with tennis trophies and school pennants and clippings of aeroplanes tacked to the walls. I spread out the lace coverlet Adrienne had gifted us for our wedding, stood back to enjoy the effect, and wanted to cry. Adrienne. Gabrielle. They were oceans away.

Beside me, Oscar reached out and lifted my chin toward him. "Darling, what's wrong?"

"Your parents don't like me, Oscar. Did you see how they looked at me?"

He tensed up. "Antoinette. It's not that they don't like you. It's not that at all. It's me. They need time to get used to the fact that I didn't marry a girl from Windsor. I'm not the same person I was before the war. They're going to have to understand that."

"You should have told me," I said firmly, shifting my head back so I wasn't looking at him anymore.

"I had hoped it wouldn't be like this. But they'll love you, Antoinette, I know they will. They won't be able to help themselves."

Adrienne and Maurice had been together for ten years, and his parents still wouldn't acknowledge her.

"And remember," he said. "We won't be here forever."

We were to move to Toronto in the fall. He was to start studying law at Osgoode Hall.

But that was months away.

Later, to prove that his parents didn't object to our marriage, Oscar showed me a clipping from a November issue of the local paper from when we were still in France, thinking it would smooth things over.

Mr. Oscar E. Fleming has just received a cable from his son, Lieut. Oscar E. Fleming, Jr., announcing his marriage on Tuesday last at Paris, France to Mlle. Antoinette Chanel... They are spending their honeymoon at the Chanel country chateau, Biarritz, France.

My wedding announcement.

He looked so pleased. I smiled, told him the announcement was lovely, and pushed away the eerie sensation I was reading about two strangers.

To win over Oscar's parents, I tried charm. I tried compliments. I was, after all, the preferred vendeuse of some of the most particular women in the world. But my English was lacking. Was I saying what I meant to say? Or something else entirely? It all felt so awkward. His parents were trying as best they could, but still Oscar's mother wouldn't meet my eyes. His father always looked skeptical, a deep furrow at his brow, whenever we were in the same room or passed in the hall.

The wedding announcement had mentioned "the Chanel country château," which really meant the Villa Larralde, the building that housed the Biarritz boutique. Had his parents intentionally obscured our whereabouts because they disapproved that I was a businesswoman? Had Oscar told them of my plan to open a boutique in Windsor? I wondered if they considered that inappropriate for a married woman.

Soon, I understood their concern, especially after meeting Oscar's friends, their wives and girlfriends during the at-homes Oscar had promised. There, I was a specimen, a curiosity in the Mother Abbess's cabinet, a butterfly pinned to a board of velvet. I smoked cigarettes. I drank. I liked to dance. I dressed like no one else. I was "showy," not to mention a decade older.

And there was the fact that Windsor, as Oscar explained, had started out as a French colony until the British took over. There were two rival factions in town. The Anglo-Protestants, like his family, and the French-Catholics, like me.

I was turning out to be the family scandal.

But none of it mattered when a cable came a few days later, just before Christmas, from Paris. From Adrienne.

CHÉRIE NINETTE. THE WORST HAS HAPPENED. BOY CAPEL HAS BEEN KILLED IN AN AUTOMOBILE ACCIDENT. OUR DEAR BOY IS GONE. POOR GABRIELLE. SHE'S DEVASTATED.

# SEVENTY-ONE

"WE HAVE TO GO BACK," I SAID TO OSCAR WHEN WE WERE alone in our room. I was frantic, too shocked to cry. "I need to be with Gabrielle."

He took my hand and sat me on the bed, trying to calm me. "You have to think logically, Antoinette."

"Logic? This is no time for logic."

"But it's impossible," he said. "The funeral would be over before we could get there."

"It doesn't matter. Gabrielle needs me. I have to see her."

He hesitated. "What would I tell my parents?"

"What do you mean?"

His voice was low. "I can't tell them that we need to rush back to Paris because your sister's lover has been killed, a married man."

His reaction appalled me. "Oscar. I have to go to her. What does it matter what your parents think? Boy is dead."

His face was tight as he admitted the terrible truth. His father controlled everything. He was generous with his children, but only if they did what he wanted. It had been his father's money Oscar had spent in Paris, unlimited funds showered on him as a reward for his military service.

Oscar had no money of his own.

He couldn't afford the passage back.

He was indebted to his father.

"You lied to me," I said, standing up, every part of me trembling with anger.

"I didn't know. I thought I'd earned my freedom. In Paris, that's how Father made it seem. Now, France and England are free, but I'm not."

He was frustrated. Embarrassed. Oscar's father didn't view him as the man he had become, but the son he was supposed to be. Soon, he promised, it would be different. It wouldn't always be this way.

He tried to pacify me, but I was too angry with him, too angry with myself. I wasn't just a *fool for love*. I was a fool. *Tricked by a man*, the voices whispered in my head. *Like your mother.*

In Paris, with the commission I'd earned since the day I'd signed the ledger book on the Boulevard Malesherbes nine years before, I took care of myself. I hadn't married Oscar for money, but he'd led me to believe he had it. Money meant freedom.

I'd trusted Oscar, trusted him enough to move all the way to Canada, to leave Gabrielle behind, and now I was so far away when my sister needed me the most.

It was agony. I sent cables offering sympathy, expressing how much I wanted to be there, to give André my love, poor André who'd lost a father figure, but she didn't answer. I wrote letters explaining Oscar's situation, begging her to send money for passage back. I could be with her as long as she needed, then I'd come back to Oscar. Oscar, I wrote, would have to understand.

Still she didn't reply.

I wrote to Adrienne, asking about Gabrielle.

*She's despondent*, Adrienne wrote. *Poor Gabrielle. She won't talk to anyone. Except that awful Misia Sert. The best thing to do is wait. She needs time, Ninette.*

I couldn't bring myself to tell Adrienne I needed money for passage back. With Gabrielle, it'd be her own money, but Adrienne would have to ask Maurice. I couldn't put Maurice in such an awkward position, and as desperate as I was, I couldn't do that to Oscar no matter how upset I was with him. Another man paying for me, especially a man who was not a relative, would eviscerate any pride he had left.

I had one option left. The seventeen trunks of clothes.

While Oscar worked as a clerk at his father's law office, Jeanne and I visited the department stores and dress shops in Windsor and Detroit. We showed them the pieces from Gabrielle's collection, the most exquisite gowns with lace and embroidery, pointing out all the fine detail and handiwork. We showed them day clothes, sports clothes. The stores could carry the collection while I found a spot for a boutique.

But the reaction everywhere was the same.

"Women here will never wear clothes like that."

Detroit, it turned out, was nothing like Paris.

Two months after Boy's death, a letter finally came from Gabrielle.

*Your duty is to Oscar, Ninette. Returning to Paris won't help me. Nothing you or anyone can do or say will make me better. I've lost Boy. I've lost everything.*

# SEVENTY-TWO

A STRING OF ROADHOUSES ALL ALONG THE WINDSOR SIDE OF the Detroit River came alive at night. The Island View Inn. The Chappell House. The Rendezvous. The Edgewater Thomas Inn.

Speakeasies. That's what Oscar called them. Places with secret passages. Hidden wine cellars. Lookouts and spotters and buzzers to warn if the police were on their way. In a matter of minutes, green felt-covered gambling tables were folded up, drinks poured out, bottles hidden away.

In the States, there was a new law called Prohibition. In Ontario, a Temperance Act. But unlike in the US, Canadians were allowed to manufacture alcohol. They were allowed to export it, just not drink it. It made no sense at all.

That spring and summer, the speakeasies were our respite from the claustrophobia of living with Oscar's parents, from the bleakness of our current situation and the tension between us. We danced to Dixieland jazz, we drank whiskey and bourbon, played roulette, blackjack, poker, my repertoire of casino games

expanding. And the people. Brash and vulgar and strangely fascinating. Automobile magnates came over from Detroit, the park-
ing lots full of roadsters and sedans that in winter drove across
the frozen river. The Fords. The Fishers. The Dodges. Bigwigs,
people called them. They were the nouveau riche but, despite
their wealth, didn't know how to dress, didn't understand elegance and taste. When it was warm enough, their expensive
boats and yachts lined the docks. Mixed in with the crowd were
always shady characters I avoided, men who flashed revolvers in
their waistbands. Others, distillery owners, flashed cash.

Oscar and I stayed out almost until dawn. What else could
we do? Stay home and listen to the radio with his parents, his
mother ignoring me, his father scowling? We were adults. Oscar
had fought in a war with the RAF. I was a grown woman used
to directing a business, to being occupied all the time.

Poor Oscar. Half of his day was devoted to making his father
happy and the other half to appeasing me. He was exhausted,
his handsome face clouded with strain. *It won't always be like
this*, he kept saying, his velvet eyes troubled. Every day, I slept
past noon, another habit that did nothing to endear me to his
mother. Only the lure of the speakeasy could get me out of bed.

I didn't care. In Paris, my sister's world had fallen apart, and
I wasn't there.

On the dance floor, Oscar and I could close our eyes, nothing but music in our heads. We could sway in each other's arms.
For a few hours every night, we were back in Paris, at the end
of the war, remembering why we'd fallen in love.

# SEVENTY-THREE

IN LATE AUGUST, ALREADY THERE WAS A HINT OF A CHILL IN the air, a precursor to the coming change in seasons.

Soon Oscar and I would move to Toronto. He'd start studying law and would be on his way to becoming a barrister. We'd live on an allowance from his father, but at least we'd be on our own, for once, as husband and wife. In Toronto, they might be interested in Gabrielle's collection. Perhaps there, everything would turn around.

But as fall neared, Oscar grew silent. Finally, a week before we were to leave, he confessed.

"Sweetheart, darling…about Toronto." He swallowed. "Father thinks it best if I go alone. He thinks…he thinks I'll have trouble concentrating on my studies if you're there."

I felt myself shake, a strange sort of quiver like the earth itself had moved out from under me. "But, Oscar, I'm your wife."

He wouldn't look me in the eye. "Antoinette…"

"Mon Dieu, Oscar. You fought in a war. You're a hero. You're not a child."

He was silent.

I shook my head, trying to understand. "You would really leave me behind?"

His lips were tight. His soft eyes looked lost. "I don't want to. It's the last thing I want to do. But he won't pay for it if I don't go alone."

I took a deep breath to calm myself. The air going down my lungs was ragged. The cooler weather had brought on a cold. "And I would live here, without you, under the same roof as a man who despises me."

"He doesn't despise you," Oscar said, stricken. "He's angry with me."

I reached for his hands. "Darling Oscar. Do you even want to be a barrister? Or is that what he wants?" I couldn't help but think of Lucho and his father. The woman he'd married for land. But Lucho loved horses. He'd had that for himself…

"It doesn't matter what I want," Oscar said. "It's the only thing to do. Father won't give me any more money unless I go."

"The only thing to do is to not leave your wife. Three years, Oscar. It takes three years to become a barrister."

"He won't insist on a separation for three years. It's just temporary, Antoinette." He moved to embrace me, but I backed away. "I'll come to Windsor every chance I can. Holidays. Summers. It's just a day's train ride away. Before you know it, I'll be a barrister. We'll have a home of our own. A large home. The castle I promised you. We can live in Montreal. You'd like it there. Everyone speaks French. We'll be as we were just after the war. We'll travel back and forth to Paris whenever you want."

I sat back on the bed in a daze. "You're really leaving me."

He reached for me again, but I turned away. "I'm not leaving you, Antoinette. I would never leave you. You're all I want. I'm begging you, please, be patient. I'm going to Toronto to study law. For us. I'll be back."

*I'll be back.*

Oscar didn't fight for me. He didn't insist I come with him.

My brave, handsome, glamorous aviator. He could defy gravity, but he couldn't defy his father.

There was so much he hadn't told me, so much I hadn't told him. In Paris, after the Armistice, the whole world had sparkled. We hadn't wanted to talk about the past. Everything up to then had been hard enough.

Marriage was supposed to be the expression of love, but could you truly love someone you didn't really know, someone who only knew the bright side of you and not the dark?

After Oscar left, my mind was a blank. I started having headaches. For hours, I didn't move. His siblings went to school. After, if my head wasn't throbbing, I helped them with their French, the girls with their sewing, a needle and thread to while away the hours.

Jeanne, my maid, had left months before. When one of the girls, trying to speak French, inadvertently called her a monkey, Jeanne snapped at her and made a scene. The next day, Oscar's father sent Jeanne away with money for a ticket back to France.

If only I were so lucky.

When Oscar's mother wasn't nearby, the girls would ask me questions. What is it like to smoke? How do you light a cigarette? Do you hold it just so? How do you get men to look at you? How do you walk in heels?

I let them try on my dresses and shoes. I showed them how to hold a cigarette, but I didn't let them light it. I taught them songs like "Coco at the Trocadero" and "Le Fiacre," a dip here, a twirl there.

A few weeks after Oscar had gone, one of the sisters was caught smoking in the bathroom. Oscar's mother blamed me.

I wrote to Gabrielle.

*They've sent Oscar to Toronto without me. I don't know what to do. This has all been a terrible mistake. Gabrielle, I'm desperate.*

I went to town to mail the letter on a stormy day. I had no umbrella, and it started to pour before I could get indoors. After, I collapsed into bed, shivering. My eyes felt heavy. I was flushed, weary, pain in every limb. I spent the next two weeks in bed with a fever.

# SEVENTY-FOUR

A MONTH AFTER I MAILED THE LETTER, A CABLE ARRIVED FROM Paris. It was from Gabrielle, addressed to Oscar's father. A family friend would be passing through Ontario. Would Monsieur Fleming be so kind as to take him in for a few days? The friend, Arturo Harrington, was interested in learning more about Canadian culture.

"Do you know this Arturo Harrington?" Oscar's father asked me, taking me aside in his study.

"Yes," I said, attempting to hide my shock. I was still weak from my illness, but the thought of Arturo revived me. "I knew him in Paris. He's from a well-off Argentinian family. He's very...presentable."

I left it at that.

Oscar's father sent a reply. The Fleming family would be pleased to host Mr. Harrington.

He might not care for the fact that his son was married to me, but he wouldn't turn down a request from the famous Coco

Chanel, especially since Gabrielle had helped his daughter Gussie make connections in Paris.

I didn't know what to think. Why was Arturo coming? He wasn't curious about Canadian culture. The only logical conclusion was that Gabrielle was sending him to tell me in person that they'd found Lucho's remains. The news would be too hard for me to hear alone via letter. I forced myself to eat. I didn't want Arturo to see me frail and thin. Then he might not tell me the truth. And I needed to hear it, as difficult as it would be. Otherwise a part of me would always believe Lucho could come back, and I would never truly be able to give myself to another, no matter how much I tried to pretend it wasn't true.

Two weeks later, Arturo arrived. "Arturo de Alba de Vallado de Irujo de Harrington," he said, bowing to the Flemings as if they were the royal family and he was a prince.

He was still a charmer, his hair still brilliantined back, a camellia occupying his buttonhole this time instead of a carnation. He still carried his gramophone in a case at his side, though it appeared to be a more updated model. The sight of him made me smile, until I remembered the purpose of his visit.

"Antonieta," he said, coming toward me, greeting me with an exchange of cheek kisses as we did in France, the Fleming girls giggling.

The whole household was in a tizzy. Arturo set up his gramophone and spun Oscar's delighted sisters around the room. He taught them the latest dances, the bear-step, the crab, as Oscar's mother watched, her face ashen. His father looked on, bewildered, not sure what to make of this Chanel family friend. I wondered if they were suspicious that Arturo might be an old lover of mine, which, of course, was impossible. Surely, they saw that.

That night, Arturo and I stood on the dock outside the speakeasies in the cold, the river frozen over, Detroit blinking in the distance.

"They call it the Paris of the Midwest," I said flatly.

"Is it?"

"No." I turned to him, my voice soft now. "Your violinist?"

He shook his head. "Gone."

"Oh, Arturo. I'm so sorry."

"Yes. So am I."

I'd waited all day for him to tell me about Lucho. Now that we were alone, I braced myself.

"Lucho's alive, Antonieta. He's in Buenos Aires."

The words rippled through me.

Lucho.

Alive.

"Your sister wrote to me a few months ago," he continued. "She wanted to know if the family had heard anything of him. When I told her he'd survived the war, she said you were unhappy in Canada. The marriage wasn't what you'd expected. She told me to come see you, to tell you about Lucho."

Oh, Gabrielle. Boy was gone. But somehow Lucho had risen from the dead, and in her suffering, she was giving me the chance she would never have. The weight of her loss overwhelmed me, while a part of me I'd forgotten, deep inside, opened up, the place where I'd once kept the joy of knowing Lucho was in the world.

"Have you seen him, Arturo? Is he…" My voice caught. "Is he all right?"

Arturo was silent for a moment. "He's not himself. He was concussed, and he suffers from it. The truth is, there might not be much time. He didn't want me to come here. But I told him about your letters to Coco, how miserable you are."

"Not much time?"

"Some men who've come back from the war, they don't have injuries on the outside," Arturo said. "But inside, the blasts have affected them. Their brains."

"What do you mean?" I said.

"The doctors don't fully understand it. Lucho's been concussed before, falls from horses, polo accidents. This is different."

"You're telling me he's alive but…dying?"

"Come back with me to Buenos Aires, Antonieta. Come, and I'll take you to him."

I stared out at the water, emotions swirling. Jazz music seeped out from the windows of the roadhouse, a chaotic barrage of horns, five melodies jostling at once, as confusing as my thoughts.

Lucho was alive.

But I was married.

Arturo slipped an arm through mine. "It's a lot to think about, I know. But right now, I have something more pressing to propose. A drink or two or five. And after that, if we're up to it, we'll show these Yanks how to dance."

He stayed for a few more days. For appearances' sake, he engaged Oscar's parents with questions about Canada, Ontario society, Windsor. He was giving me time to decide.

When he finally said goodbye, the Fleming girls were heartbroken, Arturo solemnly kissing each of their hands, his exit as courtly as his entrance. He was gone, and the house echoed from the quiet.

I waited a day. Packed only a few necessities. Left everything else behind: the lace coverlet from Adrienne, the tea set and samovar from Gabrielle, all my gowns and dresses. I wanted Oscar's sisters to have them, to play dress-up with now, to serve tea later, when they were older, hosting at-homes. The idea made me smile. They would be so much better at it than I.

I slipped out of the house when no one would notice. I left a note on the bed to tell Oscar's parents that I wasn't coming back. No one would be heartbroken I was leaving, except Oscar, and he was in Toronto.

I crossed the river into Detroit, then took a train to Chicago, where Arturo waited. I felt like myself again. The cough had mostly disappeared. The headaches too.

Together, we took another train to New Orleans and booked passage on a ship to Argentina. Soon, I would be in Buenos Aires. Lucho, Arturo said, refused to return to the pampas, and I remembered what Lucho had said in Paris, that he'd never be able to face the empty grasslands, not after what he'd done to his horses.

I wondered if people could tell that I was a woman running out on my marriage, a living, breathing scandal, my name forever soiled. Still, Lucho was alive, and I knew by now that the best thing I could do for Oscar, for his parents, was to leave. *Oscar, darling,* I wrote in a letter to him that I mailed from Windsor before I left, *you're free. We both know it's for the best.* I explained that I would be in Buenos Aires. His family would tell him about Arturo, and everyone would think I'd left to be with him. Eventually, Oscar could get a divorce for abandonment, his marriage an episode they'd blame on the war. He could marry a nice girl from Windsor, one who didn't smoke or drink or dance. Everyone would be relieved. Maybe even Oscar.

A part of me would always love him. My handsome, dashing aviator, the Oscar I knew in Paris. But back in Windsor, that man didn't stand a chance.

# SOMETHING BETTER

## BUENOS AIRES
### 1920–1921

# SEVENTY-FIVE

IN BUENOS AIRES, THE AIR WAS WARM, SULTRY. I'D GONE FROM winter to summer in a matter of a week.

It was my turn to follow the sun.

Plane trees and café terraces lined the Avenida de Mayo, reminiscent of Paris in a way that gave me hope and made my heart want to break all at the same time. It was a grand boulevard, with tall, softly ornate buildings and, on one corner, a hotel with wrought-iron balconies, columns, and a prominent clock tower.

Arturo kissed me on the cheek, leaving me at its columned entrance. "He's waiting for you."

The Majestic Hotel. The name was spelled out in enormous letters on the side and again at the top, the initials "MH" etched in the frosted glass doors, just like the hotel where Oscar had stayed in Paris. Was it a coincidence? A trick of fate to keep me from forgetting what I'd done to Oscar?

I went inside, passing through more columns, walls of boiserie, bronze sculptures, and climbed a wide staircase to the top, thinking of the Ritz in Paris, of Lucho waiting for me there, the door unlocked. Would it be the same here? We hadn't seen each other in five years.

I didn't know what to expect. Arturo had said Lucho wasn't himself.

At his door I knocked lightly, then turned the handle, relieved to find it unlocked. The room was dim, the curtains drawn, but there he was in a chair in the sitting room: Lucho.

He stood as I rushed to him. "Antonieta," he said, enfolding me in his arms.

We held each other, and that was when I knew he wasn't the same Lucho, not quite. He felt thinner, almost fragile. I stepped away, searching his face, the dark eyes that were always glad to see me, the mouth that turned up slightly at the ends, the wavy black hair that sometimes fell across his forehead. I touched his cheeks, his lips, to make sure he was real, that he was really there. He was still the man who'd taken my breath away on the polo field in Moulins. But his features were now cast in a shadow. He looked tired, dark circles under his eyes.

*Concussed*, Arturo had said, but I wasn't sure what that meant.

"You're married now," said Lucho.

The words poured out of my mouth. "It's over. A mistake, for both of us." He of all people knew about that.

"Are you sure?"

"Lucho, my love, I'm here."

He took a step back, and at first, I was self-conscious. Maybe too much had happened.

But when I looked up again, I recognized his expression and relaxed. He was taking me in as he had that morning so long ago at the Ritz, his eyes brushing over me so that my skin tingled.

"Antonieta," he said. "You remind me there's still beauty in the world."

I bent forward to kiss him. I wanted him against me, the familiar way we fit together that I'd missed. He was thinner, yes, but he still had that athletic way of holding himself as if he were made of springs, and he kissed me back with a strength that surprised me, that made me believe Arturo was wrong. Lucho wasn't dying. He was tired, he'd lost weight, but that was all.

"I remember this," he said, kissing my earlobe, the game he played in Paris whenever he'd return to me from Argentina. "And this," he said. "Oh yes, and this…"

I'd married another, but I was still Lucho's.

"There was an explosion at Verdun," he started later as we curled up in the bed. My head rested on his chest, his heart beating beneath it. "A naval gun…" He stopped. Took a deep breath. "It killed ninety-seven horses with one shot."

The blast, he said, knocked him in the air. He landed twenty meters away. That was what the other soldiers told him.

On the battlefield, every shell that burst afterward ricocheted in his head. All along the front, the slaughter had been terrible, but at Verdun it had been worse. Dead men, dead horses, everywhere.

"Can you imagine, Antonieta? Eight million horses lost over the course of the war, gone because of the idiocy of men. Eight million."

At the front, he'd had to teach others how to kill a horse. A mercy killing. A single shot to the skull. "If you could get that close," he said. "If the horse wasn't thrashing in panic and pain." He'd had to do things he couldn't talk about, things that made him turn away so I couldn't see his face.

We didn't leave the hotel. We had room service for our meals. We kept the curtains closed all the time. We stayed up all night talking, touching, making love, talking some more until we both fell asleep or I thought we did. Sometimes I would wake and find Lucho watching me as he had back in Paris.

I didn't realize at first that he was trying to protect me, to keep me from seeing how ill he was. He knew the nightmares would give him away.

But he had to sleep eventually, and on the third night, I was startled awake by his shouting, crying out, yelling at men, at horses.

Terrified, I woke him. "Lucho," I said, wrapping myself around him, his heart pounding so fast I put my hand over it as if that might calm it. "It's me. Antoinette. I'm here."

I was afraid he might toss me off, think I was part of the dream. But gradually, his breathing slowed, his body unclenched. He relaxed, and so did I.

"Antonieta." He whispered my name over and over, his head buried in my neck as we held each other and cried. Not for all that had happened but because somehow we were together, after everything.

I learned to recognize the headaches he wouldn't tell me about, the way his jaw tightened and the color left his face, how he'd grip something, the edge of a chair, until his knuckles were white. I saw how he only pretended to eat, pushing food around his plate, hiding some of it beneath a napkin. He acted as if he was reading the newspaper too, holding it in front of him, blinking because his eyes were unfocused.

"You need to see a doctor," I said.

"I've seen doctors. I've seen a lot of doctors."

"What did they say?"

He took a long breath. "I've been concussed too many times."

"What else did they say?"

He was quiet.

"Tell me."

"They said there's nothing to be done. They said it will only get worse. Antonieta, you don't have to stay."

A wave of fear came over me at the thought of not being with Lucho. "Don't ever ask me to leave," I said.

"You should be in Paris, living your life."

"Don't, Lucho. This is my life. Don't you understand? I'm happy. I'm happy because I'm with you. Even with all of this, I wouldn't want to be anywhere else."

"The headaches will get more severe. I could have trouble walking. Talking. My brain. It's dying."

"I'm not leaving," I said.

He studied my face, looking for doubt in my eyes, then turned and opened a drawer on the bedside table. "Do you remember this?" he said, his voice soft as he handed me a frayed piece of cloth.

It was stained with mud or blood or both. And in the corner, almost imperceptible, my initials. I was stunned. My handkerchief. The one I'd brought to the polo match in Moulins, the first time we'd met.

He'd had it with him at the front.

"You see, Antonieta, you've been with me the whole time."

# SEVENTY-SIX

THOSE NEXT WEEKS, WE SETTLED INTO A ROUTINE. I MADE REGular visits to a drugstore nearby and bought medicine for Lucho's headaches and Veronal to help him sleep, measuring out the doses because the chemist warned not to take too much. I went to the local markets and restaurants, always looking for something appetizing to eat, something he couldn't turn down. I held his head in my lap, rubbed his temples. I read the newspaper to him in terrible Spanish that made him laugh, I'd picked up a little in Biarritz, but not much. When a motorcar outside backfired or honked, I closed the window. When the light was too strong, I drew the curtains.

He would get better. I would make him better.

I drew hot baths, the heat and the steam loosening him up.

"Come, Antonieta," he would say, beckoning me to join him, and I would lean my back against his chest, his body cradling mine, sweet, so sweet, this watery bliss, the two of us dissolving into one.

I'd tried many times since I'd arrived to write Gabrielle, only to end up staring at the blank piece of paper, a pen unmoving in my hand.

CHÉRIE GABRIELLE. TODAY I WENT TO THE DRUGSTORE…
CHÉRIE GABRIELLE. TODAY I MADE SURE LUCHO ATE…

Everything gave an inaccurate picture of my life, as if it were all sickness and worry when it wasn't.

We went outside most nights, in the early hours before dawn, when all was quiet and even the pigeons were asleep. We strolled arm in arm along the empty Avenida de Mayo like two shadows, the only sounds then the breeze stirring the leaves, the soft trilling of an owl. The air smelled of bougainvillea and river water. This was when he seemed to feel the best, less agitated, in his head a dull ache instead of a throbbing. We sat on a favorite bench beneath the jacaranda and rosewood trees and looked up at the sky as we had in Deauville, a million stars blinking.

"That one?" he'd say, pointing up.

"No," I'd say. "That one."

# SEVENTY-SEVEN

"YOU NEED TO REST," LUCHO SAID TO ME ONE DAY IN JANUARY. I had lost my breath coming up the hotel stairs from a trip to the drugstore and was panting, trying to get it back.

I smiled. "I do rest. When you're asleep."

But I didn't. I couldn't sleep at all. I'd started taking Veronal for myself. I had pain in my chest, a weariness I couldn't overcome, a cough I tried to hide.

His eyes bore into mine. "Something's not right," he said. "You're ill."

"I wasn't well," I said, taking his hand. "Back in Canada. The climate there didn't agree with me. I'm much better now. I promise."

We didn't walk at night anymore. Instead, we sat out on the balcony, Lucho's arm around me, his fingers sometimes playing with a strand of my hair. We gazed out over the trees instead of sitting under them, the city dark and still, memories wrapping us up like soft muslin: our fated encounter at Royallieu, the music that had moved us both, the flight of the Valkyries, the goddesses swooping down from Valhalla. We remembered Paris, Maxim's, Montmartre, our nights at the Ritz or the Parc Monceau, walking along the Canal Saint Martin or the Seine in the moonlight. There was Deauville, the tango, dancing in our room to the orchestra below. We marveled at how perfect everything had been that year. Sometimes we even danced right there on the balcony, a slow swaying, the two of us leaning against each other. I would close my eyes and realize I was happier now, despite everything, happier than ever. For so long all I'd wanted was a home of my own. I didn't understand home wasn't a place. It was a person. Lucho was my home.

# SEVENTY-EIGHT

CHÉRIE GABRIELLE. ARTURO WAS RIGHT. LUCHO IS DYING.
CHÉRIE GABRIELLE. HOW DO YOU LIVE WITHOUT BOY?
CHÉRIE GABRIELLE. ISN'T IT STRANGE? I KNOW WHAT
JOY IS NOW.

Words still seemed an absurd attempt to tie everything together in a nice, neat bundle, to explain the unexplainable. I
missed my sister, but I didn't know what to say to her.

Until one February morning, when I awoke, panicked, not
knowing where I was, the sounds and smells of Buenos Aires
still unfamiliar. Then I saw Lucho asleep in the bed beside me
and was filled with a sense of peace. I couldn't take my eyes
from him, checking off every part as if to confirm it was him,
the thick black hair, the broad shoulders, the curve of his athletic frame.

Finally, I knew just what to write.

*Chérie Gabrielle,* I started, remembering that day at her apartment overlooking the Seine and the Trocadéro, just after Boy

was married. *Thank you. I would never be here, none of this would ever have happened, without you.*

Before sealing the envelope, I took off my gypsy ring, the stone that brought warmth and light to the darkest places, and put it inside with the letter. I wanted her to have it. I didn't need it anymore, but she did.

A few weeks later, a letter came from Adrienne. When I'd first arrived in Argentina, I'd written her at the Parc Monceau to let her know where I was, that I was safe. I could hear her voice, content, joyful, right off the page, and it made me tear up for how much I missed her, for how glad I was that she was so happy. When she'd moved in with Maurice, I'd thought she'd made the wrong choice. But she was right all along. She knew love was what mattered most.

*March 2, 1921*
*Chérie Ninette,*
*It's been a little over a year now since Boy left us. Gabrielle doesn't cry anymore. She went on a trip to Italy, to Venice with that odious Misia Sert, but she came back changed. She has a new paramour, Ninette—a Russian Grand Duke! Exiled, of course. Handsome. Blond. Very soigné. I think Gabrielle hopes he'll form an army and take Russia back. Then she can become empress!*

*Our dear André has gotten tall. He's a young gentleman now. He's taken an interest in rugby and he's brave and kind and optimistic.*

*Oh, Ninette, I almost forgot! Gabrielle is making a perfume! You know how sensitive she is to smells. She goes to the south of France with her Russian. He knows some scientist who puts scents together and she tries out different ones but she says it still isn't*

*right. She's very particular, but you know that. She's thrown her-*
*self back into work, her next collection.*

   *We miss you terribly!*
*Bisous,*
*Adrienne*

André—brave and kind and optimistic—just like Julia-Berthe.
It was all a relief. Any guilt I felt at not being in Paris was gone.
Everyone was moving forward, the world continuing to spin.

# SEVENTY-NINE

FOR LUCHO AND ME, I WANTED TO SLOW THE WORLD DOWN.

"Antonieta," he said one morning in April. "You're so cold." He wrapped his arms around me.

My temples throbbed. My lungs burned. My throat was raw from coughing. I rested my head against his chest, and I thought I might never be able to lift it again.

"You're ill," he said, holding me closer to stop the shaking.

A fever was coming, I could feel it, the way the aches pinched me, little flames everywhere.

Now Lucho watched over me. He called in orders from the drugstore and helped me take medicine for the headaches and Veronal to sleep. He ordered room service and tried to make me eat. I could see the concern and strain on his face, the way he tensed up, attempting to push away the ache in his own head. His handsome face, the face I knew better than my own, was gripped with pain, and I felt for him and admired his strength all at the same time.

After one week, I sat up in bed again.

After two weeks, I said I was better. It was only a lingering cough.

"You see, Lucho," I said, moving around again. "I just needed rest."

But rest wouldn't come, not for me, not for him. In April, Arturo visited, and there was a tone in his voice I didn't understand until I saw Lucho as Arturo must have. He hadn't gotten better. He'd gotten worse. Added to the headaches was dizziness, blurred vision. Lucho, who once had the balance of a centaur, swayed as he moved, putting a hand on the wall to steady himself. Despite Lucho's protests, Arturo insisted on sending for a doctor. Afterward, I overheard the doctor and Arturo talking outside the room.

"We don't know much about these kinds of head injuries," the doctor said. "Particularly when they come from the battlefield."

Arturo's voice was a whisper. "How much time does he have left?"

"Weeks. Months. It's hard to say."

I cried in the hallway where Lucho couldn't see, Arturo trying to comfort me, until finally he made me look him in the eye.

"Antonieta," he said. "The doctor wants to see you too."

"Why?"

"You're ill."

"It's just a cold."

"Maybe there's something the doctor can do for you. You can't help Lucho if you're unwell yourself."

Back in the room, I let the doctor listen to my lungs, but there was no need.

The cough. I'd recognized it. The same deep, tight cough as Julia-Berthe, as my mother. There was blood too, but I'd hidden that from Lucho. Just as Julia-Berthe had hidden it from us.

A few days after the doctor's visit, Lucho and I rose late from bed to find Arturo's gramophone in the sitting room along with a collection of recordings. He must have dropped them off while we slept. Perhaps he thought the tango would cheer us. But I couldn't imagine that kind of music doing anything but worsening Lucho's headaches. And my breath came short just thinking of moving like that.

We ignored the gramophone for the next few days, waiting for Arturo to come back and claim it, until one evening, I was eased from sleep by the sound of some kind of heavenly music.

I followed the notes to the sitting room, and there was Lucho in a chair next to the gramophone, eyes half-closed, a peaceful smile on his face, relaxed as I hadn't seen him in weeks. He motioned me over, gently pulling me to his lap.

"It's beautiful," I said. "What is it?"

"Bach," he whispered. "Prelude No. 1."

He played each of the recordings in turn. Chopin's Nocturne No. 2. Mozart, a concerto. Massenet, from the opera *Thaïs*. Debussy's "Rêverie." Each of them exquisite. The melody of angels. I thought of Arturo's violinist and wondered whether these pieces allayed or worsened Arturo's pain.

"This music, it almost makes you believe in redemption," Lucho said as we listened. "I never thought you'd forgive me for leaving and going to war. I just hoped, prayed, you'd understand."

For my father, disappearing was always the easy way out. For Oscar, going to Ontario was simpler than going against his parents. But Lucho. He could have run from the slaughter, but he didn't. He'd made the hard choice. Painful as it was, I'd always been moved by his courage.

"The fact that you went is why I love you," I said as his arms tightened around me. I put my head on his shoulder. The concertos flowed on, soft and delicate and ethereal. I didn't know what would happen tomorrow or the next day or the day after that. But here with Lucho, amidst all the uncertainty, I'd never felt so unafraid.

# EIGHTY

"I WANT TO SHOW YOU THE PAMPAS," LUCHO SAID, SITTING UP in bed. A month had passed and he'd gotten weaker. He'd been delirious with insomnia for several days but now, suddenly, looked perfectly alert. Hope shot through me.

"On the pampas," he said, "we play polo before we can walk." He told me he had a house there, a simple house surrounded by cattle and horses and that was where he was most at peace, among the criollos.

He thought we were back in Paris, before the war.

"I know you don't want to leave your sister and her hats, Antonieta. But it's safer there. We can wait out the war. We can live there and be happy."

"Oh, Lucho," I said as if I could change the past, as if I could make everything different. "Let's go. We'll sleep now. And we'll go tomorrow."

Maybe I was delirious too. Part of me thought we really would go to the pampas. Maybe that would make everything better. I recalled how he'd always described it: the symphony of the cow birds, the lowing of the cattle, the rippling of streams, cold and clear. The air fragrant with the sweet, sweet scent of eucalyptus. The plains that stretched beyond the horizon.

Neither of us had slept, really slept, for days, Lucho with his headaches, me with a fever that had returned. I reached for the bottle of Veronal. The chemist's warning ran through my mind. Already we were at the highest doses. Our bodies had grown immune.

When was the last time I'd taken some? I tried to recall but my head was blurry. Hadn't we just gotten a new bottle? No, that was days ago. Or was it yesterday?

The pampas. It sounded so nice, so warm. It was May, which meant in Buenos Aires it would soon be winter.

Just a little more, I decided, picking up the bottle, measuring another dose for Lucho, another dose for myself. We would sleep, and tomorrow we would go to the pampas. I put a disc in the gramophone. We'd moved it into the bedroom a few weeks before, hoping the music might soothe us to sleep. Our breathing always seemed to come easier when it played.

I settled back into the bed to the first notes of "Rêverie," nestling into him. His hand found mine, taking it, fingers entwined. "Dulces sueños, Antonieta," he murmured, his lips close to my ear. He was warm, so warm, and at last I felt myself drifting off, a strange, encompassing darkness pulling me in, until it felt like I was floating, weightless, iridescent. Somewhere in the distance I saw Gabrielle as a young girl, head bent, practicing her stitches in the convent workroom. I drew nearer, whispered to her, and she looked up as if she could hear me. *Something Better*, I said. *You're going to be Something Better.*

There was more I wanted to say, about how she was right, that love had nothing to do with marriage or class. It meant someone knowing and embracing every side of you.

But before I could, she faded into streaks of deepening orange and pink and red, like a sunrise or a sunset, and then I saw Lucho, smiling in the light, coming toward me, and behind him eight million horses grazing in pastures of gold.

★ ★ ★ ★ ★

# ACKNOWLEDGMENTS

FIRST AND FOREMOST, TO MY FABULOUS AGENT, KIMBERLEY Cameron, for your belief in me, expert guidance, and eternal optimism.

To my brilliant editor, Melanie Fried, for your wisdom, thoughtfulness, patience, and vision. Thanks to you, this story has a depth and polish that wasn't there before.

To everyone at Graydon House for your hard work and commitment to *The Chanel Sisters*: Pamela Osti, Justine Sha, and the extraordinary publicity and marketing team; Kathleen Oudit for the gorgeous cover art; and all those working diligently behind the scenes from sales, subsidiary rights, and editorial who had a hand in bringing Antoinette's story to light—thank you from the bottom of my heart.

To the best writing group in the world that is so much more than just a writing group: Ann Weisgarber, Julie Kemper, Lois Stark, Rachel Gillett, and Laura Calaway. Each one of you has enriched this book and my life in so many ways. And to Rob Weisgarber, Jim Kemper, and George Stark for continued enthusiasm and great wine.

Thank you also to Inprint Houston, where it all began, and

to Saint Stephen's Episcopal Church for providing us a meeting place. To Kathy L. Murphy, artist, author, and generous champion of books and literacy, you truly are the queen. And to all of the readers, book clubs, bookstagrammers, and bloggers, for celebrating authors and turning what once was a solitary endeavor into a real community.

To Philip Gross and Mary Lake Collins, thank you for sharing your thoughts and memories and allowing me to share them with the world.

To Les, my smart, handsome and, most importantly, funny husband for handling with aplomb the growing realization over the years that you married a nerdy writer, and to my children, Scott, Lindsey, and Olivia, who amaze me every day with your genius and ability to navigate this crazy world: you all are my Something Better.

# HISTORICAL NOTE

A FEW YEARS AGO, I PICKED UP A BIOGRAPHY OF COCO CHANEL expecting to read that she came from a privileged, glamorous background. What I discovered surprised me. Born into a family of peasants, Coco and her younger sister, Antoinette, had been abandoned as children at a convent orphanage in rural France, where they spent years as charity cases.

To me, this part of Coco's biography made her eventual success all the more stunning. But as I thought about how to approach a novel, Coco, famous for lying about her upbringing, didn't feel like an authentic narrator. She never would have willingly shared that part of her life.

Instead, Antoinette emerged as an opportunity both to tell Coco's story and to reveal a more intimate, honest side to Coco only her sister would have been privy to. Only a sister who had stayed loyally by her side could know, for example, that Coco's lies about her childhood were also a way to escape the pain of their abandonment.

Yet other questions still haunted me: What was it like to be Coco Chanel's sister? We know whom Coco became, but what happened to Antoinette? Details about Antoinette were sparse, and it bothered me that Coco's biographers seemed to brush her off as pretty but not as clever.

Determined to find more information, I pored through census records, newspapers, and magazines, and visited genealogical sites. And as my research progressed, a very different picture of Antoinette began to form, that of a smart, lively woman who, like her sister, was ahead of her time as an entrepreneur.

In terms of what in the novel is fact, Coco's biographers state Antoinette was at the orphanage in Aubazine with Coco, and she also lived for a time in Moulins, most likely at the Pensionnat. She was part of the trio, with Gabrielle and their aunt Adrienne Chanel, referred to as the "Three Graces."

Census records indicate that at one point Antoinette was selling hats in Vichy, where Coco had attempted a career as a singer. In January 1910, we know Antoinette was helping Coco in Paris, at Etienne Balsan's garçonnière on the Boulevard Malesherbes, where Coco began her foray into fashion by selling hats. Antoinette signed the ledger book on January 1, 1910, as *vendeuse*.

Antoinette continued to assist Coco with her business, eventually called Chanel Modes. While Coco worked behind the scenes on her designs, Antoinette managed customers from the highest echelons of society with savvy and charm. She helped establish the first boutique on the rue Cambon, then another in Deauville and Biarritz, overseeing hundreds of employees. Notices in the newspaper *Le Figaro* noted her travels between Paris, Biarritz, and the south of France. She must have been an accomplished businesswoman.

When World War I ended, Antoinette moved back to Paris. There, she met the Canadian airman Oscar Fleming, whom she married in November 1919. Boy Capel was a witness. On the marriage license, Antoinette's address was listed as the Parc Monceau, where Adrienne and Maurice lived. Oscar's address was listed as the Hotel Majestic, which is now the Peninsula Hotel on Avenue Kléber.

A Canadian newspaper announcement noted that Antoinette and Oscar spent a brief honeymoon at the "Chanel country château" in Biarritz. After that, they departed for Ontario, Canada, and from there everything went downhill.

Eventually, Oscar was sent to Toronto to study law without Antoinette, and during that time an unknown Argentinian gentleman with a portable gramophone visited the Fleming home in Windsor. Soon after, Antoinette fled to Buenos Aires. She died under mysterious circumstances in the Majestic Hotel on the Avenida de Mayo on May 2, 1921. The death certificate lists her as "Antonieta Chanel de Fleming" and the cause of death as "intoxicación." Some of Coco's biographers have taken this to mean alcohol poisoning, but in Spanish it simply means "poisoning" and is not necessarily related to alcohol. Other than the death certificate, no record of her time in Buenos Aires has been found.

Antoinette was thirty-three at the time of her death. Her mother had died at the age of thirty-one.

While Lucho Harrington isn't based on a known person, it's plausible that Antoinette had a former lover in Buenos Aires. Otherwise, if she was really desperate enough to leave Canada, it seems she would have gone back to Paris instead. Given that she was thirty-two when she married Oscar, more than likely she'd had previous lovers, and though nothing more is known of Antoinette's love life, Coco's circle of friends included many polo players, with whom Antoinette would have socialized too. I like to think there really was a Lucho. Otherwise, her death is all the more a tragedy.

Oscar remarried in 1928 and had one daughter in 1948. He died in 1956 when she was only eight. The lace bedspread and tea set with the Russian samovar is still in the possession of the Fleming family. No one knows what happened to the clothes

Antoinette brought from Gabrielle's collection or to Antoinette's wedding gown.

Adrienne Chanel met Baron Maurice de Nexon around 1906. His parents refused to accept her. Unlike many men of his class, he remained devoted to her and never married anyone else. On April 29, 1930, Adrienne and Maurice finally married after the death of Maurice's father, and Adrienne became the Baroness de Nexon. She died in 1956 and Maurice died in 1967. They had no children. A portrait of Antoinette by Tadé Styka is believed to still be owned by the Nexon family.

Julia-Berthe Chanel died in May 1910. Coco has said that Julia-Berthe committed suicide by rolling naked in the snow. According to her death certificate, however, Julia-Berthe died in Paris in May, when there would not have been snow. She died in a hospital for people of means. The death certificate doesn't state the cause of death, and it's unknown why she was in Paris at that time.

After finishing school in England, André completed military service, then worked as director of Tissus Chanel, Coco's textile company. He married, and Coco gave him the Château du Mesnil-Guillaume in Normandy as a wedding present (the first of three châteaux she gifted him). He had two daughters, one he named Gabrielle. He served in World War II and was taken prisoner by the Germans. Desperate not to lose him, Coco managed to get him released. He contracted tuberculosis and wasn't able to work again. He died in 1981 at seventy-six.

Celestine and Arturo are fictional characters. Amedeo Modigliani, or Modi, was indeed a painter and sculptor. An alcoholic and drug addict, he died, destitute, of tuberculosis at age thirty-five, having given all of his paintings away in exchange for food, drink, and drugs. His works became famous after his death. The poet Guillaume Apollinaire, despite his name or maybe because of it, was injured by shrapnel in 1916 and, in a weakened state, died of the Spanish flu in 1918 at age thirty-eight.

Throughout her life, Coco Chanel lied about her background and her family. She never talked about the orphanage in Aubazine, the Pensionnat in Moulins, or her time in Vichy. Her story was that she was raised by wealthy aunts in the countryside and that was where she'd learned to ride horses. She was, in more ways than just fashion, an illusionist. Tales she's told about her past and about her sisters may or may not be truthful.

Coco did admit to living with Etienne Balsan at Royallieu. Photographs of Etienne and his guests include Coco on horseback and in some cases dressed in costumes. In one, a fashionable group is posed wearing expensive clothing, fine hats, and serious expressions, a contrast with the donkeys they're astride. Etienne remained a good friend to Coco for his lifetime, never divulging her secrets. He died in 1954 in a car accident in Rio de Janeiro, taking what he knew of her early days to the grave.

Coco met Boy Capel at Royallieu and fell immediately in love, eventually moving to Paris to be with him. When he died in December 1919, he'd just told her goodbye after one of his usual visits and was on his way to Cannes. Some speculate he was planning to meet his wife and ask for a divorce. Because of a tire blowout, no one will ever know. Coco has said that 1919 was "the year I woke up famous and the year I lost everything."

Coco was known for wearing a mysterious oval citrine ring on her left pinky finger. In her later years, it hung from a chain hidden beneath her blouse. She said a gypsy gave it to her, but no one knows where it came from or why she wore it.

Though Coco would never admit she was raised in an orphanage, her time with the nuns in Aubazine defined her. The famous logo of interlocking Cs she started using in 1925 mimicked the interlocking loops in the stained glass. While it's assumed the initials stand for "Coco" and "Chanel," some speculate they represent "Chanel" and "Capel." I like to think they signify Coco and Antoinette, arm-in-arm. Her jewelry designs mimicked the celestial patterns of stars and moons in the stone floors. Her aesthetic was derived from the austere beauty of the structure itself, her color scheme from the black and white habits of the nuns, her use of wooly, textured fabrics from the rough-hewn uniforms, her preference for simplicity and a clean scent from the fastidiousness the nuns taught her. Aubazine never left her no matter how hard she tried to pretend it hadn't happened.

Coco died in January 1971 at the age of eighty-seven. She never married, but had many lovers, some of them controversial. Her last words were, "This is how one dies."

History portrays Coco as a solitary figure wreathed in strands of pearls. But she wasn't always alone. In the first few decades of her life, she had Antoinette, and in an era when few women were independent by their own means, together the sisters lifted themselves up.

# THE CHANEL SISTERS:
## A TIMELINE

**September 11, 1882**: Julia-Berthe Chanel is born

**August 19, 1883**: Gabrielle Chanel, later known as Coco, is born

**June 14, 1887**: Antoinette Chanel is born

**1895 est.**: The three sisters are left by their father at a convent orphanage in Aubazine

**1898 est.**: During holidays, the sisters begin visiting their paternal family in Clermont-Ferrand and meet their young aunt Adrienne, who, along with Antoinette and Coco, will come to be known as "The Three Graces"

**1900 est.**: The sisters are moved to the Pensionnat in Moulins with Adrienne

**1902 est.**: Coco and Adrienne leave the Pensionnat and work as seamstresses at the nearby House of Grampayre

**November 29, 1904**: Julia-Berthe's son, Andrè, is born. The father is unknown, and she is forced to give Andrè up to a priest

**1905-06 est.:** Coco tries to become a singer in Vichy, one of the few ways women could rise out of poverty

**1906 est.:** The younger Antoinette is finally released from the Pensionnat and joins Coco and Adrienne in Vichy

**1906 est.:** Coco leaves Vichy to live with a group of bon vivants at the Château de Royallieu, where she begins experimenting with men's clothes

**1908 est.:** Coco meets Boy Capel at Royallieu, and they fall in love

**Late 1909-10 est.:** Coco moves to Paris

**1910:** Antoinette joins Coco in Paris, where they begin making and selling hats

**May 1910:** Julia-Berthe dies of consumption in Paris

**October 1, 1910:** A portrait of Coco modeling one of her hats is published in the theater magazine *Comœdia Illustré*

**End of 1910:** With a loan from Boy Capel, the sisters open their first hat shop at 21 rue Cambon. They call it Chanel Modes

**1912:** French actress Gabrielle Dorziat wears Chanel hats in the play *Bel Ami*

**Summer 1913:** The Chanel sisters open a store in Deauville on the rue Gontaut-Biron

**June 28, 1914:** Archduke Franz Ferdinand of Austria is assassinated, setting off World War I

**September 1914:** During the war, Coco's knit jackets and straight skirts fill the need for practical attire

**July 15, 1915:** The Chanel sisters open a fashion house in Biarritz. They're making more money than ever

**Early 1916:** Chanel has a staff of 300 across its three stores

**1916**: Coco pays back Boy Capel's loans

**March 1917**: *Les Élégances Parisiennes* illustrates a group of jersey suits by Chanel

**1917 est.**: Coco cuts off her hair

**1918**: Chanel is registered as a couturière, and the sisters establish a maison de couture at 31 rue Cambon in Paris

**August 1918**: Boy Capel marries Lady Diana Wyndham but continues to see Coco

**November 11, 1918**: World War I ends with an armistice

**November 1919**: Antoinette marries Canadian airman Oscar Fleming, and in December they move to Windsor, Canada

**December 21, 1919**: Boy Capel is killed in a car accident, devastating Coco

**May 2, 1921**: Antoinette Chanel dies in Buenos Aires at the former Majestic Hotel. The cause of death is listed as "intoxicación," or poisoning

**\*DISCLAIMER**: Some dates are approximate or unknown and were estimated for the novel. For example, because Coco lied about her past, historians don't know with certainty many of the dates before 1910. The records of the convent orphanage in Aubazine were destroyed or lost (some say Coco had a hand in that), and there are no records from the Pensionnat in Moulins as far as the author has been able to discern.

# THE
# CHANEL
## SISTERS

## JUDITHE LITTLE

### Reading Group Questions

REVIEW

1. How did the Chanel sisters use fashion to escape the reality of life as orphans in the convent?

2. Discuss Gabrielle's decision to live at Royallieu with Boy and his bon vivant friends. What impact do you think it had on her relationship with Antoinette, her views on love, and her approach to fashion?

3. Did you understand Antoinette's choice not to marry Alain, the grocer's son? What might you have done in that situation?

4. How do you think growing up without a mother shaped each Chanel sister and her actions throughout the novel?

5. How were the opportunities for the Chanel sisters similar or different from opportunities women have today?

6. Do you believe fashion can empower women? Discuss how this idea is or is not reflected in the novel and in your own life.

7. How did the Chanel sisters adapt their product to current events over the course of the novel? How were they pioneers in fashion, even at this earlier point?

8. How did Antoinette's various roles, from selling hats in Vichy to opening the boutique on the rue Cambon to presiding over the first Chanel couture house in Biarritz, impact her understanding of her place in the world and her sense of purpose?

9. Did you learn anything unexpected about the Chanel sisters from the novel, particularly given what the brand represents today? Did you understand Gabrielle/Coco in a new light as a person and as a businesswoman?

10. Who was your favorite Chanel sister?

JUDITHE LITTLE grew up in Virginia and earned a Bachelor of Arts in Foreign Affairs from the University of Virginia. After a brief time studying in France and interning at the US Department of State, she earned her law degree from the University of Virginia School of Law where she was on the Editorial Board of the Journal of International Law and a Dillard Fellow. She lives in Houston, Texas, and is the author of two novels, *The Chanel Sisters* and *Wickwythe Hall.*

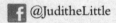 @JuditheLittle

# Bookends

## When one book ends, another begins...

Bookends is a vibrant new reading community to help you ensure you're never without a good book.

You'll find exclusive previews of the brilliant new books from your favourite authors as well as exciting debuts and past classics. Read our blog, check out our recommendations for your reading group, enter great competitions and much more!

Visit our website to see which great books we're recommending this month.

Join the Bookends community:
# www.welcometobookends.co.uk

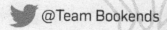 @Team Bookends    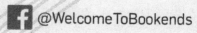 @WelcomeToBookends